The Agency Trilogy

A RICHARD KASAK BOOK

The Agency Trilogy

DAVID MELTZER

First Richard Kasak Book Edition 1994

First printing September 1994

ISBN 1-56333-216-7

Cover Art © Brian Lynch
Cover Design by Kurt Griffith

Manufactured in the United States of America
Published by Masquerade Books, Inc.
801 Second Avenue
New York, N.Y. 10017

THE AGENCY TRILOGY

THE AGENCY

Book One

INITIATION

"...Indeed, Dolmance, 'tis terrible, what you have to do to us; this at once outrages Nature, heaven, and the most sacred laws of humanity."

—D.A.F. de Sade

1.

On a balmy night, the young man, a dreamer, walks down the avenue chewing a candy bar, feeling cosmic, horny and lost. He holds a book of Chinese philosophy in one hand. He isn't going anywhere in particular. Maybe to the park, to watch the dirty-yellow swans swim through the beer cans and garbage in their pond. A soft wind works at his face.

An incredibly long, silent black Cadillac sedan draws against the curb. The chauffeur wears a black twill suit and a black leather cap. His glasses are made of one-way silver mirrors and hold the image of the young man. Two women sit in the back and the tallest of the two picks up a small phone, speaks into it.

The chauffeur nods. One of the car windows hums open.

"Get in," says the chauffeur to the young man.

"Who, me?"

"Of course. Get in. In the back. With the women."

The window hums shut.

The smaller lady opens the back door and gets out. Her face is veiled as if in mourning. The young man enters the car. He wants to ask a question but can't. The tall woman he sits beside also wears a veil. She takes the book from his hand as if to examine the title. Instead she drops it into a compartment by the window. The smaller lady reenters the car and sits thigh to thigh by the young man.

The door shuts with a resonant sound. He feels as if he is being sealed into a diving bell. The chauffeur starts the engine. They begin to move.

The young man looks out the window and finds it tinted a dark shade which makes all details beyond seem vague and shadowy. The taller lady snaps a switch beneath the door handle and the windows are covered by concealed curtains. It is almost totally dark now.

"Let's go to Carla's," says one of the women.

"Ring Max," the other says.

"Yes?" says the chauffeur's voice, crackling through a small speaker.

"Carla's."

The car swerves. A hip presses against his own and a hand rests gently upon his inner thigh. The other woman pulls his hand up and moves his arm around her shoulder, placing his hand upon her blouse so that his fingertips feel the steady rise and fall of her bosom.

He begins to notice the different perfumes they are wearing. One has a lingering quality of an erotic dream and the other is like awakening in the morning in an elegant whorehouse.

He feels his pulse pound and hears their breathing get heavy. Yet he doesn't move. He shuts his eyes as if to enter a deeper darkness than the one inside the car, which is smoothly moving across unknown roads.

The hand upon his inner thigh moves up boldly and unbuckles his belt, quickly unbuttons the top button, then unzips his fly. Perhaps the other one is the one who rolls his pants down below his knees. He feels a slight breeze as his shorts are rolled down his hips.

Involuntarily his hand surrounds a breast and begins fondling it as his exposed body is being caressed by leather-gloved fingers. It is a strange new feeling to have his cock so touched and it swells and grows beyond her grip.

"Very good. Big. You see, dear, you work on the disguises a man wears walking down the street. They're all really hiding."

A tongue burrows into his ear just as a mouth folds its lips upon his cock's crown.

"Wait," says one of them.

He is pushed to his side. He understands and stretches out on the large seat, its leather warm to his bared rump.

One of them mounts him so that her cunt rests upon his mouth and the other one is back on his cock, her mouth passing the crown and rolling up and down the shaft. Her cunt perfumed as her body is, his mouth begins to work through its fleshy curtain, his tongue reaching inner rims and nerves which makes whoever it is grab behind her back to push the other one's mouth down harder on his member.

"Enough," says the voice through the small speaker.

"But Max, we need a sample."

"Enough. Wait until we're there. Carla must prepare him."
The voice is metallic and flat.

The ladies disengage themselves from the young man. His
loins ache with the frustration and pain of withheld seed.

"I suppose it's better," says one of them.

There's no answer. Yet the leather-gloved hand goes back to
his still erect cock and begins to manipulate it. As his body arches in orgasm, he feels warm lips enfold his pulsing organ to withdraw the discharge of its love fluid. He groans when the suction
becomes more insistent. The tongue tip moves quickly upon the
tremendously sensitive crown.

"Damn you, Leonard! I told you to hold back," says one of the
women.

"Carla's a bitch."

"But you have to do these things right or we all get in trouble."

"I couldn't help it. He's so big, so much to work with," says
the other voice, the other woman. Leonard?

"We're almost there. Get your pants up."

The young man does as he is told.

A hand grabs his as he's buckling his belt and thrusts it under
skirts to a touch a hard crotch. The young man's hand withdraws
after feeling the firm throbbing organ pulsing beneath the silk
panties of one of the women.

"Yes," hisses the voice. "I'm Leonard. You'll know me soon."

The car stops.

"Blindfold him."

Silk blackness covers the young man's eyes.

The door opens.

"You can go," says one of them. He hears footsteps on the
gravel.

"Go on, move. There's a lot to be done before the night is
over."

He gropes his way out. A hand grabs his. Another hand grabs
him underneath his rear, its fingers tipping his testicles.

Someone says, "Wait!"

He's led through a doorway. He hears the sound of an elevator door opening

Then he's led into it. The door shuts and his stomach sinks as the elevator begins its quick rise. It seems as if there are more people in the elevator. He smells new perfumes.

All the way up, hands keep touching him, prodding him, as if he were a steer at auction.

2.

Into another elevator. Someone nudges him in the delicate spot behind his knees and he falls down. Immediately bodies are upon him. The elevator continues going up.

His clothes are ripped off. The elevator must be filled beyond belief with hands, hips, knees, organs. He is naked. The elevator stops.

Tongues, lips. He is licked and kissed. Hands rub an oil over his body. Slowly. The hands getting gentle as they reach his manhood. Someone nibbles on his nipple.

"Hung well."

"He'll be useful."

"For a while."

"Who knows."

"Shave his pubes?"

"See what Carla says."

The elevator begins again. Strong hands begin to pry apart his buttocks.

"No. We can't. We must wait."

"Get up."

The young man is in a daze and tries to stand up but can't function as he'd like to.

"Pull him up. Watch out. He's slippery."

"He shines."

Strong hands grab him under the armpits and stand him up.

"Lean against the wall. Hold onto the rail. There, behind you. Right. We're almost there."

It sounds like the voice of the chauffeur.

At any time he can take off the blindfold. But he doesn't. He can't. Not being able to see, he feels concealed, as if he is in a dream.

The elevator stops. The doors open. A refreshing wave of air embraces his naked body.

"Wait. A little dab more."

Oil is once more rubbed over his body. Gentle fondling of his cock, cupping of his balls.

"Oh, shine."

"Alright. Go on. Straight ahead. When you hear the door shut, take off your blindfold."

The light's dim but it still hurts his eyes. The black silk drops to the floor. He watches its slow descent onto the marble floor as if in slow motion.

A beautiful woman stands before him. Her body is encased in a skin of black leather that is slashed down the center to reveal the white flesh alive beneath the garment.

Part of her breasts are revealed. The thrust of her nipples pushes through the leather, outlined in the sheath. The slash ends right where her cunt has begun. Her pelt is a black curly triangle that dissolves into the skintight leather gripping her in such a way that it makes it hard for her to move at this moment. Each body motion stimulates her too much. She must be reserved for now. She must enact the rite correctly.

"I am Carla," she says. "Do not speak. I know who you are."

She moves to him slowly. Looking at his body, looking at his face.

"Do you know why you were chosen?"

"No," he answers.

She's the most beautiful woman he has ever seen. She is the image his sex dreams conjured when, on his knees, without a woman, he would bring out his desires alone.

Her face is the face of all the women he has wanted to love. As a young man, he has yet to love any of his dreams into a reality. All the girls, the young ladies he had hungered for, were always unreachable, sacred, beyond his means. Their pale faces, mysterious bodies concealed behind virginal lace, the red lips, flushed cheeks, the perfect grave grace of their moving—she, Carla, was all of his dreams transformed into a woman. A woman in an erotic leather outfit. Black hair tumbling about her shoulders. Her lips shine. Her eyes scrutinize his naked body with detachment.

The whip lashes out, curls around his hips and stings his rump.

"Stop dreaming," she says.

She pulls the whip back, snaps it, sets it flying around him again. Its end is thorned and as it flashes into his rump it draws a thin line of blood.

"I am Carla and you are nothing. You are dirt to trample on. You are mud. You are clay to be shaped into whatever we see fit. Down on your knees before me!"

She pulls the whip back.

He falls to his knees.

"On all fours. Like a dog."

He hesitates.

Her high heel pushes against the back of his neck.

"Down, dog!"

The heel is sharp and sudden as it digs in and knocks him off balance. He falls on his belly onto the cold marble.

"You're a toad. Crawl, toad! Crawl!"

He lies still. The chill marble is a shock to his abdomen but, after a moment, it feels pleasant.

The whip slashes across his back and he jerks in the pain of its crossing.

"Don't you understand? I am Carla, your Mistress. You are useless dung. Now obey."

Again and again.

He feels new pain and begins to like the rasping scrape of the whip across his body. Then, without warning, his bladder works against him and he urinates. The liquid spreads warmly upon his belly.

Carla laughs. A warm laugh that chills him.

"You're a child. Wetting your bed. You must be punished."

In another room.

Set up like a police lineup. He is against the marker lines in bright light. Naked.

"Alright, profile."

He turns.

The camera flashes.

"Turn around. Back view."

He turns and faces the wall.

The flash pops.

"Okay. Closeup time."

A woman in a skintight rubber jumpsuit steps onto the stage and walks up to the young man.

She takes his cock in her hand.

"Fine," says the photographer. "Hold it."

Flash.

"Okay. Now let's activate it."

She unzips her jumpsuit and embraces him. Her body is hot and her round breasts bore into his chest and her hot cunt moistly presses into his cock. Her legs thrust through his.

"Kiss me," she says.

They kiss. Her mouth drops open like a cave and as his tongue enters it, she begins to suck on it until he thinks she'll pull it out by its roots. They move apart.

"I've got five kids," she whispers in his ear. "Wanna see my stretch marks?"

"You're in great shape," he answers.

"Pig," she whispers.

"C'mon, c'mon, let's get to it! I don't have all day," says the photographer.

"He's a pig too," she says.

Then she's on her knees with the young man's cock halfway into her greedy mouth. He thought he was through for the day (but he thinks too much) and writhes in sweet pain. He wants to pull her off and get into her, into somebody.

"Okay, get dressed."

Flash.

"Turn sideways now."

He turns. Flash.

The mother of five stands up, steps into her skintight rubber jumpsuit, zips up, walks off.

"Okay, Doctor, you can have him now."

The Doctor is a six-foot-seven Negro with a white Lone Ranger mask over his eyes. He's naked except for a scarlet silk undergarment holding his massive tool. A brass armband digs deep around one of his huge biceps.

"Come on, young man, into my office. Follow me."

Entering the wings, he sees the rubber jumpsuited mother of five beneath the photographer. They're fucking deliriously. Another man races around their tangled forms taking pictures.

3.

The office is black. The walls are painted black. The chairs, sofa, magazine table, the ashtrays, all are painted black.

Tacked to a black wall is the bright yellow-and-black hide of a skinned tiger.

Tacked to another black wall is the pale pink hide of a skinned human being.

"This way," says the Doctor.

The hallways are black and on the walls are ancient figurines of fragmented bodies caught in various postures of lovemaking, tribal masks worn by savage healers, scalps and, oddly, as we enter the Examination Room, an icon of Satan embracing a golden-haired angel in a transluscent chemise.

"On the bed."

The young man gets on the so-called bed, which is a leather-covered contraption rising above the floor on iron legs. From the ceiling hangs an odd-looking X-ray machine in the shape of a circle whose center presents a phallic tube with a round glass-encased hole in its center.

"I'm going to have to strap you down. I hope you don't mind," says the Doctor.

"I have no choice."

"Perhaps."

The black Doctor hums a vague melody as he begins to strap the young man down.

"That's a song I wrote when I was in pre-med," he says. "It's my body chant. I love bodies, you know. I was a skilled surgeon from the beginning. But I was black and I was big," he hums, and his voice seems to come from the bottom of a steel drum.

"You're not going to…going to cut me up?"

"Of course not, my morsel. We're just going to examine you, use you up."

He begins to hum again.

"What do you think of when you see a big black man?" asks the Doctor.

"I don't know. What should I think of?"

"Oh, c'mon, man. What do you think of? Nine-foot cock, super-rapist, coming down the aisle to grab your tiny fiancée and defile her on the altar? Isn't that where it's at when you see me walking down the street?"

A crackling sound. The phallic tube turns blue, then a blue-edged white.

"Don't worry, baby," says the Doctor.

All he sees is the light blazing above his head.

"Now, this won't hurt much."

A needle is stuck into his arm.

"Nor this."

A needle is stuck in his thigh.

"Nor this."

A needle is stuck into his shoulder.

"…y'see my mother was all spread-eagled out on the floor an' this big ofay mother-fucker comes barrel-assing on top of her an' sticks his sick prick in her and rapes her as much as he's able an' all the time my daddy's watchin' because he's tied to a chair an' whitey's blonde whore's on Dad's lap pullin' on his pecker an' laughin' an' stinkin' of bourbon…

"…y'see, I'm a surgeon, y'see, because I passed some special tests, I mean, y'dig, besides the written ones, an' all them fag-got Dr. Kildares down on their knees before me, suckin' an' a gaggin', an' all them Dr. Caseys on top of me, boring tunnels into my rear end an' sweating on my back…

"…y'see, I'm a weird doctor an' this is my clinic. You're my guest an' I'm going to teach you what you wanna learn, y'dig, you wanna be destroyed, you wanna be reborn, you wanna be somethin' more than nothin', y'know what I'm sayin'…?"

He knows nothing.

A cartoon of the universe explodes behind his eyes. Shooting stars with enlarged, flaming tails sizzle and detonate. Rockets, fireworks, the traditional planets with humming rings around them, Buck Rogers, Flash Gordon, a cliché of stored images zoom and boom and fade away, return, smile, smile widely enough to light half the earth, then fade away again.

He knows nothing.

The levels his fragmented mind reaches have trapdoors. There's nothing to stand on that doesn't open up and drop him through a new void.

Where am I in this universe? Which universe? Whose universe?

Mayan gods on tractor-feet raise stone spear-holding claws. His mother in a wicker basket offers a rubber bottle of milk to him with a leaky nipple that dribbles warm Cream of Wheat on his open mouth.

He knows nothing.

Flashed on a mammoth screen: his tumescent penis.

Flashed on a mammoth screen: his buttocks pushed apart and stuffed with firecrackers.

Flashed on a mammoth screen: his mouth wide open, lips cracked, having a giant uncircumcised cock pushed into it.

He knows nothing.

Dreams in dreams tangle in his dislocated head and faces and forms collide, become one, disintegrate.

What is going on?

Does it matter?

Into a body-warm tub of sperm. Slowly. His muscles beginning to loosen. His loins beginning to relax. Then, without warning, he's pushed all the way under. White milky universe. Drowning in it.

Fingernails and toenails dissolve from their locations.

A tiger begins to pounce and pad on heavy, muscled legs towards him.

What is the real world?

Does it matter?

He remembers somewhere that he wants to be a poet. This is a vision, he thinks. I must I use it.

Cosmic diarrhea pours on him.

"Eat the universe, you dumb bastard!" says another faceless voice coming from outside. Or inside. Or where? Does it matter?

"Eat, you dumb bastard! Turf, open his mouth."

Turf's a karate champ with knuckles the size of pinballs. The other man's a dentist. The young man's mouth is pried open.

"Say 'ahh.' "

"Ahhrgg," says the young man, beginning to retch.

"Now."

Turf pulls out all the young man's teeth.

The young man spits a waterfall of blood into a chrome basin, splattering the white tennis sneakers of the dentist.

"Musn't do that," announces Turf in a prehistoric voice and leaps into the karate fight stance, does a quick karate dance, yells, then hacks downward. The chop hits the abdomen and goes right through. The young man's pain dissolves. Suddenly there's a cloud in the hole where his stomach once was.

"Y'alright?"

"I don't know."

The woman's breasts are tied down with a leather thong. A leather hand holds her crotch. She's holding a golden straight razor.

The young man is still on the doctor's bed, strapped down. She walks toward him and he strains to break free of the straps, arching his back, having a horrible image of this leather-held woman cutting off his manhood with one quick golden swipe of the razor.

She laughs.

He gets a hard-on.

It puzzles him. In the middle of his death, his hard-on springs to proud attention.

The girl laughs.

"You're cute. I'm not going to hurt you. Just going to give you a little shave. A little rubdown."

Holding his cock, she deftly applies sweet oil on his pubic hairs, then manipulates the oil into foamy suds. Then, still holding on, she shaves his pubic hairs off. Daintily wipes off hair and suds. His hard-on remains, saluting the ceiling.

"This won't do," she says and pulls the leather hand off her crotch.

She straddles him and guides her drooling cunt over his erection, centers it, then skewers herself to him.

"Now for the rubdown."

She begins rowing him as if he were a sex-boat. Then pumps up and down like an oil well.

The poor young man is dazzled by her pressed breasts and she, in a sweaty frenzy, catches his helpless eyes and unties the thong to let them balloon out before him. They bounce with their fullness. He tries nipping at one of the large erect nipples but misses. Meanwhile she is working her hips faster and faster and then begins a curious corkscrew motion, bouncing about. Facing him, then her back to him. Humping, bumping, squealing. And he can only watch and feel his shot, his charge, begin to gather up force as her final pump squeezes tight upon his cock tip.

On his saddle horn, she begins to feel her own release electrify the circuits of her desire until she stops riding. Shudders for a second. Then screams in ecstasy. His orgasm pumps furiously into her as if his cock had turned into a machine gun. He can't stop and neither can she. She screams and comes and comes and screams and young man Priapus screams not but keeps pumping out his hot white gravy into her steaming basin.

A voice out of the loudspeaker somewhere on the wall.

"Is that it, Marla?"

"Ohh, God, is it..."

"Is he clean?"

"He's cute..."

"Marla, you haven't been...?"

"Oh, no, I've done what you told me and he's clean there," she says dreamily, dismounting, picking up her equipment, and binding herself together again.

"Alright, Marla, you're dismissed."

She begins to leave, then turns back and blows the young man a kiss.

He smiles helplessly at her, wishing he could wave to her, but his hands are strapped down to the bed.

4.

"The plan's simple," says Carla, now in blue jeans, hanging out wash on a plastic clothesline, posing for a soap ad in a midtown advertising agency. "It's a well-organized, self-sufficient sexual underground that runs smoothly. Structured like a diagram of an archaeological chart. There's the total bottom, the disaster area for the incompetent, the unstable, those unable to adjust to total character transformation. The ultimate bone-pile."

"Uuh, Carla, turn sideways. Right," says Jack Flash, staff photographer. "Sammy, use the orange gel. Right. Good. Okay. Good girl. Fine."

Carla continues, her body rigid in its pose, exactly as it will look in the photograph in the national magazine.

"It's like a skyscraper. The top is the penthouse, the power center. We have offices all over the country and agencies in Europe, especially Germany, and in Japan. Very good place for much of our sexual apparatus. Most of our cameras come from there too."

Jack Flash walks up to Carla. Kissed her on a lovely white cheek. Pats her head.

"Great, baby. You can unwind now. C'mon, Sammy. Let's go into Studio 6."

"What's going on there?" asks Sammy.

"That's the animal room."

"Oh boy, y'mean that donkey?"

"Right," says Jack Flash. "Let's go."

And they're gone.

Carla continues, walking from the set and going into a dark shadowed area where a cabinet stands. She reaches in.

"Drink?"

"Sherry."

"Fine."

She pulls out an antique decanter and pours the amber delicacy into the appropriate glass.

He is led into a room with lights on the ceiling creating a vast spotlight in the room's center.

"Okay. You wait. The photographers'll be here in a sec. Meet Myrna. She'll wait with you."

Myrna comes out of the shadows. A small, sparrowlike lady with small breasts and smudged blonde hair cut short. Almost hipless, her lean legs are covered with a golden down that shines as she walks toward him.

"Don't tell me anything," she says.

"Okay, I won't. I don't have much to say anyway."

"Kiss me."

They kiss. Her lean body is frail as it pushes into his. He has to bend down to reach her thin lips. They part. For a moment he feels as if his tongue is too huge for her open mouth. Yet, strangely, the more his tongue burrows into it, the wider it seems to be until he can feel her lips widening as if to swallow his face. He tries not to press her too tightly because he feels he would hear bones break if he did.

They part. She looks at him, surveys his body and fixes her eyes on his slightly hardened cock.

"Let me have a man before they bring on Aesop?"

"Aesop?"

"Ask me nothing. Fuck me. Now. Here."

The thin frail-blonde girl-woman bends over, grabs her knees and offers the young man her small round butt. She stands there. A thin trail of liquid trickles down her inner thigh.

He goes behind her, puts his hands around her waist and, holding her breasts, begins to push his pulsing cock into her proffered rear.

The door opens.

"Ah, c'mon, Myrna, no cheating."

She pulls up. Her shoulders drop in defeat. Jack Flash stands between them with three cameras around his neck.

"Listen, Myrna, y'got to save your ass for Aesop. He's been waiting a week for you. And you too."

"Me?" asks the young man.

"You."

"Yes, go on," he says.

They toast each other. Carla lips quickly at the sherry.

"I've never understood why old wines are supposed to be so good. This tastes bitter to me."

"Go on."

"Yes, alright," says Carla and puts the glass down. She begins to undress, removing the plaid blouse, stepping out of the baggy jeans, standing before the man in her undergarments.

"Help me unhook. This is a special bra that makes my breasts unobtrusive but believable to the American housewife and her husband."

He walks behind her and unhooks the bra.

"Mmm," she sighs, feeling her breasts sway free, unconfined.

"Go on, please," he says. "I don't have much more time. I'm due in Paris in five hours, then Moscow in the morning..."

"Moscow? You mean?"

"Exactly. Continue."

"What do you need to know?"

"For now, just a general rundown of the operation. But, if you'll permit me, I must rewind the tape machine to get the rest of it down."

He opens his attaché case, which contains a shirt, a tape recorder, a .45 automatic with silencer, and a copy of the *Wall Street Journal*.

"You know, of course, that it's more than just pleasure, just dream-copulation, just fueling the masturbator's culture. It's a matter of control. Many-sided, many-celled, Hydra-headed..."

"What is a Hydra head?" asks Carla. She feels a draft on her breasts.

"That's unimportant right now. Why don't you put something on; your body is covered with goose bumps. Please hurry, I must get it all down. By the way..."

"Yes?"

"For the record, your dimensions."

Carla smiles and moves closer to the man.

"48-22-35. 39-26-38. 36-24-36. What are your dimensions?"

"Please, this is business of the highest order."

"What is your name?" she asks.

The man's hand blurs past her eyes and flat-palms a slap to the side of her cheek.

"That was uncalled for," Carla says, her eyes beginning to see through the glaze.

"That's unimportant. I need information, you know that. If I require recreation I know where to go. Now. How many heads of state are active in the Agency, how many senators, congressmen, generals, etc.? Do you have a list?"

"Yes."

"Good."

Carla reaches into a drawer and hands the man a folder which he retrieves delicately, belying his intense curiosity.

"Mm, so…extremely interesting…No!…mm. Good."

"I have photographs, movies, recordings, letters, receipts, assorted mementos," says Carla.

"Send them to the Main Branch when ordered. You will be contacted. You've done your job well. You are happy, aren't you?"

"It's a job," she says.

"Oh, come, we too have photographs, movies, recordings, etc., and you seem to enjoy your work beyond the normal call of such employment," he says, shutting the attaché case and moving away, toward the exit sign.

"You're leaving?"

"Yes, the helicopter's landed."

"How do you know?"

"I heard it."

"Do you ever miss me?"

"Why do you ask? I hardly know you," he says, trying to push the door open quickly.

"But you are—"

"It was a mistake," he says, shutting the door.

"—my father."

The echo of the slammed exit door fills the empty studio and causes slight ripples in the sherry in the glasses.

"Okay, kids," says Jack Flash. "I want Myrna over there. Sammy, get the stool. Right. Okay, Myrna, give the ass head while you…right, you…you let the screwed-up donkey give you head.

Sammy, get him the small ladder there. Okay, kids, great. I'm gonna experiment with some new filters today which oughta give the pics greater contrast and tone."

The young man climbs up the small ladder and sits on the top before the gray old donkey named Aesop whose snout quivers into the young man's crotch.

"Let's see now. Myrna, let Sammy make up Aesop some more. Yeah, put that slickum on his dick. Right. Okay. Hey, knock it off, Sammy, leave Myrna be now, you can have her later during rest time. Slick up the young fellah over there. Right. Oops. Really gets it up don't it?"

Yes it does, he thinks, his cock aflame and erect again, nearly poking an eye out of Aesop who stands there firm on the studio floor.

Aesop's large steamy pink tongue lolls out of his mouth and blankets the young man's erection in its heat. Meanwhile, down at the other end, Myrna begins gobbling Aesop's incredibly immense member. Jack Flash, nimble and quick, dances about, snapping pictures, crawling on his belly, shooting upwards, shooting behind her bunched-up shoulders to zero in on a new view of fellatio; then atop a high aluminum ladder, with a new wide-angle lens, to survey the landscape below; then, one arm hooked around a ladder's step, he leans out like a sailor sighting land from mast-top—Jack Flash works into position to shoot between Aesop's ears. An interesting vision of the young man, bent back, holding onto the ladder top, while Aesop guzzles the young man's resurrected erection.

"Okay, kids. Cut for a sec. Gotta switch to color and I'm gonna work out with some crazy new lights…kids? Ah, shit. Sammy, break 'em up before they come."

Sammy runs around prying, pushing, struggling. Myrna's suction is so great that when she's pulled away it sounds like the top popped off a giant champagne bottle.

He has to use a nasty trick on the young man. He flicks his fingers against the throbbing hard-on. Once. Twice. The young man groans. His erection falls as quickly as it rose.

A few bleak minutes go by. Pain subsides.

They sit, Myrna, he and Sammy, drinking tepid coffee.

"I've forgotten what I used to be," says Myrna. "I don't know how it happened or why but here I am and it seems as if here is where I've always been. I used to be twenty-five but I don't know how long ago that was. Let me hold your hand?" she asks the young man.

His hand reaches out to her hand, their fingertips touch. For a moment, the young man is in another world and romantic tenderness blossoms in his tired heart. Her poor bruised mouth, he thinks.

"Bullshit," says Sammy. "You was found in a Tijuana animal-show, queen of the reruns."

"Liar," says Myrna, her voice cracking. "I was a consulate's mistress in the jungle and then came the dreaded plague and destroyed his mind and then the natives revolted and…"

"You were born in Pasadena and never left California except when you went to T.J. for your animal act."

"Liar," says Myrna, her voice frosting over its sorrow and turning brittle. "I was born in an aristocratic family with a long lineage of royalty. My colors are royal green, jet blue, flame red…"

"Bruises and cuts on your knees from bad scenes in public men's rooms…"

"Liar," says Myrna, her voice turning into dry ice. "I was a script-girl, a governess; I was a secretary to a billionaire who loved me more than life itself but whose heart gave way before he could sign his name to the new will.

"I was a hostess in a key-club in London and was adored by a six-member rock and roll band who were all multimillionaires. They made love to me on soft cribs of pounds and silver. All at once and then each alone.

"Then I was the concubine of a Tibetan Tantric Yoga prophet and saw eternity and felt the map of my nerves illuminated when his magical love would be within me, without me…"

"Aw, bushwah," says Sammy, knocking over his container of coffee.

"Okay, kids, c'mon now, knock it off. Take two," sings Jack Flash.

"I think I believe you," the young man says.

"Oh, thank you," says Myrna and does a strange quick bump and grind for him.

"Save it for the jackass," snarls Sammy.

5.

The Cafeteria, a room smaller than the Animal Room.

The young man is led into it through swinging doors. Against three of four walls are a series of black leather saddles. Across all of the walls, all framed in nonreflective glass, are photographs of cunts of all shapes and sizes. They form an amazing calligraphy and the young man surveys the collection in amazement.

Starting off each row is a photograph of the ideal cunt: the perfect pelt, neatly curled, a perfect triangle, trim and precise, directing the eye, like an arrow, to the mysterious lips at its point. Then the shapes begin to vary in a compulsive rhythm. Some cunts are like a single swooping brush stroke, others are tangled hair jungles breaking the triangular shape into hairy extensions that reach into the inner calf; some are round-shaped, hence, the muff; cunts of delicate composition whose hairs are thin and almost translucent like the fragile chin-hairs on Oriental sages; square-shaped cunts, hence, box; trapezoid cunts, some with a hair leader growing up in a line on a soft white belly reaching the spiral of the navel; cunts whose hair have the texture and thickness of Brillo pads; white-haired cunts, red-haired cunts that explode into freckles; bearded cunts; cunts like Shakespeare's Vandyke; shaved cunts looking oddly like rearranged muffins; mystic cunts like the top of the Tree of Life; black cunts; Chinese cunts; a cunt tattooed in spectacular patterns where the hairline ends—the elaborate tattoo blossoms across the body into a magical floral display; cunts which resemble the faces of rodents...and in the center of the center wall a large photograph, thrice as big as the others, of a man's tongue, cloven, forked, sinister and inviting.

A door opens and a small platoon of naked women march out and take their places before the black leather-covered saddles.

"Everybody here?" asks a voice through concealed speakers.

A lusty cry of "Yes!" is barked out by the girls.

"Alright, get into position, ladies," orders the voice.

The ladies straddle the saddles, lying on their backs, their legs spread wide, their feet hooked into stirrups growing out of the contraptions.

"Pillows comfy?"

The girls adjust leather pillows behind their heads and shoulders.

The door opens once again and a six-foot-seven Amazon strides into the room. She is wearing a breastplate over one breast, while the other breast, a mammoth basketball of a boob, bobs freely. Around her loins she wears a metal chips. She holds a mace in one hand and metal chips. She holds a mace in one hand and a giant bullwhip in the other.

"Alright, you," she snarls at the young man, who cringes in the blast of her voice. "Get going."

"Where am I going?"

She cracks the bullwhip in the air and a small cloud of plaster sprinkles off the ceiling.

"I'm Brigette," she bellows.

"How do you do?"

"Now get to work. I want all muh girls satisfied and well-done so's my army can have their taste too," booms Brigette in a voice not unlike a rusted foghorn.

Then he gets the idea.

"Counterclockwise, soldier!" roars Brigette.

He begins at the beginning. The smallest cunt. A tiny round pink-rimmed entrance. As soon as the tip of the tongue enters the center of her, she jerks in her stirrup. "Eyiyy-yy!" she shouts. Her zone is extremely hot and burns his tongue tip, but he continues and she continues yipping her strange scream.

By the time he's a quarter of the way down the line his tongue tip's numb, his jaw stiff, his mouth covered with musk, essence, pubic hairs and tears. He falters as he faces the cave of a giant cunt.

"I get so horny," says Brigette on her mount, legs spread, sounding almost girlish. "Get goin'," she snarls softly. He's reminded of the joke about a midget. He dives into her expansive gleaming cunt, trying not to notice the muscular thighs and calves knotted in anticipation and desire. His tongue works the flaccid rims. Brigette grabs hold of the back of his head and jams his face full into the sour mash.

"Work, boy," she grumbles. Her voice a vast echo coming through the drum of her taut belly.

He works as best he's able. Nose-deep in work, mouth nibbling, nuzzling, slurping, probing, chewing; her clitoral smell a combination of a locker room and a Turkish bordello (gallon jugs of Woolworth's cheapest perfumes). He begins to feel more than mere suffocation. This is how I'll die, he thinks, and it's almost what he imagined being inside the womb was like.

Her hands push his head harder and her football-player legs circle his back and push him farther down until he feels as if her cunt is the mouth of a whale and he's to be swallowed alive in it. It's like trying to paint the Sistine Chapel ceiling with a crayon. He begins to falter, his tongue completely numb, swollen; his lips feel twice as big as they were once upon a time and they stretch into curious shapes like dough.

"Argh," groans Brigette in anguish, "there'll never be another Klaus. Okay, boy, pull out."

The young man slumps to his knees. The cool air is a precious feeling on his sweaty face.

"Y'see," says Brigette, turning on the strange saddle to rest on her muscular stomach, "that's Klaus up there."

The man with the forked tongue.

"He was all tongue," groans Brigette. "Well, there's only one thing left for you to do for me. Hop up and burrow in, buster." She slams her huge fist on the table. He gets behind her and she deftly props her read end into his face.

"Get th' picture?"

The young man gulps.

One foot bridges between his legs and lifts him half off the structure.

"Get th' picture?"

"Yes, yes."

"Fine, buster."

Gently, with delicacy, the young man is set on level ground.

He begins to work his numb tongue between the firm mounds. They part and she lies there. After a bit of exploration he finds the place and extends his tongue into it. Brigette's stomach rumbles. The young man doesn't duck in time.

How many hours the rest of it takes remains a mystery.

The last cunt his mouth fixes to begins to look like a person he once knew. So many cunts and after a while each one looks different, takes on a personal quality. To kill time, he begins to see if he can visualize what the face above the cunt will look like, what the cunt will smell like and what the smell reminds him of. Preserve the imagination, he thinks. There's a spasm of orgasm and the last lady goes through the throes of ecstasy. Expired, she presses a button.

The door opens. The ladies, in a wobbly single file, leave.

Now what?

The door shuts.

"Alright, boy," says a familiar voice through the concealed speakers, "lunch time's over. Bath time's next."

Two muscular lads in brief tight jockstraps come into the room. They look like those kids you might see on the covers of physique magazines: hair in waxy pompadours and ripply, tight-muscled forms. Their faces are bland and pale, each has the same Kewpie-doll nose, the same classic bob. Muscle-bound Barbie Dolls. They grab hold of both his arms and drag the young man out.

6.

Hurko Fist, ex-football great, Oxhead '57, stands in the center of a squad of nice young men. Fist wears a latex mini-jockstrap around his hairy middle and a silver football helmet decorated with a triad of gold phalluses.

"Hey, cover him up!" barks Fist. "Get him dressed and *then* bring him to me in my Locker Room. And wait until *I'm* finished with him. Y'hear?"

The nice young men nod.

A steamy place. The stink is the first shock. A stench of lotions, perfumes, talcs, balms, condiments, sweat and enemas. It webs the humid air.

Stone ledges line the back wall. A square pool of hot, dark water rests before the ledges. The pool is surrounded by saddle-tables similar to the ones used in the Lunch Room. No pictures on the walls. The walls are decorated with public urinal tiles. A statue of a broken torso. Soft music piped in. Maybe Johnny Mathis or Judy Garland.

The squad of nice young men wear many uniforms. One wears a black body-grabbing motorcycle jumpsuit of leather and a white vinyl motorcycle cap. He holds onto a floor-length tire chain. Another young man wears a cock-bulging tight pair of Levi's. His torso is undraped to reveal his rippling muscles which roll and tumble as he flexes them. One young man wears chaps around his naked frame. Between his chaps hangs the longest cock our hero has ever seen. It seems to reach to the kneecap.

A young man in a white silk sailor suit which is tight around the calves and groin, flaring out at mid-knee; soft fabric rustles upon a pair of soft black leather gaucho boots.

Like a young Greek god stands a blond-haired lad clad in a plastic fig leaf. His body is perfect and slightly bronzed. He picks his nose with one hand and holds a hand mirror in the other.

The last young man he notices wears a WWI flier's outfit.

Hurko Fist's Locker Room is lit with colored lights that make the lockers and the old posters and framed photographs dim and mysterious. Softly heard, as if the speakers are muffled with throw-pillows, the sound of marching bands playing school songs.

The smell of heavy lilac incense. This upsets the young man more than anything so far because he remembers eating lilacs when he was a kid because he loved how they smelled—and he never was sicker.

Hurko's wearing a bright kelly-green and yellow silk boxer's robe and reclines on a large metal cot which is covered with foot blankets decorated with Oxhead's insignia which was (and is) an oxhead resting in the center of a thorny garland.

"Come on in, kid, and sit down. There. By my cleats."

The young man sits on the floor and looks up at Hurko Fist.

"I wanna talk awhile and then we'll get down to business. Wanna drink? Here, have a drink."

Hurko hands a porcelain beer mug to the young man.

"It's filled to the brim with old Oxhead piss and vinegar. You and me, kid, chug-a-lug it."

Hurko guzzles down his drink in record time. "Like so."

Burps, farts, gasps, groans, wipes his lips and exhales.

"Ahh. Ahh."

The silence is broken only by the mug being refilled.

"By the way, kid, how old are you? I mean, you're not over thirty, are you?"

"No."

"Okay. Let's drink up, boy."

Hurko lurches his mug to the young man's. They toast.

"Chug-a-lug! Old Oxhead!"

The young man drinks the stuff down as quickly as he can, thankful to be relieved of the lilac stench. He drains the mug to the dregs.

Again, the band music, coming down some long hallway. The trumpets, fifes and drums. The tubas, triangles, glockenspiels and trombones.

"First off, now that we're blood brothers, I wanna tell you about a few things that I think I wanna say. Here, drink another mug of old Oxhead. Gimme your mug."

He hands Hurko the mug and notices how large and hairy-knuckled his hand is. Also the robe falls open slightly and he sees how the hair starts from Hurko's ankles and gets heavier and darker as it enters into the groin garden. Hurko's gone to seed and has gotten fleshy. His belly shows white through the curls of hair upon it. His legs are chunky and it looks like his rear end is packed with old Oxhead.

"Y'know, in the old days at Oxhead, I had them little cunts anytime I wanted, but, y'know, in those days, there weren't no pill and all, and I didn't wanna get married right then, y'know, I was hoping to go pro and make some money outa football, y'know, so I kept myself pretty clean, I mean, I kept myself away from them young cunts with their pom-poms and batons and tits and asses and all, y'know. About the only cunt I had was the coach's wife and that was because the coach was such a good guy, y'know, but the war fucked around with his fucker, y'know, his thing, his dingy, his dong, and he couldn't even raise a pinky, so's we'd all, for him and old Oxhead, fuck his wife, in rotation, once a week. I mean, one of us, every Sunday night, would take a blanket and meet her in the empty stadium and under the goalpost fuck her until she'd had enough.

"But, y'know, she was a strange old cunt and didn't just want to fuck, I mean, after a while, she wanted it every way we all could give it to her until she'd have maybe three or four of us out there under the old goalpost fucking and sucking and shoving, and after a while more, y'know, it kind of got outa hand and even the second-stringers would be there, standing in line, taking their turn too, and we first-stringers got tired of it and began to relieve ourselves. I mean we was big strong men, not faggots, y'understand. But it was all we could do to keep our mind on football, and after a while, y'know, we'd get hung up at big games over the other side's hips and thighs and instead of tackling we'd be goosing 'em and feeling their baskets and promising them anything. Old Oxhead had a weird year that year. We lost a few, we won a few.

"Now, boy, get up here and suck off an ath-a-leet. I woulda made All-American if it hadn't a been for that fucking coach's wife! I woulda been great!"

Hurko Fist spread his hairy almost-All-American legs and pushed aside the green and yellow silk. A small prick nestled shyly in the pubic jungle and all the young man could see attached to it was one ball.

"What's the matter, old Oxhead's got your tongue?"

"I never, I mean I don't know how to…"

"To what, y'young prick? To suck cock? Y'mean you're a cherry, some kind of weirdo? Heh?"

His arm reaches around the young man's neck. Jerks him off the floor, pushes his mouth onto the dormant tiny prick.

"Now suck on it 'til it wakes up. Then suck my ball. It's a good sign to have one ball."

The young man's tongue tips the tip of Hurko Fist's teeny-weeny.

"Suck it, y'asshole," groans Hurko.

The young man fits it between his lips until the crown rests upon his tongue, and begins to suck and lick it. And it begins to move in his mouth and widen and widen until he feels like gagging and moves his mouth back, up the shaft, now gnarled and hot and pulsing, then down again, back and forth, the flame within the inner skin of Hurko's cock burning his mouth.

"Okay," pants Fist. "Now suck my ball. I wanna come in your hair."

So he sucks on the ball, gently.

"Harder. Hurt me, y'prick."

So he sucks harder on the ball, pubic hairs plastered to his wet mouth.

Hurko Fist, former great, ejaculates a weak yellow-white stream in the young man's sideburn.

"Mmhh, mmhh, down a little lower, y'fuckhead," groans Hurko.

Hurko Fist finishes coming into the young man's ear.

"Ahh, that's the way the old coach liked it best," he mumbles, hairy hands pawing a trail down the young man's chest.

"Now, cunt, we're gonna take your ass."

And so he did.

Wearing a waxed wooden dildo around his gutty midriff, Hurko Fist pushes 275 pounds of flying tackle into the young man's unbroken butt.

The young man's eyes try to break through the blood roar of his shut lids. Hurko begins to pull on the young man's cock. Lunging, pulling, roughly handling the balls, the young man feels his erection grow in Hurko's paw. Deflowering agony subsides and he comes in Hurko's hand.

"Yay, team!" screams Hurko Fist, licking the sauce off his mitt.

The squad of nice young men walk into Hurko's Locker Room to carry our hero off.

One of them, in a pinafore, stays to wipe up the blood and

come, and also to reservice Fist, who, at the moment, is sobbing softly in a foot warmer.

They take his clothes off. Quickly.

Then drop him into the dark waters of the small pool which is hot and smells of sulphur. The heat relaxes his muscles and he floats in pleasure in the water.

A beautiful young boy in a scuba diver's helmet dives into the pool and vanishes underneath. And never surfaces.

While another young man, blond hair, mahogany-tanned by the sun, wearing a Tarzan breech clout, dives in and swims beneath the young man and begins blowing bubbles, underwater, on the young man's cock and balls.

Then pulls his leg so that he too goes underwater. They wrestle silently with the weight of oceans upon their bodies. But the bronzed boy is fast and soon is fixed to the young man's root and sucking on it like mad until the young man must bend over in painful joy. His come streams into the muddy water like a shredding ribbon. A dirty white bridge in space.

Cock raw from underwater sucking, the young man is handed over to the sailor in the white silk suit.

"On your knees, mate."

On his knees, the young man faces a twitching pink rod released from the button-down sailor-suit flap.

And his mouth enclosed it.

It tastes strangely of cinnamon.

The load finally gushed into his mouth tastes like the foam of waves.

The motorcyclist straps the young man, belly down, on his powerful cycle; spreads the young man's legs apart, straps them with thongs to each pedal, then plunges his cock into the young man, keeping balance by holding onto the handlebars.

This goes on. They all try him.

After each trial, he's bathed, rubbed down, then handed over to the next one, the next nice young man.

The Levi lad arranges them so that they are in the classic 69 position, but the man in Levi's uses teeth to punctuate his ecstasy and when he comes almost bites the other's cock off.

The last young man to have our hero is the one in chaps, the one with the incredible cock.

The others in the squad gather around, arms around slender hips, to watch the finale.

The nice young cowboy straddles the saddle table and sinks into the saddle bow. Legs around his neck, rump thrust out, and over the crack, like a handle, the impossible cock, an extension beyond the artist's realm.

"Alright, partner. Ride me."

The WWI flier pushes the young man to the stirrups.

"C'mon, buddy, kiss the bud."

The young man kneels before the cock's northern point. Its crown flares around in red sunset tints and begins to widen as the young man's breath touches it.

"Grab on, buddy, and ride."

The prick's tip widens and becomes a large as a man's face. The center of it opens and within, deep down its pink-rimmed tunnel, the fire of flares is white.

"I can't."

"C'mon, buddy, do it."

Down the shaft's tunnel into the birth of a nova.

"C'mon, buddy, ride me, ride me, ride me…"

The illusion broken, the young man begins to gobble on the tip, pushing the mammoth hose into his mouth, feeling it fold inside the wet cave.

Then, the erection, the maypole.

The young man hits the ground and is picked up by somebody.

The nice young cowboy is flat on his back to support the tree growing out of his loins.

Some of the nice young squad stand him upright.

They put the other young man, our hero, on the saddle and clamp his hands in the side-grips. His second-hand butt is pushed up and propped as a clearly sighted target for the cowboy who is across the other side of the room.

The cowboy yells, whoops, screams and starts galloping. He rams into the young man with full force.

"Yay, team!" screams Hurko Fist.

The cowboy's incredible cock is a corkscrew up his ass and crashes into his spine and he feels his nerves and discs crack and spangle with pain.

"Hi-ho, Silver," moans the nice young man in a pinafore who stands behind Hurko, jammed into Hurko's meaty rear end.

Hurko's hairy knees wobble but the young man holds him up, cupping Fist's flabby pectorals, tweaking the hair-circled nipples.

Knees dragging on the floor, they carry the young man down a hallway, through a swinging door, into a room which consists of an old sofa, a table and a chair. They leave him and shut the door. He stays slumped on the floor, his body sore, his cock a tired flower between his legs.

The door opens.

"Ha, it's you. They told me."

The young man sees only a black skirt and black high-heeled boots.

"Look up," hisses the voice.

The young man sees only a black skirt and skirt, the white blouse, and into the face of Leonard.

"Now that you're theirs, I want you to be mine. Get on the couch. Come on. Move."

The young man pulls himself off the floor and flops down on the couch.

Leonard drops upon him and begins to kiss the bruised mouth.

"Open," he snarls.

The young man opens his mouth and Leonard's tongue pushes through and waggles about inside.

Leonard's hands begin to fondle the young man's hips and slide between his legs to gently touch the abused cock. With delicate feather-light stroking around the top of the shaft and the crown's rim, Leonard manages to activate the young man's cock into a tired hard-on.

"Come on, love me, I don't want to do it all," says Leonard, his voice becoming soft, tender.

"I have the needs of a woman. It is God's fault that he made me the way I am."

The young man embraces Leonard and begins to touch his body, running his hands over the foam towers of his breasts, up the sheer black nylons that lead into the silken panties which cannot conceal Leonard's male apparatus.

"Be gentle," moans Leonard.

The young man is gentle enough and shuts his eyes and smells the perfume dabbed behind Leonard's ears and, silk and nylon meshing and frothing, the young man feels his belly being licked by Leonard. Open-mouth kisses and then plain doglike lapping.

"Darling, put your legs on the floor and lie back," Leonard whispers.

The young man does as he is told and Leonard is off the sofa and between his spread legs. First he runs his tongue from the crown down the shaft to where the balls begin. Up and down. In that same languorous rhythm of this encounter. The young man's prick springs to a pulsing attention. Leonard continues until the young man's cock feels as if there is another cock, a bigger and newer one, being born within the skin and trying to break through it. He squirms. Leonard persists. Then enfolds his wet mouth about the cock-dome and performs classic and exquisite fellatio upon the young man's rejuvenated cock. Leonard stops as the young man becomes ready to ejaculate.

"Oh, no, not that way. I'm not that kind," he says and quickly pulls down his garter belt, nylons, panties, and mini-girdle. The whole works tangles around his knees.

It's over quickly. Leonard pats the young man on the rump and leaves, walking rather unsteadily, still enmeshed in his undergarments.

The door shuts. And locks. The young man hears the bolt click into place.

7.

He doesn't sleep. There's no way to turn out the light. It hangs on the ceiling by a dusty chord, fly-specked. By the sofa (stuffed with barbed wire, wood shavings, old guitar strings, cracked bowling balls) is a small bookcase which the young man notices after his first meal of the day (the week, the month, the year?) which was brought to him on a hard rubber tray by a chunky, matronly Negress with outsized breasts bound together by a tight black bra, in a pink half-slip and nylons rolled down to her knees. Her mouth was ripe and oversmeared with a purple lipstick. When she smiled at him, bending down to place the tray on a small table, he saw that her teeth were the color of nicotine and that her breast divided into two whales and he watched their bigness and she saw him and winked.

"Y'can't eat the food, baby, until you give me some of your staff of life," she said, and he saw that there were fine hieroglyphs of age around her eyes and two strict lines running to her mouth that made her look like a ventriloquist's dummy. "Y'all ready and pink and your pecker is shining from lusting," she said, and pushed her huge breasts into his slack-jawed mug and he could smell detergent and sweat as she fell on him. She fell on him with her soft massive hulk and pushed her tongue into his ear and unhooked her bra so that those huge breasts mashed against his naked body and he could feel the burning of her cunt against his still prick.

"Y'know, when y'get this old and beat-up and used-out, y'gotta get it when you can, even when they don't want it, you want it, you gotta get it—and I'm gonna get it, boy, now!" And she tangled with him, pushed her legs through his and placed her hands on her breasts and his fist into her cunt and they rolled about until he was on top of her and somehow was inside her and she was pumping and humping and saying nothing at all, staring at him, working, as if this were like washing dishes or making a bed. More tumbling and she was on top of him, his pole still in her, and her breasts flapping in his face, his face in their shadow. Slapping his face, the nipples hard and rubbery, and he grabbed them while she squeezed his cock with her cunt muscles and rode his white frame. More tumbling and he was back on top, still kneading those brown tits and trying like hell to come, to come, to get it over with. And when he came it was painful but she wouldn't stop and drew the final seed from him and left him immediately.

"I'll be back in five minutes for your tray and you better be ready for more. That stuff there ain't much for nutrition but it's good for fucking and keeping goin' until you're done-in like me, used-up, through."

His meal was a cup of bitter tea, a vial of green fluid, a dry cracker which didn't taste like a cracker, one dried animal organ (he didn't want to guess which because it was the only thing that tasted halfway decent) and thirteen pills of various sizes and colors in a cup attached to a glass of smoky water.

Five minutes later, or maybe sooner, the black lady returned. This time their fucking was a little more animated because she had rubbed an unknown ointment into her cunt and as soon as his cock timidly entered the large slot it became twice as large and twice as greedy. It was like oil drilling. When they gushed, they gushed. She bit a neat chunk out of his shoulder and also tattooed part of his other arm with a bear-paw scratch. That was when they were coming. And coming. And that was all over now.

The young man sits on the immensely uncomfortable sofa and decides to see what's in the bookcase. He can't sleep because he is too tired and he fears that if he sleeps he might not awaken.

In a neat cellophane-wrapped package, he finds a collection of twelve photographs featuring himself and a bevy of fuck-happy freaks in a dazzling display of sexual delirium.

Magazines with pictures of women wrestling with men in brilliantly-lit living rooms. Catalogs for sexual gear such as dildoes, foam-rubber cunts with "remarkable new electronic interior nosecones to keep the comer coming as long as the charge lasts," rubber-wear, chastity girdles, spying devices (SEE THRU WALLS!), whips, racks, rods; encyclopedias of masturbation, self-buggery, alphabets of perversion. A couple of tattered volumes filled with drawings and photographs ("for the professional seeker of Truth") of the infinite varieties of positions used in lovemaking. One is printed in India with exotic drawings of temple

whores working over a bejeweled white elephant. There's a
Japanese booklet of lopsided Walt Disney woodcuts. See the little frogs fuck the little toadstool toe-dancers; watch the horny duck
hump the cross-eyed mouse-lady; see the cobra burrow between
the thighs of a deer...

The pamphlet which he decides to read has an orange cover
with black borders. Its title is stated in bold type: THE SEXUAL
ILLUSION; OR, WHAT'S UP FRONT IS NOT NECESSARILY
WHAT'S AHEAD; OR, THE MIND INVENTS ITS OWN DEATH.

On the flyleaf is a photo of the anonymous author. His naked
back is turned to the camera.

A few preliminary extracts:

—Life is short...but it can be "fun."

—Spare the rod and spoil the orgasm.

—We cooperate with the Post Office—therefore, please do not
write obscene letters. Also do not use postcards—it is in bad
taste.

—Leather Garments. Rubber Garments. Exotic Garments.
High Heel Shoes. Science Fiction. Broadminded Men. Broad-
minded Women. Female Impersonation. Homosexuality.
Swapping. Passive Women. Dominant Women. Transvestism.
Photography. Nude Photos. Discipline. Psychology. Wrestling.
Lesbianism. Divorces. Wrestling. Long Hair. Bloomers. Spanking.
Bondage. Romance. Corsets. Artists. Boots. —Check Categories.
We are compiling a list.

Many more pages, which comprise an introductory anthol-
ogy. Quotes by Confucius, Dale Carnegie, de Sade, Elbert
Hubbard, Nicodemus, Nostradamus, Thomas Aamper, Lao
Tzu, Leary, Artaud, Peale, Pike, Spellman, Sartre, etc.

—Is it the fear of the fact that makes the mind crave illusion?

—Who am I? What shall I be? Do I care to really know?

—Who leads me?

—As you know, the asking of questions forks the road into
two. Beginning, end.

—Movie stars are dead.

—Who are the gods, what are heroes?

Strange tract, muses the young man, trying to restore the lost core of his own dream. I think I wanted to be a philosopher or a poet. I was always waiting for the muse, any muse, to enter my room, my candlelit retreat from the street, my room of books half-read, my room of pennies and day-old bread. And she would be pink and real and pale and mysterious. Sometimes I saw the Universe as a great magic circle whose spirals and spins held the seeds of infinity and greatness. I, he thinks, wanted my dreams made real.

—We are more than we can realize and fear fulfillment as much as we fear loss.

(A reproduction of a drawing-insignia of a male and female twisted into the shapes of an eight-point star.)

—Bend with the wind is what the grass stalk does.

Man resists wind. Man is not a grass stalk.

The force-field center of fucking. Eyes shut to add to dark, in darkness, clamped to the mate, yet dreaming of fantasy distractions, impossible dreams further corrupted by short-circuited imaginations.

It is out of and not into that the spirit seems to go. Illusion, maya, is our mistress, our major mover.

(A cut of a circle going into a circle going into a circle until the eye tries to continue through the page and into space.)

Bullshit, he sighs.

I never wanted to be anything. I should never have been born. But, having been born, I push along.

A buzzer.

"Who is it?"

"Nobody. Go to sleep."

Bullshit, he sighs, and is instantly asleep.

The book falls to the floor.

No traditional deep sleep, a black void devouring time, then to awake, refreshed, ready to begin again. The sleep of, let's say, the laborer coming back from a 14-hour day (25¢ an hour), grabbing a hunk of leathery meat, a chunk of hardening bread, washing it down with cheap thick red wine beginning to sour.

Not for our young man. He gets the traditional inferno of dreams, the classical pulp bright-colored cover panel of nightmares. They begin in blackness. First, a red flare's eye. Then firecrackers. A display of explosions lasting for a few moments. Enough time to awaken the dreamer to his dreams.

"Give him room, give him room. He's a baby."

"Aww, shit, no; a baby, a wee one?"

Pulls him out of the muck, the baby is mud slag, eyes still sealed with womb syrup.

"What is it?"

"Let's see now."

Hands poke through the crust, the rotten rag.

"It's a boy baby. 'S'gotta little boy twig poking in his diapers."

"All right, well, let's clean him up and feed him."

Into the pot of Pet Milk.

Into the Arctic glare of icebergs and snow.

Parsley pudding. A green lens to look through. The baby's held by the heels and dumped and dowsed into pot after pot of stuffs.

"Knock it off," yowls the baby, our young man as a dreamer. But he isn't heard because infants have no words to botch with.

Oak soup. Maybe years later he is on a beach with oversize sunglasses, brown, covering his wide-open eyes trying to outstare the sun.

"Don't you hear me?"

Of course not. The two men continue dipping him until they decide to stop.

"Now what do we do with him?" asks one.

"Find it a momma," says the other.

"Where are we gointa find a mamma?"

"Mine's dead. Poor bitch. Bitten by a mad rapist when she was snooping through Lover's Lane, her nightly outing, the wretched bag. Tetanus of the tit it was."

"Terrible. Y'know mine was never found. I mean it was terrible that she got so lost, working in the factory, she got a thing about the Grinder (that eternal machine symbol, technological phallus) and one day fell into the tray that led into his three-story-high teeth. That was the fruit-salad plant and we know there was enough of her to go around. Compensate for the niggling on the maraschino cherries."

"Terrible. No mothers about then?"

"I guess not."

"All right, the hell with it."

"You mean?"

"Exactly."

The baby's taken outside and dropped, head first, into the primordial slime where he was found.

When you're pursued by all the faces that terrify your eye, your imagination, and no matter how tight your eye is shut in sleep, and no matter how tight you shut your eyes as a dreamer in a dream, the faces continue until they surround you and then they're on giant Cinemascope screens all around you and there is no escape and then their voices are amplified and you can hear them all around you in super stereophonic stroboscopic clash and clang and the car you suddenly are in won't start and when it does start it won't go fast enough and the brakes won't work and your foot's pressing the gas pedal through the floor and your other foot's pressing the brake bar through the floor and the car won't go and the car won't stop.

Up stone steps. Toltec gods on pillars. Sky rich blue. No clouds. Air hot. Just don't ask any questions. Carried above them, by them, their leather foot-bindings squeak and groan. Finally near the top. The sky and air ripple in the heat waves of the fire at the top.

It is so quickly done he is not afraid.

Into the stone altar seat, head pulled back, eyes see the temple top upside down.

The sword blade has been so well sharpened that it is only after his chest has been cut in half that he feels pain.

Dying, he sees his heart in the priest's hand. Still pumping, rich red splashes of his blood splurting out of the severed ventricles, arteries.

She comes to him in a meadow seen through filters. Glowing

and diffuse, she is a movie of herself walking to him. Her naked body sparkles and her mouth is a starburst as the sunlight catches the glaze upon her lips. Her breasts are firm and move as her legs move and as her body moves towards him. Green grass speckled with shasta daisies, yellow faces, brown centers. She comes to him from faraway and breaks through the gauze to reach him.

Under a tent made of sheets he is being handled by a fat pig of a woman who's past all of her prime and has tits that reach her ankles and a belly that's half a hemisphere and a cunt whose red lips rot beneath a tangled mat of pubic hairs and she is kissing his mouth and belly and cock and her breath smells of old books rancid in sea-held trunks and she never stops talking to him about God and the Mythical Mystic Powers that move Man and once he looks down and she's looking up at him with her eyes while her mouth is slurping on his cock and even then she is mumbling something about Powers Beyond and Mind and she's on top of his mouth whetting her cunt's lust by sticking her asshole in his tongue which poles into the incredibly musky, budded hole and her tongue goes up his bunghole and her tongue is so long that its tip tickles the base of his spine and they continue burrowing into each other's lost continents
    Selah, she burps, jamming a burning hot nipple into his mouth
    all he can think of in the maze is the lovely girl walking to him in a fade-out gait which ends a movie about love and romance

Numbers.
Count out.
One, two.
Then what?
One, two.
Who are you?

Book Two

INDOCTRINATION

"The quickest, nicest way to kill a rat or other small animal which has been caught is to put an old potato bag or feed sack over one end of the trap. Open the door which enters the bag. Grab the neck of the bag and you have him. Swing the bag hard and smack against the floor, wall, or any hard object, and the animal is killed instantly and painlessly."

—From an instruction manual
supplied with an animal trap

The Whip, The Rod, The Violated Object

His breakfast is as drab as the last meal. Two yolky poached eggs on gritty crackers, a goblet of what looks like orange juice but tastes like nothing he's ever tasted before, three vials of three differently colored fluids, and a small bowl of assorted pills.

Nevertheless, he gobbles it all down as if it were the highest of exotical cuisine. And burps. And for it all, feels not much pain. Yes, the stiffness in his back and in the muscles behind his thighs, but otherwise he's all right.

The pamphlet's gone.

Perhaps it was never there.

The bookcase is gone too.

Perhaps it was never there.

He stretches out on the funky sofa and yawns. The door opens in mid-yawn. It's not the black big lady who was his maid before he slept. It's a big white woman in a tight black silk dress wearing sunglasses and walking about on the highest spiked (gleaming image-reproducing patent leather) shoes that he has ever seen.

The big woman has big thighs, huge breasts that are coned to a fine point by a firm bra, and a floor-dragging bullwhip which she holds loosely in a fat paw. Her white meaty legs shine through the black patina of her black nylons. He can see bruises beneath both of her knees.

"On your knees, slave! I am your mistress! I am Carmen La Tour from Red Hook!"

Kapow! Smack! Brack! Whup!

Carmen La Tour from Red Hook snaps, cracks and pops her bullwhip in a series of body-shocking maneuvers.

The young man drops to his knees like a well-trained air raid driller.

"Crawl to me and kiss my shoes," orders Carmen La Tour.

He crawls along the crummy linoleum floor to her brilliant

black patent-leather toes. He sees his face grow large and then narrow in the toe-tip.

"Kiss, lick, lap and humiliate your degraded tongue upon my boot," orders Miss La Tour. The young man begins to delicately tongue the mirror-black leather toe.

"Follow behind me, my little demented degraded slave, on all fours. Hurry up, please, it's time for your ultimate degradation by the superior demanding female."

Kapow! Smack! Brack! Whup!

The young man follows behind her on his hands and knees. While waddling so, he sees shoes, boots, high heels, ankles, of people in the hallways looking down at him. Spit hits his bare back as he crawls behind Carmen La Tour from Red Hook.

Slave Training Time.

The Opus opens new horizons under the severe tutelage of Miss La Tour.

Our hero crawls through a doorway and his knees and hands hit carpeting.

"Stop," she orders.

He stops.

"Attention!"

How does one stand to attention on his hands and knees…?

"How…?!"

"How, Mistress…" suggests Carmen La Tour.

"How, Mistress, do I stand at attention when I'm on the floor on my hands and knees?"

Kapow! Whrump!

The whip wraps around his taut gut and its tip withdraws with a burning sensation.

"You, slave, inferior male, stand up when it is attention time! Stand up and be further degraded by Carmen La Tour, your Superior Beloved!"

He stands up, naked, before her and she is, oddly, three inches shorter than he and her bosom smells as if it were seeped in chintzy cologne and cunt-soup.

"Put out your hands," she commands.

He puts his hands out and, like a prisoner, she places golden handcuffs about his wrists. Attached to the cuffs is a golden chain with which to lead him about, as if he were on a leash.

With chubby delicacy, Miss La Tour rolls her panties down and quickly pees into a J.C. Penny gold-tattooed soup dish. Her yellow gush sparkles in the bowl and is like chicken soup with the same round oil bubbles glistening on the surface.

"Sup, slave. Back on your hands and knees and taste of the fluids of your Superior."

Kapow. Whump.

He sups.

"Sup, guzzle, get it down, and then thank me for my offering by sucking my toes encased in black nylons holding my lovely form-divine legs in mouth-watering beauty."

What the hell, he thinks, having supped and guzzled viler droppings, and crawls to the bowl as if it were the last great watering hole.

Every so often, Miss La Tour taps her over-high high-heel spike into his head to push his face into the yellow lake.

"How is it?"

"Superb, Mistress," says the young man.

Then he sucks her big nylon-sheathed toe until the fibers of the stocking begin to scratch his mouth.

"It's get or be gotten, slave. That's how it is where I come from. Red Hook in Brooklyn, you know, is no picnic once you get to be twelve if you're a chick and have any kind of tits to speak of. All my mother ever did was to get the shit kicked out of her by my father who was a hairy monster. Hair on his chest that spread all over his body—I once saw them fucking on the living-room floor and he was more hairy than I imagined and she was more pale than I imagined—and he'd be goosing and grabbing me as soon as my tits popped out and if it wasn't him it was Lenny Slotkin who was the gang leader of the Fuck-Offs, an underground gang who dope-dealt and pimped, and Lenny was always tearing off my cashmere sweaters. Whatever you did you had to do it before anybody else did or else you were done in—like Milly Schwab who taught me the French arts in a garage on a slab of plywood on the grease. She was a good kid and gave good head, the best, but Lenny Slotkin caught us and went after Milly, burned off her nipples with his butane cigarette lighter, then set fire to her cunt hairs then while she was writhing and moaning he stomped on her face, he stomped on her belly—I could see the life stamped out of her body and she began vomiting up blood from her ruptured organs—and in her blood, on her broken body, Lenny fucked me in the ass, face down in her dying, and he made me suck him off and spit the come out on her crushed face, then he shit on her belly and made me pee in her open eyes which would not shut again and when he finally took me from there, he took me to his pad and told me to never mess with women again because I was his girl and he took off his belt and beat me with it, then turned it around and beat me with the belt buckle, all over my ass and back—and then overdosed me with sleeping pills—and I woke up maybe days later underneath steel stairs in my waste—and here's a three-inch scar across my neck to show how close he missed, that sonofabitch Lenny Slotkin…"

"Up, debased dunce!" says Carmen La Tour of Red Hook.

He gets up and his golden chain tingles.

"You've been chosen to be my servant, to serve my needs and that of my aides and that of my other slaves, the cattle I keep penned and fed in order to fulfill their destiny and mine," she says, standing close to him so that the black silk cloth straining around her big breasts touches his naked chest in a subtle way.

Carmen La Tour's mouth is full, her lower lip is ripe from glistening with rich red lipstick and the drying spittle from her tongue, which she always sticks between her lips when she finishes a command.

She moves a little closer so he can feel the firm ribs of her bra push against his chest.

Her hand reaches to his cock and pulls it and lets it rest there while her mouth moves up to his and slowly opens. Her tongue tip appears. And he feels his cock begin to harden in her hand. Then she begins to squeeze it harder, then releases the pressure, then squeezes it again.

By now, the crown is blazing red with lust and it poles out before him.

"Now, slave, worship me while I degrade you once again!"

Whump. Kapow!

Carmen La Tour moves against him and thrusts her tongue into his mouth and hikes her tight black silk dress up high enough to push his cock between her nylon-sheathed legs. They kiss and she rubs her nylon legs against his flaming member. Her breasts flatten against his chest and his hand instinctively reaches behind her back to rest on a round wide firm ass which twitches slightly to his touch.

Carmen pulls away and snaps, "Down on your knees, inferior male, and worship your superior!"

He falls dumbly to his knees, the gold chain taut.

"Now satisfy yourself by yourself while I watch and celebrate your debasement!"

Kapow! Carmen La Tour's bullwhip ricochets about his head, the tip just missing his ear.

Cock in hand, he begins to masturbate before Carmen La Tour.

When it's done with, he is ordered to stand at attention again.

He arises before Miss La Tour.

"Here," she hands him a Kleenex. "Wipe yourself off, dumb man, feeble prick, prune balls!"

The Kleenex gets glued in the semen and it's like peeling off rubber cement.

"Who has decided that you are fit to be a slave?"

"You," he mutters.

Thwonk!

A whip handle on his rump.

Thwonk! Thwonk!

"Mistress," hisses Miss La Tour. "I am your Superior Mistress and before your time is up, I'm going to train every inch of your dumb man-body to serve me!" Thwonk!

"Mistress, Mistress," says the young man between gritted teeth.

Mistress La Tour unlocks the chain connected to her wrist, then unlocks the handcuffs from the young man.

"It is just beginning."

"Yes, Mistress."

"Come here!" Carmen La Tour orders.

He goes to her.

Miss Carmen La Tour of Red Hook spits in his face, knees him in the groin furiously, and walks out.

Our hero slumps to the rug. The moment's pain spreads through his body and jackknifes him into a silent agony. Mouth open, he can't give voice to the scream that wants out.

"Ah, in perfect supplication before me! Ah, Miss La Tour is so efficient. Ah, get up, young man, and confess your ailments, sins, debasements, harassments, tell me all, my pink-pricked honey-fuck."

The voice is clipped and with a twit of London in it. Our hero's mouth and eyes are still straining in the subsiding pain and it is a great effort to raise his head up to face his new tormentor.

"Ah, brown eyes, too, too much! Eyes the earthen color of healthy turds. Now, now, enough obeisance, my son, my weenie-pudding."

In blurry, botched vision the black habit of a priest appears in his eyes. A tall gray priest with clipped gray hair and gray flesh and his thin mouth is a pink tint against the gray.

"Arise, arise, my son, and let us sit upon this chair together, you and I, and you shall tell me everything, and I shall save your gnarled soul, reshape it, my ear-fucker, as God made Adam. Take my hand. Here."

The gray priest extends a long gray-fingered hand. A snake-shaped silver ring entwined about his middle finger. The hands are strong and chilly. Its grip is firm and final, the gray priest's long fingernails make quarter-moon scars on our hero's wrists.

Seated in his bony lap, the young man, for a moment, feels like a little boy.

"Now tell me all your sins, my little shit-hole, worm-sodomizer, tell me all."

"I don't know where to begin."

"At the beginning. Tell me how you first began to play with your dog-biscuit. Tell me about your first fuck, first blow-job, tell me about what you think of when you're shitting, what you think of when you have diarrhea, ah, tell me all, my cock-robin."

So the young man begins at the beginning and as he rambles, the gray priest's hands tighten about his thighs until he fears the blood will be shut off. Besides this pain he feels the gray priest's prick beginning to poke into his rump.

"Ah, the beginnings, ah...get off and down on your knees, my flesh-o-ramic cunt-prober, whilst I get more comfortable. Get, get..."

"But, sir..."

"You may call me Father."

"But, Father, I can't move because your hands are gripping my thighs," announces the young man.

"No, my son, see." He extends his long-fingered gray steel-rod hands into the young man's face.

It is then that our hero realizes that his thighs are frozen by nerve and circulation disasters caused by the gray priest's grip.

"Come on, now, this is ridiculous," the priest announces and with a quick twist of the wrist dumps our hero, knees first, onto the floor. He remains there, locked in place like a statue before the gray priest.

"Hurry, now, tell me more, or..."

Kachunk. Klack.

The gray priest whips out a lethal thin chain and sets the air a-cracking.

The young man continues. The young man as a heroic statue. A penitent paraplegic.

He tells the gray priest early jerk-off dreams and realities and of his first great sexual love, Marcia Tuft, who was the dumbest girl in the sixth grade but who had the biggest boobs and would take on sometimes as many as three boys at a time. But Marcia Tuft, whose legs needed depilation work, couldn't understand our young greenhorn's silent, jaw-muscle-bulging horniness. She liked the class louts and clods who gave her money and bubblegum and comic books. She'd have them in her loose-leaf notebook and would read them continuously throughout the class. Our hero would be struggling with the technicalities of the Revolutionary War, side-angling (ogling) Marcia Tuft's broad face, half-concealed by her Veronica Lake hairdo, staring intently at an E.C. Comic of gory morality and ghoulish conclusions.

"Oh, yes, yes, my son," burbles the gray priest whose fly is open and whose cock is a long narrow gray pole whose top is a pale pink ring fading into the gray flesh. "What happened, what happened? I must know it all, every sensual lustful foul corrupt lascivious immoral outrageous act and dream-act committed by your body and mind." Gray prick quivers in the air like a dowsing-rod. The gray priest's voice speeds into a higher pitch. Clacking the chain against the chair, as if keeping time, the gray priest's voice cracks into a whining liturgy.

"Everything. Describe the shape of their cunts, their rotten passageways, their foul pestholes of sinful lusting breeding, those breedways, freeways that catch and snare a man's root and ruin his dream of Heaven forever..."

The gray priest's London twang grates into a gargoyle cackle. His gray prick getting pinker and pinker, the dark blue veins throbbing, the gray-brown ball sacks supporting the upright root.

"Back to Marcia Tuft, rank sinner, trickster, cocksman, back to Marcia Tuft," his voice shifting gears, slowing, deepening, soon back to its original brittle and solemn tones. The gray cock loses its first flush.

At last the young man's thighs and legs come alive with circulation and, thus relieved, he continues telling the gray priest about Marcia Tuft and how, one day, he walked home with two thuggish types who owed him a favor (cheating on tests, etc.) and who said he could have his bout with Marcia Tuft who was waiting for them at the park where all the kids go to conduct their puberty rites. She was there and looked a little put-out when our hero appeared, but the two lugs threatened to slug her boobs and she shrugged her shoulders, muttered, "What the fuck?" and then asked for her money. "Fifty cents each," she said, looking blandly at a tree behind the trio. "No singles today," she said. "Let's go," and the group went to a cave called the Fuck Hut and stretched out on the newspapers and a shredded blanket and Marcia Tuft pulled down her pants, opened her blouse, unhooked her bra, and lay there while the two clods pawed over her, one on each side. She tells the two clods to open their pants and get their dicks out, which they do, and she grabs a cock in each hand and begins to pull them and rub them with a tremendously dull look on her face, and the two serviced young men manipulate what they can reach—one works on her jungle-thick wedge while the other mashes a full tender breast, a very white, soft-looking breast. And our hero watches as the two ejaculate their white seed in Marcia Tuft's experienced hands. "Ech," she says dispassionately and wipes her hands off on some newspaper, stands up, hooks her bra together, buttons her blouse, pulls up her panties, and walks out of the Fuck Hut while our hero stares dumbfoundedly at her ass wiggling and bouncing in her skirt...

"Yes, yes," the gray priest hisses. "Yes, yes?"

"That was it."

"Ah, apocalyptic!" Gray prick pole at full attention again. "And how old were you then, ten, eleven, twelve? Ah, the whore, the beast, the fool. Ah..."

The gray priest twines his chain around his hard-on, then bends his face down until his mouth helps itself to his cock.

"Ah, mmm, mmm."

Out of the way in time. The gray priest rolls off his chair onto the floor and keeps rolling on the floor, his mouth gripping and sucking his cock, a gray snake at its tail, making choking gurgles, bouncing against the walls, finally coming, guzzling the arctic sperm, gulping it down. Orgasm over, the gray priest stretches out on his back on the floor and with a gray cock-eyed stare watches his expired prick descend into a gray toadstool upon the hairs of his salt-and-pepper-colored crotch hairs.

"Ah, now. Back to you, my degenerate donkey. Now you must be, of course, punished for what you have seen. That was my atonement for your pubescent carnage."

Without warning, the gray priest picks up a bound bundle of twigs and begins to flagellate the young man about his shoulders and back.

"Ah, now, now! Now you know each lewd thought is pain,

each lust-provoked dream is pain, each rotten inch of your rotten pussy-lusting flesh is putrid, corrupt! Now, now!"

It wasn't so painful at first, but after a while of it, splinters of the twigs start to snarl in his flesh and his back begins to burn with pain.

"Real pain for real sin. Ah, now! now!"

"Father, Father," the young man wails.

"Yes, my son?"

"Forgive me, I knew not what I did," shouts the young man.

The gray priest stops in midswipe.

"Forgive you? But what on earth for?" he asks in a voice whose questioning edges have a Gallic lilt.

"For my sins, my sins," sighs the young man.

"But...?"

The door crashes open.

"Very smart, dumb bastard," snarls Carmen La Tour and picks up the chain and strikes the gray priest across the face, chipping the bridge of his nose, drawing a straight line of blood there.

Exit the gray priest, whimpering.

Exit Carmen La Tour, slamming the door behind her. Opening it again, quickly, sticking her head through the partial view, sticking her tongue out at the young man who does a double take.

A few minutes later, she returns, and stepping on top of his prostrate form, her spiked high heels boring deep holes in his still sore back, she lets go of a warm gush of shit which drops on him and slides off his back, across his ribs, and onto the floor.

"You know what to do with that," says Carmen. And she leaves.

"This is the final induction before training. This process divides up the lot into either the totally disabled or the properly deadened agent. How's he doing?"

"Eating lunch right now," answers Carmen La Tour.

Carla arches a neatly plucked, perfect eyebrow.

"The usual?"

"Yes. My blue-plate special," answers Carmen.

They wanly smile at the allusion.

"Cheers."

"Cheers."

And toast each other. Pink Ladies.

They watch our hero through a one-way mirror for a while, then turn their backs to him. It's a dark cozy room lit by the light coming through the one-way mirror. Pleasant mood music fills the room with monotones of schmaltzy taffy-pulling strings and muted soft trumpet solos.

"What ever happened to Marcia Tuft?" Carmen asks Carla.

"The Basement."

"Oh, really?"

Carmen La Tour still wears her dark sunglasses.

"She was too dumb, too erotically hung-up on money and got in the way. She worked well in our street organization. A good hustler: money first, a time-clock cunt, a quick machinelike affair. Like a cash register. She was also good for posing, in fact it was double-time for her. She'd bring a trick in as the male model and also get paid for the posing session. Somebody decided to promote her into the suburban wife-swapping operation. As soon as Marcia Tuft got into the upper-middle-class world, greed tangled her animal motives and she was caught running a side-operation of extortion. It's like paying taxes on dreams. Clients balked."

"Huh," grunts Carmen. "But you know what a charge they all get in paying for it. That makes it more worthwhile to so many of them."

"Yes, of course, I understand. They pay our bills. They still don't understand. But Marcia was out of hand, imposed too great a financial and fear burden on them—and many of that group, the husbands, were in the military. There was nothing that we could do for Marcia but send her to the Basement."

"You mean?" asks Carmen.

"Exactly," answers Carla.

The mood music washes through the deep silence that is between them.

"Another drink?"

"Mm, yes, that would be good."

Carla presses a button.

"It's a delicate thing, keeping the illusion working. Everyone has to play their part fully and without thought, otherwise it doesn't work. You understand that. Your line of work, your specialty. They want sex a dream, a fantasy. They still don't understand."

"Mm, yes, of course," mumbles Carmen.

"After the imagination reaches its climax, then distract them with the money-fantasy, the token of guilt. They still think sex is dirty, illicit and joyless."

The door slides open and a servant places two more Pink Ladies on the table and, bowing quickly, leaves just as the door begins to slide shut again.

"Why are you looking at me like that?" asks Carla.

"You're so young, you're so much smarter than me…"

"Oh, now, please, Carmen, don't start in again," says Carla.

"I'm so dumb, so confused, and you're so…"

"No more. I'm not that smart either. Now stop it."

Carmen La Tour's tears trickle slowly from beneath the rims of her dark sunglasses.

"I don't know, for God's sake, who you are or who I am, for God's sake."

"There's no need. I'll see that Moses attends to you tonight."

Carmen La Tour sighs.

"Drink up."

"Cheers," says Carmen weakly.

"Cheers."

They down their Pink Ladies quickly. Carmen suckles a splinter of ice cube. Swallows it. Presses a button and speaks into a microphone piped into the room where our young man eats her droppings.

"Lick it all off the rug, slave! All of it!" she bellows, feeling a warm glow spread in her cheeks.

Our hero looks up, startled.

A little boy walks in. Maybe he is twelve years old. Wearing tight white Levi's and a tight white T-shirt.

"Hi," he says. "I'm Harold and I'm gonna give you worse

than that old bag of come Carla La Tour ever thought of." And
Harold smiles. And Harold's teeth are perfect. And Harold's hair
is perfect, not a follicle misplaced. His eyes are sky-blue circles
in immaculately bright white spaces. Eyelashes, notes our hero,
are in perfect formation.

"I been reading a lot and fucking around a lot and I guess
you could say I started out young, heck—I'm only twelve-and-
a-half but I know what I want. I want you, first off, to kiss my
ass."

Our hero looks into those sky-blue eyes and is paralyzed
while those sky-blue eyes begin to darken into a slate-gray color.

"Hey, look," says Harold, "didn't you understand me? I said,
you dumb boob, to kiss my ass as a starter or else this is *really*
gonna be a bummer. Y'see these hands?"

Harold displays the palms of his hands.

"They're killer's hands, man, I'm a black-belt champ."

Harold smiles.

Our hero still doesn't move.

"Hah! Huh! Yieee!" says Harold and leaps into a Karate
stance.

The blue eyes go from blue to slate-gray to a black-ringed vio-
let.

"Man, how old are you? I mean are you over thirty? If you're
under thirty, how much under are you? I mean do you wanna
die before you get to be middle-aged? Don't you understand,
you're my slave and I'm gonna degrade the hell out of you
because you're so incredibly uncool to be here and to be bare-
assed and shit-faced and dumb."

With incredible speed, Harold hacks into our hero's neck,
chops his shoulder, pokes his chest and drop kicks a toe-slam into
the midriff.

At first, because it was so fast, our hero continues to stand
blank-eyed. Then his eyes roll up and he collapses onto the
floor in a broken pile.

Wakes up.

Harold stands over him. Still smiling that perfect smile of
perfect American teeth that salute the dark eye in magazines

and billboards and in the TV haze. Blazing white. Perfect as
the American Dream. The smile is a masterpiece.

"Now will you kiss my ass?"

Our hero tries to stand but can't seem to make his muscles
respond to his command.

"I...I can't move," he moans.

"It'll pass. Give it five or ten minutes. Anyway I can move my
ass here to you and you can kiss it, okay?"

"But, you don't understand, I can't seem to move anything
at all."

"Yeah, yeah, sure. That's what that's supposed to do, that particular sequence. Pretty neat, huh? I got better ones than that.
You know, I can kill you with maybe one rightly-aimed chop. You
understand what I'm talking about?"

Without waiting for an answer, the black-belt twelve-and-a-
half-year-old Harold sticks his white Levi's-held butt into our
hero's pale snout.

"Kiss it, asshole."

Our hero kisses it.

Harold farts in his face.

It is an incredible anti-American fart: such a rotten stench
that's found only in the bowels of cancer-devoured ancients.
Expecting a strange green-yellow comic-strip cloud to seep
through those buttocks, our hero begins to feel life in his body
again.

Harold erupts another colossal explosion of foul gas which
grips our hero's face and gives him a severely acute desire to barf.
It's a stink beyond description. It's as if this young lad eats regularly of that monstrous manna passed out to a precious few.
Presidents and generals are fed the stuff. Also a few multibil-
lionaires. Something happens to the food halfway down the
gullet and the stink begins. It's mostly the stink of fear. The
fear that cleaves a man's innards with acids that bubble in
cramped intestines and form odoriferous gut-hogs whose only
exit is that narrow channel of evacuation. (Though for some
the stench rises out and upward and everytime they talk, green
rot clouds puff out of their mouths.) Prophets and profit-crazed
businessmen, men who hold onto the American scrotum, all

eat this yeasty manna which blasts off like regularly-spaced cap-sules to fog-up board meetings and policy crisis confrontations and military-industrial haggle-fests at the Pentagon. The cor-ruptive odor of fear's blight weaves into the cigar and cigarette smoke and drops from that cloud like fallout. Nobody within those rooms escapes the touch of it. A gushing flummery com-pounded of alien chemistry which, at this very moment, is being investigated by security-checked chemical companies who are try-ing to break it down, if possible, package it and use it as a new nerve gas on the enemy (whoever the enemy is).

Harold laughs. His eyes are back to bright blue.

"How's that, boob?" he asks.

"How's what?"

"You gotta be kidding," says Harold. "Just where are you at? Man, what a boob!"

Harold's sister, Hertha, enters.

She's eleven but obviously proportioned like a seventeen-year-old swinger. She too is in tight white Levi's and a tight white T-shirt and she wears no bra because you can see the square nubs of her nipples in outline against the fabric.

Harold and Hertha embrace, French-kiss, grab each other's crotches, then pull apart.

"He's a boob, baby," says Harold, "but he's as good a toy as any, I guess."

"Gee whiz, Harold honey, he sure looks dumb, but his dingy looks nice. Lemme see," and Hertha walks over to our hero, who has managed to stand up, and pulls on his cock a little bit. "Wow, I'll bet it gets real big when it gets hard, huh!" she says and looks up into our hero's fuddled face. Her eyes are almost kelly-green and her pale oval face is sprinkled with pale freckles the color of blood dried on paper. Her mouth is a small ripe bow of flesh. "What's the matter, baby, you shy?" Hertha ask him, still kneading his prick. She smells of the sea and of suntan lotion and cloves and cinnamon and she makes our hero's heart pump with the honey of romance. "C'mon, sweety, let's go onto the bed and do things," she whispers wetly in his ear while Harold stands against a wall, watching, scratching his elbow nervously.

Hertha nestles close to him on the sofa and he can feel his manhood begin to tingle and burn with life.

"Oooh," says Hertha and looks down to watch it grow, to see the stem widen and stretch upwards, to see the crown flush and swell. "Well, look there, Harold, now that's a dong for you."

"Aw come off it, Hertha. Just do your work, okay?"

"We have no mother, no father," whispers Hertha in his ear. "I am tender, have no fear, I am an object of love and you are a bull stud and I want you to be gentle with me…"

"You are lovely," groans our hero.

"I write good poetry, too," sighs Hertha, nibbling at his nipple.

"Hey Hertha, wanna get high?"

"Groovy…say," she says to our protagonist, "wanna get high?"

Harold pulls out a collapsible waterpipe from his pocket and fills the pipe bowl with Mixture Infinite (an insidious concoction of Lebanese hashish, Moroccan kief, Tibetan opium, Oakland DMT and Chinatown pot). The pipe is passed around.

The kids do fine. Suck up the universe like old pros, while our hero has his usual problems and gags and chokes and makes Harold and Hertha laugh gleefully at his dilemma.

Years later.

Harold and Hertha turn into wolves with mandala eyes.

They pounce on our hero who is now in a new stupor. They begin to indulge in their torture and torment rituals. (Harold and Hertha established an earlier mark on the fast-moving times by being involved in a preteen ratpack of upper-middle-class Americans who freely looted, mugged, raped and destroyed people and property. When caught by the police, the reporter transmitted this quote from their leader: "Why not? Isn't that where it's at?" Since they came from a decent income class and their parents could afford lawyers and Important Friends, they were let off on parole, in the custody of their parents.)

Some of the variegated pain they use on our subject are:

1) push his legs back till his head sticks through them—

Indian Rubber Man—Hertha straddles him and forces him to
tongue her clitoris and Harold sticks candlewax up his ass, hot
candlewax;

2) Hertha cuts a bit of flesh on his chest and begins to peel
it off and our groggy savior groans while Harold chews at his
shaft's seam until his sharp teeth create a counter-stitch;

3) holding his legs up, Harold turns our hero into a human
wheelbarrow and butts his head into the wall molding—Hertha
humps onto his back and yells bawdily as she rides our hero,
whose legs are still powerfully gripped by Harold, her hot moist
cunt drooling on his spine;

4) Harold's cock in his mouth and Hertha impaled on our
hero's flaring hard-on—Harold's cock is a wide hard burning bit
and because he is sitting on our hero's head, our hero can't
move away from it or get any leverage to ease the pain of it filling his mouth and pushing down his gullet, nor can he do much
about Hertha who pumps up and down, her flat hard ass slamming his abdomen—thus at work, the brother and sister carry
on a dull conversation about last night's TV coverage of the
war;

5) a mini-flashlight stuck into the well of Hertha's pink-
ribbed cunt, held by Harold who looks at our hero and says,
"What do you see there, man? Do you see Buddha, Christ or
Moses? C'mon, man, what's there?" Hertha squeals, "C'mon,
Harold, let's make him cry. I dig seeing men cry." "Aw, heck,
Hertha, don't you have any sense of style?" "Harold, I'm horny,
I wanna get my charge." Harold was taught the de Sade version
of Chinese acupuncture by a Filipino junkie who served as the
gang instructor in various ways of fixing. With a fat hypodermic
outfit, Harold plunges the needle into our hero's unenlight-
ened cock-eye. The pain is fantastic and he faints. "Let's paint
him while he's out." "Yeah, yeah!"

As a primer coat they deposit their waste on him, then kick
his ribs—"Too much. Sounds like a marimba!"—Hertha jumps
on his hand until she heard some crunches and pops—

"Oh, God!" Harold turns to look at her. "You there?" "Yeah,
yeah." Hertha's orgasms spasm through her body and her kelly-
green eyes roll into white.

Harold catches her. Lays her on the sofa, undresses her, undresses himself. Taps her on the cheek. Hertha's eyes flutter as she returns to earth.

"Yeah, yeah, now," she whispers.

The two make love in a noisy cruel way, tearing at each other, clawing, squeezing, until their coming passes and, holding each other tightly, they cry and rock on the sofa.

What does it matter? What ever did matter? If there's nothing to matter about then what's the matter? Matter is matter anyway. Isn't it?

"Do you think he'll make it?"

The bearded physician unpeels the surgical mask.

"We'll see. Let's check out the circuitry. Area One."

A switch is pulled back.

Our hero's mouth begins to work.

"Mamma, mamma. Want milk. Want milk…"

"Area Two."

Click.

It is pink-red. Sound of a waterfall roaring far away. And golden flakes and white clouds. The cord attached to his belly floats before him like an astronaut's lifeline. Pulse.

"Try Three."

Click.

"Say, do you have a cigarette? I'm dying for a smoke."

"Sure, Doc. Here."

He lights up.

Total blackness. Dense black with no possibility of light. Blackness that is a pressure in his brain, a massive rock of blackness.

"He'll be alright. In fact, he's doing fine," says the Doc, exhaling. "Let's pull out the plugs and get him back in action. Next."

The Doctor's assistant pulls the transistor nodes out of our hero's brain map and a voluptuous nurse wheels him out.

Awakes in his grim room.

Food on the table on a tray.

Carmen La Tour sits across from him. She wears no dress but is in her webbed black silk panties which stretch across her wide hips, black nylons and glassy-black high heels. Her whip hangs from the wrist of one of her black leather elbow-length gloves.

Her black-lensed sunglasses have pale mother-of-pearl rims. Her huge breasts hang down and rest upon her belly, which is cinched in by the elastic of her panties. Her thick lips are lacquered with spittle.

"Go, slave, eat. Your Mistress will watch."

"Yes, Mistress," says our hero, needing no directive for this act. He eats the meager repast, drinks the strange fluids, yawns and is done.

"Now, slave, follow me to the dressing room."

Carmen La Tour walks up to the young man, clamps a gold ring into his nostrils. The ring is attached to a chain. The chain is given a jerk.

The two gold prongs dig into the delicate nasal membranes. The young man (doggedly) follows Miss La Tour.

2.

The Dressing Room.

Jack Flash and Sammy are there with cameras, lights and props.

"Hiyah, Carmen baby," barks Jack.

Kapow. Whunk. Wap.

"Fool," she growls, "not when we're on duty."

"Sorry, Mistress," says Jack, winding his camera, uncapping the lens-guard from another. He kicks Sammy in the ankle. Sammy looks startled and then understands and falls onto his knees.

"Hail, Mistress," Sammy announces with fervor.

"That's more like it."

The young man is taken into a small closet lit with one pink neon light. Guard of the closet is a small wiry man with shaved head shining with a vaseline veneer. His muscular chest is bare and tapers into slender hips covered with skintight pants.

"Ahh, Mistress," he purrs.

Carmen La Tour slaps his face twice, her hand flashing back and forth across his cheeks like angry fishtails.

"Pig! Wait until *I* speak to you!"

Smack-a-ty-smack-a-ty-smack.

A fine line of bloody treacle trickles down one side of the man's jaw.

"My boot, you fool!"

The man crashes to his knees and begins to lick Carmen La Tour's toe. While doing this to her right foot, Carmen's left foot rises and stamps a high-heel into the bald man's irresistible bald head. The vaseline helps to divert the impact. Nevertheless, the man nearly passes out in response to the kick.

"Ah, Mistress!"

"Alright, servile, repulsive, slop bucket of a sniveling dog-shit fucker," bellows Carmen La Tour.

"Ah, yes, yes…" sighs the man.

"Let's dress up my new slave so he can have his picture taken and registered with the universe."

"Yes, yes…"

"Wipe the blood off your cheek and chest. Here." Carmen La Tour reaches inside her net panties and pulls out a tampax and tosses it to the bald-headed, bare-chested man.

While putting on our hero's first transvestite garb, the bald-headed man introduces himself in whispering, conspiring, ear-curling tones.

"I'm Montgomery Pocket, arch-masochist. My name is legend. Slip into these panties. They're exquisite silk, the cheapest of all from Woolworth's, just what's right for the shamed penis…"

Our hero's nose-ring and chain is hooked onto a coat hook in the closet while Mistress La Tour is in the other room discussing matters with Jack Flash and Sammy.

"Your cock doesn't look ashamed enough," says Montgomery Pocket. "Here, slip into this girdle. It's at least five sizes smaller than what you'd ordinarily take. This might take some time. And…it might hurt wonderfully…"

It hurts more wonderfully than our hero could anticipate and gasping for breath as the girdle grips his midriff, he asks if Montgomery Pocket would unhook the chain from the coat-hook.

"Oh, no, Mistress wouldn't like that at all."

"But I keep lurching about because I can't breathe and I'm afraid that I'll lurch too far and rip my nose off…"

"Wonderful, wonderful, what a clever humiliation. Now let's get the nylons on and hooked to your girdle," answers Montgomery Pocket.

Our hero's toenails scrape the nylon and threaten to tear it.

"Tch, tch. That's no good," clucks Montgomery and pulls out a pair of toenail clippers.

"I'll do both feet at the same time. Be still. Quit squirming."

"It's the…girdle…it's…"

"Oh, hush now, relish it, bathe in it, become one with the Pain. Oops!"

Missing a toe, his clippers rip a slab off of the big-toe's joint which causes our hero to writhe too largely and the ring in his nose churns deeper into the nostril flesh.

Sweat beads form around our young man's pale forehead as Montgomery Pocket continues practicing the fine art of pedicuring.

"For years, you know, I've been preaching the word, you might say, about Pain, about being one with it…oh, damn!"

Not gauging the toenail's length, Montgomery Pocket clips off too much of it and, in doing so, rents off some flesh the nail stuck to for survival.

"Uh…uh…"

"Don't mess in your panties now. Don't come, for Mistress will be angry," admonishes Pocket.

"I'm not coming…I'm suffering," answers our hero through gritted teeth.

"Yes, yes, good," sighs Montgomery.

And continues his work without further crisis.

The buzzer zings through the closet.

"Slaves, what are you doing in there?"

They both whimper and whine.

"Alright, make it snappy," orders Carmen La Tour, her voice crackling through the small speaker on the ceiling next to the lone pink neon bar of light.

KAPOW! WHUMP! WEEAWHH! SMUNK!

Her whiplashes rattle the small speaker.

"Oh, God, I came…" groans Pocket. "She's such a subtle ruler. Amplified whiplashes…huh."

Pocket hands our hero the nylons and watches while he rolls them up his legs.

"Oh, my God, I forgot," squeals Pocket and opens a drawer and pulls out a depilator and shaves the hair off our hero's legs. This, too, is without incident.

Nylons finally on, it's bra-time. The bra is a structure of foam rubber, wires and clamps which Montgomery Pocket, bald head gleaming pink, straps onto our hero.

"It'll be tight too but it'll help equalize out the pressure the girdle makes."

The bra structure clutches his chest like a clamp. A band of mighty pressure around his chest and around his middle, our hero is then made-up by Montgomery Pocket, who continues to talk of his abstract exploits.

"I don't want to remember when I first realized the path of Pain…I like to think that I always knew it was the only way. My mother used to whip me most lusciously upon my tender naked buttocks with her riding crop and when I got older, I would instigate problems in order to have her whip me. Ah, when she'd whip me, I'd be stretched across her lap and my shameful penis would be nestled in her silk skirt and with each stroke on my buttocks, I could feel the life within my soft root awaken. One whipping I remember is when I experienced a shameful erection and…don't blink your eyes, this mascara streaks terribly…and it bore through her skirts and I know now that she knew, but she allowed it for a while, and then with the whipping over she told me to stand up, and I said I couldn't, and she said, 'Stand up, that's an order,' and I slid off her silken lap and stood before her in my state of rigid lusting, and she laughed and said, 'Shame, shame, what have we here?' and I blushed to my toes and couldn't answer—turn the other way, that's right, fine and instead of whipping me, as I had hoped for, she stood away from me and looked at my skinny boy's body and my infant hard-on and laughed at me and laughed at it and left the room, and she no longer whipped me, nor did she mention the incident again—yet there were times, especially when I started dating, that she'd look at me in the eyes, press her face closely to mine, smile, and then laugh softly, and I'd blush to my toes again and, after a while, I couldn't date anymore...the girls just weren't right for me. But Pain was. I'd find all methods of tormenting my flesh and even when I would experience a masturbation orgasm, I'd make sure to inflict some pain to my flesh. There, that's done, now let's get into your dress and we'll be almost finished."

The dress presents no problem. It's a gas-flame iridescent blue dress with a men's magazine V-neck cleavage. There is a problem getting it over the head without disturbing or yanking the chain attached to our hero's nose-ring.

The wig is easy too. The glue to keep it down smells like fermented apples.

KAPOW! WHUMP! WEE-AWHH!

"Coming, Mistress, our object is almost done. A few finishing touches."

"Hurry," crackles her voice.

The intercom snaps off.

Montgomery Pocket surveys his work. Our hero stands before him dressed as a woman, his face a mask of makeup and his body racked with the pain of bra and girdle vises squeezing him in an unbreakable grip.

"Here's my belt," says Pocket, yanking it through the loops of his pants. "Beat me before you go."

"No."

"Please," he implores.

"No."

"Fool. At least spit on me."

"No," says our hero, walking painfully on high-heels, feeling as if all his ribs are breaking.

"Help me!" whines Pocket.

"I can't."

Other photographs taken that session show our hero decked-out in exotic paraphernalia.

Rubber-skinned, hands tied behind his back to his ankles which are also tied, strung on a rack which moves back and forth.

"Use the pink gel, Sammy."

"Right. He's kinda gray."

Chains around a metal belt around his waist which supports a steel device, a male chastity pouch, clamped around his cock. The tube has teeth in it that would chew on the cock if it were to be excited to grow. Miss La Tour manages, despite his willpower, to stimulate a painful erection by placing one of her big boobs in his face and making him suck her nipple until it becomes erect almost simultaneously with the young man's anguish.

"Fix the strobe, will ya, Sammy," yells Flash.

"Right."

Color shots of our hero in the nude splayed out on a bed of nails;

giving head to a small tank cannon;

reversed to show the cannon poking up our hero's ass;

three faggots in jockstraps and bolero-cut leather jackets whipping our hero with aluminum mace-chains while our hero hangs by disjointed thumbs from a beam;

three bull-dykes in stevedore jackets and 'Frisco jeans force our hero to the ground (the klieg lights are fanning his body with a peculiar mazda-tan) and with ornate dildoes strapped about their girthy hips, they take turns servicing him while Jack Flash and Sammy race about shooting pictures and more pictures;

sequence-shots; formal shots; film clips; spot announcements; one-, two-reelers; situation comedies; Greek tragedies (he's put into a phallic mask without eyeholes in a circle of businessmen—it's called Blind Man's Monopoly—and whenever he bumps into one of them—they're all in ritual costumes of Hawaiian sport shirts and black leather cock-and-bull clouts and gym shoes—whenever he bumps into one of them, and they move in so that he can't miss, they take turns paddling his naked ass or tweaking his tired balls, and the small one keeps poking a long gnarled pinky up his asshole—all of this done with great laughter);—a great variety of images are taken.

"Whew, what a workout!" says Jack Flash, packing up nine 35mm cameras, seven reflex cameras, twenty-seven lenses, telephoto, wide-angle, an attaché-case of lens filters, caps and cleaner, twelve tripods, one press camera, five light meters, one camera obscura as well as one camera lucida, a stereo camera, a Polaroid camera, an aerial reconnaissance camera (that Sammy had to use in some of the ceiling shots, hanging onto a metal bridge in space), a stray periscope that Carmen La Tour used to supervise Montgomery Pocket preparing our hero in the small closet, a microphotographic setup to analyze and enlarge the various sperm counts...

"You bet, boss," says Sammy, sweeping up two hundred popped and blackened flashbulbs (which were used in many pictures to give him that amateur quality needed for the amateur dreamer). "Y'know, it's too bad you didn't have a chance to use the X-ray machine, boss."

"Ah, well, you can't win 'em all, huh, Sammy?"

"I guess not, boss."

3.

He's taken into a plain small room. The only item of furniture in it is an ebony-topped table in the room's center. Three high-intensity lights are grouped in the ceiling's center directly above the table. The table has foot-, arm- and neck-holds. There's music being piped through small speakers: calliope music and Dixieland music. From brass spigots pour a translucent pink smoke. At the head of the table is a Chinese mandarin in a white-silk brocade dressing-jacket and black raw-silk pantaloons. His yellow parchment face is narrow, the eyes a bright black, the mouth thin and barely hidden by a few black-gray wisps of moustache and chin-beard.

"Come, come, no need to hesitate," says the mandarin, his voice like a bamboo flute. "We've been through this before and we'll be through this again and when we die who will know or care?"

The young man walks to the opposite end of the table.

"I see a white tiger in your heart. Are you afraid of me?" the mandarin asks.

"I don't know," the young man answers.

"But when does one know anything except what one knows? Shall a reading aid your sense of destiny?"

"What? A reading of what?"

"The yarrow-sticks, the I-Ching. Come over here and we shall cast the sticks for you and consult the oracle. Here, under the spigot."

Not wanting to, the young man goes to the old (or young or middle-aged) mandarin. They both sit on the floor.

"Move over against the wall. We must have room to spread the sticks out on the floor."

The young man moves against the wall, the brass spigot directly over his head, the pink vapor slowly leaving it, drifting about him like incense smoke.

Dividing the stalks into two piles, the mandarin nimbly picks one stalk from the right-hand pile and puts it between the ring finger and middle finger of the left hand (the ring is a gold band inlaid with jade). And so on. Gathering, dividing, until the total hexagram is determined. The mandarin notates its process on a rice-paper tablet with a brush dipped into a stone tray of ink.

"Well, well," he sighs.

"Well, what?" asks our hero.

"Meng."

"Yes?"

"The hexagram means Youthful Folly. Entangled folly brings humiliation. Six in the fourth place. According to the oracle. Danger at the foot of the mountain—mm, good pun, relative to what's next—ah, 'To strengthen what is right in a fool is a holy task.' Yes, mm…"

The young man's attention drifts and he finds himself concentrating on the smell of pink gas trickling from the brass spigot. It smells like whatever he can imagine. Like a hallway he once walked through when he was looking for the room a girl told him to meet her at and she wasn't there, nor was her room number. Like the grass he flopped on when he was sixteen years old and in love for the first time. The grass smelled sweet and green and he sniffed it deeply and the smell of the damp rich earth it grew from made him dizzy. Or the four-leaf clover he could never find when he took her to that hill. They blew dandelions into infinity and plucked daisies and she wouldn't let him get into her. She smelled like Jergen's Lotion. He smells the ocean he discovered one night on a double date, racing down a dark sandy hill to the surf roar, holding the hand of another love; then, hitting the wet shoreline, they ran barefooted in the darkness until they were out of breath, and he grabbed her and kissed her and the tide spilled around their ankles. Smells like gingerbread men in the oven. Smells like pork-roast rind-fat crackling. Ham and eggs in a yellow bed of slime in an all-night drive-in, 5:30 in the morning, truckers eating breakfast, and he's with his mistress and she's telling him that she's pregnant but he can't figure that; it's impossible because she took his cherry only a week ago, all he can figure out is that he's madly in love with her and profoundly afraid of marriage. Only eighteen. It's like the Draft Board. Smells like a honky-tonk in a raunchy town outside his hometown where they serve beer to underage kids; plaid shirts, sawdust, jukebox, having to carry him out, shoes scraping a trail in the sawdust, heaving into a bush. Smells like his imagination. It smells like outer space. Smells like perfume, new comic books, old comic books, pulp magazines smell old forever; smells.

"Ah, come now, no reverie is worth too much pursuit," advises the mandarin. "Come now, it's time to rest on the table and renew your strength."

He leads the young man to the table and helps him onto it.

"Stretch out, legs out, yes, palms up, yes, now shut your eyes, relax, concentrate on feeling all tension leave your body, yes, starting with your toes, yes, working upwards through your body, everything loose, yes, relaxed, yes, yes, yes…"

The mandarin watches the young man fall asleep and then clamps the bands around his feet, hands and neck.

"Ah, very good," he sighs, gathering up his sticks, pen, ink and paper off the floor in a quick and easy movement. He places them in a small teak box with two sliding shelves. The bottom shelf contains small brass containers and glass vials and leather pouches.

"One *chien* of *Ch'ang p'u* (Sweet Flag for American herbal scouts) and one *liang* of *Yin yang ts'ao* (Longspur Epimedium) and"—reaching into a leather pouch—"two *li* of *I mu ts'ao* (ah yes, Siberian Motherwort) and, hm"—poking about in a brass pillbox—"a dash or two of *Lung yen* will help bind the circle into its proper width, i.e., not to overburden the young man's foolish stamina, and a taste of *Che ch'ien tze* (Rippleseed Plantain— why Westerners must use capital letters…), Solomon's seal *(Huang ching)*, *Polygonum multiflorum Thunb*, *Tsao* and a good measure of *ginseng*, of course. Now grind it all together and we have," he whispers, grinding a pestle to the various powders and branches and herbs, "enough to keep our hero fuck-happy for another light-year. Ah, well, perhaps only another hour. But what is time when you are young?"

He plucks out a chin whisker and adds it to the concoction and then leaves the room to decoct it all by mixing it into a tea base, the leaves of the tea coated with tincture of opium.

"Sinister and clever," hums the mandarin over the hibachi. "Clever and sinister." And his slight voice trills and hums in its peculiar bamboo-flute tones.

Lady Go, the mandarin's Japanese concubine, joins him in the room where the young man lies strapped down. She's a bright button of a woman, round and cheerful with a laugh and a giggle which is gradually as disturbing as a tic. She wears a brilliant floral kimono sashed about her hips by a rich brown obi. She carries a lacquered box which is quite large.

"Set it down by the foot of the table, Lady Go," orders the mandarin.

"Oh, yes, of course," she giggles, placing it against the wall, reaching into her sleeve and pulling out a bright red cloth and placing it on the floor before the foot of the table and then picking up the large lacquer box and setting it upon the cloth. "There," she sighs, backing away from it, giggling, like a pigeon cooing.

"Wake up, my young friend, and we will demonstrate to you how patience can be rewarded by excess. Come, come," orders the mandarin, nudging the young man in a strategic center of his neck.

The young man opens his eyes dreamily.

"A little tea?" asks the mandarin.

The young man nods.

"Lady Go, the tea please."

Lady Go leaves the room and returns with an earthen pot of God-knows-what tea concocted and decocted by the mandarin.

She pours some of it into a vessel glazed with a dull sheen covering a gray color with calligraphy and symbols circling it.

"The bamboo straw," says the mandarin.

"Oh, yes," giggles Lady Go and produces a bamboo straw from her sleeve.

The young man attempts to rise to drink the tea. But can't move. His eyes become wide with the shock of confinement (much like that of recognition). The young man's body becomes rigid.

"Now, now, let's relax and drink the tea, please, through the straw. Come, you can do it."

The young man sips from the straw and the warm tea slowly washes down his throat to fan out through his body. Lady Go giggles. Calliope music.

"Open the box," coos the mandarin and Lady Go races to the foot of the table, bends down, opens the long lacquer box and withdraws a radiant peacock feather.

"Ah, yes, first the peacock feather."

Giggling, bowing, Lady Go, no Maat, hands the feather to the mandarin.

He strokes our hero's belly with it. Gently, so it barely touches the skin and feels like a breeze upon the flesh and then the breeze begins to tickle and our hero's stomach muscles cramp to contain the laughter forcing its way out.

"Now, now, let it out, my young friend, let it out…"

Lady Go goes back to the box and pulls out a triad of dove-feathers and begins to run them gently over the young man's soles. His toes begin to squeeze tight to fight off the laughter, his leg muscles stiffen like pistons to push it down.

"Reach down, my lady, and hand me the ostrich plume."

Still tickling the soles of his feet the round maiden reaches down with her other hand and retrieves a fluffy pink-edged ostrich feather. The mandarin wisks it out of her hand and begins, with renewed delicacy, to dust our hero's belly button and hips, gradually stroking the dormant prick with it. Lady Go continues her sole attack. Finally the young man breaks and, straining against the straps that bind him, our hero's laughter tears through his muscles and explodes out of his mouth in hysterical nonstop guffaws which turn into gasping squawks and giggling whimpers.

He begins to suffocate in his strangled cackling and tries to speak, to beg for mercy, but all that comes out are strangled hiccups and wild guttural grunts between gargling chortles. And in this frenzy his cock becomes erect and shoots a spurt of seed into the sky.

"Pause to reflect," says the mandarin. "More tea?"

"Please, no more, I can't stand it," begs our hero.

"You must learn many things about what your limits truly are. You're doing wonderfully. Isn't he?"

Lady Go nods and titters.

Before he can protest more, the bamboo straw is pushed into his mouth and he sips down some more tea which is cooling off now and has an oily aftertaste. His stomach is strained and taut and the tea has a way of massaging the arching organs and relaxing them as well as hitting his groin like a Roman candle.

Dixieland music.

It begins again. New feathers set to work. Lady Go works with mandarin duck feathers on his feet while the mandarin alternates between dove, swallow, wry-neck and swan feathers (those birds sacred to Aphrodite).

After a while of it, blubbering cachinnating, peeing, shrieking, convulsing, he begins to prepare for death. Choking on salt and spittle and snot, he can no longer breathe. His laughing surrounds him. He is total laughter. His entire body is laughing. He suspects that even his cells and neurons are laughing, and he is at the edge of death and hysteria, poised at the cliff's end, ready to dive into the void.

"Lady Go, now!" commands the mandarin and she drops her feathers, reaches into the lacquer box and pulls out a mysterious looking feather which begins to flame and cast off a luminous light.

"Ah, the Phoenix feather!"

The young man, convulsed with laughter, doesn't realize that nobody is tickling him.

The mandarin yells, "Wake up, youthful folly!" and drives the feather point into our hero's forehead, watches it burn to a crisp in the young man's skull, leaving a small golden pile of ashes.

There's the point. The point of it. A tunnel into the brain. Fires and flares light the dome's vault. Can't get out. Why go? Earth moves like a fan belt. I just stand still. Why go out? Explore? Nothing to find when there's nothing to look for.

"He's ready for the final phase-out."

"Let him rest for a while, gather up strength."

"Of course."

"I think he'll make it."

"Of course."

4.

The Whip, the Rod, the Violated Object Revisited; wherein our hero is once again upright, clothed in a young executive's suit. He stands in a cement-floored room with white plaster walls. All over the room are instruments of torture: whipping posts, racks, straps, whips, Iron Maidens, screw, thumbscrew, treadmill, crank, crops, quirts, guillotine, a cross, and an electric chair.

A steel door grinds open and two men in black cowls bring in a small lovely doe of a girl with wide soft-brown eyes which glisten with warmth and tenderness and, now, fear.

"She's first, Master," grunts one of the guards.

The young man's jaw drops.

"Yes, Master, she's an appetizer, there's more to come. This will be a wonderful love-feast."

"But, what am I supposed to do with her?" asks the young man.

"Why, Master, you jest," grumbles a guard. "You're to punish, humiliate, degrade, sexually abuse her."

Exit the guards.

The steel door closes with a grim clank.

The girl is small and frail. Her breasts are firm and placed high on her chest. They stick straight out, pushing through the gingham pinafore she is wearing.

She looks at our hero with her incredibly round soft moist eyes and her full lower lip begins to tremble.

"Please," she begins, but her words are lost in a heavy sob which shakes her body.

Our hero looks at this most sympathetic of young ladies and watches a wide crystal sparkle of tears slowly move down each tender cheek. Then he watches the tears drop onto her gingham pinafore and spread on the fabric.

Time and silence pass by.

The girl looks up, puzzled.

Our hero walks up to her and cups her wet chin in his firm hand and punches her in the stomach.

Eyes wide with pain and shock, she slumps to her knees, still looking at him, grabbing around his knees, gasping for breath.

Our hero looks down on her quivering frame and curls his lip and snarls at her.

She unzips his fly.

He grunts his assent.

She pulls out his penis which is limp.

"No," our hero growls. "Stand up and face your Master."

Relieved, but looking suspicious, the young girl stands up and faces the scowling young man in a gray executive's suit.

Drawing her to him, he grabs the doilylike collar of her blouse and with a firm grip rips it and the gingham pinafore off.

She stands before him in her bra and panties and immediately he can see goose bumps erupt all over her exposed flesh.

The swell of her breasts in her bra excites him as well as the imprint of her cunt-hairs against the thin white panties.

He grabs a razor strap off the wall and slams it against her belly, leaving a thick red bar.

Before she can fall, he steadies her and tears off her bra. Her breasts are firm and round. Her skin is satiny. The nipples rest in pink discs and are erect. He twits each nipple and she flinches in the pain. Then he grips them tightly between his thumb and forefinger and twists them until she screams.

"No one can hear you." And he grabs her panties and yanks them off.

She is naked before him.

Her shoulders shake in an attempt to stop crying. Her hands cover her perfect triangle. Our hero feels his body webbed with a new electricity. Averting his eyes, he drags her to a whipping post and ties her hands to it with leather thongs. He grabs a paddle and starts whacking it against her small tight rear. Each smack leaves its red insignia and her legs squeeze together as if to hold off the incredible burning pain racing through her body. Whack. Whack. Whack. Until white-ribbed welts rise on her white flesh and small blood clots in the welts break into thin lines of blood.

He stops and hangs the paddle up.

She's muttering prayers to herself and this outrages our young man. He pulls her head back, grabbing her hair. Her mouth is wet with saliva and tears and is open. Her eyes are squeezed tight.

"You're my slave and I forbid your praying to anybody but me," he says, then jams his tongue into her open mouth and brings his knee up into her crotch.

He leaves her to survey the whip-decked wall and selects a suitable one for her most tender flesh.

When he returns, she looks him directly in his eyes. Her brown big eyes are deep with sorrow and beauty and love.

"You fool," she says, "what are you doing?"

Our hero looks at her beautiful face and into those profoundly disturbing eyes.

"I'm not a fool," he says. "Everybody is always calling me one. I'm nothing anymore." And he hits her right breast with a riding crop.

When he's finished with his whipping, slapping, kicking, punching and gouging, her body is bruised, bloody and distorted.

She's on her hands and knees crawling around the floor, her wrists scarred from the thongs which he tied too tightly. Moaning, no longer crying, she moves about in a strange circle, like a crippled animal.

"What are you saying?" he asks her.

"You're a fool," she groans.

He leaps up in the air and lands on her back feet first.

The two men come in and carry the girl out.

"Is she...?"

"Master, that's none of your concern."

"Right," says the other one, his voice coming from an inner drum. "We'll be back in a moment with the next one."

The next one is a pale skinned, blue-eyed, flaxen-haired beauty who is slender and large-busted, but not top-heavy. She's in a lavender gown which tints her paleness and reveals the swell of her white breasts pushed up by the bodice. Her mouth is ripe-lipped, sensual and berry-red. She wears no makeup, just a bit of eyeshadow and liner, which accent her blondeness and enlarge her blue eyes and frame them.

The guards leave. The door again clanks shut.

She stands by the door and allows our hero to scrutinized her frame. She observes him too. She sees a young face that looks old and oddly wolfish. His eyes seem stuck in an oddly-fixed focus. She is ready for whatever comes but wonders who this young man is and what he represents in her trial.

"Come to me, slave," says the young man, his voice newly resonant, his hands still aching from their recent workout.

Obediently, the girl walks to him, looking at him with her blue, blue eyes. He averts them and instead looks greedily upon her breasts.

"On your knees, slave!"

Without a murmur, she gracefully sinks to her knees and looks up at him.

"You know what to do. Now do it."

She understands. As she unzips his fly, she sees a cluster of drying blood stains on the floor and shudders.

"Do it!" our hero yells, mistaking her fear.

She unbuckles his belt and allows his gray pants to fall around his ankles. Then, with cool hands, she pushes his shorts down.

"Snap it up!"

His flaming cock in her cool fingers springs to immediate attention. She strokes it and looks into its single eye, watching the staff's crown widen as her fingers gently stroke the under-part of his foreskin.

His hands grab the back of her head and push her mouth upon the crown. He's hard on her mouth and keeps pushing the enlarged cock into it, jamming it in until she begins to choke on it.

Instead of ejaculating in her mouth, he pulls out and shoots his stream in between her eyes and laughs crankily as the gray-white fluid dribbles down her face.

"Up, up."

She stands up.

"Now go around the corner," he says, sounding like a seasoned fantastico.

"No, don't walk, slave."

He pushes her to the floor.

"Crawl."

She crawls around to his back.

"Now bore in there and be gentle with my balls," he grumbles, looking over his shoulder at her long hair.

Her tongue at first is tentative in this unknown territory until he again reaches his hands behind his back and pushes her face and tongue into it.

While engaged in tickling his musky channel, she holds his heavy balls in her hand.

He farts in her face.

Once more he loses control.

Scourges her flesh after clawing and tearing apart her lavender gown, scratching ten bloody uneven lines down her breasts, ribs, belly and legs.

Then mercilessly birches her full breasts until they're bloody and bruised and permanently scarred. He rips out handfuls of her blonde hair and stuffs it into her bruised mouth.

Sometimes, during it all, he observes himself, neat in his suit, violently ravaging this beautiful creature so that she will never be the same again. He watches, as if on the ceiling looking down, and can't stop it.

Bullshit, he snarls to himself, clawing apart her cunt's lips as if to rip it in half.

The two guards return to carry her away.

"Very good, Master, she's ready for the Basement."

"What's the Basement?" our hero asks.

The guard with the deep cavern voice says, "The Basement is the bottom. It's the end. It's when you…"

"Quiet," says the other guard.

"What is the Basement?" our hero asks again.

"I can tell you no more, Master. Besides, new treats await you."

They drag her out, each holding a leg. Her head and ragged hair drag along the floor.

When they return, they return with a tray of so-called food.

"A little respite," says the voice booming from the bottom of the big bass drum. "A little refreshment before the next discipline session."

They leave him with his tray.

The same tubes and pills and tablets and crackers. Except, this time, there's a sandwich which is delicious. And he eats it. The flavor of the meat is like no other he has ever eaten. He opens the bread to examine it.

No, it can't be, he thinks.

And if it is…?

Fuck it.

And he gobbles it down.

A progression of tender virginal girls is pushed through the iron door and he lashes, binds, paddles, rapes, destroys and defiles them with increasing efficiency. He forgets what they look like and how or why they protest his increasing violence towards them. What he can not forget is that they all have sad, intelligent eyes that look deeply into his. One of them, a tender young girl, perhaps only a teenager, made him want to tear those accusing eyes out of her skull.

During this rage, a chorus of voices chant out ethical emblems through speakers our hero cannot locate. Because if he could, he'd tear them from the walls and stamp them to bits and—

"Go forth, maids of Jerusalem,/And look, you daughters of Zion,/On King Solomon wearing his crown,/Placed on his head by his mother/To mark the days of his wedding,/The day of the joy of his heart."

He enters a young girl's anus and hears her cry aloud in startled new pain. And continues to plunge until he comes.

"'Tis better to give than to receive."

"Fear not; believe only and ye shall be made whole."

He ties a redhead to the stretching rack and starts cranking the ancient wheel.

"Smiles are always precious."

Her gums all bloody after he's punched her mouth, she spits a red splatter on the floor. This enrages our hero.

"Great, indeed, is the task assigned to woman. Who can elevate its dignity? Who can exaggerate its importance?" the chorus chants while our hero stuffs another lady into the Iron Maiden. He can hear her muffled screeches and notes blood seeping from the maiden's shut brass-piked door.

"It has been said that in sickness there is no hand like woman's hand; no heart like woman's heart; and there is not."

Virtue, virtue, he mumbles, fucking her as she lies on her back stretched out on a table littered with broken beer bottles.

"Command his attentions by being always attentive to him."

The horsewhip feels good in his hands and he chases the frightened young girl around the room, lashing her with it until the lash curls about her head and snaps her backwards to fall on the floor.

"Virtue is its own reward." "A penny earned is a dollar saved." "A stitch in time saves nine." "A rolling stone gathers no moss."

"To be or not to be." The voices continue until they speed up and sound like a field of hysterical crickets.

5.

It's a beautiful show.

The young man sits in the electric chair and Carla enters the room.

"Now, you're one of us," she says to him.

His heart leaps at the sight of her.

She pulls down the switch.

A million volts of myth burn up his nervous system.

And then they begin to enter through the opened steel door. All of them. Starting with the mother of five, the Doctor, Marla, Myrna, Brigette, Hurko Fist, Leonard, Carmen La Tour, the gray priest—they all toe-dance through the door, a weird corps de ballet, freak Rockettes. Bow, smile, square-dance around the room, then, in single file, skip out. Followed by the young girls with the intelligent and sad eyes who come toe-dancing back into the room of their ruin, all holding onto a white gossamer veil. All perfectly intact.

His spine's a blazing candelabra.

They dance around him. Blow kisses. Diddle their cunts. Bump and grind. Drool and wink. Those beautiful indestructible ideals.

Leaving, they sing a tuneless cheer.

"Fuck the fool. Fool the fucker. The fool-fucker fucks himself."

The steel door clanks shut. A dramatic slam. Carla walks over to him.

"Tomorrow we take you out into the Field."

"What?"

"You start the first course of training."

"For what? Why?"

"You are going to become an Agent. Why? Because there is nothing more for you to do," says Carla.

"You're beautiful," announces our hero. "You're the dream-woman of my life."

"The only way to have me as a woman is impossible. Unless you are a surgeon."

"You mean?" croaks the young man.

"Exactly."

"One for all and all for one. Don't shoot until you see the whites of their eyes. God bless America. The family that prays together stays together."

"Can't you shut that off?" he asks her.

They sit across the round table facing each other. In the center of the table is a Mesopotamian candelabra. The candles are umber and scented.

Each has a large snifter of 19th century brandy before them which they sip as is their wont.

"I want to marry you," he says.

"Don't be silly," answers Carla. "I'm already married."

"Let me be your lover," he asks.

"Don't be silly, I'm impenetrable," she answers.

"Let me go home."

"You have no home."

"You mean?"

"Exactly. This is your home. You have entered the Order and there's no returning."

Baroque music tinkles out of the stereo entertainment center.

"We've given meaning and purpose to your life and now you must, in exchange, give meaning and purpose to other people's lives. Do you understand?"

"No," answers our young man.

Nothing before him, nothing behind him, and he can fathom the blankness of it and realize that he has no choice, but yet feels loss and, for the moment, wishes he were alone.

"It will pass," says Carla. "Have some more brandy. Cigarette? Or, I know what, how about a pre-Castro Havana cigar?"

He chooses the cigar and clips the end off and lights it while Carla pours another, deeper sniff of brandy.

Harpsichord and strings. The violins playing music that's like mountain ranges and the harpsichord sounds like a computer.

He gulps the brandy. It burns going down and lands in his center like a small sun.

"Vivaldi," says Carla, lighting a cigar too. "Now, tomorrow, we send you to Washington with Rod Straight. You're to spend a few days there observing the high levels of enterprise that we are engaged in. I want you to take notes, if necessary, and prepare a report for me when you return. Also, try and take pictures with a specially-concealed camera we'll outfit you with and, also, be sure to try and get some tapes. Before you leave, you'll go with Rod Straight to the Russian Consulate and engage in the same sort of observation. We keep both sides supplied with phantoms."

"You know you are my muse. I never thought of it before," he says. "I never could make out her face, but now I know she looked like you." And he drains the glass.

In his cell, his new home, the young man falls wearily on the firm but comfortable bed allowed him. The room has no windows but does have a small washroom attached to it. On the washroom's door is a small chart of daily exercises to perform upon arising and before sleep.

Every inch of his body is stiff. His balls ache, his thighs feel wrenched, his arms are sore, his chest feels inflamed, and his eyelids fall upon his eyes like hot cement cups.

He dreams.

He dreams.

He dreams.

But in the middle of the night and in the middle of his dreaming, two strong men lift him out of bed and, holding him gently, carry the sleeping hero into an elevator.

The elevator goes down. The doors open when they land in the Basement.

When he awakens, he is in a pile of rags and wet broken-down cartons in an alleyway. A trio of ancient ruins watch him.

The first crony, a crooked withered lady, sits on skeletal haunches and rocks back and forth. The second old biddy, a thick-fingered man, leans against a brick wall. (In his time he led a glamorous ring of homosexual dopplegangers. Now, at forty-five, he is an outcast and drinks too much.) The third hag sits on a wooden crate. An enormous woman who is built up, layer by layer, composed of tubes of fat that start from her donut-thick ankles up to her earth-mover tire-huge bust into the receding folds of flesh that taper into her round, battered mug. They wait for the young man to open his eyes. While waiting, they pass around a half-gallon jug of "smoke," a concoction of raw alcohol and water. The alcohol is cheap and the water is free. There's always a half-gallon empty jug in the garbage or in a doorway. It's lethal and gets you high.

The smoke dribbles down the fat lady's chins and body and she looks like a grotesque water fountain. The lean and bony one pulls out a neatly folded paper cup from her shirt pocket and pours the stuff into it. The demolished faggot plants his lips around the chipped half-gallon spout and guzzles his fill.

"Shouldn't we wake him?" asks the faded faggot.

"No. Let him wake up…" begins the thin one.

"…so he thinks he's dreaming," concludes the fat one, and when she talks, the words are squeezed out. Heavy breathing and gasping punctuate each word. She's like a huge bellows.

The young man's eyelids flutter.

The three stir expectantly.

"Ah, it's just another dream," says the wasted fairy. "When their eyeballs roll around against the lid, they're dreaming. I read that in a book somewhere."

"Heh, heh," cackles the thin one. "You sure you didn't write the book yourself?"

The large lard lady laughs briefly. Her laughter is woven with gasps of breath. Her eyes begin to bulge out and her cheeks get red, that black-red flush of the dying.

"I used to write poems," says the faggot, breaking the word up so that it sounds like po-ems.

The skinny one rocks and chuckles. Her cackle is like broken glass.

"Roses are red, violets are blue/What you need is a good shampoo," drones the fairy leaning against the wall. "Pass the sauce," he adds, scratching his crotch.

The jug is passed around.

It happens that the liquid takes little time in rearranging the easily disordered mind. This trio, strangely bound, last ate an alley cat for dinner, cutting its throat with the top of a tin can. They roasted the lean wretch and managed whatever meat they could. It wasn't that they were hungry, but every so often they need food. It is to drink and to keep drinking that is their motto, their particular burden. Wind whistles down the alleyway. Topsoil whipped off the open garbage cans rattles about on the ground.

Our hero awakens.

"Ah," gargles the fat lady.

"Hee," snickers the skinny one.

"At last," sighs the finished faggot.

It's the knowledge that it may not be a dream that bothers the young man as the three of them, in clumsy order, fall upon him and begin to undress him. Not entirely, just enough to get his parts out in the open.

Assorted exclamations. A blast of chilly wind whips through the alley. His prick-tip begins to feel a cap of ice form upon it.

"Oh, for God's sake," groans the faggot, forty-five years of age, a relic of the game. "Who's going to get him first? I mean, aren't we the chosen ones?"

"Ah, chosen for what? For death?" the lean one grunts, clutching her bony shoulders and hugging herself.

"Chosen for me first, of course," the fat one wheezes. "Bring him to me. You know how hard it is for me to move. Except, of course, when necessary."

They pass the jug of smoke around. The more you drink of it, the more your taste is able to remember better things. Now it tastes like high-class octane gin. The stuff you used to fill your young heads with when it was courting-time in Auschwitz.

Grunting and grinding, a Moby hulk of a mess, the fat one pushes her bulk to the young man's open pants and gazes with rapture upon his icicle cock and seed sacs.

He can smell her ancient sex. Canned tuna and squid. He sees her drawers and they are stained and threaded. Her clumpy fingers roll them down over mastodon-wide hips and stodgy thighs and as soon as her cunt is exposed, small steam clouds hover around it.

Her bush is overgrown and gritty, leading into a hanging

gray-pink vulva, which she pushes into his face, squatting over him.

Ambushed by her cunt, he can see nothing more and is heated by its ocean fumes and lust and feels his stomach churn.

He doesn't ask her what he is supposed to do. His questioning time is done with. His tongue begins its drudgery. Pushes into her extensive slot which is thick with her lust-fudge.

She squeals, she groans, she gushes a new load at his tongue.

The lean one can't hold back and jumps upon the fat one's back to kiss the leviathan lips and push skeleton hands into her elephant clothing to mash and grab hippopotamus boobs and the fallen faggot stops chug-a-lugging the smoke and begins to suckle our hero's cock with ferocious appetite.

An alley cat idly pees on the ornate structure of people. The wind continues.

Word gets around and before you know it, there's a line hanging out of the alleyway made up of all the used-up rejects and lost dreamers. Quietly, since they're used to loss, they stand and take their turn upon our hero.

A smelly procession of cocks and cunts make constant use of our hero's mouth and parts. No need to detail the grim procession. His mouth starts to burn early in the game. Pubic hairs plastered all over his face. He forgets where he is or who he is. It's just suck, lick, squirm and gasp for breath sometimes when the stench is particularly putrid. Some old men can hardly get their withered peckers into his chapped mouth without dribbling some of their pent-up desire on his new white shirt. He's skewered, cunt-yoked, cock-bolted, come-wedged, shit-stapled, battened, hatched, teat-bracketed, coupled, bung-hole-fixed, braced, hitched, pussy-riveted, gash-strapped, spooned, sponged, drooled on, shat on, wept on, thumbtacked, fish-farted, breached, tongue-knotted, stamped and sealed, forgotten and remembered...

"Oh, my son," she croons, popping a flap of tit in his gray face.

"Oh, my astro-alchemist," groans a portly queen, raking our young man's left testicle with his purple-tinted false fingernails.

It goes on and on like this.

Our hero goes back to sleep. Cold arctic cabinet holds his broken form.

Dragged through the streets of hell.

Two crones hold a leg each and drag him out of the alleyway, cock dangling and mouth smeared with the paste of ages.

Heaved onto a stage.

A rock band (one drummer, one bass, one guitar) shatters the smoke with their endless monotony.

"Dance, you prick," gushes some art fan.

A bloated Mexican lady waddles out of stage left and does the Mexican hat dance on our hero's corpus. People pour watered-down drinks into his closed mouth.

A naked lady races out in the audience and does an obscene dance with a candle (and candle holder).

Several over-the-hill sailors pound on her, fall onto the floor with her. Sailor suits fly up into the silent fan.

Raked off the stage.

Dragged down another alleyway.

Tossed down some stairs into a new Basement.

Picked up, like clockwork, by two familiar guards who put our hero back in the elevator.

For all he knows, it is all a dream.

The next morning, he is flown to Washington.

Rod Straight sticks out a neat strong hand.

"Hi, I'm glad to meet you," he says, and it sounds like an announcement. "Here's your very own attaché case. Note," he says, snapping it open, "the tape-recording device and, here, cleverly concealed as a package of Marvel cigarettes, is a mini-camera already loaded and ready to shoot. Gosh, you look a bit pale. Had a bad night?" Rod Straight chuckles knowingly.

"When do we leave?"

"Almost immediately. Do you know what to do? Have you been told? Here, read this manual in the ten minutes we have until take-off time."

Not as big as the phone book, but as bulky, our hero takes the manual from Rod Straight whose hand, at the moment, is underneath his pants poking about in his parts to be sure they're arranged according to the crotch-cut of his new suit.

Lots of martinis on the plane. Straight giggles a lot about his "absolute madness" for martinis.

They watch a few stag-movies while aloft. One of them features our hero in the Lunch Room. The other stars Rod Straight. Our hero notices that Straight has the longest, straightest prick he's ever seen. Apparently it must cause some difficulty, because Straight's hand is always dipping into his pants to arrange the coil so that it doesn't appear too conspicuous.

"You'll love D.C.," announces Straight. "It's just like home. First stop, of course, the Pentagon—where the action is. It's a swinging place. We'll pick up some tapes, flicks and photos there and have a board meeting, a shorty, with some of the great gang there. Here, have another martooni. Special formula." Straight winks at our hero and uncorks the thermos to pour more into both of their cups. "I'm crazy about the olives myself, aren't you?" gurgles Straight, giving our hero a pretend right to the jaw. Rod Straight opens up a jar of stuffed green olives and pops them into their cups. "No picks for me. Makes it too easy to eat the olive before the drink's done. And everybody knows that the olives have to soak before they're any damned good. Right?"

Our hero nods.

"Here's to D.C."

They toast paper cups.

"Here's to more of the same. Hey, look at the neat cloud formation. Makes me think of fucking. Right?"

Our hero nods.

"You know, I've been out in the field now for nearly half a decade—makes it sound like ages, doesn't it?—and I've learned how to keep my mouth shut, but you're the tightest-lipped agent I've ever met. You must've gotten special training. Right?"

"Mm-mm," grunts our hero, looking out the window, beginning to feel a warmth towards the clouds and the martinis.

"Horny?" asks Rod Straight.

"No," answers our hero.

"Good. That's the best way to be when you're on duty. Too many distractions. But when I knock off work, you bet your ass you know where you can find me. Right? Huh? Just fucking away like an old jackrabbit. Right? Man, I been measured and even had a bronze cast made of my super-large cock. It's the biggest in the whole Agency. Make that dumb fucker Casanova look like a pipsqueak. Say," says Straight, "you show me yours and I'll show you mine, okay?"

"But we're on duty."

"Aw, come on, we're just flying now. D.C.'s a good two hours away."

"No, Straight. In fact, you'd better cool it on those martinis or I'll report you," says our hero, trying to sound like the facsimile he is supposed to sound like.

"Man, what a crummy thing to do. You must've had real special training. That's the shits. They never gave me any special training. Can I have just one more martini?"

"One more, Straight, and easy on the olives."

"But…"

"But, *Sir,*" says our hero.

"But, *Sir Sir?* Sir? Are you? Do you mean that you're…"

"Exactly," says our hero, draining his cup.

Straight salutes him.

Our hero salutes back.

More martinis are poured.

Our hero goes back to cloud-watching.

They're picked up by a silver-gray Rolls-Royce limousine driven by a chauffeur in an army uniform.

They salute when saluted and enter the car. An imperious woman in a brown tweed suit sits at the end of the seat. They salute her. She salutes back. Our hero sits next to her while Straight sits next to him, looking out the window as Washington, D.C., passes by his bleary eyes.

"You're new?" the woman says.

"Yes…and no," answers our hero.

Her eyes are gray and her nose is aquiline and her brown tweed suit cannot conceal the swell and contours of her body.

Her lips are lightly tinted with a subtle lipstick which matches her suit. He thinks that she may be in her mid-thirties because of a few lines around her mouth and eyes. Her skin is a powdery white, firm and silky.

"Need a Bromo, Straight?" she asks.

"Heck, no, I can hold my own," he answers, dark shadows under his eyes like bruises.

The young man feels his hip pressed by her hip and her toes curl around his ankle. He looks at her face and her face turns to his. They kiss.

A deep long kiss. Their tongues first start a tongue-tip duel in their mouth caves. Gradually his tongue pushes hers back and he paints the roof of her mouth with dainty sensual tongue-tip strokes.

"Mm, mm," she groans, and shifts about so that his hands can reach around to feel her breasts.

"Mm, mm," she groans again, weaving her fingers through his hair and giving it a gentle tug.

"We're arriving at the Pentagon in two minutes," announces the chauffeur's voice through the intercom.

"Ah, well, we'll meet again. I'm Miss Rake and I'm with the ICBM people. Comb?"

"Yes, thanks."

"Gosh," groans Straight, "I sure could use a drink now. This place always scares me for some reason."

The car stops and the chauffeur opens their doors.

They enter from a rear door and are immediately photographed, fingerprinted, X-rayed, frisked (Miss Rake allows the soldier delightful frisk-liberties), saluted, and finally let onto the elevator.

"He says," she says, "that the Boss'll be there too."

"Oh, God, if only my thermos weren't empty," Straight sighs.

Elevator door opens.

The guard salutes them and lets them out.

They walk down a long marble hallway that makes their footsteps sound like shuffling explosions. At the end of the hall is a colossal wooden door that reaches the ceiling. Gold military emblems are engraved in the wood. Six guards stand before the door. Papers are checked, passports inspected; more photos, more fingerprinting, more frisking (one of the guards discovers Rod Straight's specialty and he and his buddy make use of it, while the other four guards examine Miss Rake in great detail— to her seemingly lavish delight).

Thus finished, the guards resume their posts. One of them presses a button.

"What the hell is it now?" booms a loud voice.

"Chief, it's some people from the Agency."

"Aww, well why the hell didn't you say so before, you mother-grabbing ball-breaking per-vert! Let 'em in, for Christ's sake!"

The mammoth door opens, pulled back by three guards in chrome helmets. The young man, Rod Straight and Miss Rake, walk down another long hallway. This one's covered with six-inch-deep carpeting, royal blue, which leads to another door.

Along the walls of the hallway are pictures of combat scenes enlarged to epic-size, detailing specific cruel wounds inflicted upon American soldiers in all major 20th century warfare.

Wall-size photograph of a WWI doughboy's face corroded by gas warfare. Photo of a WWII G.I.'s head blown off. Color wall-scenes of mutilated sailors. A sergeant's guts hanging out of his neatly-pressed battle fatigues, shot down by a draft dodger in the barracks. A full-length poster of the draft dodger's body after it was used for bayonet practice.

The trio move quickly to the next door.

There are no guards. Just a gold bayonet door-knocker.

Miss Rake uses it.

"Come the fuck in!" bellows the Chief inside.

They do just that.

The room is smoke-filled. Maps of war-areas cover most of the walls except for one which has a blown-up flash-photo of the ex-Minister of Missiles being cornholed by the ex-Minister of Crop Defoliation.

"Can't stand fags here, right guys? American military are all men. Right?"

All the men sitting in the smoky haze nod or grunt assent.

"How the hell are you, little buggers?" announces the Chief, towering over Miss Rake and planting a big open cow-mouth kiss on her while grabbing her buttocks and kneading them with his huge hands.

"Mm, mm," groans Miss Rake.

"Ah, you little cock-teaser, how about a drink?"

The Chief looks at our young man.

"Who the elephant-shit are you?"

"He's new," announces Straight.

"What do you drink?" asks the Chief.

Straight whispers into our young man's ear.

"Tell him you want rye straight."

"Give me rye straight. No water."

"Ah, a man! Come here and let me shake your hand!" The Chief extends his huge hand to our hero and squeezes it like squeezing a lime into a drink.

"Men drink rot-gut straight. No bullshit mixed drinks or ice or fuck-piss like that. Right?"

The men sitting in the smoke around the war table nod and grunt and, as proof, raise up their shot glasses.

"Okay, let's watch the war, and then we'll watch whatever the mashed balls you got. War movies get me horny, don't they get you horny? All them brave virile men getting their fucking heads blown off and their unmentionables blown off and their blood and gore gushing all the come-fuck out of them. C'mon, Miss Rake, sit down on my raunchy lap and let's watch the war."

Lights are dimmed and war movies of real war start churning onto the screen which slides down from the ceiling.

"Hey, fart-head in the projection room, how about showing us those films where our guys get garroted in a yellow-cunt whorehouse. Something special for our guests."

"Yes, Chief," barks the voice in the projection room.

Before the screen turns white, we see a platoon of soldiers climbing up a hill. Climbing, climbing, until they get to the top. Then we watch them all shot down by guerillas. Even the chaplain.

"Y'see that?" grunts the Chief. "Godless teeny-weenies. That's the whole problem with them yellow people is that they got cock-complexes and are all jealous about white Americans who've got the biggest and best cocks in the world. Right?"

In the darkness, the men growl and burp agreement.

They watch the Chief's request.

You see eight Oriental ladies of the night at their toilet, feathery and tittery. They wash and cleanse themselves with sponges, syringes and brushes.

The door is broken down. A squad of twelve soldiers pushes through it.

The girls all look startled and foxy and lewd and pure. All at once.

No sound track, but one of the soldiers walks up to one of the prostitutes and they engage in a conversation. Meanwhile, the other girls are busy with the soldiers who were ordered to stand at ease.

"Y'see?" barks the Chief, "look at them rats go for our boys, look at them snooping into their drawers to see a pure American cock."

The glint of Miss Rake's exposed breasts.

In his excitement, the Chief has ripped off her suit top and blouse and is dandling her full erect tits in time with the movie.

Hand-held camera pans down a dim hallway where the ladies and soldiers walk, separating into separate cribs, except for two of the girls who, to be fair to the number of men, take on two at a time.

Shots of each soldier being serviced or imposing his service upon one of the Oriental ladies.

These scenes are edited in a choppy fashion. The main portion of the film details the garroting. The strangler's weapon is copper wire around the neck while the ladies bind the soldier's parts with copper wire—and yank.

"Ha, goes to show you! Make some great American trophies for them yellow slit-slot misfits."

Films are exchanged, forms filled. All of this is handled by a murky crew of men in blue-black business suits.

Rod Straight and our hero leave, leaving Miss Rake with

the Chief who was last seen under the war table with her, stretching apart her pliable legs and trying to get an erection.

Much the same kind of business at the Russian office. They watch a Soviet youth parade and missile display movie. This excites Smirnyav Murkov immensely and Straight, knocking down as many vodkas as they'll give him, starts dancing with Murkov's secretary, Olga Bulkoff. His monumental prick uncoils as they polka and stops the show for a moment. Murkov and Bulkoff and Straight retire to another room while our hero continues to watch more war movies in the company of stolid Russian diplomats who keep offering him vodka which, as Straight earlier instructed, he cannot refuse.

Both Russian and American leaders agree, our hero finds out, that the Asians have penis-envy problems.

Straight and our hero spend equal time in the airline's toilets on the return trip, heaving up Washington, D.C.

PROLOGUE

Me no know
Me no care
Push a button
And go somewhere.

—Children's rhyme

It's a job. It's all he can do. He carries out his assignments without bitterness or thought of alternatives beyond them.

After Washington, our hero was shown the various downtown aspects of Agentry. He observed the Mail Processing Room which covered an entire floor of the building. He was released into the custody of a photographer and watched a day's work schedule take place. (The photographer was not Jack Flash.) He was shown the Accounting Room and had a chance to look over some of the books and was impressed by the scope and value of the enterprise. It was then he felt a bit of pride to be a party to it, this vast network of illusions. That may have been the last time our hero felt his pride stir for anything.

His sex life has become nonexistent. He's lost thirty pounds. Much of his attention is lavished on his gun collection. He's also become a connoisseur of fine wines. His apartment is on the Agency's premise and he can, at any time, tune in to the activities in a specific room to hear the joy or agony of a new initiation. But he rarely bothers.

He no longer reads. The management gave him a TV set in honor of his first quarter's work. He decants a glass of Château Meridian Nadir Cabernet Sauvignon '59 and watches, primarily, the children's shows: the cartoons, westerns, and crime-fighter entertainments. He is most fascinated by commercials, especially when they're interspersed between the 6 o'clock news. He watches the 6 o'clock news regularly because he no longer cares to know about the outside world and the news is a pleasant way to realize that the outside world does not exist.

He also collects pipes and exotic tobaccos from all over the world. He sits before the TV when his day's work is done and drinks his wine and puffs his pipe and, thus, lets time move on.

He's always on call whenever he's needed to play a role in an initiation rite. His closet is well-stocked with an agent's stock garbs: priest, guard, cowboy, Priapus, spaceman, Napoleon, de Sade (which comes with five interchangeable powdered wigs), over-sexed hippie, etc.—a large variety of robes and vestments.

His dreams, since they feed him new food, do not bother him, nor are they real, nor are they any less real than his room, the TV, or that strange black containment which squats within his center.

Once a month, they let him take his guns to a special shooting range. They allow him a fair yield of ammunition. First it's regulation targets. Then the targets assume the circled shapes of women and men that bother him, or whom he's failed to reach or communicate with. He's become an excellent marksman.

The only writing he does is when it's necessary to write up a report. This necessity has become less frequent. His reports are dull and matter-of-fact and leave out all the salient details, the atmospheric redundancies. They don't bother him, unless it's important, to write reports.

Our young man grows older.

An incredibly long, black, silent Cadillac sedan draws against the curb.

They've been following a young girl who walks down the street holding a book of French philosophy in her hand.

Our hero and the scowling bulldyke who is his partner on this run agree that the young girl is what they've been looking for.

One of the car windows hums open.

"Get in," says the chauffeur to the young girl.

This is the part our hero gets excited about.

"Are you talking to me?" says the young girl.

"Of course. Get in. In the back, with the men."

The window hums shut.

AFTER WORDS

The Rabbi of Kotzk said: "Everything in the world can be imitated except truth. For truth that is imitated is no longer truth."

Like all printed morality, they are books of dreams.

THE AGENT

Part One

Me no know.
Me no care.
Push a button
And go somewhere.

—Children's rhyme

1.

You must understand that rarely have I felt real.

I move thru my dream with a blank head and a numb heart. The last time I cried was when I was six years old and my dog was killed in an auto accident. The accident also took the lives of my mother and father. I could only mourn for the dog. My mother and father, naturally, went to Heaven. No need to cry for them. They were good Christians, decent hard-working folk and upstanding Americans.

An orphan, I was sent to Grimrock, a military school financed by the CIA I spent my childhood and early youth there, trained to honor those high moral, ethical and nationalistic standards of our nation. I was a first-rate student, straight A's. I also became quickly adept in the martial arts, marksmanship, track, gymnastics, football, chess and, as an aside, sky-diving. I was fearless. My body developed into a handsome structure of muscle and firm flesh. My rock-hard muscles were, and are, at my instant command.

I got along alright with the other lads, but I never could, nor would, indulge in their proxy-sex games. Many a time I whipped some perverted punk of a whelp who would try to bugger me in the showers. The homos left me alone. Right there, in that shower room, so lovingly provided by our Government, were budding degenerates and dissenters. I did what had to be done. I turned them in.

Some thought me aloof. But I was merely industrious. There was much to learn and little time to learn it all. I had no time to fool around. Fooling around is for fools. Marcus Forman was always passing around girlie magazines he'd pilfer in the city when he was on leave. The other boys would put their pillows over their parts and beat-off whilst looking at the indecent, fallen flesh-pots revealing their undergarments and bulbous bosoms. Not I. I warned Marcus Forman to quit corrupting America. Forman stuck a finger in the air. I turned him in.

For their sake, I would sometimes forgo the pleasure of a leave in order to clean out their lockers of any indecent material. You would be astonished at the amount of filth they could accumulate in a week's time.

I had learned at an early age to revere and honor that shrine of purity: Woman. I knew, as a second sense, that my time would come and that it would be with the bride whose hand I would take in holy matrimony. Besides, there was too much to do then, as there is now.

Because of my exceptional physical and mental powers, I was selected by a scholarship board to be sent off to the Lodge. The Lodge, virtually unknown outside of the CIA and, perhaps, FBI, was a cement complex built into the side of a mountain in the North Central portion of America. There, young lads like myself were prepared for fundamental training in service to the organization called KOMM (Keep Our Morals Meaningful). In cooperation with leading religious leaders, businessmen, generals and government officials, we lads were given a four-year course. This course transformed most of us into totally impeccable, unimpeachable dynamos of strength, cunning and moral fortitude. Of course, a few didn't make the grade. They left the Lodge while we slept and we never heard from them again. Most of them, anyway, were homos or wiseacres.

It's cold. It's night. I'm in my office. The lights are out. A water glass half-filled with Chivas Regal. I'm looking out the window. Watching the city move. The lights. Cars, signs. Watching people walk up and down the streets, look in windows, enter doors, leave doors. The whole world.

You forget the loneliness sometimes. Earlier, with Ruby Marlowe, I forgot a lot of things. She reminded me quickly. Slowly undressing before me. Unzipping the front of her soft black leather dress. Stepping out of it and standing before me in black hose, black panties and a thin strip of a black bra barely containing those incredible breasts. It was all I could do to hold myself back. Jumping up, grabbing Ruby Marlowe in my arms and dragging her to the sack. But in my work you learn how to wait. Wait and watch. Watch Ruby Marlowe do her slow dance. Caressing her hips. Licking her lips. Her pink tongue-tip slowly slipping over her lips. Rolls a sheer black nylon stocking slowly down her long lovely leg. Repeats the same with the other nylon. Bending over, exposing even more of her bulging breasts. Rims around her nipples. It's all I can do to keep still. My cock begins to uncoil. She unhooks her black bra and it falls to the floor. Ruby Marlow's breasts are round, full and firm. Her nipples are round erect turrets. Her hands caress them. Her tongue darts across her lips. She squeezes the huge globes and sways her hips in time to a silent music. She's got a flat tight belly framed by hips that were made for riding. Ruby Marlowe falls to her knees before me.

This is what I was waiting for. I stand up and pull her up with me. We kiss. It's a good, long, tongue-to-tongue kiss. My hard-on pokes into her and she laughs. "You're ready," says Ruby Marlowe. "As soon as I saw you," I answer. And I rip off the black whispy panties and get out of my clothes as fast as I can. Which is pretty fast. She helps me unbuckle my shoulder-holster and pants belt. "Aren't you going to take off your shoes?" she asks. Talking time is over and I push her onto the bed.

All over now.

I take a stiff pull on the glass, snap on the desk lamp. Stretch my legs by pulling the black curtain over the window. Then back to my desk.

I open the bottom drawer and pull out the metal case. Unlock it and start decoding my new orders.

I graduated from the Lodge a full-fledged agent for KOMM. The college I was sent to was a beehive of moral disintegration. I made straight A's, Go Champ, football hero, Student Body President, etc. That was easy enough. But the work I had to do there cleaning up the moral rot at work on the young psyches of many of the students—that was another matter altogether. I knew that KOMM was testing my true value and I couldn't let them down, nor could I stand the disgrace of betraying their confidence in me. I did well, if I must say so. Utilizing advanced spying devices, electronic tools, a winning smile, I was able to destroy a free-love ring, a nudist group, a biology professor, a tribe of marijuana addicts, and assorted Godless wretches spewing their infection into the pure white bowl of American virtue and purity. That was my freshman year. In the succeeding three years at this particular university, I was also able to render hopeless any further moral degradation, suppressing all radical elements. When I graduated, cum laude, I knew I had done my job well. A man from KOMM was there to take me to Washington for further indoctrination and briefing.

The head of KOMM gave me a swell sheepskin American flag which, in reality, was my credential and passport to secret government organizations throughout the world. My number, thumbprint and signature were engraved on the back in gold. It folded into a neat, discreet packet. Later, I found a secret section in all my shoes to place it in.

I found out the nature of my assignment at a special briefing meeting of KOMM. I was staggered at the magnitude of the operation I was to be pitted against, as well as incredibly grateful for this most prized of all assignments.

They wanted me to infiltrate the Agency as an undercover agent and to get to its heart and break its power and influence. When they described the range of the Agency's power, I was dumbfounded. The Agency was a vast enterprise which formed a giant cartel on the sexual imagination of the world. It supplied untold millions with repulsive materials to follow their crooked dreams with. Books, films, pictures, paintings, objects, tape recordings, and finally, people.

They played a taped talk of one of their leaders, a female, part of which I blushingly offer to you as an example of their monstrous philosophy:

"Ours is a mammoth enterprise of illusion that reaches into almost all levels of American life. Our resources are great and our active membership is beyond belief. All evidence of the sexual encounter, the sexual fantasy, is circulated, annotated, duplicated and registered in archives. Our central Archive is in Washington, D.C...."

I looked at my superior and he nodded. The tape continued.

"From diaries to full-length movies in technicolor featuring royalty and heroes; from sexual emporiums in Germany and Japan, to photo-offset sex want-ad magazines; tape-recordings, snapshots, wall posters, lithographs, comic books—no item too small or too large for us to handle. We arranged, we control, we allow the sexual imagination of America a course. And, best of all, we offer a well-regulated, well-structured organization. We're a secret institution. We satisfy all as soon as we know what their satisfaction is. Our wealth is beyond measure. We are democratic to a degree. Anyone is welcome who can comprehend that water seeks its own level. We have to stress some kind of necessary class-consciousness. The poor have too rich and violent an imagination. We prefer starting with the middle class. They seem the best starting-point for recruits and members. Our services demand consumers. The beauty of the Agency is that everything, everybody is used one way or another. To consume is to *be* consumed!"

It gets harder, after a while, to astonish a guy like me. The orders take a few moments to connect. I burn them. Watch them become ash in my big brass ashtray. (A present from a Chinese Nationalist counterspy who used to help me. A small body, but she was tight and tough and insatiable.)

The micro-paper burns quickly. Something in the paper produces a small ash-count.

Another slug of Chivas Regal.

The orders hit me. A movie screen opens up in my head and I watch the magnified words appear on the screen.

Madness. Not my outfit. Not my line of work. But I remember my oath, my pledge, and I think about the Chief, and I realize that I must do what I must do.

The orders come thru the Chief via KOMM.

An agent there informs the Chief that KOMM is planning to infiltrate the Agency. The agent says it's going to be done by one man. Some kind of super-patriot tiger who's unbeatable. A cherry to boot. (How are they going to prime him?) And I'm supposed to get into the idiocy of it by infiltrating myself into the Agency. Somehow, on some level, I'm going to meet this star-spangled freak and beat him out of the race.

Another shot of Chivas Regal. This one doesn't go down too well.

The kid's twenty-one. Master of martial arts, super athlete, trained by the military, inducted and disciplined for four years at the Lodge, a vital member of KOMM.

The orders are signed by the Chief. With a postscript. "Get that dumb motherfucker in the balls for me, too."

Light a cigarette that tastes like yesterday's hangover. Hits my lungs like a sand-blaster.

I turn the lights out. Pull back the black curtain. Open the window. Hear the sounds of the city. And sit back in my chair to watch the city move. The lights. The sound. And think. And plan. Tomorrow's going to be a busy day. A hell of a busy day.

Shit.

I was given the abstract particulars on the Agency. But this was to be a singular task and I had to be more completely conditioned for the job.

My Commander then told me how I was going to be indoctrinated and conditioned for my assignment. My first instinct, to my horror, was to protest. I held it back because these were my superiors and I was their servant, their weapon.

They brought the young lady into the briefing room. As casually as a Field General works on a wall map, my superior instructed the young lady to undress. With each item of clothing she removed, my superior named it and told me to memorize its name and function. This went well until the young lady—who had a pleasing face—stood before me in her undergarments.

She stood before me and I could see the rise and swell of her handsome breasts confined within an attractive white and lacy brassiere. The skin gave off a strange sheen. And her brief undergarment was cut so low as to reveal her navel. Gazing upon her breasts and then her navel and then—and then I saw her innermost essence, a black triangle ill-concealed by the filmy fabric of her undergarment. I turned away. Mortified.

"Come, come," said my Commander-in-Chief, "I know how distasteful this is to you, but this has to be done in order to toughen you up for the major ordeal ahead."

"Now," said the Lieutenant Colonel (who looked strangely

familiar), "you must undress the young lady. And touch her."

I saluted the Commander-in-Chief and the Lieutenant Colonel. (Who was he? Why was he smiling ever so slightly? But I couldn't use my fantastic memory at that moment because of the dilemma I was engaged with.)

The girl stood at ease and looked straight ahead.

I walked up to her.

As I stood before her, the Lieutenant Colonel's voice announced, "And, after you've undressed and touched the young lady, then you must make love to her. She is an expert teacher and you have nothing to fear."

For the first time in my twenty-one years on earth I felt fear. A mist of cold sweat formed about my forehead. A chilling explosion in my stomach seemed to drain it of any substance. Behind my knees, it seemed as if somebody had snapped the tendons. My lips became parched as if I'd been walking barefoot thru Death Valley one summer afternoon. I felt a slight nervous twitch ricochet thru my right eyelid.

"We must overcome the enemy, lad," said the Commander-in-Chief with a kindly tone to his voice—which I cherished at that moment.

"Come now, we don't have all day," snapped the Lieutenant Colonel. "I believe the young lady is getting impatient and, most likely, cold."

The Commander-in-Chief fumbled about on an elaborate panel on his desk and found a button and pressed it. Immediately the room was filled with music. The National Anthem.

"Come. Come to me," said the young lady, opening her arms, stretching out her hands.

But I was at attention and in full salute.

The Lieutenant Colonel went to the board and pushed another button. More music. This was the kind of music I'd heard in restaurants. The lights in the room grew dim.

"We'll leave you to your task," said the Commander-in-Chief. "You've got—check your watches—ten minutes and thirty seconds to accomplish your mission. We've got more briefing to do today and tomorrow. Let's go."

The Commander-in-Chief left first, followed by the Lieutenant

Colonel who, before he shut the door, extended an upright finger at me.

Not Marcus Forman!

The young lady embraced me.

The dwarf leaves the back-alley door. Scoots down the alley on his thick legs. He needs a shave. He's carrying a dark brown envelope almost as big as his face. One eye's gone wrong on him. A permanent white cloud covers the eye. He has to look twice as hard to see whether or not I'm there. Whether or not anybody else is there watching us. It's alright, Buddy, I think to myself. But it isn't.

Buddy stops running and stands still. He squints at a face in the parked Mercedes sedan.

You can't hear the shot.

All you see is the small red hole suddenly appear in the middle of Buddy's forehead like a raindrop.

Buddy's expression doesn't change in the instant that the back of his head blows out. His good eye rolls up into his shutting eyelid. The bad eye stays open as Buddy falls backward onto the sidewalk.

I get out of my car fast.

The Mercedes guns its engine and starts moving slowly out of its parking place.

I zigzag across the street to Buddy and grab the envelope out of his hands which grip it tightly. I start yanking at the envelope.

A splinter of cement rockets past my eye. A cement cloud of powder. The Mercedes races by. Nothing is working right. I can't see the driver. I can't get the envelope from Buddy's grip. And I can't get my gun out of the shoulder holster. The leather clasp won't unhook.

Two more silent bullets buzz out of the Mercedes.

One goes into Buddy's stomach. The other in his groin. The car roars off. No plates.

It's hard to look back at Buddy who lies in the dark red seepage of his blood.

I've been in a lot of rank scenes and I've done a lot of rotten things in my time, but nothing to come close to the shooting-down of Buddy, the one-eyed dwarf and counterspy.

Hell. He was dead when he hit the ground the first time.

What kind of a maniac—what kind of heartless gun-happy freak would shoot two perfectly placed shots into a man already dead?

How many times do you have to kill a man to prove your point? What point?

The envelope is easy to pull out of Buddy's grip now.

Buddy, I'll find that freak. I'll find him and make him pay.

Sirens. Somebody must've seen.

I get back in my car. Push the lighter in. Light a cigarette. Turn the ignition on. Step on the gas and drive back to the office.

Because I must, I will. Perhaps words do have a cathartic effect. I must keep a log, a journal, of what is happening and what will happen to me. That, and my regular daily reports to KOMM, will hopefully give me a good cathartic experience. First of all, my new name is Kane White. KOMM designated it as suitable from now on. I am their weapon. I must obey.

2.

First Day

Helpless.

She kisses me on my lips. My lips remain sealed. She pushes her tongue thru my lips. My teeth remain firmly clamped. She pushes her tongue harder, as if knocking on a door. Then she presses her body against mine. My mouth opens. Her tongue pushes in. I want to faint in horror. If this unsanitary filthiness is considered to be love, then I'll remain a virgin until eternity.

Some female karate or judo. I don't know how it happens. But she takes my hand and places it on one of her naked breasts.

Helpless.

Can I describe the incredible outrage and shock of her living flesh? It is soft and warm and, at the same time, pliant and firm. The palm of my hand is burned with the hot boring of her hard nipple.

"Kiss it," she says in a whisper.

I try to tell her that it's impossible. I can't put my mouth on it. The nipple sticks out on the breast circle like a small missile. Her tawny flesh shines in the dim light of the Commander-in-Chief's office.

"Kiss it. It's an order," she says.

"From whom?" I ask her with a voice that is not my usual deep resonant voice. Instead, it comes out of my throat like the crackling of old newspapers.

"The Commander, of course. Kiss it."

"But why?"

"Because you are learning how to make love to a woman."

"But..."

"Oh, stop whining. This is conduct unbefitting a member of KOMM."

Helpless.

I kiss her nipple. A quick peck.

"Again. Open your mouth. Lick it. Suck it. Hurry, we have

only seven and a half minutes left and you cannot fail this most basic of all trainings."

The humiliation. Years of dreams violated by this lovely young lady forcing me to suckle her teat.

"Know the Enemy," sizzles the Commander's voice over the restaurant music.

Am I being watched by the Commander? And, worst of all, by the Lieutenant Colonel?

"Cup it in your hand," she says, "and lift it gently to your parted lips."

It feels like a live animal in my hand and has a strange bounce that makes my hand feel electrified. Her nipple has a foul salty-like taste to it. I tentatively pucker about it and attempt to suck on it.

"Use your tongue," she orders. "Let your tongue stroke it in a back and forth motion. Increase that motion. Then gently nibble on the nipple as soon as it feels firm and tough enough for your teeth. Do you understand?"

I nod. I cannot answer with her nipple in my mouth and I cannot bear having to take it out and speak—and then go back to this odious task.

"Mm, that feels fine. Let's go and lie down on the sofa."

She walks ahead of me and stands before the Commander's well-stuffed, leather-upholstered sofa. She pats it, indicating to me that I should lie down. I do. I shut my eyes so as not to have to gaze at her naked full breasts swaying above me.

I keep saying to myself, I am Kane White, Kane White. Hoping that it will absolve me from what I have been doing and what I have to do. I am Kane White. Kane White does these things. It's alright for Kane White to engage in this horror. Helpless.

She unzips my fly.

You get used to it all.

The blood, the unseeing eyes of the dead.

You get used to a lot. Changing names, faces, places. (I automatically check my car for booby traps or assassins whenever I take it out of the garage.)

If you're alive long enough, you've learned a lot. You've

forgotten a lot too. You begin to not care. You get tough. And hard. Your heart gets muscle-bound. What the hell? You go when it's time to go. That's how I figure it.

I've been lucky. That's all. Lucky and tough and hard. But I can't get Buddy's killing off my mind.

Fingernail claw-marks on the envelope I open. New orders. It's always like this. They give you a new name, new papers to match that name, a book-length prospectus detailing the new person's character, background, tastes, dislikes, etc. You read it. Try to memorize aspects alien to your own nature. Then burn it. And try to rise out of it like a phoenix.

You get the orders and read them and you know that they won't know you again until you come back with your report. If you come back.

And those little pills. They help you to never come back in case you're caught. Or if you can't take their torture, you pop the pill then.

The hell with it. I always flush the pills down the toilet.

My new name is Titus Black. I'm a pervert. I also collect photographs and movies that are pornographic. My name is Titus Black...

I pour the rest of the Chivas Regal fifth into the glass and take a stiff belt.

I've had so many names that I no longer respond to my real name. When I had to counter-provoke the peace-strikers, my name was Buzz Brown. They gave me a crew cut, real short, so short you could see a tiny pancake-sized flesh disc on the top of my skull. I felt for those dumb kids with their banners and signs, but I'd been trained in Special Services and had to shut my eyes to feeling. The enemy is what your general tells you. When you start choosing, you become the enemy. When you start thinking about what the hell you're doing shooting down strangers, then you become the enemy.

For a hell of a long time, too long of a dull time, I had to sit in college classrooms getting data on both students and teachers to send to Washington for top-secret processing. Every so often I wondered where the fuck all my crummy notes went, into what office, what machine, what file.

There was a while ill-spent when my name was Dust and I was an undercover agent in a hostel hippie heaven where heroin, LSD, marijuana, etc., were being imported in incredible quantities. That hurt too. Most of the kids still had momma's sweet tit milk dripping from their hippie lips.

I've worked for so many branches, so many departments, outfits of the Government that I no longer know which I belong to. This confusion helps me to keep telling myself that I'm a free-lance private eye. Bullshit. I'm theirs and I know it.

The thing that pisses me is that Kane White, that incredible boob, is not much different. He's theirs too but in the wrong way. Do you understand? Does anybody understand how all of this works, how you can be alright one day and then a traitor the next? Fuck it. On with the show.

3.

First Day (Cont'd)

She pulls my pants off.

She pulls my BVDs off.

"Well, you're certainly unusual," she says, gazing down at my exposed virile member. "Sit up, on the sofa, yes." I sit up. "Move back a little." I move back. She nods. "Very unusual. Alright, make room. This is zero-hour."

It's so unspeakable that I cannot write about it. She spreads her legs and then reaches her hands down into her vagina and pulls apart those fur-rimmed lips and exposes a pink oysterlike glistening area of lust. I shut my eyes.

"Now, listen to me. You must look and see what a woman's sex looks like."

I look. I try squinting my eyes to blur it.

"Now you must kiss it, for the proper kissing of a woman's sex makes her more passionate and ready for lovemaking. Kiss it and stop looking cross-eyed."

Can I tell you how my mouth begins to twist into a gnarled shape as I bend down to place it on that gleaming opening? You could never understand what immense discipline it takes for me to do this. I feel like turning around and telling the young lady of my particular heroism.

"Use your tongue. First kiss the outer rims, the outer lips. Stroke them with your tongue in a gentle caress. Ah, well, that'll do."

Thinking myself liberated from this bondage, I begin to turn away.

"No, that's just the beginning of it," announces my teacher. "Get back down there. Now, when you've finished redoing what you've just learned, then push your tongue inward and, using the same stroking motion, penetrate deeper into the folds of this most sensitive organ. Ah, yes, but not so fast. Start slow. Always. Mmm, mmm. Then, yes, a little faster, yes. Good. Uh-huh. Yes. While tonguing my clitoris, why don't you use your hands. Your lips, too. Yes, everything. Remember, you're trying to stimulate me into a frothing frenzy. Feed on my sex. Grab ahold of my buttocks with both hands and bring me closer into your mouth. Huh, hmm. Strong one, aren't you? No, no, don't say anything. Yes, continue with your lesson. Mm, mm. Inch one hand over my buttock into the crack that cleaves them both. Go on!"

My God, did any of our country's great leaders have to suffer this in the cause of freedom, morality? My head swims with the picturebook faces of great moral and military leaders and my respect deepens for them. The ordeals that purity must submit to. And still, in my heart, I know I am unsmirched. Besides, I am Kane White.

"Four minutes, two," a voice says, cutting thru the music.

I pray for time to exceed its own bounds and save me from the altar of sin.

"Alright, Kane White, now for the coup de grâce. Lie beside me and stroke my vagina and I am going to pull on your penis and fondle your balls and stimulate your sexual desire to its full maximum."

Which she does.

I cannot, I dare not, even in this, my own diary, my log, describe the shameful handlings she suffered to my flesh.

Her hands are incredibly deft and she grabs the staff of my rod and pulls the foreskin membrane down to make the dome of my staff push up and flare a flame-red color.

Helpless. I can't control the organ's swelling. It rises quickly to attention and quivers in the air as if trying to say or see something. And all the while, my teacher is handling my seed sacs with one hand and pulling up and down on my erection.

"You are now ready to enter my sheath of joy. Mount me. Good. Now, I will guide you into my cave of Venus. There, the nut of your penis is larger than the shaft which supports it and it stretches my vaginal lips, which fold over it, accept it, mm, mm, and now your...your shaft passes thru and into me and your cock's tip is nudging my clitoris and...your unusual prick keeps filling up my cunt...and I'm reaching my hand underneath your muscle-bound body and sticking my finger up your sweet ass-hole...and I'm...hm, mm, huh, mm...that's right...Like a hob-byhorse...back and forth...basic principle...you...cock...you...fuck...cunt...fuck...fuck! FUCK! FUCK! AHHHHHHHH-HH!"

"Time's up, kids. That was wonderful," the Commander's voice says thru the speakers.

A small pain in my right testicle seems to signal the instant before my seminal fluid erupts out of my penis into the steamy depths of my teacher.

Titus Black walks down the empty street. Foghorns. No stars. He walks close to the walls. It's the south side of the waterfront, near Ranger Ann's Round-Up. That's where he's going. He's heard there's a stag-movie show in the back room.

Titus Black's footsteps sound a hollow echo. He wishes he had his gun but Titus Black doesn't carry a gun. He does carry a wallet with money to buy the films he'll see and whatever else is to be sold at Ranger Ann's Round-Up tonight.

Two more blocks to go.

Walks past warehouses sealed up and boarded shut. Past a large vacant lot littered with weeds and garbage and, for a quick second, the combat of courting cats.

Ranger Ann's Round-Up is a key go-between for the Agency. Disguised as a hashjoint, Ranger Ann's has a back room and basement which serve as pleasure palaces—or, if there is trouble, extermination chambers.

Foghorns grow louder. The ocean is near. Ranger Ann's is a block away from the sea. He sees the grimy blue neon sign, then a blinking red neon sign that says "Beer" over and over again. He hears the ocean and feels the salty wind on his face.

Titus Black pushes open the door.

There's no one in the place. Nobody sits at the counter. He hears the hum of an electric clock over the cash register against the wall behind the counter. Ten o'clock. Right on the button.

He sits down and pulls a menu out of a metal rack on the counter.

At the end of the counter is a doorway that leads into the bar.

"Be right with you, buddy," says a voice.

Titus Black finds his gut tightening. (This game isn't in my book, he thinks. I've done a lot of rotten things in my life...)

"Yeah, what'll it be?" asks a bald man in a white apron standing behind the counter.

"Coffee?"

"Sure. Anything else?"

"Apple pie," says Titus Black.

"Sure. Anything else?"

"Got any ice cream?"

"Sure. You want it à la mode?"

"Right," says Titus Black.

"Be right with you. Here's your coffee."

The coffee's good and strong and hot.

Titus Black drinks it quickly, waiting for the counterman to return.

He returns at ten-thirty.

"We're out of apple pie."

"I need more coffee," says Black.

"We're out of coffee, too. I think we're gonna close."

"I was told to be here at ten o'clock and I was on time," says Black.

"I didn't tell you anything," says the counterman.

The counterman looks Titus Black in the eye with an innocent blank glance.

"I'm here to see the movies," says Titus Black, hoping he is saying the right words. (If only I knew how they talk, the sex people, he thinks, wishing he could grab the counterman by the collar and thumb-gouge his Adam's apple.)

"Does this look like a movie-house?"

Titus Black's jaws lock into a grit. His jaw-muscles flex and he feels his teeth grind and squeak.

"Okay, how much?"

"Well, that'll be twenty-seven cents, including tax."

"You know what I mean. How much is admission?" asks Black, pulling a cigarette out of the pack and lighting it.

The counterman looks again at Black, then turns his back to him and presses a switch on the grill.

"What are rates tonight?" he says into the electric grid on top of the grill.

The voice comes out in the crackling scratch of static and shortwave radios.

Titus Black hears something barked out but can't decipher it. The cigarette tastes rotten. It's stale and the last one. He looks around but can't spot a cigarette machine.

"Twenty seven bucks. Pay now," says the counterman.

Titus Black reaches into his suit-jacket pocket and pulls out his billfold. (It's a good thing the Chief gave me a big bundle of unmarked bills, he thinks. Twenty-seven bucks to get in. I wonder what it's going to cost me to get out?)

Titus Black peels off a twenty and a ten.

The counterman takes the two bills and stuffs them into his apron pocket.

"Alright, follow me."

"But what about my change?"

"Tax," says the counterman, lifting up the cash register, propping it against the wall, reaching into the space it occupied to pull a switch.

Hell, I been around, I've seen some wild flicks, like when we were overseas—Korea was great for stag films—but shit, I never saw anything as crummy and lousy and sick as what I had to sit thru in Ranger Ann's Round-Up.

Christ, good God, what's happened to America?

4.

Kane White's First Day [Cont'd/Cont'd]

Do you know who I am? I do not. At the moment I am a naked male in the Commander-in-Chief's office holding a desk blotter over my parts.

The Commander and the Lieutenant Colonel walk in rather briskly. Salute. Salute. I manage to keep a good grip on the blotter.

A good lunch at the Officer's club. I'm introduced to Capt. Rod Kneejam, an American expert on cryptography. Also, he says, an authority on Indian culture.

Grilled cheese sandwiches. Milk. Canned spinach. Pig's feet.

Kneejam is a swarthy young man of well proportioned physical presence. He's in great sympathy with my forthcoming assignment. When asked how he knew, Kneejam replies that he is a part of the training program.

"What part?" I ask him, without trying to sound suspicious or fearful.

"The best part," says Kneejam.

Before he can answer more, the waiter brings us our rice pudding.

Kneejam, after the pudding is done with, invites me to his quarters for a glass of either sherry or port. When I decline, he looks angry and insists. He tells me that not only was he an Eagle Scout but that he too was a member of the Lodge and had graduated with full honors. Besides, says Kneejam, it's orders.

"What do you mean?" I ask.

"What do you mean, what do I mean? Orders are orders and they're made by the Commander and this is Training, Kane White, not friendship. There is no friendship in Training or Combat. Merely orders. Do you understand?"

I salute him.

As we walk down the long hallway, he tells me about his Armenian grandfather who fought against the Turks. The last great Armenian warrior, says Kneejam, pushing the elevator button. Grandpa would box the parts hacked off by his mighty sword and send them back to the widows and parents of the slain.

The elevator takes us to the tenth floor.

"After you," says Kneejam.

Kneejam's digs are simple and uncluttered with material possessions.

On the wall of his living room is a large, poster-size portrait of Lord Baden-Powell. "We were born not for ourselves but to help others," is the emblem woven about his Lordship's scout-master hat.

"Have a seat," says Kneejam.

When I sit down, I notice the mirror on the ceiling.

"Strange place for a mirror," I comment.

"Helps me with my exercises," says Kneejam, going to the small bar and removing two glasses from a shelf.

There is a small statue of a nude Greek god on the table by the chair I sit in.

"Sherry or port?" asks Kneejam.

On the wall above the bar is, I assume, his grandfather's scimitar.

"I don't drink or smoke," I answer.

"Orders," says Kneejam.

"But I took a vow…"

"You must obey orders."

"What do you recommend?" I ask.

"Try the port and pretend that it's grape soda."

The shame of woman's loins cannot compare with what goes next. I've tried to hold off Kneejam's purpose. I've tried to tie the sorrow in my heart with a string of mere notes. But orders are more than orders. They are the pulse that moves me. Nobody seems to understand my pain. Kneejam's port is the color of red carnations. A thick carnelian fluid whose alcohol mist clots my nose with its alien stench. It goes down like a smooth carmine fudge. But halfway down my throat, the heat of its vileness begins to seep into my stomach and spreads a fiery spiderweb thru me. My heart becomes slow. My tongue swells. I can feel flames cup my eyes.

"Cheers," says Kneejam, quickly gulping down his glass of port.

The disgrace of my decline can only be excused by saying that I am under orders and must do what I am told because that is my way, my destiny.

"Kiss me," says Kneejam, standing before me. "Stand up and kiss me."

All I can say is nothing. My throat tightens and a wheezy gargle comes out.

"Oh, come now, Kane White. Embrace me and rub your loins against mine and kiss my manly mouth."

We embrace and I feel his member as a hard rod prodding mine. But it is kissing his mouth that repulses me more than anything. His tongue pushes its way thru my tight lips and, again, I am forced to open my mouth to allow it entry.

He pushes me off and tiptoes over to his record player, pushes the automatic play switch and returns to me.

German lieder surrounds us as he leads me into his bedroom. The bedroom is as sparse as a barrack except for the over-large bed against the wall. Braced on the wall above the bed are a pair of dueling swords.

"Strip," orders Kneejam. "I want to see what your body looks like."

Something is happening inside of me that I cannot understand and I fear it is too late to understand anything anymore. God bless America. Where am I?

"Come on, White, my cock aches to see you."

Kneejam pulls out his penis. It sticks out of his open fly like a red pole.

I undress. First I take off my shirt and neatly fold it into a square shape and place it on the floor.

"Walk around for a bit. Let me see you from all angles. Beautiful torso. Like a Greek god, like a German warrior. Shoes and socks next. Do that quickly. Then take off your pants."

I take off my shoes and socks and try to lose myself in the sound of the woman singing her song, but she rolls the r's and sounds more unhappy than I. It is as if suddenly the numb order of my life has been disturbed. I feel something inside of me, something fragile, cracking. I unbuckle my belt, unzip my fly and pull off my pants and stand before Kneejam in my jockstrap.

"Oh, beautiful thighs, so muscular," says Kneejam, his voice modulating into a softer sound. "Turn around. Slowly."

I turn around, feeling like some odd mannequin.

"Beautiful buttocks!" Kneejam whispers.

The breath of his voice is a web and sticks to my ear and I feel a strange rustling inside of my jockstrap.

"Take them off, White, take them off!"

Kneejam is busy getting undressed in a disorderly way. Clothes flying all over the place.

My tormentor is a well-built man, though much hairier than I. His chest is a garden of blackness which moves into a thick black line that blossoms into the blackness of his groin. His thighs are clustered with curly hair. His pink rod, slightly upraised, contrasts against the blackness of the hair around it. His seed pouches are dark and bearded.

"Lie on the bed, White, and take off your jockstrap so I can see your cock."

For some reason, another strange phenomenon, I lie on the bed and wiggle out of my jockstrap, feeling queerly girlish and seductive. I roll the straps off my hips slowly and watch Kneejam's eyes on me and then look down to his erection which begins to swell more. I get them down to the point where he can see my pubic hairs.

"More, more, you bitch!" he whispers, reaching for a jar of Vaseline.

My craw's stuffed with bile and disgust.

I sit in the room. It's small, it stinks of old cigarette smoke. It's hot. It's pitch black. The projectionist is changing reels. A dark slug trough. I hear the others mumbling and groaning. They're playing with themselves. Or each other.

I've had to sit thru two hours of porno flicks and my head and eyes ache. I feel like I need a bath. I feel like when I get home I'll lock myself in a shower and scrub the filth away until I bleed. If I get home.

What kind of people would do the kind of things that I've seen tonight?

I've been around. I'm not a prude. I've had my fun. But what kind of woman is it that will put the cock of a Shetland pony in her mouth and suck on it, holding his horse balls for balance? What kind of woman is it that will let herself be strapped into a difficult position and be screwed in her butt, then turned over and fucked in the mouth while a hunchbacked defective sticks his hunchbacked cock in her cunt?

Let people have their fun. I know the score. But what kind of man would make love to another man after the both of them shit on the floor that they roll in? What kind of woman and man would make love to a Negro girl who must be obviously ten years of age?

"Get your hand off my thigh or I'll have it on my wall as a trophy," I snarl at another anonymous hand that tries to feel me up.

That's what happens to these freaks. They forget their place. You know, when I was a kid, on the farm, we'd take our turn on the cow. But we were kids. It was Morris, the small one, that always missed and usually slipped and fell into cowshit. But that was kid stuff.

What kind of man would fuck his daughter while his wife sucks off his son? That was the theme of one of the movies.

A new movie begins.

Okay. I'm Titus Black, porno-crazed collector. This is my job, my duty, but, Jesus Christ...

Full-screen spread of somebody's asshole. Weird mandala. The title is superimposed on the circle: FRIGGERY, BUGGERY, I & THOU.

Room lit with too many lights. A painted window with window shade half down. A cot with a rumpled bedspread over it. A chick in her mid-forties with tired big tits hanging down and panties and black hose walks in and sits on the cot.

IT'S HARD TO BE HARD-UP.

Two German shepherds pad in. What is it with the animals? She isn't that draggy looking. Those tits still have some spring in them.

Blows off one dog while the other one buggers her buttocks.

Which is hard to do. She's on her knees working on one shepherd's cock and the other hound's around her back jamming his tool into her.

I light up a Marvel.

The next film is a surprise.

NEW MOON BULGE.

Kane White is being seduced on the sofa in a general's office. The girl is beautiful, the only really beautiful woman so far. White is a good-looking, well-built young man who faces her ripe plenitude with horror, disgust and repulsion. I get a good look at him from as many angles as I can. He's a jerk, but he looks like a tough one.

And tough jerks are the toughest. Take it from me. Dumb cunning, machine-like intensity, these are fierce qualities in a stooge and are hard as hell to combat. I sometimes think, I sometimes wonder. A dumb fuck like White never thinks or wonders. He just does. Shit, I know what you're thinking. I been around. But if you don't believe you got God on your side, the trigger-finger side, then you don't stand a chance at the showdown.

5.

The First Day [Cont'd etc.]

At least with a man, you feel that...

I don't know what I felt. It wasn't unpleasant, but neither was the woman. Both of them violated me. My ideals, my vision, my dream. I can't even tell you, my diary, my alter ego, how outraged I was after Kneejam finished with me. And he used me thoroughly. Have you ever felt the full form of another man's organ in your mouth and suckled it until it pumps out a salty white god-awful fluid that you have to spit out? Have you ever...?

I can't tell you, my inner image, what I had to do to justify my degradation. I can't tell you how good it felt. I can't tell you because I feel torn apart. I must do my job. This is training. But, dear friend in these words of my diary, I feel torn apart and I can't be truly honest anymore. Truth is beginning to lose its shape.

I was allowed a break, a time-out. The Commander-in-Chief let me use his Mercedes. I take a ride.

6.

The First Night

I dine in the Commander-in-Chief's private dining room. With us are two handsome women, one at each end of the table. Feeling exhilarated from my drive, I commence to devour the excellent blood-rare steak before me, washing the good meat down with a big goblet of wine. A hearty robust beaujolais. I'm tempted to drink the meat's bloody juices off the plate. While no one is looking, I manage to pour the bloody juice into my goblet and swirl it around into the wine. I drink it down quickly and reach for the silver-aproned decanter to pour myself another glass of wine.

Both women are dressed in black. Each dress is cut in a V to reveal the beginning rise and divide of their ample breasts. Their faces are alike too, as if they might be sisters or twin sisters. They both eat lightly, half a steak each, and dabble at the baked potato and sip cautiously at the wine.

The Commander-in-Chief eats quickly and silently, constantly wiping his mouth after each forkful, and glancing first at the one lady in black and then to the other. When he finishes, he pushes the plate away, finishes his wine and exhales a jolly sigh of pleasure. The ladies in black look at him and smile.

The waiter, in military uniform, comes in and clears the table of everything except the goblets and decanters. All the silverware, napkins, plates, accouterments and the little silver jars filled with gold toothpicks stamped U.S. ARMY in tiny letters along the golden stems.

"Kane White, I'd like to introduce you to Mary and Molly Powers. They're a team, the Powers Girls, and they are here to conclude your basic training period," announces the Commander and steps on a floor-buzzer. The waiter comes in and the Commander whispers in his ear. The waiter leaves and returns moments later with a silver tray that contains a decanter and several silver and gold jars. The Commander whispers in the waiter's ear. They salute and the waiter turns on his heels and leaves quietly and quickly. The waiter returns again, this time following the Lieutenant Colonel, Marcus Forman.

"That'll be all," the Commander says. They salute.

The lights in the dining room dim as the Lieutenant Colonel manipulates the control panel by the door.

"Strip, Kane!" he orders.

"No, wait," intercedes the Commander. "Let's do this a little more slowly. Let's get the Powers girls busy. Come on, Lieutenant Colonel, let's relax. Our student has done fine, considering his background."

The Lieutenant Colonel smiles a sickly grin at the Commander.

"Yes, Sir," he says.

I'm given a glass of liquid poured from a new decanter by Molly Powers who, when bending to pour the fluid into a goblet, displays a daring view of her breasts which are unhaltered and free behind the tight black silk of her dress.

Molly Powers catches my eye and licks her lips.

"Drink up," she says in a deep whisper whose sensual tones vibrate thru my loins, despite my instinctual repulsion for her glorious bulging flesh. I drink up. This wine, or liqueur or whatever, tastes of the sea, of cinnamon, of ginger, of bat caves, sneakers, new books, popcorn—a strange variety of tastes to my tongue. And whilst I am tasting this strange brew, I feel a pressure on my fly-zipper and look down. Molly Powers is unzipping my pants. I watch her, feeling the liquid move languidly down my gullet, throat and into my stomach. Wherever it touches, that part tingles.

My malehood is held in Molly Power's cooling hand. With the other hand she smears an ointment around its head which stings and burns for a moment. My penis burns into an erection which reaches its full dimension and then, as a gear, locks in place and refuses to subside. She walks away and I am left to stand there, my pants and underpants around my ankles, with a fixed, rigid erection sticking out of my loins like a club.

The Commander and Lieutenant Colonel seem to be putting away a lot of wine. Mary Powers sits in the Commander's lap and Molly Powers sits in the Lieutenant Colonel's lap.

"Get completely undressed, White," says the Lieutenant Colonel. "No sense standing there like that. Get on top of the table at the far end and walk to us."

I have learned to obey orders. When you are a special soldier, you learn to do what you are told. Without question, your mind may say no but it still signals the body to move. My mind screams no until my head hurts, but I take off my shirt and shoes and socks and, stepping on a chair, I step onto the white tablecloth. My erection remains hard and quivering before me like a handle of a broom.

As I walk in perfect form, I look straight ahead at the wall, trying not to see out of the corner of my eye how the Commander and the Lieutenant Colonel have ripped off the black silk from the Powers girls and as I walk, they maul the ladies about the breasts, and the ladies, loving it, tongue steamy messages into the ears of my leaders. But, in my heart, I know they are testing me. This whole day and night, a rite, an initiation into the higher order of things. I can feel it in my bones. To be so singled out is a great honor. For a moment, as I near them, still maintaining my fixed gaze straight ahead, and my fixed hard-on straight ahead, I feel a little guilt for a foolhardy outburst enacted in the late afternoon during my break. But I am a servant of perfection and part of my inner rage is against any deformity. Every day in every way I must serve the cause of purity and perfection. I am an American servant whose service is cleanliness, in cleaning up the dirt and ugliness that have a way of insidiously appearing like fungus in our pleasant gardens and groves. All lines must be severe and accurate, right and true. The human being, the good American, must be, as I have learned, perfect in body and mind, a splendid example of the inherent perfection of the American dream. If I have a philosophy it is probably: Keep clean in mind, heart and body. Thought creates dirt and tangle. I've disciplined my mind to think clearly, quickly and to avoid useless meanders and distracting ponderous rhetoric. (I have, in my will, given the orders that this, my only Journal, be given to the Archives of the CIA to be placed where they see fit.)

The Lieutenant Colonel yanks the white tablecloth from beneath my feet and I fall on my posterior right before them all.

They are, by this time, all naked. They leap onto the table and fall upon me.

I buy some flicks, paying cash. The man takes my money. Puts it into a metal cash box.

"They take two weeks to arrive," he says.

"Can I get a receipt?"

"Are you kidding? All I need is your address. They'll get there. They always do."

Ordinarily, I'd pull the punk up, hooking my two fingers into his nostrils, and slap the smirk off his mug. But I'm Titus Black and feel like a damned fool for being so uncool as to ask for a receipt.

I give him my address. He writes it down in a crummy two-bit five-and-dime notebook.

"Okay. Next."

I move out of the dark room into the bar. There's a bartender there now and some of the people who were inside watching the flicks are sitting around drinking. Infiltrate. I sit down and order a screwdriver. Might as well get some vitamin C.

A man in a plaid topcoat and shades sits down next to me.

"You Black?" he asks. His breath smells of Sen-Sen and I quickly light up a Marvel.

"Yeah," I answer. "Who are you?"

"Call me Cruncher. Buy me a drink."

"What'll you have?" I ask him, deciding to go along with it. That's all I can do now. He sure doesn't look like a Cruncher to me. Small, bald, the plaid topcoat is too big for him. His nose is huge and hooked, his chin is weak, he wears double-thick glasses behind his shades.

"Champagne cocktail," says Cruncher.

I order for him.

"Alright. What's up, Cruncher?"

"What did you think of tonight's show?" he asks, his voice a thin whine.

"I don't know, I…"

"Don't put me on. You know it was crappy, a put-on, small-time…"

"What do you mean?" I ask.

"You know what I mean. Listen," whispers Cruncher, leaning towards me, "we know who you are."

"Who am I?" I ask Cruncher and light another Marvel.

"Titus Black and you're a big-timer in the porny pic and flick biz," says Cruncher with a satisfied smile.

"What if I am?" I answer, blowing smoke in his face.

"I'm supposed to take you to Headquarters," says Cruncher, whispering again.

I signal the bartender and order another round of drinks.

"What if I don't want to go?" I ask him. "You've got to," whines Cruncher. "I'm a special agent from Headquarters and they said that you've got to come because we've got what you want."

"What do I want?" I ask. I make a big business of grinding out the cigarette in the ashtray.

"Look, Black," says Cruncher, gulping down his champagne cocktail, "what kind of a dumb game are you playing with me? I mean, I know you're a big operator and all, but, Jesus Christ, man, I'm just a stooge for the Agency. They don't tell me nothing."

"The Agency?"

"Of course. I got a wife and three kids and my wife's got a heart condition or else I wouldn't be doing this kind of flunky work because, after all, man, you wouldn't suspect it but I'm a real great saxophone player but I can't find work anymore and nobody digs jazz and welfare people keep wanting to train me for other work, like computer analysis or truck farming, man, and I tell them, I keep telling them that I'm a musician, man, I've played with Woody, Chip, Sam, Diz, Bird, Les..."

"Never heard of the band. Finish up and let's go," I say. Cruncher looks like he might start crying any minute.

"You know, I've been married for fifteen years and my aunt, it happens, is a numbers connect and she used to supply chicks for the Agency, in fact, I used to play in one of the house bands but I didn't know what was happening..."

I grab him by the collar.

"Shut up. I don't like whiners. Let's go."

"Man, I'm sorry," apologizes Cruncher.

I slap his cheek. Twice.

"I don't like apologies. Let's go."

We leave Ranger Ann's Round-Up. Two men are playing cards at a table by the door. The big-shouldered man with the thick dripping moustache looks up at me as we leave.

Cruncher doesn't seem to walk but to shuffle along. Strange rhythm. My quick hard steps and Cruncher's dogged shuffle.

"Where are we going?" I ask, and my voice is surprisingly loud.

"Follow me," whines Cruncher.

He walks into the middle of the street and stops before a manhole. Inserting a steel form into its top, he manages to take off the cover.

"Down here," he says.

Wishing I had a gun, I walk off the curb to the open manhole. There's an iron ladder and I climb down it. Cruncher follows me after he manages to pull the manhole cover back over the opening.

We walk in darkness for a few paces.

Cruncher lights a match. Finds the button. Pushes it. A door slides open. We walk thru it and into the eye-stinging brilliance of a subway station.

7.

The First Night [Cont'd]
by
Kane White
Kane White
Kane White
I AM KANE WHITE!

"Eat this, Kane White," says the Commander, "and salute." I gasp as he shovels his wide penis into my mouth while Molly Powers sits on my eternally erect erection and Mary Powers sits on my chest facing Molly and suckling her nipples while the Lieutenant Colonel stands on the table before Mary and pushes his horrible rod into her mouth until it seems lost there forever and both of her hands hold onto his buttocks. "Eat, eat," laughs the Commander as Mary Powers spirals around and sticks her pretty pink tongue into my Commander's brown dank anus.

Martyrs know it because their destiny prepares them for it. I am a martyr and I sacrifice my flesh to their testing. My eyes fix on the ceiling and after a while I can see visions of eagles, unfurled American flags, a squadron of jet bombers in formation like silvery angels slicing up the sky. The table is my cross. My body impaled to it. Yea, though I crawl in the valley of the shadow of her breasts billowing over my face, flapping and brushing over my eyes and forehead, pink flares and rust-brown nipples in the rings upon the powder-white roundness of them and I bite at one and get it between my teeth and hear her groan and feel her fingernails rake down my chest and lodge into my neck to draw blood which she bends over farther to lick while I switch breasts to chew the other nipple. Yea though I fear no night I walk in the shadow of the spread buttocks slowly sinking over my face of I know not who, and as they slowly land I shut my eyes as a small point begins to push out beyond my nose and rub my lips, and I am punched abruptly in the ribs and open my mouth to gasp for air.

Let them, let them, let my children use me so, I fear no evil, yea, though I fear no evil I know at any given instant that I could kill any one of them with my bare hands, and I grab Molly Powers' unclamped rump-length brown hair and she slips and slides and falls to her knee and my Commander's big hand grabs at her anus thru her cunt and pulls her to him, and the Lieutenant Colonel hands a strange object to Mary Powers who looks dazed and is besplattered with Molly Powers' droppings.

"Eat, eat," laughs my Commander wildly and I could kick him in that spot right above his breastbone and he would die as I walk in the valley of Molly Powers' vagina which is spread over my face to lick and chew voraciously, to suck the sea from it and the leftover seed of my leaders, and I think of St. Francis and of St. Demian and I waggle my tongue thru the red and gray folds and my tongue-tip feels ridges and ruts and lingers there while she groans and grabs the air and pushes her sex with power into my face until I fear that my nose will break from the pressure.

"SALUTE! SALUTE!" And I am holding the wall and cannot see Mary Powers with the dildo strapped around her hips come charging from one end of the table to where I stand and the first time she misses and rams the base of my spine and I do not cry out nor weep. Yea though I walk in the space between earth and Heaven I fear no evil but the evil inherent in all weak-willed men and I could kill Mary Powers by embracing her and squeezing until one by one the ribs would pop and snap and at least five of them would puncture her heart. And she doesn't miss the second time and the wooden giant phallus rips thru my rear opening and I feel great pain but I do not cry out, feeling blood warmly trickling down my legs. I salute and turn around to face them and my penis is still incredibly achingly erect.

I could kill Marcus Forman but I will wait. He is my superior in rank only but I am a special soldier and I obey orders and I could kill both of those girls in so many ways and the Lieutenant Colonel tells me to masturbate. The four of them watch me and laugh and laugh and my Commander is wise because I can see it in his eyes that he knows that I am a special martyr and that it is all right and that he is sorry for this inconvenience as Molly Powers is back on the table where I kneel with penis in hand, pumping it, and she begins to dance with a whip in her hand. "Pump, pump, get it out," she giggles and cracks the whip above my head. "Get it all out, White," snarls the Lieutenant Colonel who, with the Commander, are sticking their fingers into Mary Powers' cunt as she sits, legs spread, on a chair.

No end to night yet I know the light is within me, I feel it to be so. When they are finished with me, I will make them proud and I will do my work better than they had ever hoped for. All my life I had always seen in my head that woman who would be my wife and she would be as pure and as chaste as the snow atop Mt. Grimrock. My leaders have destroyed that image and they are righteous leaders and they know what is best for me. Yea though I've walked thru the highways and byways of the valleys and dales of time.

"This is their private subway," says Cruncher.

"How long do we have to wait?" I ask, pushing a gum machine and getting Cinnamon Chicklets.

"It runs like a regular subway. In fact it's like an underground subway, I mean, you know, it uses the subway tracks to get to certain places and then switches off onto its own tracks..."

His whining voice drowns in the rumble and roar of the subway pulling into the station. Its doors open. We get in.

It's like an ordinary subway except for the advertising. Row after row of dirty pictures.

"I'll be back," says Cruncher.

"Where are you going?"

"It'll take a minute," he whines and is gone and I don't give a shit right now.

The subway's motion relaxes some of the tension I feel. I look with appreciation at one of the girls displayed in a picture. She reminds me of Ruby Marlowe. Jesus, I wish I was back there now. After all the years of chasing around to find a babe that's really Miss Right.

The subway stops. The doors open. A gang of teenagers in tight leather pants and jackets walk in. Chains around their waists. Shades. The girls have big boobs pushing thru thin blouses and silver swastika medallions and boots.

For a second I feel the survival excitement rush thru my body and raise the hair up at the nape of my neck. But they don't pay any attention to me and they go to the other end of the car and sit down. Probably all stoned on pot or something. They don't talk or look at each other. The red-headed chick is a winner. The leather is like skin on her body and her hips and thighs and even the impression of her cunt mound all strain and push against the tight leather.

Cruncher sneaks in and sits next to me.

"She's the leader of the pack," he says, his bad eyes ogling her thru thick glasses and smoked shades, and his little tongue darts out and moistens his thin lips. "They're one of the Agency's sado-maso teams. The guys are all fags and the chicks are all super domineering types and real neat and fast with whips and chains…"

From where I sit they look like rugged fags. And the girls look wild. But the redhead is like the untamed horse in millions of horse flicks. The wild-maned untamed perfect animal creature. Her eyes are emerald green and there's a white-hot glint in them. She's the first woman I've seen tonight that's gotten a rise out of me.

"You wanna hose her, huh?" whines Cruncher.

I bring my fist down hard into his crotch.

His shades drop off and his watery eyes thru the thick glasses are wide as they look at me. Then he folds over like a baby in the womb. His skin turns gray-white and he cries his pain out.

He falls onto the floor and rolls around.

The redhead watches it all with her emerald eyes which are rimmed heavily with kohl which sets off her white skin. Her bright red lips.

"Jesus Christ," gasps Cruncher, pulling himself up, "why the hell did you do that?"

"You're a loser. Quit whining," I answer.

Cruncher returns to his seat, whimpering.

The redhead says something to one of the leather clad men. He's wearing a motorcyclist's cap with a silver eagle clipped in the center. The man stands up. The redhead pulls out her whip and snaps it around his hat, knocking it off. He stands there. She walks before him with a knife in her hand. Slashes his shirt down the middle. Slashes his belt off. Says something to him. He unzips his leather pants. He wears nothing underneath but an enlarged prick bursting upward with need. She flicks sharp fingernails on its corona. Says something. He falls down and begins to lick her boots while she paddles his butt.

The subway rattles on.

He comes crawling down the aisle to my feet and begins to lick my shoes. I kick him in the mouth. A short one. But he goes back to licking my shoes. I catch her emerald eyes and stare into them. A small smile on her face. But the eyes have an arctic glare. I kick him again. Full-force. His head snaps back and a spray of his blood splatters my pants cuffs.

"Holy cow, man, what the hell are you doing?" whines Cruncher.

I give him a quick chop across the bridge of his huge hooked nose. His shades fall on the floor again. Tears creep thru his thick glasses and roll unattended down his cheeks.

The man on the floor isn't licking anybody's boots for a while. He lays face down in his blood and a small pile of teeth kernels.

One of the redhead's henchmen, a blond-haired, hairless-faced pretty boy, comes over to his buddy and picks him up by one ankle and drags the cat back where he came from. I watch the smear of blood paint a crooked line along the floor.

The redhead says something to the blond. He gets behind her. She turns her head to his mouth and sticks her tongue in it. Then he puts his hands around her magnificent chest and fondles the redhead's ample bosom. She breaks the hiss off and stares at me. The blond pretty boy opens her bulging blouse.

"Why did you do that, man?" whines Cruncher.

"Because you're a jerk, that's why."

"What tits, huh?" whispers Cruncher, a small welt rising on the bridge of his nose.

I say nothing. I watch. I watch the firm and nearly perfect globes with erect nipple-nubs that the pretty boy strokes with his fingertips. He watches me too. The both of them watch. I can feel my tool tremble and begin to grow. Pretty boy moves one hand over her leather-covered cunt mound and leaves it there.

She begins to laugh. She laughs at me. She says something to the blond. He reaches his hand behind her to unzip her. Then pushes her leather pants down over her hips, her thighs, her knees. She steps out of them and stands fully naked. Her cunt mound is the red color of her hair. Her hips are lean and I see the firm curves of her rump.

Cruncher's hand goes into his pants pocket. I can see it poking about in his shorts. The steady motion.

The redhead dismisses the blond pretty boy who glares wolfishly at me. She stands with her hands on her hips. Then she beckons to me with her finger. She still smiles. Her emerald eyes. Her face is without softness except around the lips. Her jawline is hard and angular. Long red hair spills over the white flesh of her shoulders. She beckons to me again. I don't move. I'm not going to play the game by her rules. I sit there with a shit-licking look and beckon to the redhead.

8.

The First Night

The First Dawn

Nobody knows, I least of all. I, Kane White, with the strength of ten, rest my tired body in my bunk. My penis slowly loses its rigid shape and there is a painful ache in my testicles. I lost count of how many times I discharged my seed into somebody's mouth or vagina or anus or, God help me, the armpit of my Commander whilst he lay atop the Lieutenant Colonel's penis and lapped its crown with his wise tongue, whilst Molly and Mary Powers lay entwined like a circle, their mouths and noses buried in each other's crotches. My entire body is in pain because of having to abuse my muscles and body for such a prolonged debauch. I am to sleep, arise at dawn and set out on my quest, my task.

The dwarf was imperfect, a freak, and looked so profoundly foolish with that bullet hole in his large forehead...even at Grimrock my only vice was dreaming about killing like that. I used to daydream about being able to be in my own chartered bus and to travel the country at incredible speeds with my super-scope superpower rifle. The window would be of a special glass that would allow me to see targets instantly and to frame them for a split second, to focus my superpower rifle, and then it would be over, and my bus would be gone, and whoever I killed would be there alone in the street wondering why. Whenever I felt a righteous moral outrage, for instance against Marcus Forman, I would lie in bed at night and dream my bus dream. Marcus Forman at the downtrodden downtown smut shop leering through the filth to bring back to the tender boys of Grimrock. Forman would purchase his weekly ration of garbage and walk out and my bus would pass by and I'd sight him, shoot him, see the shocked photograph of his last look...almost like the dwarf. I wonder if the dwarf had a sick woman which his gnarled ugly body would use for foul purposes. Imperfect bodies pollute each other with imperfect seed and seedlings.

Diary, I tell you now, I, Kane White, I confess. Shooting the dwarf in the head gave me a tremendous sexual charge. My loins really became alive as I have never felt before and I couldn't resist shooting him two more times. The third shot did it for me. I can't explain it to you, but the gun, the beauty of it and the silence of its discharge, seemed connected to my loins like an extension of my malehood. I, Kane White, I confess that as soon as the third bullet entered into the dwarf's groin…I ejaculated a full load and felt complete release for the first time in my life.

I hear the dawn and the birds begin their nervous conversation. There's a knock on my door. I open it. It's the Lieutenant Colonel. We salute.

"White, here are your orders. When you finish reading them, go to 875, the Wardrobe Room, to be outfitted in suitable clothing. Then go to 963 for financial assistance. Then to 1254 for your weapon. Then back to the Commander for a final briefing. He will show you photographs of key personnel that you will memorize. Then you will be let out and driven to a central rendezvous already set up by an undercover agent. You will be allowed entry into a club meeting which will lead you into the black world of the Agency."

I salute. He salutes.

"Excuse me, Sir," I say to him.

"Yes, White?"

"Don't I know you from somewhere?" I ask.

"You knew who I was as soon as I knew who you were. Why do you think you're on this assignment?"

We salute again.

The Lieutenant Colonel opens the door for me. I pass thru it. He tries to trip me. I falter.

We salute again.

His hand drops into the crook of his arm. It's a variation of the lewd sign so familiar to his cramped mind.

Let them. Let them all. They'll all die.

Part Two

UNDERWORLD

There was a lady loved a swine,
Honey, quoth she,
Pig-hog, wilt thou be mine?
Hoogh, quoth he.

Wilt thou have me now,
Honey, quoth she.
Speak or my heart will break.
Hoogh, quoth he.

—Nursery Rhyme

1.

I remember what happened. Vaguely.

The redhead walks naked and proud over to me and passes me and falls on her knees before Cruncher and puts his frail prick in her mouth. It's over quickly. Cruncher groans and moans and rolls his eyes as she drains the poor fool dry.

While I watch, her gang jumps me.

I remember the blond pretty boy is the one that rams his boot-heel into my kidney.

I awake on the floor. The floor's cement. There's no light other than a thin long line of white under the door.

I stretch out to see if anything is broken. Of course not. But I ache and my kidney is tied in knots and my face feels as if it's been run through an old-fashioned washing machine ringer.

When I breathe, my breath crackles from my nostrils as if I've got cellophane inside my nose.

Slowly. Very slowly, I try to stand up.

When I shut my eyes, familiar pain galaxies explode against my hot lids.

"No need to get up," says a voice. A rattling of what sounds like beads. "Stay where you are and relax. Rest."

When I try to speak, nothing comes out of my mouth but a dry sound like a Band-Aid ripped off a hairy arm.

"Where am I?" I say. My voice is not my voice. An impostor. A joke about a burly man who jumps off ship and is castrated by a shark.

"In my cell," answers the voice. Beads.

"Who are you?" I ask.

"Your friend," says the voice.

Now I can hear that it belongs to a woman. It is a low voice, calm and monotonal.

"You've been here for a couple of hours. Do you remember being taken off the subway and brought here?"

"No. I remember nothing. Is this the Agency?"

"Yes," she answers, "you are here, as you desire, and I shall watch over you until you are ready to continue on your journey."

There's a heavy feeling inside my skull. Plymouth Rock replaces my brain. I feel as if I'm going to pass out again.

"Think of the Holy Mother," her voice says in the darkness. "Let the Holy Mother soothe your brow and lead you from the pain. Do you pray?"

I grunt. The grunt means no.

"The Holy Mother is a lovely woman. She is eternal in the hearts of all men. Her face is the face all men wish to kiss. Her body, the body all men wish to return to," says the woman.

"Look, lady, no offense, but why don't you knock it off? That's not the kind of talk a man wants to hear here. That's not the kind of talk a man who just woke up out of a bad sleep wants to hear," I say, happy that my voice is beginning to sound like my voice.

"The Holy Mother is not the Holy Mother that most men think of," answers the lady.

Beads. Or maybe she's got a handful of seeds and keeps shifting them from hand to hand. Who cares?

"Where's the light switch?"

"Do you think your eyes are ready for the light?" she asks.

"Yeah, sure. For God's sake, stop talking holy to me and help me."

"Surely," she answers. I hear her stand up and feel her body moving past me. A perfume lingers in my nose. The light goes on. In my eyes. I put my hands over them.

"Can you stand up? There's a cot against the wall," she says.

I roll over on the floor and push myself up onto my knees. I can see the picture of me looking like some dumb club fighter down for the count in the first round, staring cockeyed at the ring floor. I sight the cot's legs and slowly crawl to it. I lift myself up and, with great effort, I sit down.

She stands before me as I sit on the ledge of the cot. It's a nun in a scarlet habit with a white cowl. The emerald eyes are unmistakable.

It's the man in black clothing: the black topcoat, the black scarf, the black pants, black shoes, socks, the black thick leather gloves. It's his spring and summer uniform. Underneath it is a black jacket over a black shirt with a black tie. Black T-shirt and black shorts. The man in black is never warm and walks stiffly because of all the black clothes he must wear to insulate himself from the cold that he imagines to be outside of him. Actually, as we all know, the man in black is cold from within. All the better to spy on you. All the better to kill you, if necessary. He prefers to take you to his special room called the Oven by Agency regulars. The man in black eats the coded message from Headquarters. Then he chews a dried red pepper which burns his tongue and burns his throat and burns all the way down to the pile of previously eaten dried red peppers. Food is heat, especially hot food. He follows that with a handful of candy which is rich with chocolate and caramel and, best of all, overburdened with sugar. Sugar is energy. Food is energy. Energy is heat. Followed by some glycerin tablets. Followed by a snort from his hip flask of soup stock, brandy and pork fat. The man in black is very fat. He is six foot nine inches tall and weighs over four hundred pounds. He is well-paid by the Agency and by Headquarters. The man in black is a counterspy. He is lonely and fat and constantly cold. He is dangerous.

Every room in the Agency's central structure except, of course, for the room at the top (which, unknown to all, is bugged by Headquarters, the CIA, the FBI and SDS)—every room in the Agency's central structure has concealed openings for the trained and cryptic eye to peek thru and supervise any unusual events transpiring therein.

The fat cold man in black watches Titus Black confront the scarlet nun with emerald eyes. He sees Titus Black on all fours sucking every toe on the nun's dainty feet.

When Titus Black reaches the last toe, her smallest one, the scarlet nun calmly makes water in his hair. He looks up angrily, urine running down his face, and she laughs at him, hiking her scarlet skirts up to allow enough leg room to push him back onto the floor.

The man in black who is always cold has always wanted the scarlet nun with emerald eyes. But she is a favorite of the Agency and she has a force of brutal men at her command and the man in black does not like dealing with groups.

Long has he longed to bring her to The Oven, where the man in black can finally peel off the layers and layers of black clothing that surround his bulky frame. It is only in The Oven that the cold man in black can stride ponderously in his sludgy flesh to partake of his rightful fill in sensual pleasure and delight.

He sadly watches the nun torment Titus Black. Black will get it in due course. That doesn't bother the man in black. What bothers him is that he, in his chilly heart, will never be able to get his due with the scarlet nun. Unless…

I'll get that girl. And when I get her, she'll be taken the right way. My way. Christ, what a prize she is! I'll get her before I get out of this carnival. If I ever get out.

No girl gets away with what she did to me. I'm putrid with her droppings and piss. My scalp itches with her filth but I can't scratch because my hands might get tangled in the crap she shat on my head.

She's gone now. Just like that. I look up from the floor after having to lick up her mess. The door to the room is wide open.

Her beads on the floor. I get up and stomp on them.

I hear a door open and peer thru to see if it's her coming back to degrade me some more. A tall fat man dressed in black waddles down the hallway with speed and delicacy.

Where the hell's the men's room? I've got to clean up and get moving. I leave the room and walk down the hallway looking for the old familiar sign. No signs. All the doors look the same.

I'll get that girl and when I get her, I'll give her a ride for her money. No girl treats me like that.

I case the floor. There are no staircases, no elevators. There's only door after door and the doors are all unmarked.

The only thing to do is to go from door to door. I press my ear against each door to hear some kinds of sound within. The only sound I hear is my own impatient breathing. I try the door handles. Locked. Locked and empty rooms. I hear a door shut. I know it's the door to the room I just left. I wish I had my gun.

There's something in me, a checking device, which doesn't

acknowledge defeat. For some reason, I always know I'll get through. If I didn't have this checking device, I think I might give up right now.

Then I hear something behind a door. A deep pulse in regular meter. Then I hear, as if in another building, the murmur of voices and laughter. I try the handle of the door. It opens.

There's a small foyer which leads to two large doors like those in movie houses. I push the release bar on the door and suddenly I'm in this large dark dance hall. My ears bombarded by eardrum-puncturing rock and roll.

It takes a while to get the layout.

The music is a meat cleaver smashing my skull. Long-haired men and long-haired women tangle, twine, and mill about the dance floor. A strobe-light catches a couple and freezes them in a strange stop-motion neon frenzy. Dark blood-red blobs of science fiction ooze, bulge and explode on screens ringed around the platform where the band is playing.

The musicians wear black silk robes with black pointed hats. Plugged into eight-foot-high amplifiers, they look like weird lamps. Living lamps. (You've got to have a sense of humor. Especially in the middle of the absurd. I've been around, but I've never been in anything like this.)

A little long-haired beaded child mongrel uses my ankle for a teething ring. I kick him away. He slides into a circle of dancers who are dancing as slow as ancient taffy. They dance around and around the kid until the kid crawls off.

Incense is burnt in large pots boosted from churches. A mottled-faced young lady walks towards me holding two twigs of burning incense, one in each hand. Her nipples poke thru the gossamer flapper dress she wears.

The floor vibrates with the electric music. I feel the bass tones move thru my body like an electric bath. The young girl with pimples and no brassiere is a snake crawling up my legs and opening my fly with her teeth. Dancers move by us. My cock is pulled out and gets hard under her touch. In the strobe light it seems to pulse in a brand-new way. I watch it grow in fits and spasms. Larger and larger. She watches it grow, looking with intensity upon the crown. The tip of her tongue upon it looks like a windshield wiper in the light. She waggles her hot tongue-tip across the crown until I can feel the fire raging and the need to fuel her mouth gets strong.

I watch my hands push her mouth down around my cock's shaft. In the strobe-light I lose sight of what I am used to seeing. She draws great delight out of my pulsing cock, sucking me in a way nobody's ever sucked me. And I've been around. But the girl on my cock is at it like an infant to its first teat. It's as if she's trying to drain me dry. And in the light I see her head and mouth move up and down in a frantic pace, her mouth distorted with my cock's wide hardness.

"Got any dope?" she asks.

"No," I answer.

"Fuck me," she asks, grabbing me by the hand and burning a finger of it with the incense stick.

"Does that hurt?" she asks, as we walk thru the people dancing and standing and shuffling about.

"A little," I answer, her hand a wet oyster in mine.

"Good," she says, trips me, and I fall on a mattress.

I start to get up but I'm caught in the time-warping flash of the strobe light. She pulls it over our mattress and sinks upon me like a slow-motion movie of a deck of cards shuffled in midair.

"I dig older men," she says, her mouth opening and closing on the words. The light makes it look as if her voice is being dubbed in.

I'm hung up opening and shutting my fist, watching the fingers blur and fan under the light. It's over and we are in a darkness away from the strobe light. I ask her how old she is.

"Seventeen," she answers. "I love older men. Their cocks are so much meatier and tastier, man."

If I had a daughter, she'd probably be seventeen.

"That's my shot. Giving head," she says, "and dope."

"How do you get by?" I ask.

The music is no longer music but is an ocean that we lay and listen to as it surrounds us with tidal wave after tidal wave.

"Why worry about getting by?" she says. "I manage. I get by."

She leaves me, too. She sees a Hindu in a white gown pass by.

"Oh, man, that's Subu Sub Hump. Giving him head is best of all. He never tires. His cock is a brown uncut pole. As soon as he comes he's hard again. I can suck him all night. He's got hashish, too, to smoke between sucks."

And she's gone and I get up.

The colored slime humps and bumps over the screens. A new band is on the platform. Seven bare-chested men in beards. One plays electric maracas. The other plays an electric ocarina. The guitar player's guitar has lights around its form. Colored lights like a Christmas tree. Even the drummer is electrified. The band has larger amplifiers to play thru than the last. They're stacked on top of each other.

I've got to find a bathroom. To clean up, pee and get moving with this caper. A cowboy slides over the dance floor and tackles a chick who looks like a maharajah's daughter. They wrestle on the floor in time with the band's incredibly loud music. I feel on the bottom of Grand Canyon as ten millenniums of slag and rock are dumped on me.

"Howdy," announces the cowboy, passing me by, hugging the chick. His both hands squashing her boobs. "Shh, don't tell anybody, but I know who you are but you don't know who I am. Y'hear?"

"Ah, shut the hell up, Lester," says the girl, bumping her cunt hump into his blue jeans.

"You must be Titus Black," he says, holding onto her tits as if they were the combination locks to a safe.

"Who are you, cowboy?" I ask.

"Haha," cackles the cowboy, "I'm Lester Lumpkin and I'm sure as shit pleased to meet you. I'm a great smut collector. Let's swap shots sometime. I'm in town for the Rodeo."

"Glad to meet you, Lumpkin. Where's the bathroom here?"

"Fucked if I know," answers Lester Lumpkin.

"Oww!" yips his lady friend.

The band reaches a new cosmic level of noise. Its sound is a bus running me over. I'm impaled against the colors.

I'm surrounded by four girls who have flowers strung over their naked bodies. They dance around me.

"Y'all sure got some good-ass fuckin' luck," yells Lumpkin.

"Come on and join in," I says.

"Why as shit sure not?" says Lumpkin.

"What the hell about me?" whines his lady.

"Well, what the hell about you?" answers Lumpkin and leaps into the circle.

We continue talking while the girls dance around us.

"Now, buddy, don't the name Lumpkin ring any cow-barking bells in your head?"

"No, at least I can't think too clearly now," I answer.

One of the girls is a redhead but her eyes are merely blue-gray. Her breasts jiggle tautly in their halter of daisies.

"Ain't you Titus Black?"

"Yeah, I'm Black," I answer.

Another girl has gray hair and the body of a goddess. Her cunt, seen thru the rose girdle, is silver-haired.

"I believe we're in the same kind of work," says Lumpkin, starting to yell.

The drummer is taking a solo on his electric drums and his drumsticks are as large as baseball bats. When he smashes into the cymbals, the sound is enough to make my eyeballs feel ready to pop.

"My dad's ol' Luther Longfellow Lumpkin of the CGTA."

"What the hell is the CGTA?" I yell into the electric void.

"Haven't they told you?" screams Lumpkin.

"Who?"

"Headquarters, y'dumb cross-eyed bat-toothed rank stranger," Lumpkin hollers into my ear.

"You mean?" I scream into his ear.

"Exactly," he barks into my ear.

We lock arms and do-si-do.

The light show biochemical display changes from colors into projected images. A vulva mandala which starts as a small pink dot in the center of the curved screen spreads until it covers the entire screen.

"C's for Clean an' G's for Girdled an' T's for Trussed an', for Christ's bloody knuckles, A's for America. Y' get it? The society for a Clean, Girdled & Trussed America. Y'get it? My pappy runs it an' he's sick. But ain't we all, and..."

Now it's two bass players that follow the drum break. The bass-amps are earthquakes.

The girls surround us and the harder they dance, the more flowers they lose. Lumpkin and me begin to step on flowers and leaves and slide about in the colorful smear until we're both on our asses.

"...But I think that's where that ol' fuck spine mother-ass Kane White comes in, an' I don't know about you but I'm fuckin'-A scared," howls Lester Lumpkin into my ear.

White watches the dance from the projectionist's booth. He surveys faces and bodies with an unmounted superpowered telescopic rifle-sight.

So far so good, he thinks, remembering the first man he killed today. It wasn't as neat as using a gun, but the wire finally did its work. The next time he'll use a thinner wire. He didn't realize his own strength and the man put up such a struggle. Screaming and hollering. It's a bad way to die, thinks Kane White, screaming against it. He pulled the wire with all of his might and the man's head fell from its base. Mouth still open in protest.

"Hey, man, better stop digging the action down there and get into it."

"What do you mean?" asks White.

"You got a hard-on that's about to rip thru your pants."

White smiles and turns back to surveying the crowd.

Indians scalped victims. Rotten filth of a young degenerate hippy looked like an Indian. Breech-clout, beads, pouches, moccasins, feather...White couldn't resist it and hacked the long hair off the young man's skull. A messy business but worth it. He stuffed beads and feather into the bloody head's open mouth. (At college, White foresaw this new aspect of moral breakdown. The ideal American male betrayed by the slovenly long-haired lout who does no work, who serves no Army, who impregnates countless women that he doesn't marry, who reads and writes poems and plays on lutes and flutes. With beards and thongs and dark glasses and motorcycle, driving to the Unemployment Office to drain the great U.S. dollar further. White could sense the plague before it started.) He put the bloody pile of hair into a Baggie, the Baggie into a manila envelope, and then mailed it off to the beheaded youth's parents.

Yet there was something wrong inside of him and White wondered what it was. Then it came upon him. A signal in his loins. And then he knew. He pulled out his weapon, a mini 30-30 pistol with silencer. He shot three bullet holes into the naked skull. A triangle.

The golden bull is brought on stage.

"Ain't he a winner?" says Lumpkin. "All meat and muscle and look at that whang. Wow. Damn!"

Upon the golden bull are two naked girls. One black and one white. Both girls are draped in flowers. Red and golden ones. When the bull comes to a rest, the two girls dismount.

"Man, look at the tight lovely butt on that spade chick! Holy shit spectrum, hallelujah!" says Lumpkin, swatting my spine with his open hand.

"Cool it," I snarl.

The music begins again.

The band is rolled out on a float. It's cowled with a giant plywood cock which serves as the bandstand. All the band members are naked. Their guitars are cock-shaped. A cunt is painted in shining colors on the bass drum. When the drummer steps on the bass drum pedal, the cunt bulges in the repercussion.

A smear of sky-blue dye streaks across the screens.

Another band is rolled out on a float. The float is bedecked with flowers. Day-Glo painted crucifixes surround the floor. A giant cross rises above the band. On top of the cross is a white neon star of David which blinks on and off. There are four musicians: a rhythm guitar, lead guitar, electric bass and a drummer. The stringed instruments are plugged into gargantuan amplifiers. Each has four apiece to play thru. Painted on the gridwork of the amps are Chinese, Hebrew, Christian and Hindu signs and symbols.

It starts with the drums. Then a guitarist strikes a chord. They're off. The cock band is already going. All the amplifiers seem like lost animals mating each other with screeches and whines of circuitry.

Two bands going at once, and, at once, my head seems split

in half. My ears are in a spiral void of pain. I put my hands over them.

The golden bull snuffs his snout into the spread legs of the black girl who lays on the stage. Her head cushioned with flowers. The white girl feeds on the golden bull's golden cock which grows and grows and finally is too big for her mouth to fit around.

Something happens with the overhead lights and they all switch over to strobe beams which shatter the bull and the girls into splinters of light and action.

"YAHOOOO!" screams Lumpkin.

I'm bent over, cramped with pain. Both bands roaring into electronic Heaven. Feedback overtones and rumble avalanche and grind into my head, slam into my body. I begin to dance the dance of death. Sound jabs my gut. Sound jams vibrating sound-cocks up my colon. My ribs rattle with sound that's let loose inside of me. Feedback crash and high-intensity overtones saw apart my cock. Chopped down by sound. I'm on my hands and knees. The floor is charged with sound vibrations. Earthquake rumbling. Shut my eyes. Riding sound surf. Ten miles high. Then let down. Smash into hardwood. Headfirst. Volcano burps earth-cracking gas. Flames barf beneath my palms. The whole floor should crack apart like a mirror struck by lightning. All music becomes one tone. An organ tone. The last chord hit at the end of a church service. The chord gets fatter and fatter, wider and wider, the floor trembles beneath me. The chord is a train carrying me in its belly. I stand up. Open my eyes.

The man in black is colder than he has ever been. He watches Kane White watching the last dance. He stands in the projection room doorway watching Kane White shoot bullet after silent bullet into the projectionist's body. Kane White masturbates with the other hand.

All color slides off the screen in a slow gradual spill-off. Imprint of thrown strobe-light beams ricochet off the luminous white fabric of the screen.

Her black legs around his throat, the snout laps and licks her pink-rimmed black entrance. The white girl is on the cock-band's bandstand. The leader's prick is in her mouth as he sings his song and plays his guitar.

Lester Lumpkin takes me to the Rodeo.

It's a good hour and a half before I can hear. A roaring in my head as if someone let the sea live there.

When we leave, everyone is tangled with everyone else and cameramen are suddenly everywhere.

Lumpkin first finds the right door. Opens it and ushers me into the men's room.

Peeing hurts. Then the pain turns into a warm pleasure.

"Sure as shit and hell and fuck feels good to let her go!"

Then it's more doors.

We walk down a metal staircase. I long for a window. Just to get a taste of whether it's night or day. Whether it's sunny out or raining. Our footsteps clank on the metal steps.

"Y'see, my daddy's alright, but he's a horny cuss an' he feels the best way to get pussy is through God. Y'understand?" says Lumpkin, hopping down the stairs with a bow-legged snap.

I grunt.

"But you know how it is in Texas, it's a strange weird place an' what they grow there doesn't take too kindly to exportin', y'understand?"

"Yeah, sure. Look, I don't want to sound dumb, but how much longer are we going to be walking down these stairs?"

"Man, y'sure are nowhere on patience," sighs Lester Lumpkin. "Y'know, in Texas, patience is your sixth sense. I mean where I come from in Texas. Man, where I come from it's an event when a kid's born. Y'know, we all livin' miles away from each other on flat desert land with lots an' lots of oil wells. But where we lived every well dried-up and' mammy died an' pappy got himself horny just thinkin' about what he's missin' and found God. God's my daddy's pimp, but you gotta understand that daddy's a good old cuss."

"Look, Lumpkin, why are you so interested in me getting to know about your father and his weirdo organization?" I ask.

"Here we are. I'll be hog-butchered an' popcorn fucked," says Lumpkin, pushing open the door.

Metal coffee cup in hand, I sit behind the fence and watch the Rodeo. The cup's filled with a strange brew which I don't question. I'm hungry and confused and I'm getting to that point where I can't do anything else but accept whatever happens.

2.

FROM KANE WHITE'S ANNALS

Watching the snakepit dancers grovel in their slime. Strange that it doesn't bother me. A great feeling of detachment is mine now. Seeing Titus Black on the dance floor didn't move me at all. I trained my sight on him and observed every detail of his face. He has a small C-shaped scar on his chin. He looks like a strong capable opponent. Broad shouldered but he looks like he might be a little out of shape. He must be forty or so. He has a broken nose which is actually quite becoming.

Unless absolutely necessary, I have restricted myself to one killing a day. Just knowing that I am free to kill gives me a sense of judicious prudence. There are, after all, two kinds of killing. The personal and the impersonal. The hippie garroting was personal. A way of striking back at the enemy quickly. Shooting the projectionist was impersonal. A victory of my detachment.

Mingling with the living carrion on the dance floor. A young lady wrapped in furs from head to foot walks up to me. "You there," she says in a husky voice. "Yes, you. Come here," she says, "I want you and I need you." I walk up to her and she takes hold of my hand and leads me into an alcove off the dance floor. She tells two young men to leave because it is her turn now. They pull on their stretch Levi's and leave quickly. "Be with me," she says and there is a heavy musky perfume all around her which at first shocks my nose and offends it. But as I move to her, the smell becomes incredibly exciting. "Come on, man," she says, "lay down with me now and let's get high together." I sit down on a mat on the floor. Her furs fall apart to reveal the portions of her body most appealing and, also, most gross. She hands me a pipe which sends off a unique odor. "Puff," she says, "puff and hold the smoke in your lungs and then slowly let the smoke out." I tell her I don't smoke. She tells me that it is time to learn. Infiltrate. I puff a small puff on the pipe's curved brass stem. The smoke burns my throat but I get it into my

lungs. (I'm in great physical shape and every morning, upon arising, do a quarter-hour of calisthenics and another quarter hour
of breathing exercises.) The smoke proceeds in, puncturing the
sensitive skin that lines my lungs. Water rises to wash my straining eyes. "Keep it in." I tell her I can't. But I pride myself in not
coughing it out, which is my first desire. I slowly let the putrid
clouds trickle from my mouth. "Beautiful," she says. We pass the
pipe around for a while.

Everything is all right. I tell this to myself as I lay on my back,
eyes shut. Everything is all right. Then I'm lost in my breathing. I feel my lungs stir to absorb the loud air I am breathing into
them. I hear the air filling the lungs. My heart. I feel my heart
pounding. Or is it the music? No, it's my heart. I feel my heart
pounding too hard, too fast. Shall I die like this? Is she, in reality, a counterspy? "In reality…" What does that mean? To be "in
reality." Help, let me in, says a child's voice. Let me into reality. Then it's my laughter that is loud in my lungs and in my ears.
"Beautiful," she whispers in my ears. The sound of her voice is
a fur waterfall. Help, let me. Let me help reality. Help me in. Let
me. Let me. In. In. I think of In. Everything must be all right.
I'll get better soon. Everything wears off. I'll be down again.
Down to earth. I am laughing louder. I am a balloon, I see
myself like that, descending to earth, streamers and sandbags
wrapped around my midriff. "I'm descending. I'm a balloon,"
I say to her. "Beautiful," she says, her mouth on my chest. She's
unbuttoned my shirt. I look down to see if my heart is going to
break through my chest. "Will my heart break through?" I ask
her. "You're too much," she says and guides my hand to one of
her breasts. My knuckles brush silken tufts of fur around her.
Warm flesh. A loaf of bread. I laugh again. Her mouth opens on
my nipple and her tongue rubs against it. Incredible feeling.
My nipple is threaded within me to an immense web of nerves
and they are all activated by her tongue-tip. "Beautiful," she says,
rolling down my pants. "Beautiful…" Her hair strokes my belly
with a thousand feathers. Slowly sliding down until she reaches my dormant parts. Door meant. Which door? Laughter in my
head which doesn't come out of me. Suddenly I am bound

around my chest with a girdle of disgust. Tempted again. The constant test. The constant trying-out as she avails her mouth of my limp penis, and it rises, and her hands reach under to caress my seed sacs in a gentle sensual cup. My body is so trained as a weapon but it cannot, as of yet, resist other temptations. I grab some of her fur wraps off of her while she works upon my penis. I wrap them around my body and over my face. Smothering in fur and then I see my first vision and it is a triad, the triangle, and then I realize that the dwarf was thrice shot and that the hippie Indian was shot thrice and the light-projectionist was shot three times. Threes. 3. 3. 3. My mini-30-30. Take away ought. 3-3. Yes, of course. My sign. Everything in threes. But her mouth tires of me. I don't care. I clutch the furs around my head and laugh and cry into them and have an abrupt orgasm.

Six men grab me and yank me off the pallet. I accept. I cannot refuse. They take me down a hallway. All six of them wear motorcycle-military leather uniforms with knee-high shining black boots and black leather jodhpurs and black leather jackets and black leather ties. Silver ornaments decorate the black hides: swastikas, numbers, crosses, circles, etc. I assume they denote rank. They're certainly a well-disciplined squadron. Holy Patton, strapped on a hump that rises my rump up high while my legs and arms are strapped down. I am naked and the hump I'm strapped to presses hard into my chest and abdomen.

I'll tell you what you want to hear because you are following this with your hand in your pocket fondling your manhood, your dong, your cock, your thingamajig—I'll tell you what happened with saintly simplicity. They let a golden bull into the room and the six men say nothing until a seventh person joins them. She is a striking redhead with emerald eyes. "He's mine," she says in a cold snake hiss of a voice. "After the bull. He's first." They let the bull loose. He snorts and does nothing. "The essence, pig," snaps the redhead in a quiet iron voice. Someone smears an ointment around my upraised rump. "Spread his cheeks farther. And spread and strap his legs farther apart. This is not Kneejam, Kane White." The men unstrap my legs and strap my ankles into floor-posts. It is very painful to be so splayed. The bull clomps over to me and sniffs at the ointment around my rear. I can't see him, of course, I can just feel his wet bull-snout poking around. There is no preliminary warning. First I hear his hoofbeats from the back of the room grow closer and closer. I know, as St. Sebastian knew, and grip my hands together as the bull's log of a cock rips thru me again and again.

I do not know how long it takes me to heal but the time is not ill-spent. I am attended to by a beautiful blond-haired boy whose cheeks are free of any beard-hairs. His body is almost as perfect as mine. I know this because of his habit of nursing me directly after he leaves the steam bath. He wears only a black leather jockstrap which bulges fully with the young man's obviously potent parts. His eyes are almond-shaped, his pale cheekbones high. His lips are pale, red and full. I think we understand each other. At first, I could not speak nor could he. But soon he began to tell me a little about what was going on. It seems the right people have found me. The redhead with the emerald eyes wants Titus Black and is willing to act as a counter-espionage operator for KOMM in order to get Black. I don't like taking orders from women but this is an extremely peculiar assignment. I must learn to allow myself more room in dealing with people. If only I could partition myself in such a way that one portion would be smoothly manipulating someone and the other portion could coldly supervise, while yet another portion could be taking notes and supplying correct data to the other two portions. My mind is divided into three compartments. If only I could utilize them all.

The blond boy is beautiful but cruel. Yet we understand each other. The day before last, for instance, he comes into my cell as usual with food, water, pills, all on a red rubber tray. He's in his black leather jockstrap and he has a leather pouch twined to one of the straps.

When I'm finished with my repast, the blond boy asks me if I am ready for something special. "Yes, of course," I answer. Good, good, he nods. When he smiles I notice two small wrinkles. One at each corner of his mouth. The blond boy unthongs the leather pouch and opens it up. He withdraws a glistening Smith & Wesson .38 Police Special which is partially wrapped in a chamois cloth. "Look," he says, and holds the gun at arm's length. The gun glitters in the overhead light's rays. He snaps out the cartridge cylinder and holds it up so that the light shines thru the six empty well-oiled chambers. I can smell the perfume of gun oil. (At Grimrock, I was a fanatical gun-maintenance man. The sight of a can of Hoppe's Lubricating—"High Viscosity-Very Penetrating"—Oil would sparkle my latent aesthetic sense. Orange, yellow, black and red. What magic colors!)

The blond boy sits at the edge of my cot and places the .38 by his hip. His body is hairless like his chin. It's covered with a strange sheen as if flecks of translucent crystals were lodged through his flesh. Firm-muscled, beautiful form. His thighs bulging with power. The gun beside his white-fleshed hip slashed by the black leather jockstrap binding. The beautiful blue-black gun. I can feel my loins begin to tremble as they awaken.

He reaches into the pouch and slowly withdraws a bullet from it. He holds the bullet, as he did the gun, at arm's length. Then brings the bullet's tip to his lips. I feel faint after that. But the blond boy is not over. He waits until my eyes are back upon him before inserting the bullet into the cylinder's empty chamber. Very slowly. Then he clicks the cylinder into place and that clicking sound is one of the most sensual noises imaginable. My penis pokes thru the blankets and it looks like a small tent growing from me.

"Shame, shame," says the blond boy.

I can feel the blush work up from my toes into the roots of my hair.

The blond boy laughs in a reedy way, then reaches into the pouch and pulls out a silencer.

He makes a very deliberate slow motion to put it onto the .38's snubby nozzle. The silencer's phallic shape becomes more meaningful when the young boy puts the barrel to his lips.

"This will be yours when you go to Texas," says the boy.

"Texas? What do you mean? What are you talking about?" I ask him.

He pulls the blankets off me and looks at my erection.

Then he gets up and slips out of his jockstrap and stands before me with his erection. His is the superior to mine and he knows it. It is also uncircumcised. His testicles are round and large and hang fully from him. His pubic hairs are thin and his pale flesh is seen thru them.

"Like it?" he asks.

I can't answer and his face hardens for a moment.

"Oh, well, she'll be in tomorrow and then you'll know more," he says, and pulls his jockstrap up.

I don't understand but I know that I feel as if I might have hurt his feelings somewhat and I am sorry, but I can't do anything about it. Someday, we'll all understand.

He puts the gun and silencer back in the pouch, picks up the tray and opens the door to leave.

"I'll see you tomorrow," I say.

"No, I don't think you will. She'll be here in my place."

"I'm sorry if I offended you," I say, feeling the sunrise of beatific compassion warm and radiate within.

"I don't know what you're talking about," says the blond boy and shuts the door.

One hell of a rodeo. That's all I can say. One hell of a rodeo. I've never seen more livestock buggery and fuckery in my life.

Followed by curdling events like setting this club-footed buxom babe alone in the arena with a wild bull. People hollering and laughing themselves sick watching her limp and stumble away from his constant charging. At one point, some punk ties a red scarf around her middle and the bull gets back to work.

I want to jump in there and get her out before the bull kills her but Lumpkin tells me that the bull's horns are made of rubber and that the bull's harmless.

"She digs it," says Lumpkin. "It's her thing, being chased by a big bull stud like that. Gets her all lathered up an' ready to roll. See, there's the rollin' chute over there. Rolls right into the hay downstairs where we keep the horniest orneriest old buggers and gaffers. They give it to her good."

A cowboy on horseback races around a pair of lesbians who are bumping each others' boxes on the ground. He lassos the bulldyke. A squat square-framed chick with a D.A. haircut.

The rope digs into her small breasts. She's dragged along the dirt.

A western swing band starts playing out with *San Antonio Rose* when the bulldyke hits the cowshit pile. Head-first.

The horseman returns to the bulldyke's partner, lassos her, drags her and dumps her into a trough. Much laughter all around as the two smirched babes are forced to form their cunt and tongue wheel once again.

"This is a once-a-year only genuine heterosexual rodeo for real men," says Lumpkin, ripping the key off a beer can. "Yes, sir. Wanna beer, buddy?"

I accept his offer and open a can of almost-cold beer and take a pull.

One lean cowboy with leathery skin, a pole of a man, slowly whips the tits of the bulldyke with a few strands of rawhide.

The bulldyke's fem has to suck a sextet of bronco-busters. They all take it in good humor. Each of the six range riders pours some beer on the girl's bobbing head. Each of them, when she gets to them, grabs her by the back of the head and rams his cock full force into her open mouth. Up to the hilt. They give no room for her head to resist the concussion.

Two fags are next.

One is in a black wig which shines like a chandelier. Lipstick, eye shadow, false eyelashes (double-set), bra and panties that pull up nylon hose and high heels. He walks rather edgily past the cowshit.

The other fag is in leather cowboy chaps with a neat hunk cut away where his naked cock and balls hang out. Cowboy hat, T-shirt and a saffron colored scarf around his neck.

"Watch the fun the boys have on them pansies," says Lumpkin, spilling some beer on his Levi's.

The fun, like all the fun here, consists in degrading the two fag-gots mercilessly.

"Are you sure he likes what's happening to him?" I ask Lumpkin when the black-wig fag is dragged over to the branding section. He squeals in real fear and the cowboys laugh and goose him along.

"You know how fags are, man, they just really dig getting the shit beat out of them. It's how they pay their dues. Just like women, for God's great cornholing tremen. Don't women like getting the shit kicked out of them?"

I have no answer and take another pull on my beer.

His screams fade into the hysterical laughter of the cowboys standing around him.

"We all put our mark on him now. Every fag in town'll know who he is. Hot mustard damn and piss!" Lumpkin slaps his knee. Spills more beer.

But, as usual, the cowpokes take their time. First they make the fag in drag do a striptease while they shoot off their six-shooters at his high heels.

All of his paraphernalia is peeled off and the young man in a black wig and false eyelashes and lipstick and too much pancake stands trying to put his hands over his parts.

The cowpokes laugh about it. Shout abusive remarks. Then get down to the business of branding.

While all this is going on, the faggot's buddy is held over the chute where a wild horse is penned. The men holding him let him slip every so often. He is very pale.

When they brand the young fag's rear end, I have to turn away. Quickly. Hoping Lumpkin won't notice. The kid bucks and it takes five of them to hold his rump down. I can hear his skin sizzle as the permanent mark is set into his flesh. They let him go and he races madly around the arena for half a minute. Then faints and falls face down into the dirt. They drag him off. The audience cheers.

"Y'know what they fried in his sissy ass!?"

"No, what?" I answer.

"This'll kill you. The brand says 100%. Doesn't that beat everything?"

I drink more beer and watch what they do to the fairy's lover.

They drag him to the arena and, to the accompaniment of "Wildwood Flower," they jam firecrackers up his ass and set the stems burning.

I don't like this job. I like it less and less. I can't accept this world. It's not mine. I get to thinking that it is the whole world.

It can't be.

I'm fed up and I sit in a folding chair in the Rodeo locker room. Lumpkin's gone off to participate in his event. I didn't ask him what he does.

I light up a Bull Durham ready-made. That's all the goddam machine carries.

What the hell am I doing?

The Chief tells me to kill a kid named Kane White which is not his real name. And the Chief knows me well enough to know that I will. Or die trying. And they give me the name of Titus Black which isn't my real name.

I'm tired of killing.

It was alright in the war. I knew about it in the air in the bomber. No people. You can't see who you kill. It's just patterns, abstract targets. Maybe it's a field or a strategic rice paddy or a small cluster of squares which are buildings. You nose down to a low altitude. You drop your bombs and that's it. Before the bombs hit, you're back up high in the sky and zooming off to another target, another pattern.

I was tired of killing the first time I saw what was left on a battlefield. It didn't make any difference whose side the bodies were on. They were piled up like timber. I'd never seen so many dead and never smelled the smell of wholesale rotten flesh. I've been around but that got me sick and I had to turn away. I didn't give a shit who was watching me.

It got to be more numbing in Special Forces.

I did my work. Hell, we were fighting a war. But some things don't blank out that easily. Some yellow gook leaps out of a bush when I'm walking alone. He's small. They're all small. Small and taut and all he's wearing is some kind of raggy underwear. He's smiling because he sees the expression of fear and surprise on my face. He bows and smiles as he pulls up from his bow with a knife in one hand. It was a dirty silent fight that was over quickly. But not too quickly. For a moment we were lovers. My hands over his naked shoulders. Grunting, breathing hard. He on top of me. Me on top of him. Holding his wrist which holds the knife away from me. His sweat mixed with mine. When I got him down I knew that he wasn't going to be taken a prisoner. I knew I would have to kill him with his own knife. That's what the fight was all about. One of us was to die. This was war. We were enemies. He bowed again and smiled. He could've run away. He didn't. He waited for me to kill him. I'd stabbed a thousand sandbags during training. That was the first time I'd stabbed a human being. It didn't go well. I was clumsy and missed the mark. Hit bone. Had to pull the blade out and try again. The second time was better. I jammed the knife into him until the hilt stopped the blade from going any further.

I'm tired. I'd like to be in Ruby Marlowe's apartment and spend the first hour touching every inch of her magical body. Then spend the next hour kissing every inch of her. Then spend the rest of the night slowly fucking ourselves into oblivion.

Maybe the Chief forgot that I really didn't do too much killing as an investigator. I tried to talk fast. I killed when there was no other choice. When there was no other bluff.

Christ, I still wish I had a gun. Some kind of brute talisman. Dumbo's feather.

"Black?"

I turned around. Quickly.

Standing over me is a fat giant dressed in black. A black whale with the face of a child. The infant face rests in the center of fat like a grotesque moon.

"What if I am?" I answer.

"Get up and let's get going."

"Look, fatty, what if I don't want to…"

He lifts me off the folding chair as if I were a towel.

"Please, let's get going. I've got information for you."

"Where are we going? Why can't you tell me here?" I ask.

"I've got my reasons. I'm taking you to eat. No one will overhear. Come," says the fat man in black. "It's very drafty in here, isn't it?"

"No. Are you kidding? It's overheated like all locker rooms are."

"Don't joke me," says the small child's face in the moon of fat. "Follow."

When he talks, he seems to be gasping for air.

We sit in a booth in a dark dismal food mill which is reached walking up an endless sequence of iron steps. It's an all-you-can-eat-for-$1.79 joint. I'm familiar with this kind of cuisine. During bad times I used to hit a place like it. You learn how to eat what's worth eating and pass on the kind of food that hits the stomach soft then hardens like plaster of paris.

My host, the fat man in black, is on his third plate of appetizers: potato salad, macaroni, pickled herring, garbanzo beans in vinegar and oil, coleslaw, pickled beets, raisin and carrot salad, and black and green olives. All of this is piled together on his plate. He pushes the stuff into his soup spoon with stale round rolls which he smears thick amounts of margarine on.

I know the score. I nibble some coleslaw and olives and eat a minute amount of the starch salads. That's how they think they'll get you. The starch doesn't seem to bother the fat man.

"You're going to have to eat an awful lot, friend, before this meal's over," says my mammoth host, his lips wet with food juices.

"What do you mean?"

"Just what I said. I try not to overstate anything."

He continues eating, pushing a hard round roll into his mouth. Like sealing the opening to a cave.

He exhales, drinks a glass of milk. Fills it to the brim and drinks down another glass of it.

"Eat. The more you eat the more I'll tell you."

"Look, I'm not too hungry," I say.

"Get hungry. Come. Let's go to the counter and start on some of the main courses. Do they have the air-conditioning on?"

"No. Are you kidding? This place is more overheated than that locker room," I say.

He uses the tongs to pick up five hunks of prime rib which he puts on his plate. He gets another plate to put the meatballs, mashed potatoes, succotash, baked onion, canned spinach, and another plate to put the fried chicken, beef stew, fishcakes and French-fried eggplant.

"Yours," he says, sliding the overloaded tray towards me. "Now for me."

I take the tray back to the table, while the fat man loads two trays, six plates, with food.

"Look," I say to him, as he sits down. "I'm not going to eat all of this."

"Yes you are. For many reasons. One, you called me fatty. I want you to be punished for it. Two, Kane White. Three, the girl with emerald eyes. Four, Lester Lumpkin. Five, Ruby Marlowe."

He starts chewing the meat off a prime rib. He keeps his thick black leather gloves on. The meat juice sparkles on the leather.

"What about Ruby Marlowe?" I ask.

"Eat. Eat everything on your plates. Maybe," he says, pausing to suck some marrow from the bone, "maybe, I will tell you some of what I know."

The food is stacked so high inside me that I can feel the last shred of prime rib tickle the roof of my mouth.

At first I thought the pain was more than I could bear. It was like having my stomach pumped up with balloon gas.

After a while I figured that if I didn't move, if I sat still, the pain would localize itself. Right about where my navel is. I can handle it.

The huge fat man in black is back with his third trayload. He's slowing down and tapering off. Now he's down to just the meat dishes and those damn lead rolls.

"C'mon, Black, eat that parsley and finish up those rolls. They're delicious. As soon as you finish, I might feel like talking a bit. Go on."

He holds his black-gloved hand over his mouth to block off a rumbling belch that I can hear as it moves up through his larded guts through his throat and towards his mouth.

Our waiter returns with another glass pitcher of milk. He is looking distressed and panicky and as he leaves the table, he keeps looking back at the fat man in awe and terror.

"How does it feel?" the fat man asks.

"Rotten," I answer, my voice sounding slushy.

"Good. Don't ever call a fat man fatty. Now. What do you want to know?"

"What do you have to say?" I ask, lighting a cigarette. The smoke has a hard time going down.

"Alright, before we eat our dessert, I'll tell you what you want to know about Kane White. But first, milk."

He pours a glass of milk, drains it, pours another one and drinks it half down.

"Ahh," he exhales. "Cold. It cuts through some of the grease. Very fatty ribs. Now. Kane White is being held by the woman with the emerald eyes. Soon she will convince him to kill you. He's in love with her right-hand man. A vicious bisexual who is, I suspect, psychopathic. She will set White against you. She will tempt White's latent gun-fuck syndrome and finally break through his dumb hide."

The fat man in black pauses to chew some meat off a rib.

"The milk chills me. I wish to hell they'd learn how to heat public places. Always trying to cut costs. The swine.

"The girl with the emerald eyes wants you first. She wants you alive before she kills you. You bother her. Now look. I want her too. Maybe we can work together. Give me her and I'll get you White."

"What about Ruby Marlowe?" I ask.

"What about Lester Lumpkin?" he asks.

"What about Lumpkin?" I ask.

"Okay. Now listen. Before she gets White onto you she's going to try him out on Lumpkin's father. Jehovah Merce Lumpkin. She's going to jam all White's circuits with drugs, shock and general. All out. Brain. Washing."

The fat man's belch breaks thru his speech and shatters the air with its power.

It raises the napkins and moves the surfaces of milk in the glasses. Incredible. I duck. He does it again. A one-two. Combines it with an earth-cracking fart whose draft whooshes under the table and brushes against my ankle.

"Ah. Joy!" he sighs. Emits a small machine-gun racket of subdued belches and farts. "Ah, blissful gas. Now I can eat one more round before dessert."

"What's happening to Lumpkin's father?"

"She's going to have him exterminated, even though he's in cahoots with KOMM, the group White works for. Her reasons are complex. She's a complex girl. Dangerous. Lovely. I want her. Badly."

"What about Ruby Marlowe?" I ask.

"She's going to get your Ruby Marlowe as a bait to get you. You've got to, first, head off White from assassinating Jehovah Merce Lumpkin."

"What do you mean, she's going to get Ruby?" I ask, feeling the cement in my belly, feeling the chill of fear and sweat break out on my forehead.

"She's probably got her already. In storage."

I try to get up.

His huge gloved hand shoots out and clamps onto my wrist like a vise.

"I'm not finished. You're not finished. Sit down."

understands me. Understands me. understands me everybody understands me. Nobody knows. nobody nobody

taking me out. Under. Round electric moons above me. Operating. Good. Bad. Nothing. No good no bad all is well five oclock all of it all of it is all of it well. Understand. understands me. To kill is to understand the power of life kill the power of life. Tomorrow is another power godly lordly men in khaki kingdom dress-ups. Uniform uniform line curve Nobody nobody. moon. moon. Grows in my belly. Pull the trigger. Kill God in face. Bang bang bang. God, you're dead. Dead god. God dead. It. God dead it. you understand nobody understands. Understand the moon is God is dead that I kill him with the gun that grows out of me in the morning if only I could be free of it on the grass fell feeling the dewbeads break on my skin to let the earth grow thru me. Understand the moon. Nobody nobody

—You love him.

Who do I love?

—Him. The lover. Black.

I love Black.

—Like you love the Others.

The ones gone.

—Yes. You care enough to let them go.

Love them out. Love them off the rock.

—Yes. But first you must kill God.

My source? The father.

—Yes. You must let him go.

(sonofabitch when I was three years old letting me roll on the grass and smell earth stepping on my hands reaching for marigold sonofabitch)

He has let me go.

—Yes. But you must let him go. Love him.

God, the father?

—The rifle range.

Life is a rifle range.

—Soon all targets gone but one.

What?

(rifle range motherfucker four years old with the first .22 a facsimile of soldier carbine on the rifle range flags all around it his painful knuckle rapping when I miss the center poor mother who couldn't do anything anymore) What's left?

Because he can't have her sexually, because his sister, the redhead with the emerald eyes, must have her first, he pushes the over-large electric artificial penis into her exposed cunt. She's strapped down to the bed, legs spread, gagged, and still blindfolded. The blond boy with the hard face, the face without face hairs, throws the switch to its extreme notch and holds onto the handles feeling a strange exhilarating vibration work through his hands. He must be careful not to draw blood. He yanks it out roughly. She tries to bend in the abruptness of the pain. He hits her soft belly with the side of his hand.

"Everything is destroyed. It is your turn, Ruby Marlowe. I hate you," says the blond young man in a high whimpering voice.

He spits on her face and on her belly. He snaps off the lights and leaves the room. For many reasons, he is very depressed and heads to the steam baths for some kind of momentary relief.

It's another arena filled with noisy people, plain people with crafty eyes and cheap dresses and threadbare suits. Besides the hawkers with the usual popcorn and hotdogs and soft drinks etc, there are hawkers in blue-and-gold sashes selling hymn books, testimonials and tracts, as well as holy water, healing seeds, American flags, records of sermons and sacred singing, lockets with Jehovah Merce Lumpkin's photo in them. Everyone is busy with their waiting and they all wait noisily, talking to each other, stamping their feet, chasing their filth-faced brats around the floor.

I mean these are decent good people who have faces carved out of vellum and teabags. Pouchy, stern pigeon ladies in thin cotton dresses with flower patterns popping around their round large forms. Tall, cranelike women with dried-up wombs and pinched faces and long spider fingers which are always nervously busy with something like knitting or rolling tinfoil into little pellets or madly scratching powdery hair. These are moral upright people. Plain, poor and righteous. For the meek shall inherit the earth.

The meek rough-jawed laborers holding delicate burdens in their hairy paws: children to cure, a wife in a wheelchair to heal, deformed twins in an iron lung to reshape. Everyone brings their Christian hopes here. Reed-tinted cheeks of bawdy yet repentant hussies greedily narrow heavy made-up eyes at single men standing stiff and fidgety in their black suits.

Kids chasing each other to the back where they can grab a quick touch at a hip or rump or maybe, like the lean wedge of a gap-toothed pimple faced boy, poke two thumbs into the tender new nipples of a flushed-faced metal-wired buck-toothed parochial school drop-out.

"God in man is Jehovah Merce Lumpkin. For nearly two decades, Jehovah Merce Lumpkin has healed, cured, resurrected, freed, liberated, given luck, given love, hope, happiness to millions of righteous, upright, moral Americans..."

I'm on the top balcony and see how the womenfolk, young and old, separate and move in a group toward the front of the stage where Jehovah Merce Lumpkin will appear. I pull out my pocket super-telescopic sight to get a good bead on the pulpit lectern where Lumpkin will deliver his sermon.

The organ plays the National Anthem. I salute and, as usual, have to restrain myself from weeping unashamedly as visions of our country's great military leaders flash through my mind like the furling and unfurling of Old Glory herself.

I feel the comfortable pressure of the .38 against my ribs in its chamois shoulder holster. I feel the less comfortable weight of the high-power rifle which is folded into a heavy tube and hangs heavy in my left pants pocket.

The lights are lowered in the arena and a spotlight widens on the powder-blue and gold-robed choir which sings sacred songs to the accompaniment of a giant theatrical pipe organ.

"O Holy is the name of Mother, Flag, and Lumpkin..."

They sing for a long time. Too long, as far as I'm concerned. I don't like music too well. Outside of the National Anthem and a few school anthems and marching songs, I suspect that there is something dangerous and tricky about music.

A man walked onto the stage to sell copies of the CGTA'S weekly magazine, *The Lumpkin God Love Gazette & Holy Reader*. This week's copy features, he says, a centerfold, three-color, full-length photo of Jehovah Merce Lumpkin in his Cosmic Coronation form-fitting white suit with gold braids and a powder-blue sash.

This is followed by a woman who walks onto the stage with her crutches under her arm. She tells how the Lumpkin Touch cured her of a lifelong paralysis. She throws the crutches on top of a spotlighted section on the stage which is fenced by a small white fence. It falls upon wheelchairs, crutches, and other cripple paraphernalia. The audience gasps as one and cheers wildly as the lady walks off.

A clean-looking kid with neat blond hair and a white shirt and black tie walks up to the lectern. His blue eyes are a bit moist with emotion.

"Look," he announces thru the microphone which bounces his voice all over the arena. "Look at me now. Do you know what I was only, I said *only,* one week ago? No, of course not. You can't tell. But let me tell you. I was a Communist! I spat on my flag and burned my draft-card..."

My stomach tightens. The audience groans and gasps.

"I stood in line before the White House holding signs that denounced our President. I called the police fascists..."

His voice is trapped in a thousand caves. The audience is groaning.

"I was a user of insidious drugs that warped my vision and robbed me of my senses..."

Hosanna! Tell 'em, brother!

"And then, picking me out of the gutter of my despair and tragedy was the only man who could help me. That man, that God-essence, was Jehovah Merce Lumpkin!"

The people cheer wildly. I notice some young girls falling on their knees in the aisles.

I grow weary from watching, from waiting. I'm on the desert again. The heat, the light, surround me. Crucified, yet I can see myself struck down to the rude wood cross. An orange-crate cross in Nevada. High noon. Surrounded by laughing naked hippies and their whores. Washing my mouth with brine.

Then I bring myself to the arena. Now giant slides are filling the huge screen. Captured Viet Cong. Large cheer as the next slide is of the Viet Cong's shot body. Great cheer and foot stomping. More women in the aisles. Some are beginning to undress in a writhing frenzy of patriotism. A slide of a Lynched Negro. Foot stamping, hooting and glee. Replaced by a slide of a beat-up looking blonde placing her thick lipstick-primed mouth around the glistening black penis sticking upright through his open fly. The gospel singers, assisted by the pipe organ, continue to sing throughout the entire slide show. It hurts my head. Slide of a burning A&P with crowds of black rioters standing before it. Foot stamping, hissing and moaning. One woman's on her back on the floor with her flowered skirt around her waist. She is inserting an American flag in her opening with some help from a pious looking gentleman in a black suit. The next slide is a police photograph of the twelve bodies of slain Negro school children after their elementary school was bombed by ACT (American Citizens for Terror). A great roaring jubilant hurrah from the audience.

Trying to remember what I have forgotten about the time when I was young and could not think ahead but just made do with what came up. You must know by now how it is in my eyes that I saw my mother naked when I was five years old and I watched her through the bathroom keyhole how she slowly took off all her clothes and then stood there by the mirror O beloved with her tender breasts in her lovely hands as if to offer them to the glass O you must know by now how it is in my eyes that I saw too my naked father upon my naked mother upon their bed and how his hairy hands were over her innocent whiteness and how his broad back moved over her shadow upon her darkness and she O she with her eyes rolled up into herself to know nothing see nothing of it was groaning and panting and whimpering and I was terrified for her she sounded like my dog when he hurt his foot and I ran to the dresser drawer where my father kept one of his pistols and pulled it out and went to the room to kill him but they were done and quietly lay together as if asleep...

O that I would want to kill him and O that they should all die the next day as if I had willed it so.

Texas is down some steel stairs, through a series of doors, then up more steel stairs.

"Like everything here," puffs the fat man dressed in black. "Texas is a state of mind, another illusion. Oh. God. It's cold. Here we are."

He points to the door.

"Good luck," he says.

He checks his watch.

"Better hurry. Lumpkin begins his sermon in ten minutes. You must get to White before then."

The audience is aroused to a fever pitch. A rake of a woman keeps grabbing hold of my ass. She stares up into the klieg lights. Ten suns reflected in her glasses. She's probably either blind or in a trance. I move on.

Steps over writhing women who are sprawled in many ungainly positions on the floor. Moaning, spit trickling from their open mouths. The men either watch the women inertly or watch them with their hands in their pockets or one old gaffer's got his old gray cock out and is frantic trying to get it up. I move on. Kids are asleep or rolling around with each other under the chairs. The popcorn vendor hits on me. I give him a gentle shove which catches him off balance. Popcorn spills onto the floor, rolls into open ecstatic mouths and into hair and cunts and ears. I move on. Some of the kids dive onto the dirty booty.

Jehovah Merce Lumpkin doesn't look too much like his raunchy son. He's a big man with a full white beard down to his belly button and broad shoulders and blue eyes with deep black centers. He's all in white. White shirt, tight white pants which bulge provocatively around the crotch, white socks and shoes. When he walks onto the stage, the audience goes wild. The women leap up from the floor in order to see him and then faint once again.

His skin is bronzed from either a healthy outdoor regime or a damned good sunlamp. He's a winner, this Jehovah Merce Lumpkin. And he scans his audience with a professional eye. And begins.

"Brothers, sisters, children of freedom, right, purity, ecstasy,— my children, my seed shoots, my garden of fleshly delirium—how we all doin', tonight? Are we all fine? *(Yes, we're all fine, chants the audience.)* Have we been good an' true to the Flag? *(O yes!),* to the eye of America—has the eye of America been served well by my children? *(O yes, yes! We have served it well!)* Testimony then, testimony, who will testify? You, you there, young lady with your dress half off an' them ripe melon breasts a'breakin' through your garment—you, c'mon up an' testify…"

The young girl staggers onto the stage and embraces Lumpkin who pats her messed hair paternally.

He holds a hand mike to her mouth.

"Name?"

"Sarah Jean Billy Mae Sue Anne Lily," she gasps, ripping off her bra.

Her breasts spring forth full and firm with the pinkest nipples I have ever seen.

"God is good," says Jehovah Merce Lumpkin. "Now testify."

"I hereby testify that I got twenny-five Reds run outa Milburn High…I hereby testify that I got fifteen niggers lynched on charges of watchin' me do my vestal virgin strip-tease…"

Great cheers from the crowd.

"Ah, my daughter, so you're the one?"

"Yes, sir, I'm the one," says Sarah Jean Billy Mae Sue Anne Lily, stepping out of her tight skirt.

"Yes, sir, Sarah Jean, you can go backstage and be one of tonight's Lumpkin Handmaidens," announces Jehovah Merce Lumpkin.

"Oh, mercy, God, glory, hallelujah," she squeals, grabbing Lumpkin's hand and licking his knuckles.

The audience applauds and groans and American flags whose

staffs are dildos are selling like crazy to frothing Lumpkinite women. I move on. Upstairs.

Break thru a Lumpkin revivalist youth fuck. This sallow, tallow-complected hank-haired snot nose lad's busy passing his raw red tool into the all-embracing quim of an eye-fluttering lady three times his age. Her breasts flop out of their halter like great flour sacks.

"Oh, God, oh, God, boy, fuck me to Heaven!"

"Shut up, woman, I'm tryin'," answers her tender drooling lover.

Her hands grab ahold of his rump and dig into the pale flesh.

"You're hurtin' me," he mumbles.

"Keep fuckin'," she murmurs.

I try to walk around them but they block the stairway. They are sprawled before the steps, writhing in their grunty workout.

One of her knobby fingers pokes up the boy's asshole which makes him squeal a tiny flute sound.

"Mash 'em, boy, mash my tits for God!"

One of the boy's dirty-knuckled paws plops onto one of her flour-sack tits and pounds on it as if it were a tortilla. Then they roll about and she's on top of him and he's groaning with her weight and the strange sensation burning thru his cock.

Then they roll about again and he's back on her, half sitting, as if in a saddle, and bouncing on her belly until she looks ready to shout for help. Instead she comes and grabs ahold of his ears and he screams.

"Hallelujah," I say and try to pass on to the stairway.

"Wait a minute, brother," says the eye-fluttering over-the-hill earth mother. She reaches her hand up and gently grabs ahold of the meat between my legs. Her fingers stroke the length of my cock.

"Hey, what are you doin'?" mumbles callow youth. "I ain't dropped my load yet."

She unzips my fly and reaches her hand under my shorts and fingertips my balls and then grabs hold.

"Stick it in for God or you'll never get up the stairs to Heaven, boy," she says.

"Hey, goddamit, I want mine too," gripes towhead.

"Oh, hell, move up and stick it in my mouth and let a real man fill me."

Which he does with rabbit speed.

Which gives me a quick escape dance to do. I leap over them and race up the stairs.

"Infidel," she hollers and tries to scream something else my way, but grubby horny sallow youth fills her mouth with his aching prick.

Selah.

Her voice in my head like a fly buzzing unwanted. You must kill the man who is God.

Nobody knows. Nobody understands.

The blond boy's face. His body. That black leather jockstrap. The incredible shock of seeing his full staff rise up bigger than any I'd ever seen. So taut and wide and large that it looked like it would rip from its roots and fly out into the sky like a winged myth animal.

Nobody understands. Nobody knows.

I want to forget everything.

On the cross. They throw lit matches into the pile of dry faggots around me and shake their tambourines and ring their bells and chant their dirty songs and watch me burn to death for their world to be reborn again and again so that they kill me again and again and why do they want to kill me again and again...

Snipers seem to like high places near exit doors. Don't ask me why. Maybe it helps them feel out of touch, detached. Who knows? Quick shot, quick getaway. As if he wasn't there. Snipers are shadowy people. They like it that way.

The balcony is a frenzy unto itself. No one's in a chair. They're all on the floor writhing, twisting, drooling, while Lumpkin's fat full Texas voice soars and slides and cajoles and echoes and clangs in the arena.

"Let's burn the draft-card burners! All the way with U.S.A.! C'mon, now, let's hit it! ALL THE WAY...WITH U.S.A.!!

C'mon, now, let's keep on purifyin' the white stream of American grace. C'mon, now, let's all of us get together an' make more an' better American girls an' boys to help stamp out that evil blight of Communism. Let's caress our neighbors an' touch our brother with love an' scrutiny an' if he's true-blue, let him have a piece. A piece of the future. A hunk of America. Aww, ahh, you women, you women who keep the secret of abundance in your God-blessed womb, how can y'refuse a real-blooded American who's there to give you the seed shoot of another red-white-and-blue American citizen-patriot, king of th' earth!"

I spot him. Sitting in a chair in the last row. He holds a rifle to his cheek.

Jehovah Merce Lumpkin's voice gloriously intones his lusty hopeful message as I edge up to the last row and start to tiptoe towards Kane White.

Surprise him, catch him off guard. Grab the rifle out of his hands. But something is wrong.

I stand beside him and he doesn't move. He is staring out into space. He is crying.

I pull the rifle out of his hands and they fall limply into his lap.

"Kane White?" I ask.

"No. Not Kane White," he answers.

"Come with me," I say.

"Who are you?" he asks, still looking out, wiping his nose with his sleeve.

"Titus Black," I answer, unloading the gun and pocketing the bullets.

He turns to look at me.

"Do you love me?" he asks softly.

I think fast. He is not alright. There's something wrong. His eyes are achingly open and don't seem to fit in his head.

"I like you, White. You're alright. I don't really know you. Come on, let's go."

"I love you, Titus Black," says Kane White in a voice like porridge.

"Good. Let's talk about it as we walk. Let's walk out of here."

I help him to stand.

He quickly turns after his elbow jams into my gut. He slams down on the back of my neck with the side of his hand. It hurts the moment it hits. And then it hurts no more.

It's a small room and the walls are insulated with soundproof tile. The floor's covered with thick pile like the mats used on gym floors. Four pairs of handcuffs hang on chains from the ceiling. Ruby Marlowe hangs from one of the chains, her wrists clamped by the cuffs. She wears a black dress with a brass zipper running down the middle of it. Cruncher Leans against one wall and hums to himself. Some archaic jazz riff. Or some lost chant. He has lousy intonation.

CRUNCHER: [*to himself*] Doesn't mean a thing. Nothing at all. Just doing my job. Guard the fort and bring in containers of coffee when the night gets long. Ah, who the hell am I kidding? Forty-one years old and I'm still a fucking stooge. I could've been great but I had bad luck. That chick sure's got a nice set of knockers. Aggie tells me she's pregnant again today. She's a winner, my Aggie. Even with the pill she gets pregnant. You see what I mean about bad luck? I wonder if I were to just inch over to that chick and cop a feel of her boobs. Man, those are real prizes. All my life I never scored any prizes, especially with the chicks. It was either nice girls engaged to dumb cats with muscles and no talent, or skeleton junkie chicks wanting to turn a trick. Once there was a Martha Beebush, once upon a long draggy time ago and I blew it. We were laying in bed and she asked me, just before I was going to slip it in, if I believed in astral projection, and I said what the hell is that? Is it like immaculate conception? And she got uptight and the lights went on and it was time to go. I thought all jazz musicians were turned on, she said as I buckled my belt. Man, what boobs she had. Hers were melons which stuck out without give, like those *Playboy* chicks whose tits spring out as if they're held up in the air with invisible wires, and they got no beer belly, and beautiful ribs, slender legs, and such a beautiful unearthly pink skin glow.

No one would see me. Why should I be afraid of nobody?

But you never can tell when she'll be back or when the blond stud'll be back. Hell, I could've had a feel by now if I hadn't been so busy thinking about it.

The door swings open. Two men in black leather hurl Black into the room. He puts his hands out to break the fall and lands on the soft pile.

Cruncher is startled and tries to vanish in his mind. His nose still hurts from his last encounter with Black.

The door slams shut.

"We meet again, man," says Cruncher.

"Ah, go to hell, punk," snarls Black, shaking his head, trying to stop his eyes from rolling around in his skull. The two black leather boys worked him over as they dragged him down the hall. Short fast jabs to the neck and cheeks and temples.

Part Three

OPERA OUT

1.

The door opens again and the redhead walks in with her brother, the blond boy.

"You can watch for a while," she says to him, "but then you must go and take care of White. Get him off the floor."

The blond boy grabs Black under the shoulders with surprising strength and pushes him against a wall.

"Stand up, you dumb stumblebum," whispers the blond boy.

"Listen, you warmed-over puke," growls Black and doesn't brace his body in time for the knee that rams into his groin.

The blond carries the slumped body to the middle of the floor and cuffs Black's hands to the chain hanging from the ceiling.

"Perfect," says the redhead. "You can go."

"Let me wake him up."

"Oh, alright. We're in no hurry. I'll wake up Miss Marlowe."

Black comes to.

"Ah, you're awake," she says, patting his cheek with her gloved hands. "Look who we've brought for you to destroy. Look!"

She slaps his face.

Through groggy eyes, Titus Black sees Ruby Marlowe hanging from chains across the room from where he hangs in chains.

They look at each other.

"I'm sorry," says Black to Ruby Marlowe.

"I'm sorry too," she answers.

"Ah, dear, how lovely," sneers the redhead with her emerald eyes blazing. "Cruncher, take the chains off her cuffs. Good. Now bring her to me. Good."

Ruby Marlowe stands before the redhead, her hands in shackles. The redhead reaches out and pulls the zipper down on Ruby Marlowe's dress. Ruby Marlowe wears nothing underneath it.

"Come, Miss Marlowe, with me. Down to the floor, Miss Marlowe, and allow me to make love to you. If you try anything at all out of the way, Cruncher will find something amusing to do to your boyfriend."

Cruncher is transformed into a killer, seeing that Black is powerless to strike at him, and he glares a deadly glare into Black's eyes.

The redhead stands above the body of Ruby Marlowe and looks into Black's eyes.

"She has a beautiful lush body, doesn't she? I will enjoy her thoroughly," she says in her chilly voice and lies down beside Ruby Marlowe.

The redhead strokes Ruby Marlowe's thighs and reaches the hairy mound leading into her cunt's lips. Still looking at Black, the redhead pushes her finger into the lips of Ruby Marlowe's cunt and, once in, begins to probe around the hot walls to reach the clitoris. He can see Ruby begin to move slowly and shut her eyes.

"Wonderfully warm," says the redhead.

Cruncher gulps as he watches the redhead work over Ruby Marlowe, touching her breasts, kissing them, nibbling at the nipples.

The redhead then kisses Ruby Marlowe and lies upon her. Cunt to cunt, they writhe together. The redhead works her mouth down to Ruby Marlowe's mouth. Their tongues and hands work furiously as they hump and bob and twist around on the floor. The sound of Ruby Marlowe's jingling chains.

Black watches dispassionately, trying to hold down his anger and rage.

Oh, shit, Ruby Marlowe, the one truth in my life. My lady, my love, oh, shit. The only one to know me, to know my name. Christ, the history of it is a fast TV film clip in my head. Ruby Marlowe married once to Lt. Col. Fartangel, USO goldbrick, head of special entertainments which usually meant animal shows or abusing native prisoners, cowards, patsies. Ruby Fartangel danced on tabletops in Vietnam, Korea, Kyoto, wherever USA and USO needed a Lt. Col.'s wife to bump and grind and tear the hearts of servicemen apart. Calendar spreads of Ruby in bunks and locker rooms all over the place. I met her in the Officers' Club, sitting with Fartangel whose eyes hardly showed between his lids because he was so goddamned juiced.

"Help me carry him home," she asked in her husky breathy voice.

"Officers should learn by now how to walk," I said, trying to sound tougher than even I could believe.

"Words sometimes mean nothing, soldier," answered Ruby Marlowe. "I need help." And she let her tongue run over her lips, leaving the sparkling glitter of her spittle along the lower lip.

Well, what the hell? I dragged the fucking Lt. Col. (who weighed in at maybe, that night, 500 pounds) to their quarters and hauled him into his bedroom (they slept apart) and damn near tossed him onto the bed.

"Want a nightcap or some coffee?"

"Both."

"You sure talk a lot," said Ruby.

"What do you mean?"

"You know what I mean. You think words make you sound like a tough guy."

We had a few drinks. Ruby knew how to knock them down and look as sober and sound as straight-headed as the best.

"What are you doing?" I asked her.

"What do you mean, tough guy?"

"What are you doing with Fartangel, what are you doing here? You could do better."

Ruby laughed.

"Sure, I could. And what, tough guy, are you doing here? You could be doing an awful lot more and be doing a hell of a lot better."

"I don't think so."

Maybe I clenched my jaws, maybe I looked into her big gray eyes and tried to read ten romantic novels in them.

The first time we made love was in the afternoon. Later we joked about it. The one bird in the backyard making all that racket, hollering and chirping its feathery head off.

Ruby went through hell when the old man found us and I was sent off to certain death advising guerilla forces in an Asian jungle outpost. I never knew and she never knew until a year later. When I got off the boat, weak from a strange tropical disease, she was there to pick me up. I don't know how she found out. We went to her place. It took us two days before we actually talked about ourselves. Most of the time we fucked and ate and drank and fucked some more. Christ, she was good to fuck. Her skin constantly a surprise: sometimes glass smooth and other times meaty enough to want to bite into. Her wonderful cunt was an oven that held onto my cock and massaged its pulsing fatness with fiery manipulations. Her long fingers would cup my balls and gently stroke them.

Ruby Marlowe's on her knees before the redhead. And the redhead turns around so that her rump faces Ruby Marlowe.

"Do it there now," says the redhead, looking at Black, who grits his teeth.

"Go on, or your man will be made useless to anybody."

Ruby Marlowe faces the powdery white globes of the redhead's rump and waits while the redhead juts her bottom towards her and rests her weight more heavily upon Ruby Marlowe's face. The redhead widens her stance and lets the separate halves of her buttocks sink down against Ruby Marlowe's cheeks and nose and mouth.

"Get to work," says the redhead.

The redhead reaches her hands behind her back to push Ruby Marlowe's tongue farther into that musky tunnel.

The redhead's eyelids flutter over her emerald eyes.

"Oh, yes, yes," she groans as her orgasm reaches its last major ripple and begins to subside electrically through her loins.

Then she opens her eyes and looks at Black who looks back at her with hatred.

"Cruncher," says the redhead. "Come here. Pull down your pants."

Cruncher fumbles out of his pants and shorts and stands seminaked before the ladies. As it were, his socks don't match.

Black tries to break free of his bounds.

The redhead laughs to see such sport.

"Crawl to him, bitch," orders the redhead.

Ruby Marlowe crawls over to Cruncher who is beginning to

salivate. He feels his body pulsing with horniness. His thick glasses steam up. He wipes the lust-fog off the lenses.

Ruby Marlowe faces Cruncher's prick which is quivering up and down in excitement.

"Suck it," says the redhead, pulling a whip off a ledge and cracking it in the air.

2.

KANE WHITE:—and he is here sitting at the cot's edge all taut and tense and I cannot understand.

"Are you still angry with me?" I ask the blond boy.

He shakes his head. His jaw muscles are flexing furiously.

"Do you pray?" I ask him.

The blond boy turns around, open mouthed and fire-eyed.

"What the fug are you talking about?" he asks me. "Why don't you just make love to me? That's all we have to do."

But when I ask him if he loves me, he says no. And I can't ask him why because inside the boulders of darkness roll over to block out the sunlight.

After I ask him for love, he undresses and stands before me, as before, naked and erect and waiting for me to begin—and I don't know how to begin because he said he didn't love me and I don't know anymore and I leap off the bed and embrace God's traitor in the hug of death.

My arms around his nakedness, I can feel the first rib pop and he tries to break away from my embrace when he realizes that he is to be punished for betraying my love and he begins to gargle out a scream but he has no breath to shape into a sound and all that comes out is a choked sob.

His incredibly formed large penis remains erect and pushes thru my legs which squeeze around it as I continue to embrace him hearing more ribs pop and feeling my face suddenly splashed with his blood spurting out of his mouth.

When it is over I hold him under the arms and let him slide to the floor slowly so that he knows no further hurt. And I don't know anymore. His penis is still erect and I kiss its tip which is still burning hot with his desire for me and the hot flesh against my lips is silken to feel and I feel my own member swelling inside its confinement. I don't know but I know that they must love me if I love them or how can we create our holy love-chain of heroism and strength (I can see the new army of lovers who face the enemy fearless and with love's power of divine outrage. Celestial warriors, we'll win all wars united by our love. Love is the foundation for true murder).

His dead penis cap fits part of my mouth and I nurse it a final time while unloosening my pants to give my own manhood air and freedom to weep its liturgy. I pull out the .38 and place the silencer onto its gleaming nub shaft and pull the trigger three times. The bullets form a perfect triangle in the blond's muscular chest and as his blood drains from him, I feel the spasm of my pure fluids back up and let go. A white spurt of my seed splashes into the red offering of my dear dead Judas.

Two men in black leather drag Ruby Marlowe out of the room. This is after having to fuck Titus Black in the rear with a large wooden penis strapped around her waist. (A strange experience which shatters Black momentarily. The pain of her entry was intense and he bit down on his lip so as not to scream. And after a while of it, the pain became a queer pleasure in his gut and then Ruby Marlowe reached her hand around and found his zipper and pulled out his cock and began handling it until, despite the pain of her pushing the wooden dildo into his ass over and over again, he came. And as he came the redhead laughed viciously. And then the two men in black came in. "She's dead, Black. I'm turning her over to the Pack. They'll make her an old woman in one night." And Ruby Marlowe, herself in a fixed trance and no longer responsible for the content of her thought, looks blankly at Titus Black. He tries to see life in her eyes but cannot connect with any light there. "You fucking bitch," he shouts at the redhead. "Yes," she laughs. "At last. Now, we're ready. Now, me and my brother will finish with you. Now, you'll crawl to me. I must get my brother. Oh, this is wonderful!" "Fucking bitch," Black yells at her as she leaves. But even he doesn't believe his own voice anymore.

The redhead comes screaming back into the room.

"They've killed him. They've killed him," she wails.

She rakes her fingernails across my forehead.

"Dumb bitch," I holler.

"It's all your fault," she screams and pulls the whip up and wraps it around my neck.

Each cut of the lash hurts less than the last until I begin to want it more. Fuck it. The pain isn't real anymore.

Her emerald eyes are wide and wet with tears and rage. Mascara washes down her white cheeks.

"All your fault," she screams again.

Pushes the whip handle into my gut. Hard as she can. Which is pretty hard.

She grabs ahold of my head, holding a handful of my hair. Pulls it back until I feel my neck begin to stretch to the breaking point.

"Ohh!" she screams, letting go.

It is then that the fat man in black walks through the open door and gingerly lifts the redhead up. Cradled in his huge black-cushioned arms, she looks like a sleeping child. Her eyes wide open. She stares into his strange childlike face. He stares back at her. He carries her out. Both in their trance.

Cruncher's long gone. I'm alone. All of the pain I feel is the aftermath of my workout. My body throbs. My cock hangs out of my open pants. Blood from my slashed forehead trickles into my mouth and sometimes gets into my eyes. And I can't unlock my chains and I can't sit down and my arms are trembling.

"Oh, my beloved," moans Kane White, entering the room. "What have they done to you?"

comfort him first of all, wipe away the blood and tell him not to worry, everything is alright

"Cut me loose," he says to me and I tell him that I don't have the key, and he says, "Get Cruncher to get the key," and I tell him I don't know who he is and he says, this Titus Black, my enemy that I love, that the pain is going away

White sits on the floor, on the soft mat-covering, and talks to Black who shuts his eyes and listens as best as he can.

—Nobody understands but I know that you must understand *(Yes, yes, he says)*—ah knew you'd understand because that is the way it is, that is our lot, our destiny *(I understand)*.

I speak softly so to calm his turbulence and I tell him how they trained me and how they mistreated me so that I would learn, through sacrifice, my true nature and how grateful I am to them *(Yes, your teachers are always right, even when they hurt you)*—I knew you'd understand.

And I tell him of my visions and how everything is three and how one is three too *(Yes, of course, won't you try and find someone to cut me loose?)* add the component together and the one is of three, and he listens so knowingly.

Surely you must understand about killing.

What do you mean? he asks.

About how it is to kill someone, what happens inside, the incredible transformation, the meaningful experience.

He nods his head and asks me if I have a cigarette.

No, I don't smoke, nor drink, even though they forced me to partake of alien matter. I'm sorry, my friend, I wish I had a cigarette. But the killing, do you really understand? *(Tell me about it, he says.)* Some men chase lines over a blank canvas and when the image is brought together they have a moment of great creative joy. It's a feeling that's almost sexual. It's life. It's a feeling of life, that life is something around and beyond us, and that we move through it trying to have moments where we are unaware of it. Do you understand. You don't? Why not? Let me try to explain it like this. I can't do anything except kill. That's my way, my art. I create through destruction.

Isn't that what you do? I ask him.

No, it isn't. But I don't know anymore. Cut me loose.

I can't. I don't have the keys. The key to all understanding is always momentary, isn't it? I mean, when I am altering the life within another person, I am in the process of revelation. Nothing is important except the actual fact before me of the man's death. His breath, his spirit, the energy that moved him up and down dumb streets, I see that I have altered this. I rearrange life. I make death. Oh, don't you know what I mean? I love you.

I don't understand your love, he says to me.

Don't understand my love? What do you mean?

I don't understand it.

I punch him in the belly very hard, perhaps too hard. Some

bile pushes out of his mouth and yellow drool dangles from his gray lips.

YOU MUST UNDERSTAND MY LOVE!

I pull his head back grabbing his hair and looking into his eyes. They are dark eyes suddenly dull. But I know the diamond fire in them. He needs a shave. But that's irrelevant.

YOU MUST UNDERSTAND MY LOVE!

He turns his head back and forth. No, no.

Why not? Why not? And I bring the side of my hand down hard against his neck. His eyes roll up into his fluttering eyelids.

You see, I am a troubled seeker for the pure well-formed truths and yet my revelations lead me to the knowledge that I am surrounded by truth and the truth is life and I can't get in. Do you understand? I can't get in unless I create and I can only create death. I want life and love…and…aren't you listening? *(Yes, yes, I hear you.)*

So it's going to be like this. I knew it. A stupid, absurd, incredibly idiotic conclusion. What a life. In the rattle of fucked-up projections racing thru my skull, I try to grab onto one grain and pull it out of the swirl. Something to lay my hands on. Something to touch. Something to pass on to somebody. Fuck it. Why didn't I ever marry Ruby? My work, that was it. My bloody fucking work and all the loneliness of it. I never knew what I'd be doing, where I'd be, whether I'd be coming back. I never knew anything and I didn't want to hang her up. Christ. I never gave her a photograph of myself (she once really got upset about that).

This piss-poor wiped-out psycho. Kill for love. I've heard it all.

Review the crummy vista. Is this the reckoning time I always heard of? Hell, our instructors always told us to use Super Spy Cop-Out Number One: the death pill you pop on capture. Rules of the big game. When you're caught, you're caught, buddy. Pop the death pill. Confess nothing. Jesus Christ. What fucking secrets did I ever have to confess? All those years, I never held a plan, diagram, code, or map. I worked in the Secret Service as a muscle-pushing public relations man.

I see his manhood poking through his opened fly and it is a good member, a big one, not as big as the blond's but big and manly and I tell him about how I killed them all, going backwards, starting with the blond. (Yes, it's good that you killed him) yes, he was cruel and didn't love me when I asked him and I tell him about the hippie and the projectionist and I tell him about the dwarf (What? Say that again.) I tell him about the dwarf, how that was when I began my liberation (Oh, God, poor Buddy) No, no don't feel sorry for me any more. (Poor Buddy) deformity is against God's way (Poor Buddy) Shut up! Please! Listen to me!

White talks on.

Sometimes he doesn't say anything when he thinks that he is. The words get lost in his mind and never get out.

Black is beginning to slump.

The hell with it, he thinks. His kidneys ache and he has to pee and finally pees onto the floor.

"Why did you do that?" I ask him.

"Because I couldn't hold it in any longer," answers Black, his voice cracking.

"You're pretty ugly looking," I tell him, suddenly seeing his beaten face as if through a giant magnifying glass: the scratches, beard stubble, wrinkles, bloodshot eyes, dried parched lips, baggy suit all wrinkled and stained, penis hanging out of the fly.

Black says nothing.

"Do you love me?" I ask him.

Black says nothing.

I go up to him, looking him in the eyes.

"Do you love me?"

Black turns away.

The big fat man dressed in black begins to undress in the Oven.

The redhead, her clothes torn off, is strapped onto a table in the Oven's center, no longer sobbing but staring at the man as he undresses.

The Oven is like walking into the sun. It is like leaving an air-conditioned movie in the summer and, feeling cool and crisp, walking into the steamy, throat-stuffing heat of summer.

Before he takes off his shirt and tie and pants, the fat man in black turns the dial on the heat-control up a few more degrees.

Sighing, he unties his tie.

The redhead's hair wilts. She stews in her sweat, no longer fighting to free herself of the straps that bind her.

Steam vapors begin to fog up the room and the man in black is finally naked. His flesh is piled upon his flesh like custard poured from a spigot into a cone. Roll upon roll of fat upon fat compose the fat man's body. His knees roll into the tubes of his thighs and roll into the tubes of his hips. His rump is a sagging drag of gray-white flesh that seems to hang, wanting to fall to the floor like uncooked dough. His belly is enormous and falls in tiers, folding into the wild fur of his groin.

As he walks to her, she is startled to see how tiny his prick is, as if the rest of it is lost in the folds of his flesh.

He pulls up a chair before the table and sits down upon it. "Ahh," he sighs, grabbing ahold of her ankle.

His face is radiant and unspotted with sweat. The redhead's face and body glisten with millions of salt crystal sweat beads.

"Ahhm, I've wanted you for so long," sighs the fat man, feeling her ankle and leg. "I just don't know where to begin."

"What are you going to do to me?" asks the redhead, her voice slow and thick with the overwhelming heat. The table is beginning to burn her back and she has to shut her eyes because the heat is beginning to roast her flesh.

"You'll find out," says the fat man.

"Tell me," implores the redhead, her voice sounding as girlish as she can make it sound.

"If you must know," says the fat man, licking his chops, "I am going to eat you."

And he begins with her leg.

There is nobody. There is nothing.

"No, I don't love you," says Black. "I don't hate you either. I just don't care."

He doesn't love me. Nobody loves me. I, who have given my

love so that all men should love me more, I, stand there and can no longer understand what love is if love cannot be offered between people.

"Who do you love?" I ask him. "Is it that girl?"

"No. I love nobody. I don't care. I don't love."

"You're a monster," I say to Titus Black.

"Yes. I'm a monster," he says.

"I thought you understood," I say.

"I thought I did too. I understand nothing."

"I thought you were strong. You were my enemy and I loved you."

"I'm not strong, I'm not the enemy. I'm a monster. Jesus Christ, help me," he yells. And I am returned to Heaven. My orders are golden in my heart.

There is nobody. There is nothing. And I begin firing bullets into him. And when the pistol runs out and the bullets for it are gone, I unstrap the bowie knife tied to my leg.

The General, the Lieutenant Colonel, the troops, after conducting other business, finally find the room where White is. They open the door.

The General, the Lieutenant Colonel, the troops, all get sick according to their own natures.

No need to detail, as we end this book, the destruction of Titus Black's flesh.

No need, either, to detail the events leading to Kane White's promotion, his Presidential citation, and his orders to serve in Vietnam, Cambodia, Laos and North Korea.

No need, for that matter, to tell you anymore.

Kane White is alive and well and plans to run for office when he returns from his tour of duty.

HOW MANY BLOCKS IN THE PILE?

I.

MAIL DREAM BELT

(A preliminary odyssey)

I don't care if you don't want me
I said I'm yours
I'm yours right now
Anyhow

—Screamin' Jay Hawkins

1.

Mrs. Diana Frank usually goes to her post office box in town every day just before she does her shopping at the Safeway. She has it timed so that when she gets back home, the laundry is ready to be put into the dryer. Then, when the groceries are put away, Mrs. Diana Frank will mix herself a gin and tonic and walk to her room, unlock the door, shut it, and sit down at her desk to read the mail.

Dear C-1532—I am twenty-five and eager to learn all the arts, especially French and Japanese. I'm 135 pounds, 5 ft 11 in, and as you can see I am well-hung. Your boobs in the pic are really magnificent. I'll start by sucking on those nipples & drawing them out into my mouth until they get hard enough to chew, then I'll move my tongue down farther and farther until I reach your Treasure. I'm a real good Lover even tho my wife doesn't understand my needs I know you will because you look so sensual & sexy. I look at your pic & my organ burns from within & its all I can do to hold back until we meet again.

                                        Yours truly, Harold Forge.

A Polaroid snapshot of Harold Forge shows him lying on a terrycloth rug. Except for black socks, he is naked. His cock is a dark long tube resting on his inner thigh's flesh and nearly reaches his kneecap.

Dear C-1532—I see your ad in Hot House of which I subscribe to for years & you have got me hornier then all the others including the one from Ontario who had tits as big as farm fresh watermelons & sent me great snaps of her sticking corncobs into her snatch & also at the same time she'd be sucking one of her mammoth tits in the snap she sent. First off, got any pics? I got some to swap too. Mainly French & Greek art stuff. But I'd sure like to see you in action.Old Horny Fred (M-983) Here's my phone number too because I travel. I sell. Sure gets horny on road. Like three-somes, 4-somes? I'm good for anything you want & I got my own photo equipment too. Yes, you sure've got glorious tits.

Old Horny Fred, again.

Mrs. Diana Frank has three metal wicker baskets stacked upon each other on her desk. The first one has a small sign on it that reads "NO." The middle basket's sign: "?" The last one: "YES!" She places Old Horny Fred's letter into the No basket and sips on her gin and tonic.

Dear C-1532—Say youre a knock-out—I'm AC-DC and live in your state—I've got a girl-friend whose tongue has plastic surgery done to it so it can get into those great places much easier than any old ordinary tongue also have a boy-friend who is available in case you want a 3 or 4 or even 5—this is me in the picture forgive the smudges but I didn't have a good enlarger then & I didn't know how to handle negatives I'd get so excited looking at how the negatives looked blown-up on the table—also available for animal-training also love posing as well as taking pictures and am always looking for pictures to swap or buy— I collect lots of things to do with you-know & I'll bet you know a lot—you sure got great balloons that my boy-friend gets all hard over & your hips hold a luscious looking twat even tho the magazine blacked-it-out I know my girl-friend would like to use her new tongue on it—I'd I'd like to be there taking pictures of it and joining in—or something—whatever's right—how big are you around? just for my records—I always looked thru all the ad-mags like Hot House, Help Mate, Hook-In, Birds 'n' Bees &tcetera &tcetera to see first of all who has got the biggest knockers—Once had the honor of co-responding with a lady with a 50-32-36 body I couldn't believe at all—Here's my phone number what's yours? P.S. Return snaps when done.

Manny First.

A group of three wrinkled, badly-centered photographs.

1. One girl has her back against the wall, sitting on the bed, her legs spread wide so her lover's tongue-profile can be clearly seen as the tongue reaches into her, whose lips are spread wide by the girl's hands. The girl's lover is a squat man with pubic thatchery sprouting from his ankles up to his neck. He has both of his hands stationed on the girl's breasts. Their white bulge pushes thru his wide fingers.

2. The hairy squat man sits on the edge of the bed. The girl is on the floor on her knees before him. His penis is in her mouth and her eyes are open and stare into his navel. She's a stubby female with a mole on her cheek which bulges with the width of the squat man's penis. Her hair's a home-dyed blonde page-boy cut that makes her round face all the rounder. Her breasts are small flaps with erect nipples.

3. The squat man, the stubby girl are joined on the bed by a lean teen-aged boy in Keds. The stubby dirty-blonde lady sits on his loins. The squat man with his hairy body sits at the head of the boy jamming his penis in the lad's thin-lipped mouth.

Mrs. Diana Frank puts the photos in her desk drawer. Once a month she sorts through the photographs and files the ones she wants to keep and sends the unwanted ones to other correspondents.

Manny First's letter goes into the No basket.

Dear C-1532:
    We're planning on taking a cross-country trip, visiting as many Hot Line people as we can, exchanging notes and bodies. We've got a VW mini-bus and scored for a kilo of Tropicana Green. I'm six foot and weigh-in at 195. I'm more than well hung, you could say that I'm super stud hung and ready to go. My old lady, as you can see, is beautiful and sensual and built for loving. We've both studied under Eastern and Western masters. We've both perfect-

ed many techniques of prolonging sexual joy and pleasure. We are also accomplished photographers and, as you
can see, our photos are artistic as well as erotic. We are
available as a couple or as singles. Whichever is suitable to
your needs. Your photograph excited us both. You have a
magnificent body. Much like those incredible Indian tem-
ple-whores sculpted in those famous temples. May we visit
you when we come to your town?

(C195) Jim & Juno Mab

There is one photo. At first, Mrs. Diana Frank cannot see
what it represents. But after a while of squinting she sees the bodies twined together. The woman's hair is long and hangs over
the bed like a flag. That's all Mrs. Diana Frank can discern. She
puts the letter into the Yes basket and takes a long gulp on the
gin and tonic.

She lights a cigarette and inserts it into a unique cigarette
holder which her husband gave her as a birthday present. It's a
miniature phallus, a tiny facsimile of her husband's organ. Inside
is a radical new filter invented by a young scientist who works
in her husband's nuclear laboratory.

Mrs. Diana Frank opens up the usual odd selection of sexual junk-mail:

1. A mimeographed letter-advertisement for sex films and stills—
"Speaking frankly, I'm a dealer of, shall we say, SEXY films." A
list of films and still photos from the films. Also an add listing
of playing cards ("69 Different Poses & Positions"), 20 different Illustrated Comic Books, French Ticklers ("The Best USA
Made"), Prophylactics Super Thin Nipple-End, &tc.

2. A special bulletin from Class Publications of "highly prized
and most wanted" novels including these titles which amuse
Mrs. Diana Frank's sense of absurdity: Groovy Scenes—Billy
Bulge makes out with busty teenyboppers. No limits to search-
ing for kicks. Incredible Nymph—She couldn't get enough but
she couldn't find the woman who could give it to her. Set in
Alaska. Lust Carnival Pleasure Annex—The new kind of swinger,

anything for kicks: dope, motorcycles, leather, rubber, plastic, steel. A lusty winner. Then non-fiction titles: Dog Lovers; High School Orgy Seminars; The Nymphomaniac: True or False; Incest, Taboo and Brotherly Love: A Manual for the Maladjusted; Bizarre, Bizarre: A Peek into Pervert Fetish Case Histories With Illustrations; Smut Empire: Factual Exposé (w/introduction by Walter Winchell), &tc. Male nudist magazines: Basket Cases, Leather Lover, Sword & Rod, Gay Gambol: Counter-Spy, Jack Jock Grecian Quarterly, &tc. Assorted magazines: TapeBreakers: 45″ & Upwards; Hippie Dope Love Orgy Bondage Bash; Three On A Stick & Four On the Floor; Gash Galore; Thighs & Guys: A picture romp thru the Parisian Underworld; Beat Me, Kick Me, Draw Blood; &tc. "All orders over $25.00 are entitled to a Special 5 percent discount. Postage extra."

3. Latex catalogues, contraceptive catalogues, dildos, whips and chains, electric gadgets, announcements for a new magazine, Cannibal—"with ads and photos that are out of this world and the next," &tc.

4. And copies of magazines Mrs. Diana Frank subscribes to and in which her photo and advertisement appear.

It's been a pretty dull load of mail. There are two more envelopes of personal correspondence. She decides to go back into the kitchen and add some more gin and tonic and ice to her drink—and to check and see if the clothes are dried.

Mrs. Diana Frank walks through her well-prepared home. Everything is tasteful and correct. The rug is all over the place, on every floor portion except the kitchen which is set in a muted pearl-gray tile. The living room is spacious and does not reveal the inner lives of the specially prepared furniture that rests in elegant simplicity on the deep-pile rug. Everything is paid for, she thinks as she surveys her holdings. Again she reminds herself that she is leading the life her mother could never dream of.

Mrs. Diana Frank opens her large icebox and reaches into

the automatic ice tray and pulls out a few perfectly round cubes to pop in her glass. She also takes out the bottle of tonic.

Dear C-1532—I'm new to all of this and I would like to learn and nobody wants to teach me how it's done, all the tricks and ways of writing the right kind of letter. I can feel the right instincts in my loins but I can't seem to get the right words out. You are the twenty-first person I've written. Either they send me a form letter and ask if I'm over twenty-one, or they hand-write me a letter and ask me if I'm over twenty-one, and they all always ask me for money for pictures of themselves. I'm over twenty-one. I'm twenty-two. I'm single. I go to school. I'm six foot, one-hundred-seventy-five pounds. Enclosed is a picture of myself. I don't know what kind of pictures to enclose so I've enclosed just one of my face that I took in a machine in Woolworth's. I don't know anybody with a camera to take more exotic pictures. I want to learn and I am in love with your picture and your body and since we live in the same state, I would be glad to travel to where you are. I'm interested in all the arts and I'm not jealous and I love you.

Ronald Rowe

Ronald Rowe goes into the "?" basket.

Dear C-1532:

Your mind's got to be in your cunt where my mind is.

They can't help me. Nobody can. Here are pictures of my triumph and how I give the old wet stinky finger to all of you fuck-freaks and Communist cocksuckers who didn't have to fight in any war like I did and have to lose what I lost or nothing like that. They can't help me.

It doesn't make any more of a solitary difference that you've got big huge meat bag tits and good hip width girth and long legs and all your fleshly bulges and dips and bends and twits and twat and I bet your dum prick husband has counted every single hair on your cunt.

Women don't know how to help me but little girls do.

Nobody can really help me but I wish they'd let me re-enlist but I'm too wounded to go back again.

So all I can do now is to listen to the transistor radio talk shows and wait for the mail to bring the magazines and I can read the ads with my cock in my hand and when I can get out of the house I go to my old buddy's and see if instead of talking he has got some little lady for me to violate and they have to be willing. I'm no pervert. I'm a veteran and I think your cunt should be a tunnel jammed with old foreskins, rubbers, barbed wires and dynamite.

If I got my hands on you I'd rip off your tits as if they were cotton candy...

Mrs. Diana Frank's hand is inside her panties and her finger pushes into her wet slot.

...and make you eat the ripped-off nipples while I shit all over your face and kick you in the stomach and then I'd make you suck up my cock and I would shovel it into your mouth and instead of coming I'd piss in it and I'd show you what it is to be a whore, you fucking red asshole sucking Babylonian whore of a tit balloon. Drop dead, cunt.

Carl "Doc" Krantz

Two pictures. Carl "Doc" Krantz is being sucked-off by a girl no older than ten years of age. The man in the other photograph must be Krantz's "old buddy." The ten-year-old girl is splayed on an Army cot. A gnarled old gaffer in fatigues pushes a crooked cock into her posterior while Carl "Doc" Krantz shits on her spine, standing over her, holding his prick. Mrs. Diana Frank increases her manipulations until her cunt walls ripple in a short orgasm that shakes her clitoris like an earthquake.

Her hands smell of lust juice. She puts the Krantz letter in the Yes basket.

She wonders if Jim and Juno Mab are real hippies and if she dare invite them to a weekend with the Franks.

I'll meet Krantz outside, at his place, she thinks. As an afterthought, she puts Ronald Rowe's letter in the Yes basket. Balance & Harmony.

Mrs. Diana Frank gets up, leaves the room, locks the door, walks on the deep-pile carpet into the kitchen.

It's 4:30 and time to put the roast in the oven and iron the clothes.

2.

Mr. Kendrick (Anglo-Saxon: "royal ruler") Frank is called Ken by the guys at the lab and Kendrick by his secretary, Miss Whitenoon, and Mr. Frank by the president of the bank and Kenny by M-609, who services Mr. Kendrick Frank every Friday afternoon in the sauna bath attached to the Club that Mr. Kendrick Frank belongs to.

"Honey, I'm bringing a client over before dinner."

"Business or pleasure?"

"Business. It's a man with pictures and movies. You never can tell. Have the projector set up so we don't have to waste too much time small-talking with him. Any prospects?"

"Perhaps. Some hippies called Jim and Juno Mab."

"Hippies? I hear they're all extremely oversexed. It might be fun."

"I'll write."

"Fine."

The usual silence between them which, when they're on the phone, sounds like an electrical surf murmuring at mid-morning.

"How are things at the Lab?" she asks.

"Oh, secret, secret. But I can tell you one thing."

"Yes?"

"Some of the boys are hard at work on your next birthday present."

The silence again. Miss Whitenoon raises her skirt up to her panties which Mr. Kendrick Frank took off before he called his wife. He nods. Miss Whitenoon takes the pink prosthetic artificial penis with raised clitoral stimulator (attached to a battery-operated vibrator unit) and works it into her cunt. Miss Whitenoon's cunt is a constant source of incredulity to Mr. Kendrick Frank. It is perhaps the widest, deepest female organ he has ever seen or known.

"What's for dinner?" he asks his wife.

"Pot roast."

"Potatoes?"

"Yes, scalloped."

"Should I bring anything home, any dessert?"

He nods.

Miss Whitenoon pulls the pink battery-operated dildo out and inserts the Big One: an ebony-colored replica of an elephant cock in a state of erection. She has to slouch in the chair, her feet firm on the floor. The device hums as she presses the starter button.

Its immense crown quivers.

Miss Whitenoon holds it with both hands. There are two specially designed hand grips on each side to make insertion easier.

"Anything new in your box?"

"No, dear. In fact, come to think of it, I haven't gone down yet."

"It's close to five. Don't you think you'd better?"

"Yes, yes, you're right."

"Oh, yes, *Scientific American* came today."

Miss Whitenoon allows the ebony monster to push thru the long drooling lips of her exceptional vagina. When the pseudo-cock is halfway into her, a gush of cunt juice squirts out and sprays the pulsing transistorized shaft.

"...the usual bills."

"I'll check them out tonight."

The silence.

"Well, I better hurry to the post office box."

"Do."

"Good-bye."

"Good-bye."

He listens to the dial tone. It blends into the sound of Miss Whitenoon's delirious scream of release.

Mr. Kendrick Frank's inner office has only one key and that belongs to him.

It is a small room with an air conditioner, tape recorder, desk, lamp and bookcase which holds his collection, neatly organized, of magazines, books, records, tapes and photographs. Everything is categorized, alphabetically, and Mr. Kendrick

Frank has only to go to it to find immediately what he wants.

He puts the pill on his tongue and swallows it with the aid of a paper cup of bottled water. The schedule no longer interferes. One at breakfast to get him thru to lunch when he can take the other pill that turns his nerves and brain into warm honey (which makes him peculiarly attractive to the generals who visit the Lab to check on top secret projects) and this pill to soothe the edge of the other two pills when they wear off. Even if he were to consciously forget to take them, his body reminds him.

Flips the intercom on.

"Yes?" asks Miss Whitenoon.

"If a gentleman caller comes to the office, tell him to wait."

"Yes," answers Miss Whitenoon, her voice thick and creamy and sleepy and dreamy and, to Mr. Kendrick Frank, incredibly dull.

Dear M-778;—See me as I really am, as I was really meant to be. The Real Me. All corseted and crotch-grabbed with tight ball cock squashing latex bonds and bindings so the satin panties show nothing unusual when I raise my Apache skirt to show my lovely long shaved legs.

It was Woman that made me into a Woman, that made me know my True Self. The Woman beat me and kicked me with her high heels until my head had a half-inch dent in it. But here I am, a TV, and damned glad of it. I take mini-tit hormone pills to burn out the great dangle between my legs. Hideous Interloper. Also have pictures of my True Opening being closed by some local Saturday night sailors. Those boys are the meanest lovers imaginable and they have the most flaming cocks ever. They're dong kings. Nobody knows, nobody understands, except those very few people who care to know my services deeply. I'm only a petite 5' 5" tall which makes men want to either protect or beat me. In heels I stand an erect 5' 9". In bed, for the Purists amongst you, I wear a special harness electronic cunt strapped around my slender waist. It holds your manpower wang in it and its inner sheath has thousands of tiny vibrating rubber tips. My great love is fellatio. I cost nothing but time. You must listen to me. I hurt easily. I am, after all, a delicate confused Sparrow in a dark cloud.

Sincerely, Robin Klamp.

It's a poorly taken picture with too much flashbulb glare. The blaring light makes Robin Klamp's heavily made-up face shadowy and mask-like. Klamp's lipstick seems laminated with a brilliant lacquer. His wig is at an unfortunate slant.

Mr. Kendrick Frank keeps everything.

He puts the picture into his 10th Degree file and puts the letter into the 7th Class folder. Each degree and class is designated by numbers, except the Personal Files which are alphabetized by name and cross-filed by specialty and by Frank's grading of the subject's abilities. Number 1 is penultimate and grades down to Number 10 which is, as you might have guessed, the dredges.

The package is bulky and soft and Mr. Kendrick Frank instinctively knows what will be in it. He pulls on the string until it breaks. He tears apart the brown paper wrapping, the tissue paper, and grabs out a trophy. A large stained pair of panties. Mr. Kendrick Frank's cock stirs in his BVDs. He sniffs the crotch where the stain begins and spreads. Mr. Kendrick Frank's cock aches in its confinement so he unzips his fly, unbuckles his belt, pushes his pants and underpants down around his knees.

Mr. Kendrick Frank's prick is slightly below average in length and width, a physical fact that has always bothered him. (In junior high school he was called Teeny Weeny by the boys in the locker room, including Mark Forth, whom Mr. Kendrick Frank would masturbate before when they were alone in the basement of Mark Forth's parents' home.)

An envelope falls out of the wrappings.

Dear M-778. Hiya lover boy, boy do you look good to me, you sound right up my alley which is big and hot and endless and waiting always for as many as you want to bring along, boy I cant ever get enuf of it ever, you know how big my bazooms are? theyre bigger then any Topless dancer youve ever seen, they're a good 48" and when my nipples get hard they go to sometimes 52" which is big and theyre soft and I know what you want and I can be giving it you while youre giving it me, lover boy, you know I am older than the rest, I am 48 yrs old and Ive been around and around the worlds, you know what I mean, here is my phone number and heres just a small sample photo of me and thanx for the $5.00 plus 5 per cent tax for enclosed weekold panties which I thought of you all the time and that is why they're so well broken in, lover boy.

Your lover woman, Hertha 'Big 'n Busty' Blax

Mr. Kendrick Frank reads Hertha "Big 'n Busty" Blax's letter while pulling on his rigid prick. She seems to be all that he always looks for: huge breasts, middle-aged, animal and ready for service, yet maternal and tender. He feels the pulse of his release begin to signal within his hot shaft. Mr. Kendrick Frank stops manipulating. He sees Hertha Blax also as the kind of brute woman he can degrade and who will love it all. His hands tremble as he looks at the photograph.

Hertha "Big 'n Busty" Blax stands in profile next to a small table with a chintzy lamp on it. Turning to face the camera with a big smile bright with teeth, her breasts hang on her chest as if huge cannonballs were stored in each tip. Her belly is a round bulge rolling into the swell of her bush, a wild-haired eruption. Hertha Blax's ass is an incredible half-earth of white flesh chopped at mid-thigh by black nylons. Mr. Kendrick Frank goes back to rubbing and pulling and tweaking and comes within seconds. He watches the first spurt shoot up and plop into his shorts while other drops hit his pants and land on the floor. Mr. Kendrick Frank wipes off with Kleenex, pulls his pants up, buckles them, sighs. He puts Hertha's panties into a gray tin locker which has the best of his collection. He puts a red tag on them. (The best have the red tag.) Hertha's letter goes into the 1st Class folder and her picture goes into the 1st Degree file.

Dear Fan of the Unusual:

Now for a limited time only, a complete set of 15 photos and these are only the very best of a large collection of material. I offer 20 sets of 15 photos each. Each set is $12.50. Some of the sets are: Dachau, Auschwitz, Hiroshima, Saigon, and others. Please tick appropriate group when ordering:

GROUPS (Mixed) ( )

COUPLES (Fem) ( )

BONDAGE (Male) ( )

SINGLES (Female) ( )

COUPLES (Mixed) ( )

GROUPS (Female) ( )

No need to impress upon you the care we've gone to to produce these sets for you. Detailed pictures of mutilated children, women and men, as well as incredibly accurate enlargements of bonfire mass-burnings, including rare photos of the Showers and Soap Work interiors, a special set of Buchenwald crafts, and a unique set of Nagasaki stillborn mutants. Some color sets are available at $25.00 a set. Also confiscated 8mm. Nazi films depicting erotic behavior in concentration camps. Write for List X for more details. Enclosed is your request sample photo. You'll find that though our rates are high, our product is more than worth it. Special rates available on large sales. Allow two weeks or more for delivery.

Glad to be of service, X-Tra Eklektic Sales Co.

A color photo in a cardboard folder. It shows a large muddy ditch filled with naked bodies piled up so high that they grow out of the ditch like a pyramid of flesh. It is hard to distinguish the sexes at a glance. Mr. Kendrick Frank picks up his magnifying glass and surveys the body pile.

The intercom.

"Yes?"

"Your visitor is here."

"Tell him I'll be out in, oh, ten minutes."

"Yes, I'll do that. A strange one."

"What do you mean?"

"Oh, nothing," says Miss Whitenoon. "Nothing really."

"Can he hear you?" asks Mr. Kendrick Frank, who does not like to insult anyone before he knows them.

"No, of course not," answers Miss Whitenoon. "He's in the outer room."

"Well, what do you mean that he's 'a strange one'?"

"I said to forget it, Kendrick. I don't know why I said it. There's just something about him which I cannot, obviously, describe," she answers, stretching out the word "obviously."

"Alright, alright. You can go home now, Miss Whitenoon. It's past five. Tell him I'll be out in ten minutes. Offer him a drink…"

"I did and he refused."

"Oh, I see."

"See you at ten, Kendrick."

"Yes, of course," he says and snaps the intercom off.

Dear M-778. Look…Whatryou afrayd of? Ts my 2d letr & i mnot going to rite no more of them. Yu didn't kahl me from the 1st letr evn wen i told you abowt how i beet you w/chayns & whips so Now i give you last chance & here sa photoh of me in my rite dress…Wayt 4 you at yr box number. Whatryou afrayd of? Beet you & bet you got a wyfe & I beet her 2 & make you suck my self in frawhnt of her…6 ft 3 in tall & hardon gets to 1 ft 2 in & bigger if better…I am yr MASTR!!!!!

…Oscar

Mr. Kendrick Frank looks at the photo of Oscar who stands with his huge arms folded over his hairy chest and in each fist is a whip. His face is covered with a leather-looking Batman mask. His parts are covered with a white silk low-slung swim-suit. They bulge within the silk like a goitered udder. The vision of Mr. Frank on his knees gobbling the giant's mystery mile-long prick makes cold sweat form about his lips. Another letter and photo to enter into the Top Form files. Tomorrow, Mr. Kendrick Frank will answer his two correspondents.

3.

"Lincoln Hawk, my wife, Mrs. Frank," announces Mr. Kendrick Frank as they enter the living room.

"Yes," answers Lincoln Hawk and nods abruptly.

"Would you like a martini?" she asks.

"No. Of course not. Well, good, I'm glad you've got your projector all set up and ready to roll. Let's not waste any more of our God-given time. Let's get down to the work of seeing, of vision, the task of coping with mysterious images which don't settle in the mid-mind too well..."

"Mid-mind?" asks Mr. Frank.

"Yes, the mid-mind which sorts out the darkness from the light and which assists the eye in responding to what it sees. The mid-mind's eyes color the colors in all images and visions of images..."

"Would you like some hors d'oeuvres?" asks Mrs. Frank.

"No. Of course not. I'm still fasting. Why don't you both sit down. What a lovely home you have provided for yourselves. Any children?"

"No," answers Mrs. Frank.

"Yes. Of course. No children. Would you bring me my suitcase, Mr, Frank? Thank you."

Mr. Kendrick Frank leaves the living room for a moment in order to bring Lincoln Hawk's satchel.

"Why don't you have any children?"

"I beg your pardon?" she asks.

"You heard me. Is it him or you or both of you?"

"That's none of your business," she says, flushing.

"Do you want children?"

"I don't know...I...Listen, Mr. Hawk, that is none of your business," she answers and gets up to mix herself another martini.

Lincoln Hawk putters with the projector. He is a small wiry man with a long pale face. The chin is smeared with a constant five o'clock shadow that no razor can erase. Hawk's hands are long and slender and he bites his fingernails. Hawk wears a black suit and a white shirt and a black tie and black shiny shoes with black hose stretched and hooked to a garter belt about his leg. Neat and seedy at the same time, he reminds Mrs. Frank of a clerk in a mortuary.

"It's him," she says, halfway thru her martini. "He never told me until years later that he had a vasectomy done when he was twenty-one years of age. He said that it was his manhood present to himself and to woman. But he never told me until years later…"

"You mean, all the time it was all right with you because you thought that it was your fault, that you were failing him and deserved to suffer?"

Hawk's voice is toneless and crisp and quickly engages and baffles a listener's tongue into instant submission.

"Yes, yes. What do you want from me?"

Mr. Kendrick Frank comes back with the suitcase.

"Over here, please. Thank you."

He places it at Lincoln Hawk's feet.

"Go. Sit down. Keep your wife company. Mix her a drink. Mix yourself a drink. Get comfortable. And, by the way…"

Mr. Kendrick Frank is mixing a martini.

"Why did you have a vasectomy?"

"Diana, you dumb bitch…"

"Come now, it's a simple enough question. We're adults, we live in hard times and simple questions are rare enough."

"Look, Mr. Hawk, my sex life is none of your damned business," says Mr. Kendrick Frank, gulping down his martini, hardly tasting it at all, except for the quick burn of its transit.

"Yes, it is, Mr. Frank. In fact, it is my main business. What is your business, Mr. Frank? Do you know what you are doing at any given time? Is your mind in functioning order, clear and sure and alert to the instant, the immediate perception?"

"What does that have to do with…" stammers Mr. Frank, mixing another martini.

"Why not one for your wife too?"

"Look, you…"

"Go on, man, it's not going to break your spirit. Do it. Give it to her with care and respect. Now. Why did you have the vasectomy?

"I didn't want kids," snaps Mr. Kendrick Frank, pouring out two martinis.

"Why?" asks Lincoln Hawk.

"If you don't want to show us those damned films, then get the hell out of here! You have no right..."

"Tell him, Kendrick," says Mrs. Diana Frank, who long ago forgot what an immediate perception was or how to be alive and alert to the moment. For Mrs. Diana Frank it is a matter of before and after. She anticipates what she has never experienced: the ultimate joyous fuck of total fulfillment, of complete and thorough satisfaction. The pictures, the letters, they help her get by the death of dreams.

"You said it yourself, Hawk. It's a rotten world we live in and who'd want to bring kids into it. Have you any kids?"

"Of course not. I'm sterile."

Mr. Kendrick Frank puffs a half-laugh.

"Where's the light switch, Mrs. Frank? Where's the screen?" asks Hawk.

"Why didn't you bring in the damn screen?" gripes Mr. Kendrick Frank.

"I couldn't find it," answers his wife, her voice thick.

"Oh, shit, I'll find it."

He walks out, reaching into his coat pocket for his pills.

Mrs. Frank slumps into the sofa with a new martini.

The First Movie:

Red hissing tail of a flare on the freeway.

The title superimposed on the image.

BAGFUL OF BREAK-UP.

Fades into pan.

Pan up the white freeway dividing line.

Zero into the car wreck encircled by flares. Two teen-age couples mangled inside the station wagon which has collided with a truck. Zoom-shot: driver and date. Their faces smashed against the front window. The car roof squashes down on their heads. Front window glass is cracked in a semicircular design. Imperfect spiderweb. Driving wheel thru his chest.

His glasses cracked, knocked askew. Blood in the cracks.

Camera moves around other side of car.

His girl friend's face slashed from forehead to chin. Skull cracked. Blood in the roots of her blonde hair.

Cut.

Highway Patrol car. The revolving red light on its roof.

Cut.

The two patrolmen exit from their car and go to the wreck. Front view. Walking towards camera. Back view as they face the ruin. Both men grip their pistol butts.

Cut.

Both draw and fire into the car. Cut.

Bullet holes bore thru glass and steel. Cut.

The two patrolmen put their pistols back into their holsters. Each one has a strange smile on his perfect face. They look like brothers. Both are six-feet-two, broad-shouldered, blond-hair cut in neat crewcuts, narrow waists, their uniforms creased and spotless.

Cut.

Side view. One of the patrolmen gets on his knees before the other.

Cut.

Camera moves closer.

Cut.

Hand unzips fly, unbuckles belt, jodhpurs pushed down to the boot tops. The officer wears a jockstrap. It's pulled down. Slowly.

Cut.

Close-up of the patrolman's erect cock. Pulsing and throbbing. Veins wrapped around it like vines. Cock fills screen. In far right-hand corner, the pink tip of a tongue.

Cut.

Back view. Patrolman's buttocks grabbed by the hands of his partner. Close-up of the fingers kneading the cheeks.

Cut.

Long shot: patrolman performs fellatio on his partner surrounded by the ring of flares.

Cut.

Buttocks flex and jerk as the officer comes into the mouth of his partner.

Cut.

Close-up of cock pumping sperm into the mouth around it. Fade.

"Now that's just a sample," says Hawk. "An excerpt from a longer movie. A two-reeler, as a matter of fact. Too bad you don't have equipment for sound movies. The sound track on this one is tremendously inventive. No talking at all. Just the sounds, the silence."

"Were those…those kids in the car…were they real…I mean," stutters Mrs. Diana Frank.

"Of course," says Hawk.

The Second Movie:

Long shot: a city block. The faces of apartment buildings. Superimposed on the shut windows:

PELT & LOVE RIBBON. The letters fade. Cut.

Long shot: a girl walks from the corner towards the camera. A wild-haired man in a leather jacket steps out of an alleyway.

Cut.

Close-up of his hand over her mouth. Her eyes wide with horror.

Cut.

The eyes of a family watching the man push the girl onto the sidewalk. The family is looking thru a window.

Cut.

Close-up of girl's mouth open in a scream.

Cut.

Venetian blinds snap shut.

Cut.

Between two garbage cans in the alleyway. A shot of the wild-haired man in the leather jacket slashing off her blouse until it is in tatters. Camera moves closer. Cars drive by. A person walking on the same side of the street crosses the street to the other side and walks on. A young couple stand in a doorway across the street and watch.

Cut.

Close-up of wild-haired man's face. His eyes are small and brilliantly lit with madness. He needs a shave. His beard is sparse. Small sprouts of hair in clusters around his chin and beneath his nose. His teeth are perfectly even. Lips thin and wet. He has the habit of licking them as he works.

Cut.

He grabs the girl by the hair and forces her to her knees. She continues screaming. He slashes off her bra straps. Grabs the tattered blouse and rips it off.

Cut.

Close-up, slow-motion, the ragged white blouse thrown out and slowly fluttering onto the cement.

Cut.

Grabs the bra and yanks it off. Cut.

Window-shade opens. Binoculars peer thru the window glass. Image of the wild-haired man forcing the girl to lay on the sidewalk.

Cut.

The wild-haired man unzips his leather jacket. The inner lining contains many implements of torture: chains, pincers, saps, brass knuckles, thumbscrew, rope, a rawhide thong whip, and assorted cutlery. He pulls out a transistor radio from a shirt pocket and puts it on the sidewalk and turns it on.

Cut.

With knife and chain he begins to damage the girl's naked flesh.

"This is a sample," says Hawk. A white flash of leader. "The rest of the reel is devoted to his further abuse of her flesh, her mouth, her other openings. A fine shot of a little boy masturbating across the street. Ah, now, as a special visual and artistic inducement, a few samples from the second and last reel."

Zips up his fly.

Cut.

There's a line of boys and men that have formed by the body of the woman. Camera moves along from face to face, then goes to the face of the wild-haired man. He winks at them and nods.

They wink back and nod.

Cut.

Camera above the girl's body which is spread on the sidewalk. Dwells on the crisscross hatchery of stiletto nicks on her thighs and belly. Whip welts on her breasts. Moves up to her bruised face. Eyelids flutter. Open slowly.

Cut.

A giant Negro sledgehammer worker is first. His cock is already stiff and twitching in the air thru his open workpants fly.

Cut.

She bites her lip. It begins to bleed.

Cut.

Shot of two teenage boys. One is fucking her. The other is making her suck him off.

Close-up. Montage of cocks pushed into her cunt. A minute-long sequence. Like the turning of calendar pages to denote time passing.

Cut.

Close-up. Another montage: cocks in her mouth. Cut.

WHAT'S LEFT OF A GOOD THING. Black letters on white screen. Fade.

Cut.

Dog sniffs her foot. Lifts leg. Pisses on her knee. Camera moves slowly up her body. Garbage has been dumped on her belly. Flies nervously attack it. Flies cluster around her bloody, ripped cunt. Camera moves up to her breasts. The nipples burned off by some kids who used lighter fluid. Camera moves up to her face which is covered with her panties. Cut.

Camera dollies down the block. Some kids shooting marbles. One of the marbles rolls out of the ring and down the street. Camera follows it. The marble gets tangled in the girl's hair. Cut. Top-view. Arms outstretched, her hands are spiked into the cement. The Project work-crew used a sledgehammer. She'd given head to most of them and passed out before she could service the crew boss. It was his idea. Beer cans, sandwich wrappings, candy bar wrappers &tc. People ate lunch and watched.

Cut.
Apartment windows. Skyline.
Fade-in: FIN.
Blank screen. Hum of projector.

"As you see, our samples are deliberately frustrating. We leave out details and demand that your imagination endure the process that leads to whatever conclusion it can claim. This, I think, shall be the last sample. It's getting late and I have much to do and more customers to consult with," says Lincoln Hawk.

Mr. Kendrick Frank sits in his leather-upholstered easy chair. His hand still massages his cock, which became activated by the last movie. Excitement and dream-lust pump electrical pulse beats thru his glands.

Mrs. Diana Frank sips the last of a new martini and her mind is split into slanted image panels. She cannot sort them out nor see them clearly. Christ, I hope the roast doesn't dry up, she thinks. She also thinks about the young girl in the movie. Was her death a glorious adventure, a triumph, or was it a cruel chance outrage? Poor Mrs. Diana Frank, thinks poor Mrs. Diana Frank. Life is a movie to watch. Mrs. Diana Frank wants to touch reality and devour it. She chews the olive and goes to the bar to mix a new pitcher of martinis.

The Third Movie:

Explosion. Title fades into the rising smoke. VIET FIRE ROT RUN.
Cut.
Hilltop. Barren. Twigs, pebbles. A naked Vietnamese woman. Small uptilted breasts and a neat pubic triangle. Legs are a little stocky. Her hands bound behind her. Two men in G.I. uniforms cover her body with napalm jam.
Cut.
Foot of hill. A naked man. American. A Vietnamese guerilla fighter rubs napalm jam on the American's limp cock. Rubs it into his pubic hair. Rubs the jam around his balls. His cock fills up and sticks out. The Viet Cong laughs.

Cut.

The woman lays on the dirt, legs spread. One of the G.I.'s swabs napalm jam around her cunt's lips and shoves a fingertiful into her cunt. Cut. Close-up. Match strikes against fingernail. Ignites.

Cut.

Flames for ass and cock, the American races up the hill (long-shot).

Cut.

Medium-shot. Soldier in flames plunges his fiery cock into her cunt as if it were a watering hole. She ignites in his embrace. Fire spreads over their bodies in the same time it took the match to flare. The flames rise. Their bodies become black forms which support the white fire. The two bodies explode.

Cut.

The G.I., the Viet Cong, sweep away the ashes. All turn to the camera, bow and smile, then stand at attention, salute, give the V for Victory sign, bow again, then go back to sweeping.

Cut. End.

"That's just the finale of one of our most ambitious movies, a history of erotic war-play from WWI thru to this most recent escapade. I think, for your sake, I'll show one last film-clip sampler. Then I must go. This sampler was put together by our top editor, a veteran of many wars, a visionary of mid-mind tactics. By the way, am I wasting my time and yours? I am used to some kind of exchange, some kind of interplay."

"Not at all," answers Mr. Frank, slowly zipping up his fly so the sound will not be heard.

"Not at all, what?" asks Hawk.

"You're not wasting anybody's time, Hawk. I will buy at least one of the group from you. Perhaps more."

"Not buy, Mr. Frank. I take that for granted. You are obligated to. What I would like to know is what do you think about them? Are they meaningful images to consider?"

"Very well done," says Mr. Kendrick Frank rather brusquely.

"The contents, Mr. Frank, what do you think about the images, what do they mean?"

"I don't know, Hawk, I'm not an intellectual, I'm just a collector," snarls Mr. Kendrick Frank. "Hell, what do you think, honey?"

"I don't know," answers Mrs. Diana Frank, her words slushy.

"Can't you tell Mr. Hawk anything about his movies?" asks Mr. Frank.

"Not now," answers Mrs. Frank. "Are they real? I mean, did they really happen for real?"

The Fourth Movie: A sampler:

MAYA MARZIPAN MOTHER & CHILD

Title letters flash on and off. A strobelike flash. Image memory retains title after it ceases flashing clashing Day-Glow colors on the screen.

Cut.

Grainy black-and-white footage. Round young girl. Small tight breasts, square-shaped nipples. A cluster of moles on her rear end. Hand-love to an Afghan hound. Rubs his belly. Close-up: his concealed prick pushes thru its hairy sheath, red, erect and shining. She strokes it with her fingertips. Her fingernails are bitten. Cut.

Dog's long snout lapping and guzzling at her pussy, standing over her while she puckers her lips beneath him to suckle his sex.

Cut.

Race riot. Mid-shot: frontline of young blacks with bottles, clubs and chains. Jerky camera action.

Cut.

New Chrysler sedan overturned by mob. They drag the couple out of it. Two white people.

Cut.

Several black men rape the woman holding the man back.

Cut.

Bonfire.

Black men throwing newspapers into it, breaking up TV sets, throwing kindling into the flames.

The couple are set on the pyre's top.

Cut.

Orgy scene in airliner crashing into the Atlantic ocean.

Cut.

Motorcycle gang runs over a naked woman. Repeatedly.

Cut.

Cosmonauts fucking in their bubble.

Cut.

Nun daisy chain.

Cut.

The Pope buggered with a crucifix.

Cut.

Shooting-down of Che Guevera.

Cut.

JFK's head blown apart by the bullets.

Cut.

Looney Tunes ending. Porky Pig silently stuttering out, "Th-th-that's all, folks!"

Fade.

Leader numbers.

Blank screen.

"Alright. That's enough. May I remind you, once again, that the clips are snipped from full-length films. The last few clips are from sources that I can not reveal. They are extremely expensive. Perhaps beyond your range of capital and imagination. Now, Mr. and Mrs. Frank, what do you need, what do you want? Please turn the lights on."

The Franks eat a late dinner in the living room and watch TV while they eat. A war is on the TV screen.

"Well what do you think?" asks Mr. Frank, his voice woven with the sounds of bombs and machine guns.

"I don't know," answers Mrs. Frank, sipping her liqueur, feeling sleepy and bored with images, words.

"I had to have that one about the girl for the collection. It's a two-reeler. Hawk says he'll deliver the print next week. Strange, isn't he?"

"Yes, I suppose so. I don't know," she answers.

"You don't know too much tonight, do you?"

"No, I don't. I'm tired…"

"You're drunk," says Mr. Kendrick Frank. A linoleum-polish commercial interrupts the war.

"So what?"

"I'm trying to talk to you," says Mr. Frank, taking another pill, washing it down with coffee.

"I'm listening. I'm listening."

The war segues into a militant student riot.

"Where did he get those assassination movies? Boy, I'd sure like to see them. Haven't you ever wanted to see what it really looked like? They never would show you that in the newspapers or on TV."

Mrs. Diana Frank sips nervously on her liqueur and watches the President of the United States gesticulate before the Congress.

"…or that Spic or Wop, you know, the brother of Castro, those shots of him being shot like that…honey, are you listening?" asks Mr. Kendrick Frank.

"Yes, I'm listening. Why do you always ask me whether or not I'm listening? I hear every word you say. Every word."

"But you're not answering me," he says.

"You're not asking anything of me," she says.

Another wheel, another round, a cycle of talk which is their dinner word-ritual. Perhaps, she thinks, we never had anything to say to each other. Mrs. Diana Frank tries to remember when she and her husband had ever talked together, listening to each other's secret selves as she had imagined lovers would do.

A little girl with a stage-lisp gargles tenderly about a loaf of white bread enriched with megatons and vitamins.

"Where are you going?" he asks.

"To get a drink," she answers.

"Another one?" he says.

"Another one," she says and walks to the bar.

Mrs. Diana Frank walks as straight as she can but her footing is unsure. She's reached the state in her drinking which is dangerous. She is unsure of her body and her body is unsure of her.

"Unsteady on your pins, huh, honey?"

"I'm alright," she says, not trying to conceal her contempt for him. Mr. Kendrick Frank takes great delight in pointing out to his wife the various stages of her drinking. This is done when they're alone together. With company, with guests, it is another matter.

By now, to balance the record, Mr. Kendrick Frank is beginning to hear the old familiar barbiturate hum in his head and he feels his body starting to melt. He stares at the TV which shows a white-robed minister behind a lectern delivering the station's sign-off sermon.

"Now, more than ever, we need to face the heavy load of our times with a strong embracing faith..."

They lie in bed after trying to make love and failing to. Her lush body is tangled in sheets and blankets and his girthy spread lies heavy on top of the covers.

They don't try too hard. It's the same nearly every week night. He's too stoned to function properly and she's too drunk to offer him much help. To his narcotized fingertips her flesh is strangely plastic and alien. To her heavy reeling head his cock is a ridiculously inept dab of flesh which she has grown tired of having to manipulate into a passable hard-on. When he thrusts his tongue into her mouth, she smells the dirt in his teeth. Her breasts bother his hands with their ripeness. They are firm and big, not huge and flaccid like Hertha "Big 'n Busty" Blax's. She's not active enough for him. He wants his women to crave him enough to rape him. She wants to be taken by a man who is willing to take her, who desires her beyond reason.

They lie in bed after trying to make love and failing to. Mr. Kendrick Frank is listening to a talk show on the transistor radio he sleeps with.

"Honey, why don't you get under the covers?" He doesn't answer because he can't hear her. His ear is plugged up with an earphone. His wife pushes him. He stirs and pulls the earphone out.

"What? What?" he asks, sounding like a child caught at shoplifting.

"Get under the covers. Let's go to bed."

"Alright, alright, you didn't have to to startle me so," he says, getting under the covers.

"Why do you sleep with that damn earphone in your ear listening to the radio?" she asks him.

"It helps me to sleep better," he answers and sticks the earphone back in his ear.

Soon he is snoring.

While thinking about whether or not she should masturbate, Mrs. Diana Frank falls asleep.

II.

INTERMISSION

(A shuttle)

Don't leave your book on the shelf
For nobody else to read,
No, sir

—Joe Tex

1.

"My name's Diana. Like a drink?"

Ronald Rowe stands at the threshold of the living room looking pale, nervous and much thinner than the photograph would indicate.

"Sure," he answers, his voice not his voice. "What do you have?"

"What would you like?"

Sometimes he drinks beer after work. Once he drank a bottle of Phoenix Feather Wine and was sick for three days.

"Whatever you're having," he answers, walking into the living room.

"Two gin, and tonics then. Sit down on the sofa. I'll mix our drinks."

On her way to the bar, Mrs. Diana Frank turns on the tape deck. The hum and throb of sensual mood music pours out of the stereo speaker system.

"Are you married?" Rowe asks, sinking into the sofa.

"Yes."

"Any children?"

"No."

He sighs with relief.

"Mind if I smoke?"

"No, Ronald, of course not. There are some cigarettes on the table in that black lacquer box," answers Mrs. Diana Frank, stirring the gin and tonics with nervous vigor. The challenge of the game always excites her. Each one is different. Or seems to be, in the beginning.

Ronald Rowe lights up a cigarette that Mrs. Diana Frank has made for her by a tobacconist who also sells her fine sets of Arab pornographic photos.

He puts the silver lighter back on the table when Mrs. Frank comes to him and hands him his drink.

"Mind if I sit down?" she says.

"Of course not," answers Ronald Rowe, trying to laugh nonchalantly. His laugh is not his laugh but some strange strangled chuckle that sounds as if he's trying to clear his throat.

Mrs. Diana Frank has always dressed well. Even before she met her husband and was struggling to meet one, she would rather go without food than to appear at work in unattractive attire. Now her closet is crammed with clothing which she replenishes seasonally. She has another closet which contains her shoes and boots, and a small selection of rubber and leather bondage-wear. They sometimes come in handy, though she prefers it when they bring their own for her to wear and have to force-fit her into the binding hides.

For Ronald Rowe, she decides to dress simply. Skintight burnt-orange pants and a provocative pale saffron shirt-blouse whose top three buttons remain unattached to the woven button loops. She wears no bra and her nipples are erect from being rubbed by the thin fabric of her blouse.

She sits next to him and he feels the pressure of her hip against his.

"Cheers," says Mrs. Diana Frank to Ronald Rowe.

"Cheers," he answers, looking away from the cleavage she reveals.

Ronald Rowe gulps down his drink. The ice cubes and lime cool his fever briefly.

"I like to see a man drink," says Mrs. Diana Frank. "I'll make you another one and refresh mine."

Ronald Rowe smells her perfume. It surrounds him. He swears to remember it forever.

"When do you graduate?" she asks him from the bar.

"I already graduated. I'm going for my Doctor's."

"What's your major?" she asks.

"Physics."

"Very interesting," says Mrs. Diana Frank and walks around the bar back to the sofa. "Here you are, Ronald," she says, sitting beside him, handing him his drink.

"Thank you."

"Tell me about the others," she says.

"What others?"

"The other women you've contacted through *Hot Line*."

"Well, you're the only one that'a answered me for a—what would you call it?—a rendezvous, I guess."

"Do you have a job?" she asks, reaching for a cigarette, bending in such a way as to reveal the fleshy swell of her magnificent breasts.

"Yes, I work part-time in an atomic lab," answers Ronald Rowe, blinking his eyes, feeling the fire of his blush burn his face.

"Have you ever made love to a woman before?"

"Why do you say that?" Rowe's voice can't get into gear and cracks before he finishes his question.

The gin and tonics work with velocity on the untrained system of Ronald Rowe. It's all she can do to get him up the stairs and into the bedroom.

"You know, I don't really drink," says Rowe, sitting on the rug-covered staircase. "I just make bombs," he says, laughing dangerously. Mrs. Diana Frank wonders whether he will throw up on the rug.

"Take my hand and come with me."

"Where are we going?"

"To my bedroom."

Rowe laughs again. It is an unpleasant laugh unintentionally harsh and infantile. When he reaches for her outstretched hand, he lurches and slumps to his knees with a giggle.

"Wow, I sure am drunk," he announces to Mrs. Diana Frank's shoes, which happen to be the nearest objects in view.

Ronald Rowe manages to pull himself up on the second try and, holding onto her hand and using his other hand to hold the rail, he follows her to the doorway of the bedroom.

She goes in first and pushes a button on a box on the wall which produces mood music out of small speakers that line the room's walls.

"Come on in, Ronald," she says.

He's propped against the door frame. His body against the door resembles an almost perfect triangle. Then he's on the floor again on his knees.

"Wow, I sure am drunk," he says once more, his voice pushing through the cement in his throat.

Mrs. Diana Frank's blouse is thrown into his face. He looks

up and watches her undress. For her, this is the last round. If he fails to respond, then the afternoon's shot.

Our novice revives quickly. The chilling thrill of Mrs. Diana Frank's striptease sends sobering tidal waves through his body.

By the time she's out of her panties, Ronald Rowe is on his feet and dry-mouthed, and his eyes seem to be stretched out on stalks.

"Come to bed," says Mrs. Diana Frank, drawing the curtains. The bedroom becomes dim. Afternoon sunlight muted through the thick curtains covering the windows. "Come to bed and let me undress you."

"I love you," says Ronald Rowe as she unbuttons his shirt.

Mrs. Diana Frank says nothing. Her hands explore his bony chest. His skin is smooth and white and reminds her of a boy she knew a long time ago. The sparse hairs on Ronald Rowe's washboard chest form the design of a strange calligraphy.

"It's a tough one," says Rowe in a whisper when her hands reach his belt buckle.

No belt buckle too hard for Mrs. Diana Frank to unbuckle, she thinks, trying to remember the face of that boy, many years ago, who took her to his bedroom and told her not to worry, not to cry, that it would be beautiful.

Mrs. Diana Frank pushes Ronald Rowe's pants down to his shoes, then gets off the bed to untie his shoes.

"You don't have to do that," he says.

When his shoes and socks are removed, Mrs. Diana Frank pushes his pants off. Ronald Rowe lies quietly on the bed and watches her return to lie beside him.

"Kiss me," she says.

They kiss. Ronald Rowe is cautious and his lips are shut. Mrs. Diana Frank pushes the tip of her tongue through his shut lips which startles Rowe. But he responds and, opening his lips, allows her tongue entry into his mouth.

Rowe shuts his eyes when Mrs. Diana Frank rolls his BVD's down and his naked manhood is there for her to see. She is pleased. It's a good one. Just right for the afternoon when the sun is still out. An afternoon cock. Not too large or wide, nor with slanted crown or gnarled curve. Ronald Rowe's balls are compact and will easily fit into the palm of her hand.

She moves down to kiss his cock.

Rowe opens his eyes in horror and delight.

Mrs. Diana Frank looks up at him with his cock half into her mouth, her large firm breasts hanging free and full upon his knees.

"I love you," he groans.

Mrs. Diana Frank is satisfied with the flaming erection and moves up to him and another kiss. For the first time they embrace and the fleshy impact of her naked body's softness against his body is a revelation.

"Touch me," says Mrs. Diana Frank.

Ronald Rowe's fingers are long and they reach out to touch a breast.

My God, it's alive, he thinks as her nipple bends to his touch.

"Kiss it," says Mrs. Diana Frank.

Ronald Rowe kisses the breast.

"Suck it," says Mrs. Diana Frank.

Ronald Rowe purses his lips and begins to suckle on her nipple which grows hard in his mouth. Her nipple is very hot.

Without being told, Ronald Rowe begins to chew on Mrs. Diana Frank's nipple and, for the first time this afternoon, Mrs. Diana Frank groans with desire.

They begin to respond more mindlessly, shedding images easily. Entwined together, they are directed by the heat in their sexual centers, and become lost in its fury.

Ronald Rowe's hand is madly probing Mrs. Diana Frank's drooling cunt while her fingers massage his aching stem.

There's a pause. Ronald Rowe remembers that he doesn't know exactly where to stick his cock. The truth being, as Mrs. Diana Frank assumed, that he is a virgin.

"What's wrong?" she asks dreamily.

"I…"

"What?"

"I…"

The shame of his declaration throttles his throat. It's stuck there. The simple statement won't come out.

"Ronald, what's wrong?" she asks.

He wants her not to worry. To tell her that there's nothing wrong. He doesn't want to hurt her but…

"I…well, I'm ashamed to tell you that…I…"

"You're a virgin?"

"Yes," he says and in saying it, is freed of it and clear of it. At last.

"How old are you, Ronald?"

"Twenty."

"Twenty? What a wonderful age. Come. Let me show you how."

And Mrs. Diana Frank does. Suddenly the mood music is a glorious sound track. She guides Ronald Rowe's erect rod into her sheath. His eyes are shut but Mrs. Diana Frank watches his face as he enters her fully. Ronald Rowe smiles. Her cunt is a warm bath of unexplored delights and Ronald Rowe begins to move his cock deeper into it as if to probe its end. Finally he can go no farther and he then begins to withdraw and plunge, withdraw and plunge. Mrs. Diana Frank wraps her legs around his back to give his cock more depth to work in. He grabs hold of her firm buttocks and pushes her onto his cock.

Mrs. Diana Frank watches Ronald Rowe's face when he comes. Surprise and joy on his face. Then, at the last shot drop, Ronald Rowe opens his eyes and looks at Mrs. Diana Frank and he laughs with delight and his newfound manhood.

"Let's do it again," he says after going downstairs for some gin and tonics to bring up to the bedroom.

And they do.

The telephone rings. She picks it up.

"Yes?"

It's Mr. Kendrick Frank and it is his usual time in the late afternoon to call his wife. She looks at the clock in astonishment. Ronald Rowe lies beside her, smoking a cigarette.

"I'm busy now, dear, I'll see you at dinner."

Mr. Kendrick Frank sounds a little wound up over the phone, as if he's trying to tell her something.

"Alright, I'll see you then. In an hour. Have him gone by then."

"Of course, dear," she says.

The familiar, traditional static and silence.

"Alright, good-bye."

She hangs up.

"Your husband?" asks Rowe, putting his arms around her.

"Yes. You'll have to leave soon."

"Will I see you again?"

"That depends. I have a very busy schedule. We'll see."

As he dresses, Ronald Rowe looks longingly over at Mrs. Diana Frank as she dresses. That sonofabitch, he thinks about her husband. He doesn't deserve her.

Over coffee, Ronald Rowe tells her that he works for the same company that Mr. Kendrick Frank owns.

"I love you," he groans, standing in the doorway, not wanting to leave, needing some reassurance of her feelings. "You're beautiful, a goddess."

Mrs. Diana Frank smiles.

"Why do you laugh?"

"You'd better hurry, Ronald. He's due home any moment."

For a second he thinks that he will dare to wait for the husband. Confront him, beat him to the ground and run off with Mrs. Diana Frank.

"But, when can I see you again?"

"I don't know. Maybe never again. Don't worry. There'll be others."

"But I don't want others, I want you," says Ronald Rowe too loudly.

"Better hurry. I think I see his car."

Ronald Rowe freezes in a pose, then breaks into a sprint to his motor scooter. He jumps on the saddle, slams his foot on the pedal, guns the vehicle and rattles off into the sunset.

"I'll call," he yells at her. "I love you!"

Mrs. Diana Frank shuts the door and goes to the bar to mix a gin and tonic and think about what to make for dinner.

2.

The Club's façade is that of a nondescript health spa for the affluent businessman. Handball court, sauna, steam bath, massage, physiotherapy, a gym for weight lifting, &tc. It takes a stiff registration fee to join the Club and, even then, you have to be thoroughly screened to qualify.

Mr. Kendrick Frank makes it a point to go to the Club at least once a week. He usually goes on Thursday because that's when he's assured of Hans Von Gumnode's services.

After a draining steam bath, sitting on the hot stone steps watching the mid-morning Greek wrestling display performed by beautifully formed young boys in loincloths, Mr. Kendrick Frank walks shakily down the hall to Room One. There awaits Hans Von Gumnode, the Viennese masseur, cracking his knuckles.

"Ah, Mr. Frank," snaps Gumnode, slapping the leather table with his powerful hand, "let's get down to business."

Hans Von Gumnode is a tall, blond, blue-eyed, bronzed ex-Hitler Youth whose father, Kommandant Shrike Von Gumnode, now operates an international chemical-warfare complex in South America. He was one of Hitler's top authorities on chemical expediency in the concentration camps. Hans once told Mr. Kendrick Frank how his father took him, a little boy, in his well-pressed Hitler Youth uniform, touring through Blaurottenkompf Concentration Camp, Kommandant Shrike Von Gumnode's model extermination center.

"Ah, yes," said the powerful, square-jawed Von Gumnode, "room after room of bubbling stainless steel vats and tubs. All rooms were air-conditioned. In fact," he chuckled, "my father, the Kommandant, found a way to make a deodorizer from the ground-up Jew bones which he sprinkled through the air-conditioning system. Pretty good, huh?"

As a joke, the Kommandant picked his son up by the ankles and held him over one of the bubbling cauldrons. They were on a ramp, high above the row after row of vats and tubs. "I showed no fear, naturally. The Kommandant was so pleased he gave me my first Luger and let me shoot a few Jews to feed the Police dogs. Pretty good, huh?"

Hans Von Gumnode always wears a skintight black T-shirt over his magnificent torso of ripe and hard muscles, white pants and white sneakers. Narrow hips which spring into his powerful thigh muscles which seem to be breaking through the white cloth around them.

"First, your massage," he says, patting the leather-covered table once more. "Off with your sheet, Mr. Frank. Here, let me."

There's no need for Mr. Kendrick Frank to conceal, nor feel ashamed by, his sudden flowering. His cock, as a conditioned reflex, swells into a hard scepter as soon as Hans Von Gumnode pulls the sheet off his body.

"Ha, be patient, Mr. Frank."

Mr. Kendrick Frank gets onto the table.

Hans Von Gumnode begins to manipulate Mr. Kendrick Frank's unmuscular back.

"Yah. War is war," begins Von Gumnode, whose monologue is a soothing counter-rhythm to the prodding of his powerful fingers. "And man will fight forever, which is good if you're a soldier and, let's face it, some people are meant to be soldiers. So."

Mr. Kendrick Frank's bones pop and grind under Hans Von Gumnode's hands and Mr. Kendrick Frank sighs in sweet agony and, as often happens, he breaks wind.

"Besides, with the world overflowing with useless people, it is right to find efficient methods to dispose of them. We must return to our perfect order. No?"

Mr. Kendrick Frank grunts his assent, wondering if he would ever be included in the perfect order.

When Von Gumnode is finished massaging him, Mr. Kendrick Frank's body throbs from head to toe in a total pulse of agony and & light. One side of his head rests in the sweat, wet comfort of the leather. He begins to doze, to let the inner waves of muscles and tendons unbunch and relax. Von Gumnode hums a tuneless measure.

"An old childhood song," he mutters, tidying up his shelf of liniments, lotions and assorted accouterments. "The Kommandant would sing it to me during the early days when the easiest way to dispose of the Jews was in bonfires."

But Mr. Kendrick Frank, for the moment, hears nothing and dozes off. One arm hangs over the table's edge. He dreams about being dropped into a vat of boiling blood. It is like looking through a red filter.

As is their tradition, Hans Von Gumnode lets Mr. Kendrick Frank sleep for fifteen minutes before waking him up for the second phase of their weekly ritual.

M-609 knocks on the door.

Von Gumnode opens it and nods.

"Right on the nose," he says.

M-609 nods and takes off his bright yellow and royal blue boxer's robe and hangs it on a hook on the door.

He is naked and is smaller than Von Gumnode. A short, trim man with a nose broken in two places and a cross-shaped scar on his rippling abdomen. His hair is short and his hairline is low so that it sometimes looks as if his eyebrows grow into it. His eyes are small and narrow and set deep into his head.

"I have the whips here," says Von Gumnode and opens the footlocker under the table. "And the other stuff. Of course."

M-609 nods.

"Yes," says Von Gumnode, "I'll go into the other room and get undressed. You can wake him up."

M-609 nudges Mr. Kendrick Frank rather harshly.

"Up," he says, and yanks the sheet off Mr. Kendrick Frank's body.

Groggily, Mr. Frank gets off the table and stands before M-609, who is a head shorter than he.

Von Gumnode reenters the room nude. His cock has two tiny swastikas tattooed on each side of the prick's eye. His organ is formidable and Mr. Kendrick Frank awakens quickly.

Today, it is his turn to be the Object. Every third week he is the Object and Mr. Kendrick Frank begins to tremble with dark joy. What a grand day today will be, he thinks with glee. After lunch he plans on a rendezvous with Hertha "Big 'n Busty" Blax.

M-609 straps the elephant-cock dildo around his waist.

Hans Von Gumnode says, "On your knees, Jew, and Heil Hitler, Heeb!"

Whimpering, Mr. Kendrick Frank falls to his knees before the two tiny swastikas which begin to widen as Von Gumnode's member starts to swell. And swell.

Von Gumnode lies on the floor to get a better grip on Mr. Kendrick Frank's head and, also, to give M-609 a better target to aim for. M-609 has been circling the two, a bit top-heavy with the elephant-cock dildo held in both of his hands.

Mr. Kendrick Frank's mouth is barely able to cover Von Gumnode's crown ("The balls. Ah, yes, hold them gently in your hands.") and cannot scream when M-609 rams his pole into him. The impact helps Mr. Kendrick Frank to widen his mouth some more and gobble an extra inch of Von Gumlnode's cockmeat.

As he comes, Hans Von Gumnode screams in German and starts clicking his heels, which is extremely painful to Mr. Kendrick Frank who is locked between his thighs, choking down the hot hose-thrust semen.

Von Gumnode is finished and stands up.

"Ah, wonderful," he grunts.

As is the custom, M-609 looks down upon Mr. Kendrick Frank and starts to spit on his face and chest. The bubbly sputum warmly runs down his cheeks and pectorals. Mr. Kendrick Frank has his first orgasm of the day.

The pearly fluid shoots up and then dribbles down Mr. Kendrick Frank's raw red tool. M-609 spits on the hot throbbing flesh and Mr. Kendrick Frank feels tears of joy dim his vision.

M-609 turns away, takes his robe off the hook and leaves Room One, slamming the door.

"Well, time's up, Mr. Frank. See you next week."

"Of course," mutters Mr. Kendrick Frank, ignoring the clean white towel Hans Von Gumnode waves in his face.

3.

Hertha Blax feels lousy. A hangover throbs in her head and wants to crush her skull with pain. Small memento from last night's carouse at Dock 9, a hangout for longshoremen who drink beer and cheap whiskey, usually together, and play endless games of dice, half-size table pool and the two pinball machines. There's also a jukebox there which the bartender turns up full notch at night.

Hertha Blax lost her dubious cool halfway through the night and became her usual lusty, loud earth-mother self, barking obscenities back and forth with the men and, all the while, trying to figure out which one was going to spend the night with her. (It turned out that five of them rented a hotel room for the engagement and it didn't break up until dawn when the docks opened their iron gates. Hertha doesn't remember that they left. For an hour the man she thought was giving her head turned out to be a pillow.)

Her flat is in an alleyway in Chinatown. It consists of a living room which enters into a bedroom. Her kitchen's in a closet. Hertha doesn't do much cooking on her hotplate but secretly yearns for the day when she'll be able to have a kitchen of her own. Often, looking out the window at the bricks of the alley wall, Hertha Blax wonders if being an earth-mother is not a costly role.

Flash photos of Hertha "Big 'n Busty" Blax decorate her living room walls. They are photos of Hertha in action, in every kind of action involving almost every kind of position and passion. The pictures are the main decoration, outside of the muddy-colored sofa rotting and dripping springs and stuffing. The floor is linoleum-covered and is swollen to conform with the floor's structural defects. There are two straight-back chairs in the living room and in front of the sofa is a chrome-based, black, formica-top table with an ashtray on top of it.

A Chinaman coughs his lungs out next door. He's been coughing like that for years. There's nothing Hertha can do for him. He doesn't speak English and whenever they meet in the hall, his TB-flaming eyes widen and the Chinaman cheeps and whines percussive words to her. Oh well.

This Kendrick Frank fellow. Oh God, how she wishes he wasn't coming today! Besides the hangover, her cunt is still sore from last night's debauch. (It's a drag, she thinks, when you can't remember who the bloody hell you were with. Especially if there were five of them and, who knows, one of them might have gotten the wrong impression about what kind of lady I am.)

Arnold, the cat, pads into the room mewing his irritating sound. Hertha gets up and goes to the window and opens it. There's Arnold's Half and Half on the window ledge. (No ice-box in her closet kitchen, just a hot plate and a few shelves.)

"Alright, you bloody ingrate," she says to Arnold. Whenever she pours the Half and Half into Arnold's bowl, she grits her teeth at the cost. Ordinary fucking cats drink milk and like it. Arnold will only drink Half and Half and, twice a week demands a pound of calf liver in his bowl. The rest of the time he settles for ground-round patties.

Hertha Blax opens a warm beer and drinks as much as she can without tasting it.

Her head and eyes are so seeded with pain that Hertha cannot even go through her mail, other than to check for money orders, cash or checks. And that bothers her too. About the money. Goddamn that William Blake Rothenstein. Rothenstein, like it or not, and she no longer likes it, is Hertha "Big 'n Busty" Blax's exclusive photographer. He takes all the pictures, process-es them, and, once a week, brings over a supply and a stack of mimeograph photo-offer sheets which Hertha has to enclose with all of the first-time letters she mails off to various correspondents requesting more information about her.

Her breasts ache. Each tip has an insistent pain core that pulses regularly, which keeps time to the racket in her head.

Goddamn that William Blake Rothenstein. He doesn't even give me money for postage stamps.

Mr. Kendrick Frank parks his silver-gray Lincoln Continental a few blocks away from her address. He walks slowly, observing the depressed streets and rat-eyed folk who glance at him as he walks. This excites him all the more. To be able to gain admittance to a woman whose services belong to the scum of mankind. Ah, what a day today is. Lean-faced groups of men loitering before the pool hall know who Mr. Kendrick Frank is before he sees them. A little urchin in a Batman T-shirt and short pants grabs ahold of Mr. Kendrick Frank's sleeve.

"Wanna fuck my sister? Three bucks an' two bucks for a blow-job," the urchin announces, digging at his crotch for lice.

Mr. Kendrick Frank walks on.

"Tsst, tsst," like the sound of a cobra and it's a tiny Filipino in a tan suit too big for him and a snap-brim hat and shoes sparkling with a new shine. "Fucky, fucky, fucky?" he whispers, his pink tongue the cobra's tongue, spinning across his wet thin lips.

A drunk slides into him, breathing distilled nose-melting fumes.

"Look," the drunk begins.

Mr. Kendrick Frank walks on. Or starts to. The drunk stamps his foot on the cement.

"Now, look," he says, and Mr. Kendrick Frank looks at the man whose fly is half-open and whose coat doesn't match his pants. The drunk's face is puffy and red and speckled with the unshaved white and black sprouts of beard.

"Look, I want you to listen. You hear?" Mr. Kendrick Frank nods.

"Alright. Look, I want you to know that I know everything there is to know an' I want a quarter so I can keep alive with my wisdom an' knowledge an', look, make it a buck. A man's gotta live."

Mr. Kendrick Frank reaches into his pocket and finds only a nickel there. All the rest of his money is paper.

"Look," screams the drunk.

But Mr. Kendrick Frank walks on.

Then it's Chinatown and Mr. Kendrick Frank's glands and hopes are near bursting. All the Charlie Chan mystery of the Chinese drifts in his mind. The opium dens, the concubines, the Tongs, the chopsticks, ivory, gold and incense. And the sinister dirtiness and corrupt insidious nature of the mongrel race. Oh what would a Chinese whore be like? Or a Filipino one? He sees himself surrounded by cobras while she opens her dark thighs and smiles and all her gold teeth gleam and her pimps pull out whips and slice silver dollars in the air. They're probably too small for an American cock, he thinks. Then sees him forcing some Chinese lady's jaws apart with his cock. Or in an opium den; to lay there in the sweaty dark, the sweet sick stench of the simmering ball, and Fu Manchu, the pimp, fingernails as long as umbrella handles, extracting the pellet for his pipe and all of them, like in the movie, Slack-jaw dreamers on dirty cots.

Flash of her tits, her hips, her magnificent maternal air to violate and, at the same time, be violated by. Mr. Kendrick Frank is at the alley entrance and wipes the sweat from his brow with a $3.00 handkerchief.

"Ah, Hertha Blax," he says when she opens the door.

Then Mr. Kendrick Frank asks for a glass of water and Hertha has to leave the room to walk down the hall to the community bathroom. That's where the sink is.

When she returns, Arnold is in Mr. Kendrick Frank's lap and Mr. Kendrick Frank is looking at some of the photographs of her on the wall.

He takes three pills, swallows them down with the water which tastes of rust and trace minerals whose value is not yet known to man.

"Ah, Hertha Blax," he announces again.

"What can I do for you?"

"Ah, what can I do for *you?*"

"What, are you a whip freak?"

"Sometimes."

"Wanna see my bullwhip?"

"Later," says Mr. Kendrick Frank.

Hertha Blax sighs. For a moment she thought the afternoon would be over quickly if all he wanted was a whipping.

"Were them asprins you took? I could sure use an asprin right now."

"They're just as good, even better," says Mr. Kendrick Frank.

"They untie the knots."

"I could sure use an ice-cold beer," says Hertha.

"Say, so could I. Why don't you take a few of these pills for your headache and I'll be right back with some beer."

They both stand up together.

She's almost as tall as he is and, before she can duck, Mr. Kendrick Frank is poking his hot tongue into her mouth and jamming his foot through her legs. She notices that he smells of cologne.

"See you in a flash," says Mr. Kendrick Frank, his mouth a smear of Hertha Blax's dime-store lipstick.

What the hell, and she takes the pills, washing them down with the water left in the cup.

The beer is cold and they both sit on the sofa ripping off can-keys. She's first to guzzle down a good half of the half-quart can. It scratches and chills her throat and, lo and joy her headache's gone.

Mr. Kendrick Frank sticks his tongue in her ear while fondling a large breast.

"Say, let me finish my beer," says Hertha huskily. "Don't be such a goddamned eager beaver. There's a right way to do everything. Goddamnit."

And Mr. Kendrick Frank grabs her head and puts it in his lap.

"Suck it," he whispers into her ear.

"I ain't standing up or kneeling down for nothing until I finish my beer."

Mr. Kendrick Frank feels the fire of forbidden orders and secret ice in the belly overwhelm him.

"What do you do for a living?" she asks.

"Eat pussy," snarls Mr. Kendrick Frank, trying to sound like Victor McLaglen.

"Aw, come on. Let's have another beer, Mr. Frank."

"Call me Ken," he says and hands her another half-quart can of beer.

She rips off the can-key and swallows the cold numbing beer with a little less passion than before. Hertha's getting to feel more comfortable. The pills hit and, for the moment, it's as if all of her bones are suddenly pulled out of her body.

"Wheww-eee," she sighs. "Gimme a kiss, lover-boy, before I faint."

Mr. Kendrick Frank kisses her and Hertha grabs hold of him and hugs. Her hug robs him of immediate breath. She has a tangy odor about her body. Smelling of burnt chestnuts, sea salt and beer, Hertha Blax thrusts her tongue into his mouth and pushes it halfway down his throat.

Her hands to the magnet and they pull on his hardened cock-stem while she continues her kiss. Hertha presses against him until she's on top of him and he cannot move. Smothered in her heat and odor, he manages to get one hand free to grab hold of Hertha Blax's meaty buttocks. Mr. Kendrick Frank digs in.

"Oooh, nice," burbles Miss Blax.

"Ohh, God," he groans on her bed.

Arnold, the cat, on her naked back while she suckles Mr. Kendrick Frank's raw cock. Her suction is so intense he can feel blood blisters burst along his shaft.

"Don't come," she says, pulling her mouth off of his cock with a popping sound.

"No, no," he mutters.

Arnold springs onto his chest, forgetting to pull in his claws.

"Oww."

"Shh."

Her forest cunt is in his mouth and the oven of her inner thighs burns against his cheek. Her oven door, open, sends forth waves of earthy stench into his nose gone wet with her juices. At first he wants to suck in his breath, but then, because he must suffer, he smells it deeply into his lungs while sloshing his tongue through the fields of her vaginal acres. Tip to clitoris which awakens her alarm system. She screeches and, as a habit, grabs her pillow and covers her head so she can scream all the louder.

Arnold, the scoundrel, begins to pick at a thread on Mr. Kendrick Frank's black stretchsock.

And with her other hand, Hertha Blax reaches behind to feathery feel Mr. Kendrick Frank's burning rod. With practiced fingers, she barely touches the straining organ, increasing his stimulation, giving more thrust to his tongue.

Finally into her inferno with his cock wanting to relieve its need.

But not so quickly, Kendrick Frank, suddenly gripped in a new death-hug of legs wrapped around his neck, wants to be driven into her like a plow-share.

"Eyoww!" says Hertha Blax.

His cock sinks into the burning wet silk of her well-used cunt and seems to get lost in the spaciousness of it.

Then she's riding him, his cock still jammed up to the juicy hilt. Her expansive buttocks slamming upon his belly.

Then they're sideways. One of her fleshy meat-slab legs slung over his hip and one of her hands boring a tunnel up his arse while the other hand tickles his aching balls.

The more they fuck, the louder Hertha gets. Her grunts and groans and squeals and moans become a sonata—nay, a symphony of bed-spring twanging, earth-opening, lust and heat.

And when his mistress celebrates her ecstasy Arnold joins her and, if you listen closely, you'll also hear the Chinaman coughing.

Mr. Kendrick Frank is delirious with sweat, stench, blind fuck-madness and hysteria. The noises, animal or otherwise, drive his timing off and the pills drive his timing off and the reality of Hertha Blax's momentum drives his timing off.

"My fucking timing!" he screams.

There's a profound silence.

"Is that your shot?" asks Hertha. "A fuck-tight can't-come tease?"

She's breathing heavily. Her flesh rippling with the orgasm seeking out.

"Suck me," he says.

"Go to hell," she says.

Arnold pads out of the bedroom to his bowl of Half and Half.

"Beat me, I'm terrible," he whines.

"Go to hell," she says.

Then she massages his balls and his cock returns to action and they're back into it again.

"I could come forever," she screams at the end of her orgasm.

"Forever and ever."

Mr. Kendrick Frank looks glumly down at his shriveled cock. The bed sheets are dirty with their spilt juices. It feels as if there are cracker crumbs beneath him.

This is the way it always is with this kind of woman who just wants to fuck. Mr. Kendrick Frank lies there thinking how rotten the room smells and how gross and unkempt her body is and how stupid sex is.

"O, I could fuck a million of 'em all night long," she says to herself, still luxuriating in her subsiding orgasm. "A million different shapes and sizes of peckers and each one doing the same thing to me, yet each one different. O, I could come forever. Couldn't you see Heaven as just one continuous coming? Like stars. Couldn't you see that?"

Mr. Kendrick Frank feels as if he is going to vomit. He can smell catshit and poverty and, suddenly, flashbulbs.

William Blake Rothenstein emerges from the cardboard closet in the bedroom.

"Great, guys," he says. "See you later, Hertha, baby. I'll notify you when the prints are available."

4.

"Doc" Krantz sits on a ratty cloth-back deck chair chewing on a half-lit, bitter-smelling Italian cigar. Krantz grunts, breaks wind with the sound of a ratchet, and kicks an empty squashed beer can into the sheet metal wall of his living room.

"Anyhow," says Grubb, his crony, "the Parker kids'll come if you give 'em some Xtra-Pop Super-Red Bubblegum. A case of it."

"Fuckin' kids," snarls Krantz. "Give 'em a taste and they want a feast. Okay, Grubb, here's a fin. Go out and get their fuckin' bubblegum and a sixpack of cheap beer. And a poorboy of white port."

General Le May, cut out of a Sunday magazine supplement, is tacked onto the wall next to a dime-store framed portrait of General MacArthur.

Krantz goes to them and gazes at the color-faded square-jawed Le May. Other pictures nailed into the sheet-metal wall: Shirley Temple Black, Jackie Kennedy, Lyndon Baines Johnson, another photo from *Life* magazine of LBJ, Lady Bird, Lynda Bird and Lucy Bird in full color now fading, and brown-toned snapshots of Krantz in Sicily, Krantz in North Africa, and Krantz in Berlin. (The group of Krantz in Moscow he destroyed in the late '50s after swearing his sins away to the five o'clock shadow glare of Senator Joseph McCarthy.) In fact, one entire sheet-metal wall is covered with photographs and drawings torn out of magazines, as well as snapshots and dime-store ikons. It's a map of Krantz's dreams and history. He is obsessed by Camel cigarette ads and all through the weird collage are ancient Camel cigarette ads (Ronny Reagan endorsing them, white-frocked MD's endorsing them, football players endorsing them, the T-Zone, and, finally, a weird poster of the engraved camel standing near the engraved pyramid). Oddly enough, Krantz only smokes gnarled, black-leaf-wrapped Italian cigars whose tobacco is as dry as desert sand and smells, perhaps, like burning camel chips.

"Doc" Krantz pats the skin circle on his skull. A habitual

fondling of that pink island surrounded by wisps of gray and black hairs. It's as if Krantz still can't believe that he's bald.

Krantz tries to remember Margot's face, his ex-wife. All he can remember is her body. Margot had boobs almost as big as the broad coming over in the afternoon. But Margot's boobs were freckled with clusters of moles. While Krantz was off to the war, ridding the world of the Nazis, bringing the lights back, the white cliffs of Dover, a Sentimental Journey, killing Krauts to make the world ready for Democracy, Margot Krantz was getting herself knocked-up by flyboys who hung out at a local cocktail lounge. Margot must have had two dozen abortions during Krantz's tour of duty. The last one proved her undoing. A Mexican doctor, he said he was a doctor, with dirty hands and his breath smelling of bourbon, did the job while a hard-faced dyke nurse held Margot down on the table. The Mexican doctor was all Margot could afford. Luke, the bartender, told her about him. Oh, he's alright, said Luke, he does it for everybody. No antibiotics, sulphur, penicillin, just aspirin to fight the massive infection in her uterus. Krantz, the conquering hero, returned home expecting, at least, a flag in the window or some ribbons on the door, something like his buddy Furstworth got. Krantz would have been home sooner but he got involved in the Furstworths' block-party and was drunk for two days and laid about everybody's hot-cunted daughter on that block. God bless America, all those pink-cheeked hot pants said, and shoved a burning tit into his hand and filled his glass with black market booze and plopped more black market steak on his paper plate. Krantz would have gotten home sooner but the hangover and heartburn laid him low in a YMCA for a couple more days. When he was able to fit into his uniform again, Krantz took the Greyhound home. Margot didn't answer the door. The house was dark and smelled of rubbing alcohol. All the windows closed, the shades drawn. Hey, baby, yelled Krantz, I'm home. She was in the bedroom. Ten church candles were burning before the Madonna on her dresser. He thought she was dead and that this was the funeral parlor. She wasn't dead, she was dying. The disease had burned away all of her flesh until she was shriveled to a child's gaunt form. She was delirious and when she talked, it was baby talk and babble.

Grubb walks in with the bubblegum, beer and port.

"Gimme a shot of the port first," says Krantz.

"I'll get your cup," says Grubb.

"Out of the bottle. I need it now."

Grubb unscrews the bottle cap and hands it over to Krantz who drinks from it making guttural gurgles as he slops it down.

"Pheww. It tastes like they got this out of a gas tank."

"Gimme a pull," says Grubb, grabbing the bottle away from Krantz. "Say, wheww, it sure is rank. Ain't it, anyhoo?"

"When're the Parker kids coming?"

"After school. I don't know. Maybe three or three-thirty."

"Hey, that'll work out fine, Grubb. The cunt is coming here at two an' we can give her a one-two before the kids come."

"Yeah," says Grubb, a metaphysical student. "Everything has a way of workin' out."

"You bet," says Krantz.

And when he went to the icebox to give her some ice to press upon her fevered brow, Krantz saw that one tray was filled with jars. I wonder what Margot's been pickling? he thought. When he realized what was in the first jar, it fell from his hand to the floor.

Krantz had never seen a fetus before except in high-school textbooks.

"Women are pigs and cows and whores," says Krantz, drinking down some more white port. "They're out to get you and cut off your balls if they can."

"Amen," says Grubb.

"You got to get them before they get you."

"Right. Gimme the port."

"If you let them get you, you're a goner."

"You better believe it," says Grubb. This is a ritual incanting. Something like a morning hymn. "My first wife, Edith Shark Charlotte, was as vicious a shrew as ever lived. Ever. She'd be breaking my stashed bottles and calling up my boss to check on me and always makin' our bed a place of carnage."

"Rotten luck, Grubb."

"Fuckin' her was like boring into a barbed-wire tunnel. Her old nasty mean an' dried up cunt must've been lined with sandpaper and fiberglass. Anyhoo, after her, I took it easy for a while. Quit the job, left the state, got caught by cops and sent to jail for not payin' Edith Shark Charlotte's alimony. Hell, she had everything, the fuckin' house, the goddam car, my beautiful short-wave Zenith radio, shit…"

"I hear you, Grubb, tell it like it is."

"Out a jail an' into the street. Skid Row Paradise…"

Krantz hands him the bottle.

"Ahh…then this social worker, Christ, with the face of Mary found me in a doorway an' took me to her people an' they fed me, clothed me, got me on the go again an', before you know it, I'm drafted an' I got a gun in my hand an' I'm fightin' off Japs who are yellow monkeys who are everywhere I look. And in Japan, I court Miss Sukifuzi Quimzo, who's a geishy girl in the Ginza an' I can't tell you how great a cunt worker she was. Man, now them Nips got a way of trainin' their women to be humble to the man an' act as if the whole world belongs to him—and the way she'd fix me up when I got home from war. Yeh, an' she had the neatest box I ever stuck my cock into. All fire and muscle and not a trick in the book she didn't know. Yes sir. Well, anyhoo…"

Krantz remembers the ninth time at the Clinic for his penicillin shot. That was France. Paris, France. Those girls in rags still had a kind of class the way they'd peddle their ass on the street. Ass for a Hershey bar, that was for Krantz. And almost all of those sweet teenage hustlers gave him the clap. The last one, Madame LaBaul, let Krantz stay a weekend at her ratty château outside of Paris and there he was inducted into the realm of sexual deviation. Krantz was an ass man. A quick kiss, a solid jab into the cunt with his cock, a quick friction, a fast come. Madame LaBaul was a fetishist, a retired AC-DC madam who decided to educate Krantz to sado-masochistic rituals. Krantz, a primal Catholic, was suddenly elevated to realize how moral shame was. Madame LaBaul was an eager dominatrix. She nearly keelhauled him into submission. Made Krantz a snack of her turds which he had to eat or else be bullwhipped. And Madame LaBaul was no feather. Nearly six feet tall, she had a broad back, mammoth breasts, and rock-hard muscles where it counted. The first time Krantz was whipped, he came thrice. Naked and chained to the basement's whipping post and Madame LaBaul was there to catch his seed in her mouth, then spit it on him. It was wonderful, after he understood the rules, and on the last night, she let Krantz be the master. Five birdlike French whores were brought in and it may have been a ghost-play of DeSade. There was buggery, friggery, punishment, pain and assorted shameful debauchery. All of this led Krantz to the Clinic for his ninth shot. He got to the Clinic too late and they had to remove one of his balls and scrape off some strange mold from his cock.

"...she says to me an' I punch her in her fuckin' mouth with the bottle, six stitches, a three-hundred-dollar bridge, an' it's back to the can for a couple of years. Just because I wouldn't take the fuckin' dog for a walk. Of course we was drinkin' a little," says Grubb, on his third wife now. Grubb's been married four times and wears khaki workshirts.

The more they drink, the quieter Krantz gets. Grubb, after a while of monologue, shuts up too and they turn on the radio to hear the Reverend Billy James Hargis deliver his noontime sermon.

By midafternoon, Krantz and Grubb are on their third bottle of white port and second sixpack of beer.

"How many Japs'd you really kill?" asks Krantz.

"Barehand or with my gun or with a knife?"

"All of the ways."

"Jeez, who knows! You know how, after a while, they all look alike."

"You know the first Kraut I killed," says Krantz, breaking wind which turns into a dribble of loose shit smashed in his underpants. "The first Kraut I killed looked like that kid in the Yearling movie, that Claude Jarmon, Jr. Never forget it because we'd seen the movie the night before."

"How'd it feel?" asks Grubb.

"I don't know. Good, I guess. It woulda been better if I hadn'ta seen that movie the night before."

"How'd you do it?"

"Two bullets in his face an' a bayonet to his gut."

"First Nip I killed, I used a flamethrower. Cleanup squad…"

"Yeh, sure," says Krantz, opening a new can of beer. "I saw it in newsreels."

"Sometimes you can't tell how important them Japs are. All charred up like that. You never know how old they are either. But the first one I figure was a general. I gave it to him straight on an' he just blew up into flame an' all them other monkeys come scramblin' out a the cave an' I just keep the flame pointed to the opening an' burn 'em all up. Got a medal for it. Sure, my captain was a little pissed. For a while. But, fuck, he says later, a dead Jap's the best."

How many men did Krantz see dead on the field with hard-ons saluting the sky? How many men did Krantz know who jerked-off while dying?

Or the men pissing in their fatigues in foxholes when the mortar and shells start flying. Or the kids shitting in their BVDs. Or crying with their guts all tangled in the dirt. Shit, where was Erroll Flynn—in North Africa?—when the mine nearly tore off Krantz's leg? Instead, Krantz's knee is heavy with a plate where the bone was.

Krantz didn't care after two months on the front about who he was killing or why. The sound track of war no longer bothered his ears. It was best to be able to get a Jap from behind and kill him with your hands.

What is moral to a man who has taken another man's life? Krantz got into war's pace.

"Hey, Krantz, what are you thinkin' about?"

"I'm thinkin' that that cunt better be ready to take whatever we give her."

"Ah, Krantz, you and them cunts from the magazines. Them magazines are for freaks."

"Kill freaks. Ain't that what we fought for?"

"Times are strange," says Grubb.

"Freaks are cunts an' they should get whatever we can give them."

"Sure. Sure. She sure got knockers, huh? Hell, each of us could get lost just feeling her tits."

Grubb drains the third bottle's half-inch of port. Smacks his lips.

"Fuck, I'm out a money," he says.

"Here, Grubb, here's a buck. Get a fifth of the shit. The kids like the shit too."

Krantz sits back in his old cloth-back deck-chair and looks crookedly at the pictures nailed onto his sheet-metal wall. They blur together like the smoke inside a crystal ball.

5.

"Come in, cunt," growls Krantz.

Mrs. Diana Frank opens the door. She is dressed in bright colors, reds and oranges, and shines in the doorway. She smells wine and beer and sweat and stale urine as she shuts the door.

Grubb grabs her from behind. One hand digs through her dress and presses against her mound. His other hand mashes into one of her breasts.

"Ha, she ain't wearin' panties or a bra," says Grubb and rips off her skirt. It swirls in his hands, a red matador's torn cape, and floats serenely down to the floor.

Krantz squints at her bush and the black hose on her legs and her soft white belly flat and firm between her hips.

"Turn around, cunt," he growls.

Mrs. Diana Frank turns around and faces Grubb.

Krantz analyzes her rear end.

Grubb looks into her eyes and she looks at Grubb's ravaged face. One eyelid is lower than the other on Grubb's face. There's a small white chip of a scar denting the contour of his upper lip. He needs a shave and his eyes are wet and bloodshot and his breath comes out heavy facing her. His breath smells of beef jerky, port, beer, raw onions, yesterday's compost, a mulch of rot and time. Mrs. Diana Frank winces slightly. Grubb takes that as an expression of her passion for him and rips off her blouse.

"Turn around, cunt," orders Krantz.

Mrs. Diana Frank turns around. Naked, outside of her black hose and pumps, she looks at Krantz while Krantz observes her breasts which are swollen in their ripe time and whose nipples are a dark red.

"Come here, cunt," says Krantz to her, and she walks to where he sits.

He pokes his thumb in her bush.

"Wanna drink before we get to work on you, you flesh bag of old cum?"

She nods.

"Grubb, give her some of th' old cunt special brew."

Grubb nods cheerfully and pees into a milk bottle. Steam of his emission curls over the bottle's glass lips. He hands it to Mrs. Diana Frank.

"Drink."

Mrs. Diana Frank shakes her head.

"Go on, cunt, drink it."

Grubb grabs her by the neck, and bends her back and attempts to pour it down her closed mouth. Instead the yellow liquid splashed down her chin and onto her breasts and drips onto the floor.

Krantz laughs darkly.

"Here, cunt, have some port," he says and hands the bottle to her.

Mrs. Diana Frank puts the bottle to her lips, cautiously smells it, then takes a long swig off it.

Grubb's on his hands and knees before her, chewing her cunt lips.

"Grubb's hungry, cunt."

Krantz laughs again.

Grubb tries to push the port bottle into her cunt and Mrs. Diana Frank squirms away, trips on spilled pee, and slides into Carl "Doc" Krantz who grabs her head and pushes it into his lap.

"Chew on it, cunt," he orders.

She chews around the firm form that is hidden by the cloth of his pants.

Grubb watches with his cock in his hand, pinching her buttocks with the other.

"Get up, cunt."

Mrs. Diana Frank stands up and so does Krantz.

"Take my pants off and suck me," says Krantz.

His underpants are stained yellow and haven't been washed for a while. When she pushes them down around his knees, the smell of his body is overpowering. One knee is scarred. His legs are thin and knobby. But it is his cock that fascinates her with its deep brick-red flush poking out. And the one ball dangling beneath it.

"Start on the ball," says Krantz.

Mrs. Diana Frank gets on her knees and, holding her breath, begins to tongue the hanging sac, trying to duck Krantz's feverish cock which keeps twitching and banging into her forehead. She moves under the ball. His hairy brown and black rectal geography is in view. Opening her mouth, and exhaling, Mrs. Diana Frank slowly, gently, suckles Krant's one ball until it is almost totally inside her mouth.

"She's alright," says Grubb.

"She'll do," groans Krantz. "Go back. Get in my bunghole. That always stops 'em. It's alright when they're kids to play with shit but they get so fucked-up double-crossed when they get older, grow up. Right, Grubb?"

"Sure, sure," he answers and stumbles to the bottle near the canvas chair. Grubb's cock hangs out of his open fly.

"Get going, cunt."

Mrs. Diana Frank props her back against a large coffee can filled with sand that Krantz squashes cigars into. Holding onto his thighs, she maneuvers her mouth under his butt and pushes her tongue thru the hairy cheeks.

It is a purge. Guilt, shame. Guilt, shame. She is punished the way she has always thought her punishment should be given her. Her tongue tastes sweat salt and fecal particles. Her tongue pushes thru tiny bum-hairs and probes the hot bottom which parts.

Krantz lets go with one of his ratchet farts. The stench burns her tongue, jams up her nostrils, pushes down her throat. Grubb kicks the coffee can from under her and Mrs. Diana Frank falls, backward, onto the floor, gasping and gagging.

Krantz spits a phlegmy blob on her belly.

"Ah, you cunts. You dumb animal fuck-freak cunts..."

"Hey, Krantz, the Parker kids'll be here in forty minutes. Why don't we get some of our load off on the broad? Just a little, huh?"

"Horny, Grubb?"

Grubb nods brightly, his prick still dangling out of his pants.

"You know me, Krantz, I can't keep out of a bitch's box, especially when she's right in front of me just waitin' to get her quim banged."

There was always somebody to tell her she was wrong. Diana was brought up in that fashion. Her father was weak and cruel. His anger was always soft-spoken. He'd tell her how much she disgusted him, how fat her flesh was, how pale her cheeks—saying it all in a little voice, quietly, politely. "You're the curse of my days. Clumsy, oafish, meaty, nothing but a toadstool."

And mother was a wiry whining woman who screamed all day and all night. She would look at advertisements and hunger for the glories that money could obtain. All of the mail-order catalogs were kept in a bookcase under glass obtainable only by a key. The key worn around her mother's neck. The midafternoon, housework done, Diana would hold as a strangely sacred time. Her mother would unlock the glass case and pull out the mail-order catalogs. A cup of coffee, a cigarette, the radio tuned to a station that played soft cloudlike music. Mother would, thus prepared, journey through the slippery catalog pages.

And the father took to drinking when he came home from work and, then, he would come into Diana's bedroom always stepping on something fragile on the floor, or knocking into something made of glass. Diana was becoming more physically dynamic and the father would fall beside her on the bed and croon to her his agony.

"Nobody knows but God how hard I work and how hard my work is to do. Day after day I work at a job that takes me nowhere and gives me nothing. And nobody to come home to."

One night, a new rite. The father would touch her breasts which were beginning to swell into their exciting form.

"You must beware of false lovers. They take advantage of your flesh and are wrong and bad and immoral."

His hands were gentle upon her breasts and his fingers were curious about her nipples. They would gently stroke them into erect turrets. And all the while, Diana would be silent, eyes shut, pretending to be asleep. The father never spoke of it.

Dirty. Dirty. Shame.

The mother comes home earlier than they thought. The mother had one of her chronic headaches and left the father to get loudly drunk with their neighbors. Finding Diana and Lenny Grove, her first boyfriend, necking on the sofa, listening to cloud music on the radio. The mother watched for a while. Then started screaming. Dirty. Dirty. Shame. Filth. But, mother, we were just kissing. Lenny Grove trapped in a dream. Paralyzed. Iceberg of fear in his heart. Red shock explosions in his cheeks. Dirty. Horrible. Using your tongues like that. Diana flushed so intensely you could almost see steam rising in waves above her head. This was love. All summer they had talked and dreamed together and slowly, because the need and the love grew speechless, they began to kiss and slowly, because the body was such an incredible new discovery in the hands of a lover, they began to press together, softness and hardness. The mother suspected something was wrong. Diana was always in her room, or outside, at the beach (she should've known), quietly sitting, or abruptly standing and charging out of rooms. The mother suspected something. It had to be. The beginning of the pain and darkness. The filth of tongues and thumbs and knees and the ugly man worm stuffed inside of you. The mother suspected something. Another failure. Another woman easily led into failure by another man just interested in infecting the womb with babies and living in squalor and filth and having to bear it all, a broken animal. Filth, rotten, horrible, she screamed, her eyes distended and illuminated with explosive light. What are you saying? What do you mean? Diana asked. You whore, bitch, screamed the mother and Lenny Grove felt his heart ripped apart. What you think is all wrong, he stammered, his voice trying to sound convincing and manly. You, the mother said in a fearful solemn voice, you get out of here and don't ever see, look, touch, do anything with my daughter. She will not be polluted by you anymore. They had talked outside in the summer night on the noisy floor swing about getting married after high school. Going to Europe and maybe living in a pink stucco villa in Spain. You rotten scum of man. Get out of here and if you try to call Diana or if I hear you saw her in school, I'll have you arrested. I'll tell the police that you molested her, that you raped her. Mother, mother, what are you saying? muttered Diana, her insides churning and squeezing and draining life out of her. What are you saying? Then maybe go to Switzerland and live in a chalet and be served big inexpensive breakfasts in bed by cheery, round, red-cheeked Swiss maids. Are you deaf too? Deaf and dumb and helpless like all of them are, all of the men? Their first kiss took two days to achieve and when it happened, they both trembled in the wave of what had been revealed. Stupid, dirty, shameful, pig, pig. I'll send her to a convent. I'll protect her. Pig! The mother shrieking at Lenny Grove. Cords in her neck pressing against the flesh transforming her face.

Grubb's teeth on her nipples make her want to scream in pain. Her legs around his bony shoulder, Grubb fucks her in the cloth-backed chair while standing up, bending down to chew on her nipples. He nibbles on one of them, grinding his teeth into the flesh. Mrs. Diana Frank is cramped and squashed in the chair. His cock jams quickly in and out of her. He comes quickly and doesn't bother to wipe himself off.

"Have her lick it off," says Krantz, who has been watching and drinking.

Grubb's a bit glazed from his coming and staggers to her with his shrinking, wet cock. Mrs. Diana Frank obediently licks off the residue. Licking the crown and along the seam of the stem into the seed pouches whose hairs are wet with juices squirted there during their fucking.

"She's a good ol' cunt," sighs Grubb.

"She'll do," says Krantz. "Okay. Turn around, cunt. Grubb, get her set up on the chair."

The seat of the chair is used as a support for her belly while her palms support the weight of her shoulders. She feels the blood rushing to her head. Krantz enters her from the rear and painfully pushes his prick into that opening. And comes almost immediately. And laughs. And slaps her butt's cheeks.

"I'm not through with you yet, cunt. Don't worry."

Billy and Betty Parker knock on the door.

"Where's the stuff?" asks Billy.

Billy Parker is ten years old and models for homosexual photographs.

"You an' Betty come in here first," says Krantz.

"Got any dope? Any booze?" asks Betty, Billy's twin sister, who has an active and profitable sex-trade at grade school.

Grubb laughs.

"Here y'go, y'little wench."

She swallows a goodly portion of White Rage port and passes the bottle to Billy. Billy quaffs his share.

"You've got to at least show us the carton of Xtra-Pop Super-Red Bubblegum, or I don't unbutton a button," announces Billy.

"Grubb, show him the box."

Grubb steps over Mrs. Diana Frank and pulls the box off a shelf.

"See?"

"How do I know it isn't empty?" asks Betty.

Like a TV salesman, Grubb opens the box and it shines with Xtra-Pop Super-Red Bubblegum.

"Who's the lady?" asks Billy.

"Another dumb cunt that wants to get her ass burned and her mind erased."

"Has she got any diseases?" asks Betty.

"We'll find out later," says Krantz.

"No go," says Billy. "The last time I fucked a broad of yours I stunk for days."

"Examine her," says Krantz.

Betty Parker stands over Mrs. Diana Frank. She is wearing a gingham pinafore and her blonde hair is braided. Betty's skin is peach-colored and her lips are red and glisten with saliva.

Krantz hands her the big flashlight.

Betty gets on her hands and knees.

"Spread."

Mrs. Diana Frank spreads her legs and Betty Parker pushes the huge flashlight into her cunt.

Billy Parker parks his mouthful of bubblegum in Mrs. Diana Frank's cunt. Then he stands on her belly, which hurts, and pees over her breasts and face, which stings.

The kids get carried away and proceed to attempt to destroy Mrs. Diana Frank's body. Betty tries ripping out her pubic hairs by pulling out Billy's bubblegum. Billy takes Krantz's lit cigar and begins burning small circles in her flesh. Grubb gags her after

Mrs. Diana Frank's first scream. Krantz and Grubb spread her legs as far as they will go so Billy Parker can see if he can stick his foot into her cunt. His toenails cut into her quim and she begins to bleed.

Betty Parker sits on Krantz's lap. Krantz's cock is poled into her hairless cunt. Grubb sucks little Billy Parker's cock. They both sit on top of Mrs. Diana Frank. She awaits crucifixion and, finally, bores them all.

"Get her out a here, she's too sick for me," bellows Krantz.

Grubb grabs hold of her hair and pulls her across the floor and out of the door and into the alleyway. It is raining outside.

"Godammit," says Betty Parker, "I forgot to bring my umbrella." Krantz has Billy Parker on his lap. His cock into Billy's bud. "Only kids really know what I know," he groans, erupting. "Kids are great."

Mrs. Diana Frank lies in the alleyway. The rain, a fine misty rain, falls on her body. Her black hose are rolled and rumpled to her ankles. One of her black pumps is missing. A rat scuttles out of a garbage can, lands on her belly, wanders off into another garbage can.

Semiconscious, her hand feels her bloody cunt and then her finger goes into it. The rain on her bruised body. Gray skies. Feels the torn flesh and feels, at last, the pulse of her orgasm begin to move through her body, electric impulse along her spine, into the bowl of her womb, down into her clitoris, the coming, the coming, the pain subsides, her body is washed, absolution, absolved, dissolved, she is green and feels the green fluid replace the blood network through her body woven there, her torn hair is fur that grows, like a beard, over her body, an animal skin, the bear, the deer, and clash of garbage cans smashed together like cymbals, and the children running upon her green furry hills, a march, a dance upon her, no longer flesh, the skin so damaged, but a cloud, silver, a cloud, shame, a cloud, filth, a cloud torn and gray and black, sin, evil, wrong, and her tears slide past her eyes and into cement blended with the rain which falls harder, door slams, what the hell can we do with her, pilgrim's progress, good will win the bad from bed, the bed will win the clouds from hills which haunt the mind, labyrinths, lost there, grove, grotto, Lenny Grove, the love, love, we do not talk, we do not touch, we violate each other, oh, wrong, evil, filth, dirt, damnation, shame, guilt, cloud, blood in the water the oil the rainbow slick shine, dumb cunt, what d'you think, I don't know, call a cab, wrap her up, in feathers and unmilled cotton, fleece of the lamb, the lamb bleats cut throat, spots grass blood, water, sunlight, clothes the color of sunlight, rags wrapped around her body, around her head, chunks of her hair ripped out by children and old men without dreams, how sad, violated, sacrificed, guilt, shame. Lace of dove fur folded together, feathers in harmony, churchspire, break into heaven, dirty shame, guilt, drink, if she could only be forgotten then she could begin again, in a leather seat, water on the floor, lady, Jesus, why do I have to get all the strange ones, dying from the sea, the fish left out of the ocean, mumbles how it was to be the sea, between my legs I am the sea, see me, ah lady, what a mess, you a hippie, take LSD, all the papers, take you to a hospital NO TAKE ME HOME alright forgodsake where's home, it's a number, didn't tell you, the number, ah it's in a house where I have to make dinner, forget it the food isn't there, no house, empty skeleton, forget it, FORGIVE ME I AM ASHAMED the whole world should be ashamed, what happened lady, you're all wet and bloody, try to fly, cut your hair, what happened, hey you ain't got any clothes on I AM SORRY I AM ASHAMED

she remembers and tells him over and over, forty-two Cross Street, 42 X St., 42 Cross Street, over and over, I'll get you there, I'll get you there

"What a dismal mess," says Mr. Kendrick Frank, helping the cabdriver carry her into the house. "Don't you know how to handle yourself?" he whispers into her ear.

"You look awful. We'll have to cancel this weekend."

"I'm ashamed, I'm dirty," she groans.

"Yes, you're awful and I'm hungry and now I'll have to call a doctor and get involved with you and getting you well. You know I loathe sickness, blood and weakness in you."

"I'm ashamed, I'm guilty."

"Oh, shut up."

He pays the cabdriver.

"She drinks too much," he tells him. "A hopeless alcoholic."

"Hopeless shame," she groans.

The door shuts.

"Goddammit, what can I do for you until the doctor comes?" he whines.

"Dirt. Wrong. Shame."

"Shut up!"

"Guilty."

"You're making a mess on the rug."

"Filth. I'm filth."

He dials the doctor.

"Hurry. Emergency. YES, it's awful. She's done it again." He swallows his pills.

"Ruined my whole day," he says.

"Forgive me," she says.

"No."

"Please?" she blubbers.

"No. No. Shut up."

Mr. Kendrick Frank drags his wife up the rug-covered stairs.

"Oh what a mess."

And, panting furiously, he manages to get her onto her bed and cover her up.

"I'll get the maid tomorrow."

"Make me a drink."

"I'm not your nigger," says Mr. Kendrick Frank. "I'm your husband."

"Forgive me."

"Go to hell. I'm going downstairs and wait for the doctor...and, listen, if there's anything really wrong with you, I'll...I'll make you suffer."

III.

TABERNACLE ROCK & ROLL

Oh I asked her for water
Oh she brought me gasoline
Just the terriblest woman
That I had ever seen

—Howlin' Wolf

1.

His breathing is heavy and punctuated by constant gulping and throat-clearing.

"I've got to see you again," he sobs. "Don't you understand?"

It's Ronald Rowe. She was a fool to give him the number. Mrs. Diana Frank will have it changed as soon as he hangs up.

"Don't you know how I'm suffering to touch you again, to tell you how great and endless my love is?"

She lets him go on. Her gin and tonic is fresh and tart and cold and she sips on it.

"How I hate your husband! If I ever saw him I would...I would kill him."

"Oh, come now, Ronald, let's be adult and sophisticated. You're acting quite childish."

"I know, I know," he groans. "I'm torn up inside of myself. Nothing fits together. I quit school..."

"That was foolish."

"I'm working full-time now to make more money so that we, so that I..."

Her wounds have healed. Her torn hair has grown back. Everything submerged once again. New letters to write and read, new photographs, people to meet.

"Ronald, it's all over. It's all part of a game. It has to do with bodies. Not hearts and souls. Give that to another girl."

"Why are you talking to me like that? Is it your husband?"

"No. It's not him..."

"I hate him," snarls Ronald Rowe. "The fool doesn't know what a treasure he has. Is he cruel to you?"

"For God's sake, Ronald, he's an adult sophisticated human being able to play the game according to the rules."

"Is he better than me?"

"No, Ronald."

"I was not good in bed. I'm sorry I was a virgin."

"Ronald, don't be an ass."

"I'm sorry. I'm more than a body. I'll learn. Teach me."

"You're getting hysterical," she says, and lips her gin and tonic.

"I'm a human being too," he says, choking. "I'm more than just a body. I have feelings and dreams and I love you and need you and want you."

"Ronald, you've been calling me almost every day now for a week and, if you care for me, if you care for yourself, I must ask you to stop and leave me alone."

"Impossible. I'd rather kill myself," he announces.

"Oh, Ronald, you're killing yourself by loving me. Please, leave me alone. I don't want you…"

"There are others, aren't there? I knew it. I'm not good enough…"

"Ronald, Ronald, why do you play with me this way? Let me go," says Mrs. Diana Frank.

"Give me a chance to prove myself, my worth. I'll save up enough money and we can run away and live together somewhere, maybe in Europe, or maybe Mexico…"

"I don't want to run away. I'm happy the way I am, Ronald. Don't you understand?"

"How can you be happy when you have to love such an immoral life?"

"What do you mean?" she asks, jaws clenching.

"How can you be happy when you have to sleep with dreams out of magazines? You took me on your bed, the bed your husband and you make love on, and I'm sure I wasn't the first, and that's immoral."

"Ronald, you're a swine."

"At least I've graduated from being an ass."

"Is this how *you* love?"

"Forgive me, forgive me, but I want you."

"I can't be had."

And she hangs up.

And then calls the operator to have her unlisted number changed to another unlisted number. While talking to the robot sing-song voice of the operator. Mrs. Diana Frank has a foggy image of Ronald Rowe swallowing a large bottle of sleeping pills or putting a gun to his soft head. This is ridiculous. He is a young man. A fool. He doesn't understand. The world isn't love.

2.

"Wow," sighs Juno Mab.

"Beautiful," exhales Jim Mab.

They sit in the back of their VW microbus smoking Guatemalan Chrome, a rare pot scored in San Diego. They watch the Richfield gas station's neon sign.

"Too much."

"Right," says Jim Mab.

"Incredible."

"Right," says Jim Mab.

"Wow," they say in unison, both spotting the red "Eat" sign over the drive-in.

The baby's asleep in the basket in a corner next to the brass incense burner. When they're silent, they can hear the baby's smooth breathing in the air. Thor, their German shepherd, sleeps by Juno's feet, snorting and growling softly.

"Are you diggin' the sounds of breathing?"

"Wow," says Juno Mab.

They listen to their baby and dog breathe.

"Snowflake sounds so beautiful," says Jim Mab.

Juno listens to the sounds and with the proper high instinct sifts and sorts breaths until she can beam into Snowflake's breathing.

"Beautiful," she sighs.

"It's a sound of eternal peace."

"Right. Wow," says Juno Mab, contemplating the glory of eternal peace.

"Children are where it's at."

"Wow, right."

"They really got it covered," says Jim, sucking on the water-pipe, drawing more Guatemalan Chrome into his well-seasoned lungs.

Jim Mab passes the pipe to Juno Mab.

She places the hot brass stem to her soft pink lips and inhales a lung-shattering explosion of Guatemalan Chrome.

He turns the AM-FM transistor radio to the rock station.

Meatpacker & the Hooks are in the middle of their two-record composition, *Power Rock Castle Boom*. It's the theremin solo backed-up by bass-amp feedback and a bottleneck electric violin background screech.

"Outta sight," exhales Jim Mab.

Juno Mab nods. A ribbon of smoke wanders out of her half-open mouth.

When the theremin reaches a mad hollering wail, Meatpacker, the leader, returns to the words of his song. Meatpacker, a twelve-year-old rock genius, sings in a voice buckshot-speckled with cement chips and avalanches.

"Don't shove/What love/Will do/For you," he croons thru a web of Grand Canyon echo-chamber speakers throwing sound in circles up into the cosmos. The sky breaks.

"I never thought they could beat their last record."

"They're too much."

"They'll never stop."

"Wow."

"Yeah," giggles Jim Mab. "Eternity. Wheww."

Snowflake stirs in her basket.

"Should we move on?"

"Mm, mm," groans Juno, rolling over to Jim.

Thor, the German Shepherd, stirs as Juno's foot grazes his ear.

How she loves to place her cool small hands upon his hard and muscular torso. Especially when they're both high and the fingertips are electrical feathers connected with all the body circuits.

At first finger fall, his organ is activated and swells and fills itself in a sensual tingling sequence of growth. It strains to be free of his custom-tailored jeans.

Jim and Juno Mab kiss on the blanket-strewn floor of the VW microbus. It is a long kiss. A slow one. He pushes his tongue into her mouth which opens to receive it. Her tongue recedes to give him room to explore the sensitive cave. When his tongue is deep enough into her mouth Juno begins to, pressing her hips against his, suckle the tongue-tip, drawing it deeper into her mouth.

The Yab Yum Jug Band plays "Anti-Anti Negativia Ragtime Obstacle Course." "No, by God, by Ghost by the light of the

silvery moon/Life must always be no more no less than a forever open room."

Arched back, her hair in an arc touching the floor, Jim rubs
the palm of his hands over her outthrust breasts. Then pulls
her back to him and a longer, slower kiss. His hand reaches
under her mandala-patterned blouse to cup the firm, taut, full
breasts.

How she loves to unbutton his jeans and watch his cock
spring free. So firm, hard and wide, yet so soft to touch. Its
silken skin so gentle to stroke. On their first acid trip it looked
like a branch, a gnarled cane. The throbbing network of veins
were living ropes holding the seed ocean in the flesh covering.
All of it larger than her eye knew it. Endless hose of cockmeat
pulled to her mouth.

Thor stirs, grunts, and moves out of the way of the bodies
twining and twisting on the floor.

The dome of his cock is an intense light burning into her
well-lubricated cunt. She feels the heat of the light within her.
Without looking down, she is sure the light shines thru the
flesh of her belly.

They lie, locked together, feeling muscular vibrations shim-
mer and bind their parts together in a delicious fever.

"They can't kill love/That's the only thing they can't/Shove
up God's heart," sings Moses Marco, lead-singer of The Hermit
Crabs.

Her hands dig into the firm flesh of his buttocks. His cock
pushing deeper into her sheath until it feels as if it will break thru
her cunt into the sky of eternal pain/pleasure reality. Juno Mab
would like to rip off the flesh, to devour her man, so great is her
physical passion for Jim Mab. To rip him apart and have him rip
her apart. For the both of them to explode into fragments, into
atoms, to be nothing but air. And the orgasm grows between
them and separates and unites them, and Jim lets go and Juno
lets go and Thor yawns.

They put fifty micrograms of acid in Snowflake's bottle and get
back on the road.

It's a good time to travel. The best time. Late at night and right thru the sunrise. The highways are not crowded. You are often the only car on the road. Sometimes trucks are also on the road. Great dark forms that rumble by.

They smoke some more pot and listen to the AM-FM transistor radio.

Juno thinks that she has something besides mother-love to give to Snowflake. It's a tradition. A new tradition, a new legacy. Whereas her mother stuffed and mounted the cocks of her dead husbands, Juno stuffs pillows with the hair of rock musicians. Snowflake won't have to worry about being uncool. She'll be hip before she's even a year old.

Everything's wonderful. Everything's cool. No moral hangups. It's all free. That's why studding out for square sex freaks is harmless. There's no sin. It's all good.

All the shock-treatment in the world never gave her what her first acid trip did. Total vision of the world and its irrelevancy. Everything is cool. Nothing to worry about. Everybody's out of it. There is no law. Just be cool.

Jim's eyes cock and glaze and watch the road lit only by his headlights. The whiteturning center-line of the highway is roofed by dark shadows and trees.

"When you touch earth/That's only birth/ Keep goin'/'Til you're knowin'/Nothin' but Everything," sing the Stranglers, a New York sock-rock group.

3.

Mr. Kendrick Frank co-sponsors his assistant, Ronald Rowe, in applying for membership in the Club. Mr. Kendrick Frank feels a lecherous fondness for his troubled star. And Ronald Rowe finds some of his dark torment eased in the hands of masseurs and in the relaxing baths and in watching the ingenious homoerotic tableaux provided by the management.

Now nothing matters but the work at the Lab. There is the wild secret project Mr. Frank has given Rowe to complete for his wife's birthday gift. Lucky man, to have a wife, a wife odd enough, loving enough, to be able to make use of the secret project. Nothing matters but the work, the books about the work: the circuits, wiring, transistors, reactors, &tc.

When he thinks of Mrs. Diana Frank, he thinks that she must be suffering now that she has not heard from him. (Despite the fact that she changed her number. The shocking agony of the operator interrupting his phone call. "What do you mean she's changed her number?" "I'm sorry. I find no listing for a Diana…" "Diana!" "Diana what?" He doesn't even know her last name. "I'm sorry. We cannot give you a phone number on the basis of an address.") When he thinks of her, he thinks that one day he'll return to her, a rich man, top man in his field. He'll be incredibly suave and liquid, well-dressed in impeccable elegance, and she'll be older and hungry for him and he'll refuse her.

They're alone in the steam room. Mr. Kendrick Frank and Ronald Rowe. Since the work goes to overtime, Mr. Frank has been in the habit of inviting Ronald Rowe to the Club.

"Do you have a girl?" asks Mr. Frank, who is trying to be tactful.

"No. I'm getting over an unhappy affair."

"Too bad."

"Maybe," sighs Ronald Rowe, sweat falling into his mouth.

"Were you going to get married?"

"No. She was married. I'll never get married. Sorry, Mr. Frank, no offense."

"No offense, Rowe. My wife and I have an understanding."

"Oh? How nice."

"Let's hit the showers, what do you say?"

In the shower room. They are alone. Mr. Kendrick Frank offers to soap Ronald Rowe down. Ronald Rowe accepts. He accepts with a partial recognition of what will transpire.

It is hard to be buggered on the bottom of a shower stall, the water on full blast, suds up to your chin. It is hard, but not improbable, and that is exactly where Ronald Rowe, on hands and knees, was introduced to the Greek arts.

Afterwards, both he and Mr. Frank have decidedly more improved business relations. Mr. Kendrick Frank is delighted to know that Wednesday nights Ronald Rowe is available for soapy frolic at the Club.

Ah, he thinks, driving home, if I could manage the rest of the weekday nights as well.

4.

Snowflake is rarely fully awake. Thor paces in the VW's back, guarding Juno Mab who is half-asleep inside the sleeping bag. Jim's got his shades on and is driving the microbus. He took some speed half a day ago and is still going strong. Hands on the wheel, feet on the floor, responding automatically to the brake, the clutch. The freeway is a small one with shops and markets on either side. It reminds him of Stark, Georgia, where he drove the Love-or-Death party's panel truck during an unwelcome love-in set up in the black slum community. Unwelcome by black and white alike. It may have been the first time in Stark, Georgia's history that both black man and white man (and policeman) worked together. Jim became the getaway driver. Buckshot splintered the rearlights. Three bullets in the front window, shot by a black minister of the Flaming Rose Church. The minister wanted all the girls to stay and serve as handmaidens for a black folk mass. The girls got scared when the large fieldhands came lumbering into the Flaming Rose Church to get a look at the white handmaidens. The Flaming Rose Church's icons included crude paintings of slaughtered lambs with copious blood founts spewing into overflowing buckets. It's a drag that nobody can just do their thing. That's where it's at. What a beautiful day. Not a cloud in the sky. Just pure blue, so blue you want to dive up into it. Turn the world upside down. Shake all the people into the blue. Float. Nice.

Hillybilly music coming thru the AM-FM transistor radio. A gift from his father. It's worth over a hundred bucks. Can't buy love. No sir. It eats up batteries like Cadillacs eat up gas. Battery is running down. Tex Somebody-or-other sounds like he's gargling pebbles.

"You been gone with so many other guys/'n' yet I apologize/for not bein' a better guy than them…" Why get hung up? Everything's cool. It's all good. William Blake Rothenstein. What an operator. He's the cat. What the hell. William Blake Rothenstein. With a name like that, he's got to be cool. He's the one that got us into this bag. The only way to make a living. Loving. That's how.

5.

Did I really let him slide into me like that and then later, after he washed the soap off his cock, did I really have it in my mouth and delight in how it felt there and in the taste of his coming?

thinks Ronald Rowe, soldering an intricate grouping of transistors. The secret project is coming along fine.

Did I really return the honor to him, holding onto his flaccid sunken chest?

O Diana! See what you've done to me.

But Ronald Rowe is smiling to himself.

6.

A loving living. Love for cameras, artists, for squares, for anybody who wants and needs it. We've got it. Jim's face feels a little frozen. It's the speed. Velocity. There are times when he's going so fast his jaws ache from gritting down so hard.

One of these days maybe Juno and me can fuck in front of my father and mother and show them where it's at. What do they know with their phony world and phony values. They don't even know how to meditate. Scheme, lie, cheat and rob. No love. That's why they're so hung up. No love.

Liberty, brothers. Liberty. The road turns onto a cloverleaf ramp which leads into a flat gray freeway. Scenic view of defense plants.

He sees the flare and doesn't recognize it for a split second. Wow. A wounded falling star. Beautiful. Black-and-white cop car. Ambulance. Red revolving lights. Jim snaps out of revery quickly. All traffic has slowed down.

Everyone is consciously, or unconsciously, driving slowly in order to catch a glimpse of fatality. Groovy. It's all misted in the powdery smoke of smashed engines whose fires have been extinguished. Everything's cool. Doing their thing. The sky is smeared with smoke. Three men in gray clothes stand around a Highway Patrolman. Inside a smashed white Chrysler sits a woman. Highway madonna. Vellum-complected, brown eyes open too widely, holds a baby in her arms. Driver seat side is smashed in. I wish I had a camera on the car to zoom in and take the shots I see in passing. Like that chick holding the baby. Three gray men. Cops. Motorcycles. Flares all around.

We're stars. Underground stars. Rothenstein got three full-length features featuring us and others. *Hippie Love Cult, Acid Love-In,* and *Rock Love Bed.* All shot in the same room with the same people over a seven-hour stint. Lots of dope and speed and Myrna on the wall with acid. Also stills show up in magazines of nude hippies loving living. Postcards. Sold some stills to sex-book paperback publishers for covers. Paperbaby. Snowflake's cool. Albino dreamer. First and last time Juno missed her pill.

Balling a black militant leader. Infiltration. But it's all good and cool. Everybody's got their own thing. Right.

We're pinning it all on the future. Man, we're pioneers. Love break-out, breakthru. No shame no guilt. The body's a temple, the mind's a shrine. Give our kids everything our parents were too fucked-up to give us. Snowflake digs acid. You can tell how she coos. Kids know more than we do. They're really cool and if you're a cool parent, your kid'll be all the cooler.

Sky blue. Beautiful.

Ugly road. On and on. Ruin the land with stone. Cement cities are not rolling hills. Rolling stones. Right. He reaches into the glove compartment and pulls out a little ivory pipe which has a minute sediment of hash left in it. Lighting a match with one hand, he puffs on the pipe and steers.

Will we be there soon?

Juno Mab stetches in the sleeping bag and pets the wet snout of Thor, who stands above her.

7.

The Mabs will be at the Franks next weekend, which is alright with Mr. Kendrick Frank. He will invite Oscar for their party. Oscar's letters have gotten more violent. Mr. Frank wants to see Mrs. Frank degraded by him.

"Rowe?"

"Yes, Ken?"

"How's it coming?"

"Almost. Almost. We'll be needing the nuclear device tomorrow."

"I'll send for it immediately."

It might be fun to invite Ronald too. That will come in time. He reads Oscar's latest letter:

M-778. Bullwhip yu w/mi cock. hewmutilate tit & cunt wyfe Make her eet shitt love it Ripp out your cock if yu dont wryte Make date I'M YR MASTER!

Mr. Kendrick Frank writes a short note to Oscar giving time, place and date.

"Miss Whitenoon."

"Yes." Hiss on intercom static.

"Will it work?"

"It barely fits."

"But it fits."

"Yes. It hurts."

"Good."

Snaps off the intercom.

Everything as planned. She will learn. She must learn.

And life is so rewarding when there is work to do. For the first time in years, Mr. Kendrick Frank feels in control of himself and his domain. He swallows three pills, drinks a paper cup of water, and sorts thru the day's mail.

8.

Juno is sorry she could not meditate earlier. When she tried to kill herself the first time. Her mother never understood her. Never. It was early in the morning and there was no love in the world and her boyfriend enlisted in the army and there was nothing to hope for. Mother was out hunting another man, another trophy. Mother strong. A teacher of health and body strength to middle-aged people. But fascinated by fucking. A great fuck contortionist. William Blake Rothenstein remembers Mother. Showed the kids some incredible photographs of Mother fucking a young yogi. Both of them entwined beyond description. Married four times and four bronzed, stuffed cocks on wooden boards on the wall. Wilbur, Rod, Mark and Spike. Trophy room. Mother tower. Leathery sun-tanned face with wrinkles and bright white teeth shining in the dark skin. No muscle left undeveloped. Yet an ageless physique. Nothing mannish about Mother. Mother earth. How many times did Juno Mab try to kill herself? She is, after all, a mere twenty years of age. Four times. Each time a father died. If only she had known how to meditate then. To bore into the center and be one with the void. Great white endless, beginningless void. No guru then. The old days. Uncool days. It should all be music, dope and loving. Magic. Wonder. People who have ended should not be allowed to stand there in our way. The first time was with Wilbur's single-edged razor. Wilbur was the kind one. A health-food store owner who juiced carrots for her breakfast. The sight of blood on one slashed wrist sent her screaming down the stairs for help. Mother was in bed with Rod. It bugged them both. They got her to the hospital in time. If it wasn't for your mother, said the doctor, I'd have to report you. Killing yourself is against the law. Mercy. Mercy. Powder burns still scar part of her forehead now covered with long hair. Rod's pistol slipped and the bullet charred and grazed her. Oddity that Mother was fucking Mark at the time. No pills ever in the house but Rod dug sleepers after marrying Mother and when Rod went over the hill, she gobbled the sleeping pills. That was the best near-death.

She dreamt that she was Winnie-the-Pooh's mistress. Stumbled down the stairs in slow motion. Mother fucking Spike then. Both of them gliding out of the bedroom door. Muscular, bronzed bodies. Mother slapped her face until tears came but she couldn't feel any pain.

Shock treatment like a meditation. Spasm of dreams. Abducted. That was it. Held back. If they could only understand that there are many worlds and maybe, she screamed in a hall that was carved out of ice, I live in mine but I'm not bothering anyone. I want to be. Slammed against the wall with electrical energy. Waterfall to fall down. Rocks. Slammed to the floor, the floor a lagoon, birds watch, fall down again.

"It doesn't matter."

"What doesn't matter?" he asked. Question Man. Well, baby, I've got no answers for you. Give me a pill.

"I am what I am."

"Of course."

"You are what you are."

"I hope so."

Well, give me a pill. Dreams are levels of what I am and I want to dream and ascend. And the Question Man was a fag. Saw him with an attendant.

"You see. You live in different places," she shrieked.

Stopped, as in a photograph, the Question Man looked up from his work.

Junior College. Juno coed. What was that all about? History is fiction. Literature a newspaper. Art fun. All the guys there looked different because they were artists learning how to do it. You've got to learn somewhere.

Thor pokes his snout into her crotch, sniffing and panting. She kicks at him and he shies away. Back to his pacing.

Do your things. I am the everything, she announced to Raphael Clavier Grope III, her first lover after the boy who enlisted in the army who didn't really ball her anyway. They'd lie and rub and touch and come but never ball. But Raphael Clavier Grope III had a French hornpiper's beard and drove a Corvette and smoked grass and listened to jazz and had a weekend retreat at Malibu that his parents bought for him. His parents owned the world. It seemed. Raphael's pad in Malibu was where they'd go. Ocean surf roar outside. Fireplace going inside. Fucking on the Arctic-white bearskin rug. Abstract paintings on the natural wood walls. Stereophonic jazz on the automatic record player. Smooth and raucous pot. When she came the first time, she saw the face of her guru imprinted in red and golden light upon each eyelid. It was the form of his face. She is sure of that.

I'm the everything.

And the nothing.

All.

Right.

Thor lies down beside her, edging to get closer to her body. Without thinking, Juno Mab begins to stroke his hairy cock sheath. His pink glittering cock pushes thru and she continues stroking the pink power dog cock. Thor whimpers and pokes his snout into her crotch.

O alright.

Animal, woman, space, void.

Thor mounts her from behind as she positions herself on her hands and knees to allow him better entry.

Don't knock over the baby.

Jim Mab catches the action in his mirror. Out of sight. Doing her thing. He begins to massage his cock trying to watch them and the road at the same time.

9.

Watching the dusk shade the lawn in late afternoon. One feels old enough. Watching the lawn sprinkler spin about. Jets of water shoot in arcs over the grass. A rainbow spray falls a steady mist on the grass, the flower beds. A quality of light: fire orange and burnished gold. Mrs. Diana Frank feels old enough. As old as light, as old as the sunset. It feels like all inner colors are drained out of her to feed the dying sun. More gin than tonic on birthdays. Stirs the mixture. More sorrow. Not sorrow to be a year older. It's the old sorrow born with her. When she was younger, the loneliness would overwhelm her and fall upon her body as a demon lover. Sometimes the sorrow took her soul away and left her in a void whose form knew no edges.

The caterer will bring the food soon, she thinks. At least there will be only one guest tonight. And that is fine. Two men are easy to handle. Her husband gets incredible pleasure out of watching other men make love to her. And her husband gets incredible pleasure out of having her watch other men make love to him. And, sometimes, as it was in the beginnings, all three of them would make love. The trouble is, most men always want to disengage from one position into another one too quickly, as if they were merely posing for photographs. There was the insurance agent from Toluca Lake who went slowly and with care. Kendrick was pill-boxed and slobbered and mumbled on the sofa while the insurance agent's wife sat on his lap. "If I had you," the man said, "I wouldn't want anyone else." Tender and caring. It should be slow. Fucking should find its rhythm slowly.

The doorbell rings. It's the caterer.

Happy birthday.

They drink champagne. They toast.

"To you. To tonight."

Glasses tinkle as they barely touch.

"Oscar will be here in a short while," says Mr. Kendrick Frank. "I'd like you to open your present now."

The present is in a large box wrapped in plain brown wrapping paper with a factory-made bow taped on its center.

"Here. You must wear these when opening the box."

Mr. Kendrick Frank hands her the lead-lined gloves.

Mrs. Diana Frank looks strangely at her husband. His face is glowing and reverent and fixed on the box.

"Go on," he says. "Go on."

She goes to the box and tears off the ribbon. Then rips off the wrapping paper. A khaki-colored lead box with handles stamped FRAGILE, RADIOACTIVE, and other nuclear warnings and admonitions.

"Go on, go on."

She slowly opens the lid of the box and gasps.

"Yes, yes. Look at it. It's yours."

"Not tonight?" asks Mrs. Diana Frank.

"No. Of course not. This is your birthday party."

She shuts the lid. It clunks shut and she clasps it tight.

"A remarkable object, heh?"

Mrs. Diana Frank nods and drains her glass.

"That Rowe, he really worked himself into a lather getting it done. Nice boy, that Rowe, he'll go places. We should have him over here soon."

Mixing herself a new drink. She changed her box number because Ronald Rowe was writing novels of love letters to her. Each one getting uglier and more petulant and threatening. God, if he were to find out.

Then she sees the object in the lead box. And shudders.

"Why is it radioactive?" she asks.

"To help you be more satisfied," he answers.

"It's awfully large."

"Yes. It's ultimate."

There's a heavy fist-smashing pounding at the door.

"Oscar. That must be Oscar," says Mr. Kendrick Frank, swallowing his pills and drinking down his glass of champagne. "I'll get it."

Oscar pushes thru the door before Mr. Kendrick Frank has a chance to open it fully.

"Ahhh," he grunts, stomping into the living room. Six foot

four, near 300 pounds, Oscar gets out of his suede riveter's jacket and throws it on the couch. His blue workshirt is open at the neck and tufts of black body hair push out over the collar. "Ahhh. Gimme food. Drink. Cock and cunt."

Oscar has a style of his own. His size and hulky bearing of it cause him to constantly bump into things. He sits down on the sofa after knocking into the coffee table and brings his foot up, as he sinks into the softness, and kicks under the coffee table, jarring the bottle of champagne.

"You're the cunt. C'mere."

His hairy hand grabs her pale neck, marking it with red fingerprint imprints.

"Kiss."

He pushes his stubbly face into hers and kisses her ferociously, nearly breaking her jaw with his tongue thrust.

"Good," he grunts and twists at her tits.

Then picks up the champagne bottle, knocking her glass over, and drinks from it.

"Fuckin' soda. Gimme booze."

"What do you want?" asks Mrs. Diana Frank.

"Not you. Him. He gets it. Gimme gin. Straight. Make it snappy. You. C'mere. Feel my cock, cunt."

She manages to get the zipper down the fly of Oscar's black twill 'Frisco jeans. And she unbuckles the well-weathered wide leather belt. And unbuttons the top button.

"Here you are, Oscar."

Oscar drains the glass of gin at a gulp.

"Bigger glass. C'mon. Feel cock, cunt."

Her hands get lost in the endless steamy tubing of Oscar's cock and balls. First they get tangled in the pubic explosion. Then her fingertips touch the slack log and try to feel towards the end of it, the head of it. And gets lost and then tries to get her hand around it to measure its dormant width. And gets lost as it begins to widen and get hard and shuffle its form.

"Dumb."

And Oscar stands up and drops his pants. He wears no shorts. Mr. Kendrick Frank cheeps a strange whistle when he sees Oscar's cock in semi-tumescence.

Oscar steps out of his pants. Throws them on the sofa. Knocks the champagne bottle over. Its liquid hisses as it hits the floor. Then he takes off his blue workshirt and tosses that onto the sofa. It manages to scrape off some clam dip out of the dip bowl in its flight.

"My God," groans Mr. Kendrick Frank.
"Mm-ff, fmm-gg," gags Mrs. Diana Frank.

"Brawwwhh," bellows Oscar.
His cock needs a blunderbuss stand.
Mrs. Diana is reduced to tongue lapping around its width and length which only aggravates Oscar more.
"Brawhh, suck, suck," he grumbles.
"Let me. Let me," pleads Mr. Kendrick Frank.
Oscar sideswipes Mr. Kendrick Frank in the neck and he slumps to the rug, weeping in joyous pain.
Grabbing his immense rhinoceros balls in her hands.
"Brawwhh, suck. Mmm-suck."
He pulls the cock in his hand and slams it against her cheek.
Oscar bumps into the coffee table and breaks one of its legs. It lists at an odd, wounded angle.
Happy birthday.

Her husband holds her ankles and tries to keep her legs spread far apart as Oscar, standing on the sofa's arm, directs his base-ball-bat cock towards her cunt.
"Mmm-grhh—awrry."
And he flops upon her. Luckily the sofa is soft. She swears to her spine that it's the floor she feels when he falls upon her.
"No," she groans. "Don't."
"Mmhh. Mmhh."
She can hear her husband tittering madly at the other end of the sofa.
Oscar's cock gets partially inside of her cunt before the pain begins to bother her. Split in half. Happy birthday. Giant demon. Torment. Shame. Fault. Guilt. Filth.
"AYYYYYYYY !" she screams.

Her husband puts the pillow over her mouth.

"Ayyyyyyyyyyy," she screams beneath the pillow.

Will it push thru her intestines and break her heart apart and finally push out of her mouth tearing her face in half?

"Blargg. Mfhh. Plotch."

His hands pin her hands down. Her husband holds her feet down.

Humping up to bend with the pain corkscrewing thru her innards is no good. Oscar flattens his bulk upon the hump, breaking the tension.

Had any Christian gentlewoman so defied her God and met a weary wild death in rut-wound crucifixion, the scream has a tone of its own, a solemn earth hum, floating in her head, the pain, the pain, O God, descend upon my brutalized flesh and form it into space O shame on my filthy brute-fucked skin O

"GLAWWWWWWW! WAHH! WAHH! WOOSH!"

Half-lid open landscape.

Mr. Kendrick Frank holding onto the bar-rail while Oscar guides his weapon into Mr. Kendrick Frank's twitching buttock cheeks.

Half-open, semi-conscious, drift agony vision:

Oscar sitting on her husband's knees. Feeding the length of his monster hose into her husband's open mouth. Lips splitting at each crack. A bloodburst.

Tearing apart the bar to find more

"Booze, booze, rrrggghhaaaahh,!,!, mmmph, mppphhoooo."

knocking over ashtrays, bottles breaking, glasses crashing to the floor;

Mr. Kendrick Frank babbling in his bubbly bloodbath, laughs, crawls towards the khaki box.

Smashes his fist into the mirror behind the bar to tear away the image of his hairy flesh mountain.

Picks up Mr. Kendrick Frank, kicks over the coffee table, and throws him onto the sofa upon Mrs. Diana Frank.

"Mmmffggg. Fuck her. Fuck. Fuck."

"You're mad."

"?!?!"

Oscar throws a broken ashtray wedge at Mr. Kendrick Frank's head.

It misses the head. Spears into the lamp base, shattering it instantly.

"Fuck her. Mmmm-othr-fugg-kk-rr-aummrawwhhh."

Death, my lover, spits blood on my forehead.

Hairy hand slapping Kendrick's back as he comes inside her shredded cunt so that he coughs instead of coming. His forehead knocks into hers. Death stars.

To wake up and find Oscar sitting in the easy chair with his beanstalk still reaching up out of his pubic jungle. And Oscar holding onto it with both his hairy paws, rubbing it like one would rub a pole. And when he comes it is like an oil well of come. Hits the ceiling. Sprays the room. Like the water out of the lawn sprinkler. Her husband in it. A Maypole dancer. Showering in it. Laughing. His bloody mouth a bloody smile. Splotches of it in his hair. Gobs on his nose and cheeks and body. Soaps himself in it.

They wake up to the sound of rain.

Oscar is gone. The door is wide open.

IV.

A WEAK END IN THE COUNTRY

Standin' at the crossroads,
I tried to flag a ride,
Didn't nobody seem to know me,
Everybody pass me by

—Robert Johnson

1.

"Don't worry. The baby's cool," says Jim Mab to Mr. Kendrick Frank.

"Let's turn on," says Juno Mab, sitting next to Jim on the sofa.

Mr. Kendrick Frank sits in his chair and Mrs. Diana Frank stands behind the bar mixing herself a drink.

"Smoke dope, grass, marihuana, dig?"

Mr. Kendrick Frank nods. The familiar chill of forbidden ritual begins vibrating in his center.

"Kids are a groove. How come you don't have any?" Juno asks the Franks.

"You've got a classic and beautiful body," says Jim, lighting a joint. Mrs. Kendrick Frank smiles wanly.

Mr. Kendrick Frank puffs on the marihuana tentatively.

"Suck on it, man. Right. Way down."

"Join us," says Juno.

It's an uptight scene. Almost like home, he thinks, on the second joint. The old man's got something on his mind. Weird vibrations. His old lady's kind of groovy. But she's got a weird fugitive look. Man, I sure hope we can cop some time together alone. The pot is fragrant, cut with hash, and Jim Mab exhales slowly, with deliberation.

"What do you do for a living?" asks Mr. Frank.

"Love," says Jim Mab.

"Yes," giggles Juno. "That's our living. Loving."

"Are you an artist?"

"Yeah. We're love artists."

They pass the pot around.

Soon Mr. Kendrick Frank begins to feel like a paraplegic. From the waist down, his body seems numb. It's not unpleasant. And his cock swells and hardens.

Mrs. Diana Frank shuts her eyes for a moment and keeps them shut for eternity. Pink eyelid novae merge and vanish. Leads into an abstract tunnel into her soul. Her body begins to think cellular thoughts. Nerve serpents charge and feed on new electric current moving around her spine.

Jim Mab could be Pan. His hair is curly and long, spilling over his mandarin collar. And his beard is rich and his thighs and legs look firm and muscular in the fabric of his custom-tailored tight jeans. His teeth are bright and his eyes are the blue color of water seen around coral reefs.

Her eyes linger on the bulge between his legs. And he catches her glance and smiles.

Mr. Kendrick Frank watches Juno Mab yawn. Watches her woman-child body push her breasts forward. Watches the hem of her blouse rise up to expose her white flesh and dainty belly button. Juno is the dream he had of woman when he was a young boy living in his mother's house. Living in his room which was equipped as a laboratory. His mother spared no expense. A blond-haired princess. Long blonde hair in a solitary braid down the tower's brick-rusted wall.

The baby stirs and there is a scratching at the front door.

"Thor. It must be Thor," says Jim lazily.

"Let him in. I'll check Snowflake."

"I'll show you to the door," says Mrs. Diana Frank dreamily.

"Take off your shoes."

She does. They walk barefoot on the grass and down the gravel of the driveway and onto the grass of the backyard. The grass is cool and slightly damp. Thor pads behind them.

"Stop," says Jim Mab, behind her.

Mrs. Diana Frank stops. A slight breeze moves around her body. Jim Mab puts both hands on her buttocks. It is a sensational feeling for her and she nearly comes. One hand moves over her hip bone and presses upon her mound. The other moves slowly around her ribs and presses gently upon one breast. She catches her breath.

She's a tiger. All over him. Her innocent mouth of ripe cherries covers every inch of him.

Mr. Kendrick Frank lies on the rug of his living room while Juno Mab seemingly worships every area of his sagging body.

Snowflake whimpers in her basket, which irritates Mr. Kendrick Frank somewhat.

Juno Mab is heavenly. Her breasts are perfect, not the hamhocks of his wife. Her cunt is a beautiful triangle leading into the nicest hole he's ever entered. His tongue was busy swabbing it earlier. Juno Mab's skin is porcelain, is made of clouds, is the purest white. She stops to relight some pot and pass it to Mr. Kendrick Frank who, by now, is somewhat of an expert at smoking it.

"O, let me check Snowflake," sighs Juno Mab.

Her naked body bounces past him and he watches her tight firm ass bounce slightly as she walks.

Damn the baby. He smokes some more pot until he feels as placid and calm as a lake in summer.

"Here, man," says Juno, returning to his side on the rug on the floor.

"What is it?"'

"It's potcake. It's out of sight. It'll really blow your mind. Go on, eat it."

He puts the flat square of cake into his mouth. It tastes of trees, earth and chocolate. While he chews, Juno starts sucking on his nipples.

Thor pokes his snout into their parts as they roll on the grass. It doesn't matter. They both laugh.

Jim Mab's hard chest and strong body weave with hers and they tumble and fuck simultaneously.

"Beautiful," he says as they reach their climaxes. "Beautiful."

Mrs. Diana Frank laughs. The intense explosion moves thru her body. My toes will blow off in its wave, she thinks. And laughs again. It is an easy loonlike laugh in the night. Crickets seem to surround them in the darkness.

2.

Fragmentary drift of voices: The dreamscape. Hashish potcake barbiturate acid cola alcohol fizz slush and wow.

It has never been hard. It's what we all want to do with each other. Fuck and laugh and get high. Jim Mab lies between Mr. and Mrs. Kendrick Frank. Juno's with Thor and Snowflake on the floor. All the women want it as much as the men. That's how it works. First one, cherrytime, was my grade-school teacher. Miss Arlene Beaulieu. In the clothes closet. Because we wanted to. It's never been hard. Talking's hard. Words mean nothing. You say them but they are not true. Hello isn't the right word to say to a woman you want to fuck. You say hello afterwards. Even then it isn't the right word. Way, word, what does it matter? Christ, her breasts are filled with myth-bird feathers. Her nipples bright red. Great tantric mamma. Dumb like all the square animals. But soft and fuckable. Like momma. Dumb soft fuck freak. Everywhere you look, there she is balling some clod she'd grabbed off the street, and dad just took it, another dumb square clod. You don't have to take or give anything. Fuck laugh get high...

Mr. Kendrick Frank fondles the young man's cock.

He'd be a nice daddy.
   She curls up in the sleeping bag on the floor. Juno Mab is half-awake, half-asleep, totally stoned again on pot, potcake and some of Mr. Kendrick Frank's pills.
   Nice daddy. Poor mamma. Poor Jim. Just doesn't understand. None of them do. I don't either. That's funny. Even when I do understand, I don't understand. Meditate.
   Wide golden circle. That's my center. Ringed with medieval-woodcut frame of flames. Al-chemical design. Like a groovy collage. My center. I'm a mommy too now. Got a baby. Sleeping baby. Babies should be sleeped and not stopped. Laughs to recall rifling Mr. Kendrick Frank's pockets for his change and dol-

lars. Everything's free. Shock treatment is free. I can't be shocked anymore. I'm a mommy too. I'm an adult.

In the morning, they have a naked breakfast together. Smoke more grass, finish up the potcake, and watch dirty movies until the afternoon.

One of the poses they try is both ladies on the floor and both men, propped over them, feeding their mouths cock. Then;

another pose finds them engaged thus:

Juno's cunt in Jim's mouth, Jim's cock in Mrs. Diana Frank's mouth, Mrs. Diana Frank's cunt probed by Thor's tongue, Thor's pink shaft sucked by Mr. Kendrick Frank;

re-shift, shuffle bodies:

Juno lets Thor service her while Jim Mab stands and fucks Mrs. Diana Frank in the rear while Mr. Kendrick Frank, facing her, fucks her in the cunt.

"Fuckburger," yells Jim Mab.

Later, after more pot, more wine, some methedrine, a pause to let it settle and rearrange their bodies and minds, they engage in more improvisations.

Mr. Frank holds Mrs. Frank like a wheelbarrow. His cock is jammed up her cunt. She has to walk on her palms. Walks to Jim Mab's cock and stops there. Takes it in her mouth and starts sucking it while underneath her, Thor laps at her pussy and also laps the edges of Mr. Frank's cock, and beneath Thor is Juno.

But all in a dream.

Slowly. As if sinking. Their faces begin to dematerialize, to decompose into golden flaming particles. Faces emulsifying. Bodies undone. Bones fly from the body frame. Nerves, tendons, all the loose foliage woven about bones.

"Now," says Jim Mab to Mrs. Diana Frank. His voice has slowed down. It sounds like mud slowly moving down a hillside. "Now, for your first trip. Your first trip." She swallows the capsule with the purple powder in it.

"Will you be my father?" Juno Mab asks Mr. Kendrick Frank and hands him his cap of Lysergic acid. Lyso. Genesis. Mr. Kendrick Frank pops it with three of his own pills.

The Mabs sit in the kitchen eating an orange. The orange is

a scale model of God. Jim cuts the meat out of the skin and the orange curtain is a glass curtain parted by his body. He walks thru it. To the other room. There's a honkytonk angel in her peacock feather dress and red silk stockings, stretched out in a Victorian chaise longue, beckoning to him. The orange beaded curtains click as he moves thru them.

It's her paired womb. Orange ovaries. Glisten in the light. The life light. The mother's morning juice. Blood of ovaries. Sparkling in the juicer. "Drink your juice." Drink your ovaries. I am always afraid to. If I die, will anyone remember that I lived? You know Juno. Juno Mab. She died before her time. Jim's cock is spliced on the block. Like a diagram of it. Point the ruler to the tubes and layers of fat and veins and nerves. If I die before I awake, will I know the dream? The mother took the men before they became fathers. Took them away. Animals and babies understand. Jim's a good animal sometimes. Become an animal. Child animal. No words, no promises, laws, lies. No. Orange eyelid burns the distended eyeball with its citric fever.

Mr. Kendrick Frank stares at the monster in his mirror. His face is lined with endless wrinkles that open and shut like minute wounds. A network of pulsing light holds the fleshy mass together, binds it, prevents his face from sliding off of his skull. I am gray. The color in between. He watches his face for hours then concentrates on his mouth. It is a horrible mouth. Lean-lipped, the lips throb. They begin to pull apart, like trembling gray-pink flesh curtains to reveal his teeth. Gray, dark growths. Like bones. Skeleton in my mouth. He opens his mouth wide and tries to look down his throat and see his heart. Ahh. Ahhh. His face is a skull. The flesh falls off it. In the skull's eye-sockets are yellow-white flames. I want to kill her. I hate her. Mr. Kendrick Frank screams. And screams. And screams. And sinks to the floor which is soft and breathing and inhales Mr. Kendrick Frank.

I am too late. I am afraid. I am too late. I won't help. I won't. Help. Help. And screams going thru the floor into a spangled darkness.

There's no sure device to order the next sequence of events.

Mrs. Kendrick Frank:

Not a martyr. Beyond shame and guilt. Not alive. Not alive to the life in me. I cannot go on. I am ashamed to be alive. All I've ever wanted was to die. To die. To die again. Forever.

And she goes to the khaki box and opens it.

Mrs. Juno Mab:

Rubs Snowflake's powdery albino skin to her naked body, kissing the baby's curly pink hair. Thor, who ate a leftover hunk of potcake, is furious and jealous and jumps on the baby. And begins to devour it. Juno screams, but the scream won't escape her mouth. I'm too high, she thinks. I'm too high. This is all wrong.

Ronald Rowe:

As if called by the full moon, decides to try and see Mrs. Diana Frank tonight. To see her, to meet her husband, to face it all. He had been disturbed about the device he completed for Mr. Frank. During the time, it seemed logical. A strange sexual contrivance. A nuclear dildo. Except, not thinking, or thinking beyond his mid-mind, to paraphrase Lincoln Hawk, Ronald Rowe installed a detonating mechanism in the dildo. Mr. Kendrick Frank smiled and said it will have to do. It's a birthday present.

Jim Mab hears the dog tearing apart the baby, his wife whimpering, moaning, hears Mr. Kendrick Frank come screaming down the stairs.

O My God, don't do it! he yells to Mrs. Diana Frank. She does and he runs out of the house, nearly tripping on the dog and baby and Juno. Jim Mab hears all of this inside the clothes closet and won't come out. Everything is cool.

It hums. It is beautiful. A chrome phallus larger than most. It hums. It is the cock of an angel shining in her hand. It is a hard fit and partway in she hears it click and stop humming. There is only one death, she thinks, writhing as the dildo begins to vibrate within her cunt. There is only one death. And suddenly, for a moment, she is reborn.

About the Author

David Meltzer is the author of many books of poetry including *Tens,* edited by Kenneth Rexroth (McGraw-Hill), *Yesod* (Trigram Press), *Six* (Black Sparrow Press), *Bark: A Polemic* (Capra Press), *Karps* (Oyez), *The Name* (Black Sparrow Press), and the forthcoming *Arrows: Selected Poetry, 1957-1993.* He has edited various thematic anthologies including *The San Francisco Poets: Interviews* (Ballantine Books), *The Secret Garden: Classical Kabbalistic Texts* (Continuum), *Birth: Texts, Songs, Prayers, and Stories* (North Point Press) and, recently, *Reading Jazz* (Mercury House). *Orf,* one of ten erotic novels he wrote in the 60s, has been reprinted by Rhino*ceros* Books; Vanguard Records has reissued his 60s rock band's first album, *Serpent Power,* on CD. Current projects include an anthology of culture war texts, *High/Low Browse,* a critical work on popular culture, *Everyday Myth,* and a biographical study of the influential Los Angeles artist, Wallace Berman. With poet Clark Coolidge, vocalist/songwriter Tina Meltzer, and assorted musicians, poets and artists, he is part of MIX, a performance ensemble. He was a recipient of an NEA grant, in 1974. Meltzer currently teaches in the undergraduate Humanities program and the graduate Poetics program at New College of California.

SAMUEL R. DELANY

THE MAD MAN

For his thesis, graduate student John Marr researches the life and work of the brilliant Timothy Hasler: a philosopher whose career was cut tragically short over a decade earlier. Marr encounters numerous obstacles, as other researchers turn up evidence of Hasler's personal life that is deemed simply too unpleasant. On another front, Marr finds himself increasingly drawn toward more shocking, depraved sexual entaglements with the homeless men of his neighborhood, until it begins to seem that Hasler's death might hold some key to his own life as a gay man in the age of AIDS.

This new novel by Samuel R. Delany not only expands the parameters of what he has given us in the past, but fuses together two seemingly disparate genres of writing and comes up with something which is not comparable to any existing text of which I am aware.... What Delany has done here is take the ideas of Marquis de Sade one step further, by filtering extreme and obsessive sexual behavior through the sieve of post-modern experience.... —Lambda Book Report

The latest novel from Hugo- and Nebula-winning science fiction writer and critic Delany... reads like a pornographic reflection of Peter Ackroyd's Chatterton *or A.S. Byatt's* Possession.... *The pornographic element... becomes more than simple shock or titillation, though, as Delany develops an insightful dichotomy between [his protagonist]'s two worlds: the one of cerebral philosophy and dry academia, the other of heedless, 'impersonal' obsessive sexual extremism. When these worlds finally collide ... the novel achieves a surprisingly satisfying resolution....*— Publishers Weekly

hardcover 193-4/$23.95

THE MOTION OF LIGHT IN WATER

"A very moving, intensely fascinating literary biography from an extraordinary writer. Thoroughly admirable candor and luminous stylistic precision; the artist as a young man and a memorable picture of an age." —William Gibson

"A remarkably candid and revealing...study of an extraordinary and extraordinarily appealing human being, and a fascinating...account of the early days of a significant science fiction writer's career." —Robert Silverberg

The first unexpurgated American edition of award-winning author Samuel R. Delany's riveting autobiography covers the early years of one of science fiction's most important voices. Beginning with his marriage to the young, remarkably gifted poet Marilyn Hacker, Delany paints a vivid and compelling picture of New York's East Village in the early '60s—a time of unprecedented social change and transformation. Startling and revealing, *The Motion of Light in Water* traces the roots of one of America's most innovative writers. *133-0*

KATHLEEN K.

SWEET TALKERS

Kathleen K. is a professional, in the finest sense of the word. She takes her work seriously, always approaching it with diligence, imagination and backbone; an exceptional judge of character, she manages both customers and employees with a flair that has made her business a success. But many people would dismiss Kathleen's achievements, falling as they do, outside mainstream corporate America.

Here, for the first time, is the story behind the provocative advertisements and 970 prefixes. Kathleen K. opens up her diary for a rare peek at the day-to-day life of a phone sex operator—and reveals a number of secrets and surprises. Because far from being a sleazy, underground scam, the service Kathleen provides often speaks to the lives of its customers with a directness and compassion they receive nowhere else. *192-6*

ROBERT PATRICK
TEMPLE SLAVE

...you must read this book. It draws such a tragic, and, in a way, noble portrait of Mr. Buono: It leads the reader, almost against his will, into a deep sympathy with this strange man who tried to comfort, to encourage and to feed both the worthy and the worthless... It is impossible not to mourn for this man—impossible not to praise this book
.—Quentin Crisp

This is nothing less than the secret history of the most theatrical of theaters, the most bohemian of Americans and the most knowing of queens. Patrick writes with a lush and witty abandon, as if this departure from the crafting of plays has energized him. Temple Slave is also one of the best ways to learn what it was like to be fabulous, gay, theatrical and loved in a time at once more and less dangerous to gay life than our ow
—Genre

Temple Slave tells the story of the Espresso Buono—the archetypal alternative performance space—and the wildly talented misfits who called it home in the early 60s. The Buono became the birthplace of a new underground theater—and the personal and social consciousness that would lead to Stonewall and the modern gay and lesbian movement. **Temple Slave** is a kaleidoscopic page from gay history—a riotous tour de force peppered with the verbal fireworks and shrewd insight that are the hallmark of Robert Patrick's work.   **191-8**

LUCY TAYLOR
UNNATURAL ACTS

A remarkable debut volume from a provocative writer. *Unnatural Acts* plunges deep into the dark side of the psyche, far past all pleasantries and prohibitions, and brings to life a disturbing vision of erotic horror. Unrelenting angels and hungry gods play with souls and bodies in Taylor's murky cosmos: where heaven and hell are merely differences of perspective; where redemption and damnation lie behind the same shocking acts.   **181-0**

DAVID MELTZER
THE AGENCY TRILOGY

With the Essex House edition of *The Agency* in 1968, the highly regarded poet David Meltzer took America on a trip into a hell of unbridled sexuality. The story of a supersecret, Orwellian sexual network, *The Agency* explored issues of erotic dominance and submission with an immediacy and frankness previously unheard of in American literature, as well as presented a vision of an America consumed and dehumanised by a lust for power. This landmark novel was followed by *The Agent*, and *How Many Blocks in the Pile?*—taken with *The Agency*, they confirm Meltzer's position as one of America's early masters of the erotic genre.

...'The Agency' is clearly Meltzer's paradigm of society; a mindless machine of which we are all 'agents' including those whom the machine supposedly serves.... —Norman Spinrad
216-7

CARO SOLES
MELTDOWN!
An Anthology of Erotic Science Fiction and Dark Fantasy for Gay Men

Editor Caro Soles has put together one of the most explosive, mind-bending collections of gay erotic writing ever published. *Meltdown!* contains the very best examples of this increasingly popular sub-genre: stories meant to shock and delight, to send a shiver down the spine and start a fire down below. An extraordinary volume, *Meltdown!* presents both new voices and provocative pieces by world-famous writers Edmund White and Samuel R. Delany.   **203-5**

BIZARRE SEX

BIZARRE SEX AND OTHER CRIMES OF PASSION
Edited by Stan Tal

Stan Tal, editor of *Bizarre Sex*, Canada's boldest fiction publication, has culled the very best stories that have crossed his desk—and now unleashes them on the reading public in *Bizarre Sex and Other Crimes of Passion*. Over twenty small masterpieces of erotic shock make this one of the year's most unexpectedly alluring anthologies. Including such masters of erotic horror and fantasy as Edward Lee, Lucy Taylor, Nancy Kilpatrick and Caro Soles, *Bizarre Sex and Other Crimes of Passion*, is a treasure-trove of arousing chills.   213-2

PAT CALIFIA

SENSUOUS MAGIC

Sensuous Magic is clear, succinct and engaging even for the reader for whom S/M isn't the sexual behavior of choice.... Califia's prose is soothing, informative and non-judgemental—she both instructs her reader and explores the territory for them.... When she is writing about the dynamics of sex and the technical aspects of it, Califia is the Dr. Ruth of the alternative sexuality set....

—*Lambda Book Report*

Don't take a dangerous trip into the unknown—buy this book and know where you're going!
—*SKIN TWO*

Finally, a "how to" sex manual that doesn't involve new age mumbo jumbo or "tricks" that require the agility of a Flying Wallenda.... Califia's strength as a writer lies in her ability to relay information without sounding condescending. If you don't understand a word or concept... chances are it's defined in the handy dictionary in the back....   —*Futuresex*

Renowned erotic pioneer Pat Califia provides this honest, unpretentious peek behind the mask of dominant/submissive sexuality—an adventurous adult world of pleasure too often obscured by ignorance and fear. Califia demystifies "the scene" for the novice, explaining the terminology and technique behind many misunderstood sexual practices The adventurous (or just plain curious) lover won't want to miss this ultimate "how to" volume.   131-4

SKIN TWO

THE BEST OF *SKIN TWO*   Edited by Tim Woodward

For over a decade, *Skin Two* has served as the bible of the international fetish community. A groundbreaking journal from the crossroads of sexuality, fashion, and art, *Skin Two* specializes in provocative, challenging essays by the finest writers working in the "radical sex" scene. Collected here, for the first time, are the articles and interviews that have established the magazine's singular reputation. Including interviews with cult figures Tim Burton, Clive Barker and Jean Paul Gaultier.   130-6

GAUNTLET

THE BEST OF *GAUNTLET* Edited by Barry Hoffman

No material, no opinion is taboo enough to violate Gauntlet*'s purpose of 'exploring the limits of free expression'—airing all views in the name of the First Amendment.*

—*Associated Press*

Dedicated to "exploring the limits of free expression," *Gauntlet* has, with its semi-annual issues, taken on such explosive topics as race, pornography, political correctness, and media manipulation—always publishing the widest possible range of opinions. Only in *Gauntlet* might one expect to encounter Phyllis Schafley *and* Annie Sprinkle, Stephen King *and* Madonna—often within pages of one another. The very best, most provocative articles have been gathered by editor-in-chief Barry Hoffman, to make *The Best of Gauntlet* a most provocative exploration of American society's limits. 202-7

MICHAEL PERKINS

THE GOOD PARTS: An Uncensored Guide to Literary Sexuality

Michael Perkins, one of America's only serious critics to regularly scrutinize sexual literature, presents an overview of sex a seen in the pages of over 100 major volumes from the past twenty years.

I decided when I wrote my first column in 1968 that I would take the opportunity presented by Screw *to chronicle the inevitable and inexorable rise of an unfairly neglected genre of contemporary writing. I wondered if I would remain interested in the subject for very long, and if the field would not eventually diminish so there would be nothing to review.... Every week since then I have published a thousand-word review, and occasionally a longer essay, devoted to discovering and reporting on the manifestations of sexuality in all kinds of fiction, nonfiction, and poetry. In my columns I cast a wide net (a million words so far) over a subject no one else wanted to take a long look at. It has indeed held my interest.* 186-1

LARS EIGHNER

THE ELEMENTS OF AROUSAL

Critically acclaimed gay writer Lars Eighner—whose *Travels with Lizbeth* was chosen by the *New York Times Book Review* as one of the year's notable titles—develops a guideline for success with one of publishing's best kept secrets: the novice-friendly field of gay erotic writing.

In *The Elements of Arousal*, Eighner details his craft, providing the reader with sure advice. Eighner's overview of the gay erotic market paints a picture of a diverse array of outlets for a writer's work. Because, after all, writing is what *The Elements of Arousal* is about: the application and honing of the writer's craft, which brought Lars Eighner fame with not only the steamy *Bayou Boy*, but the profoundly illuminating *Travels with Lizbeth*.$12.95

JOHN PRESTON

MY LIFE AS A PORNOGRAPHER

The erotic nonfiction of John Preston. Includes the title essay, given as the John Pearson Perry Lecture at Harvard University, and the legendary "Good-Bye to Sally Gearhart," and many other provocative writings.

...essential and enlightening...His sex-positive stand on safer-sex education as the only truly effective AIDS-prevention strategy will certainly not win him any conservative converts, but AIDS activists will be shouting their assent.... [My Life as a Pornographer] is a bridge from the sexually liberated 1970s to the more cautious 1990s, and Preston has walked much of that way as a standard-bearer to the cause for equal rights....—Library Journal

Preston's a model essayist; he writes pellucid prose in a voice that, like Samuel Johnson's, combines authority with entertainment.... My Life as a Pornographer...is not pornography, but rather reflections upon the writing and production of it. Preston ranges from really superb journalism of his interviews with denizens of the S/M demi-mond, particularly a superb portrait of a Colt model Preston calls "Joe" to a brilliant analysis of the "theater" of the New York sex club, The Mineshaft.... In a deeply sex-phobic world, Preston has never shied away from a vision of the redemptive potential of the erotic drive. Better than perhaps anyone in our community, Preston knows how physical joy can bridge differences and make us well. —Lambda Book Report 135-7

· HUSTLING:

A GENTLEMAN'S GUIDE TO THE FINE ART OF HOMOSEXUAL PROSTITUTION

John Preston solicited the advice of "working boys" from across the country in his effort to produce the ultimate guide to the hustler's world. *Hustling* covers every practical aspect of the business, from clientele and payment options to "specialties," sidelines and drawbacks. No stone is left unturned in this guidebook to the ins and outs of this much-mythologized trade. 137-3

ORDERING IS EASY!

MC/VISA orders can be placed by calling our toll-free number

PHONE 800-458-9640 / FAX 212 986-7355

or mail the coupon below to:

Masquerade Books, Dept. Y54A 801 Second Avenue New York, NY.

QTY.	TITLE	NO.	PRICE
			FREE
			FREE

All transactions are strictly confidential and we never sell, give or trade any customer's name. **Z54**	SUBTOTAL	
	POSTAGE & HANDLING	
	TOTAL	

Add $1.00 Postage and Handling for tthe first book and 50¢ for each additional book. Outside the U.S. add $2.00 for the first book, $1.00 for each additional book. New York state residents add 8-1/4% sales tax.

NAME —————————————————————————

ADDRESS ————————————————————————

CITY————————— STATE ————— ZIP —————————

TEL. (   ) —————————————————————————

PAYMENT: ❑ CHECK   ❑ MONEY ORDER   ❑ VISA   ❑ MC

CARD NO. ————————————— EXP. DATE —————————

PLEASE ALLOW 4–6 WEEKS DELIVERY. NO C.O.D. ORDERS. PLEASE MAKE ALL CHECKS PAYABLE TO MASQUERADE BOOKS. PAYABLE IN U.S. CURRENCY ONLY